# SPINE CHILLERS

## TALES OF TERROR THAT WILL TURN YOUR BLOOD TO ICE

## MARK L'ESTRANGE

*For Effie Winifred Nolan, welcome to the world pretty girl.*

# CONTENTS

# THE WEEPING WOMAN

Darren Clough checked the time on his watch. He had been out now for forty-five minutes. Time to head for the home straight.

In the last six months, jogging had become both his hobby, and his only form of exercise. Having tried everything from sports, to weightlifting, and even ice skating, jogging after work had proved to be the only recreation which he managed to stick with without losing interest after ten minutes.

What was more, as he worked the 4pm to midnight shift at the care home, it was the ideal activity for him to enjoy uninterrupted. All he needed was a decent pair of trainers, and off he went. Everything else he had attempted always seemed to involve having to join a team of some sort or the other, and it soon became apparent that the vast majority of members only joined as a way of improving their social life.

A couple of hours on a Sunday afternoon, and they expected him to join them in the pub for the rest of the day. Not to mention the endless invites for birthdays, and anniversaries, all of which involved drinking copious amounts of alcohol until a fight usually broke out.

Over time, Darren had become increasingly fed-up with having to make excuses as to why he could not attend. For one thing, he had never been a big drinker, and after a couple of pints he was ready to go home. Not to mention he did not appear to have an awful lot in common with the rest of his fellow team-members.

Most of them had high-paying jobs, and they were always boasting about the latest killing they had made, whether it was on the stock market, or because of something they had bought for a pittance at a house sale or auction, which they then went on to sell for an absolute fortune.

Some even boasted about how they had diddled some old lady out of a fortune because she did not realise what she was selling was so valuable.

As someone who worked in a care home, Darren had always felt that people who needed help were the most important, regardless of their status, and he had dedicated the last ten years of his life in a job which paid very little but due to the satisfaction he received from looking after his trusts, made him feel as if he were the richest man alive.

Of course, he realised that his circumstances allowed him to remain in his present position without needing to seek alternative work elsewhere. Since his mother had walked out on them when he was in his late teens, it had just been Darren and his father in the house, and although they had always been the best of mates, since Darren volunteered to work the late shift, they barely saw each other.

His father worked at the local car plant, and started work each day at six, so he was usually asleep by the time Darren arrived home after midnight. But at least on Darren's days off they usually managed to share a take-away and watch whatever sporting fixture was on the telly.

At least Darren no longer had to feel guilty whenever he tucked into their take-away of choice.

As a child, Darren had always been on the plump size, and nothing he ever tried to do, or eat, or not eat, seemed to help. His mother had never been much of a cook, preferring to spend time down at the local bingo hall to sweating over a hot stove. Therefore, most of his meals came out of tins and packets, or, more often than not, from down the local chippie.

But the way he saw it, his mates all ate the same food, or so they said. So, it was still a mystery to him why he always seemed to be at least four inches ahead of them around the waist.

Then when he began shaving at the tender age of fourteen-mainly because of an embarrassing-looking clump of peach fuzz which sprouted out under his chin-he developed acne. The combination of the two assured him of never having a girlfriend when his mates paired off with the girls from the school across the road to go to the pictures, or the local fairground.

Inevitably, if there was a film he desperately wanted to see-especially a good horror flick-Darren would make an excuse, then go by himself, ensuring that he was not discovered by sneaking in after the lights went out, and leaving before the end credits.

So it was that his life continued in a never-ending spiral of failed diets and pointless exercise classes. It was only when he began to work his present shift at the home, that he discovered his new passion for jogging. As he finished his shift at midnight, it was always several hours before he had unwound sufficiently to contemplate falling asleep.

It was seeing a couple of other joggers pounding the streets on his walk home that gave him the idea. There was hardly anybody else around, and somehow, due mainly he supposed to the lack of traffic on the roads at that time, the air felt cleaner and crisper as he breathed it in.

His initial attempt was not exactly a great success. He managed to keep going for just over ten minutes before collapsing in a great heap, unable to catch his breath. But even so, the experience made him feel alive, and left him with a real sense of achievement. So much so that he found himself back on the streets the following night.

It was a long struggle, but eventually Darren managed to reach his goal of running for a full hour without stopping.

This became his nightly routine, five days of the week, straight after his late shift.

What's more, as time passed, he began to notice his clothes becoming looser, and within a year he had dropped a full six inches from his waistline, and best of all, he had not even bothered to alter his diet.

To add a bit of variety to his routine, Darren began to plot different routes so that he did not have to see the same old sights each time he went out.

Tonight's course took him out across the old railway depot, and back via the abandoned cemetery by the canal.

He kept to the lit paths as much as he could, for although he had never encountered any trouble, he did not wish to tempt fate by being too foolhardy.

As he came around the side of the railings which encased the old cemetery, he glanced at the house which had once been the home of the custodian. Word around town had it that once all the plots were full, the church tried to buy up some land on the other side of the cemetery, but they were outbid by a developer who intended to build an estate of luxury flats.

As time went on, the church decided that there was no need to keep a full-time custodian on site, and as the man who held the position was in his mid-seventies, they pensioned him off and placed him in a home.

Everybody presumed that the church would bulldoze the house and make way for some new plots. But to everyone's astonishment, they gave the place a new lick of paint and ring-fenced the property from the rest of the cemetery, then put it up for sale.

People in the town often joked that no one would ever want

to live there, because who wanted to look out of their bedroom window and see a lot of headstones staring back.

But the house did sell, and quite quickly.

In truth, it was a very spacious property, and if one could forget for a moment that it lay in such close proximity to a grave-yard, it made for a rather splendid abode.

No one in Darren's circle knew anything about the people who eventually owned it, partly due to the fact that they had no immediate neighbours, and you never saw them outside the house in the garden, other than when one of them drove through the main gates on their way out.

After a while, as with most things, people stopped contem-plating who lived there, and carried on gossiping about other matters.

But still, that house had always fascinated Darren, especially when he saw it bathed in moonlight as it was now. It always reminded him of something out of an old horror film.

He glanced to one side as he was running. Through the rail-ings he could see the silhouette of the house in its full glory. All the lights were out, as usual, so he presumed that whoever lived there had retired for the night.

As he was about to turn back to face ahead, he saw some-thing move in his peripheral vision. He continued running, although it was becoming awkward to do so with his head turned at such an angle, but he was convinced that it was not his imagination playing tricks on him. He had definitely seen some-thing white contrasted against the darkness.

As he neared the end of the road, he turned right and continued running alongside the main entrance to the cemetery. From here he could see the front of the house and having checked ahead to make sure that there were no obstacles or other joggers ahead for him to crash into, he turned his head to the side once more, to see if he could ascertain what had caught his eye moments earlier.

As he was about to pass the entrance, he saw it again.

From this distance, it appeared to be a figure, moving between the gravestones.

It was a woman, he was sure. A woman dressed in what looked like a nightdress, which billowed behind her, in the wind.

He watched her for a moment, then stopped running before he was too far along the road to be out of sight. The woman almost seemed to him to be drifting, rather than walking, between the graves, never stopping for more than a second or two, before moving on to the next one.

As she made her way along the path, she suddenly looked up towards him.

Darren felt a cold shiver run through his body.

The woman reached out her arms and began to move towards him.

There was something about the approaching figure which really put the fear of God in him. Even so, there were still a couple of hundred yards between them, so he felt like a complete coward for being afraid. For one thing, she was only a woman, and no match for him should it come to a fight.

But what if she had a weapon concealed behind her back?

As she drew closer, Darren could feel his knees starting to shake. He knew that he could sprint off at any moment, and he was confident enough that she would not be able to catch him. But still, he could not stop the feeling of impending terror which was building up inside him.

As she drew closer, Darren noticed that it was in fact a night-dress she was wearing. The weather had been incredibly mild for early October, but even so, it seemed odd to him that she should be outside, dressed as she was.

Also, he noticed that her feet were bare. It was one thing to come out in her nightie, God knows he had seen several people in his local supermarket at night who all seemed dressed for bed, rather than shopping. But for her to walk out without first putting something on her feet, he thought particularly strange.

"Please help me."

The sound of the woman's voice caught him unaware. She was now only about fifty yards away, moving closer with every second.

Darren found himself unable to move. It was as if she had managed to cast some kind of spell over him, binding him to the spot.

Even if he did now decide to run away, it was too late. She had him!

Desperately trying to take control of his situation, Darren stood straight, and stared directly at the approaching woman.

Within a few feet of him, she stopped in her tracks.

He could see straight away that she had been crying, and tear tracks streaked her face.

"Please, can you help me?" she implored. Her voice cracked from crying.

Darren cleared his throat. "In what way?" he asked. "Are you lost?"

The woman shook her head. "No, nothing like that. I live over there," she indicated to the house in the cemetery, behind her. "And I've managed to lock myself out. Please would you be so kind as to help me get back in?"

Darren thought for a moment. Her excuse actually made sense as to why she was dressed the way she was. From his first impression, she certainly did not come across as some homicidal maniac. Just a poor woman who had locked herself out in the cold.

Darren put a hand against the zip at his thigh, then realising nothing was there, he checked the other side as well. He could feel his own house key inside, but it was then that he remembered he had stopped bringing his phone with him, because his latest one kept slamming against his leg while he jogged.

He looked up at the woman. "I'm really sorry," he said, "I seem to have left my mobile indoors."

The woman let forth another stream of tears. She bent her

head, almost as if in shame for her reaction. Her long dark hair fell down around her face, masking it from him.

She was clearly distraught. At this time of night, he was probably the only other living soul she had seen, and thus, her only chance of rescue, and he had let her down at the first hurdle.

Desperate, Darren looked around to see if there might be a car on the road about to pass them. Even if he had to run out in front of it like a madman, he was willing to give it a go to try and make it up to the poor woman. But there was no car in sight.

"Listen," he began, trying to sound comforting, "I don't live that far away, I could probably run there in ten or fifteen minutes. I could call the police for you once I'm there."

The woman wiped her eyes and looked back up at him.

Her latest flood of tears had left her eyes red. But even with that, and her bedraggled hair which she hastily shoved back out of her face, she was still captivatingly beautiful.

She moved forward a couple of steps until she was close enough that he could smell her scent. Darren breathed it the intoxicating aroma and felt an overpowering urge to lean in and put his arms around her.

The woman shivered, loudly, placing her arms around her to keep out the chill.

Darren looked down at himself. He was only wearing a T-shirt and a pair of jogging bottoms, and under them, only his underwear, so he had nothing he could reasonably offer the woman to help keep out the cold.

That made him feel even more guilty than him not having his phone.

The wind picked up and pulled the woman's nightie hard against her. Darren could tell straight away that she was naked underneath, but then, what did he expect?

Above her crossed arms Darren could see her nipples protruding through the flimsy fabric. The cold had doubtless made them erect.

When he looked up, the woman was staring directly into his eyes. Darren felt his face flush with embarrassment. There was no way she had not noticed him staring at her breasts. The man who was supposed to be helping out a damsel in distress, and here he was ogling her, taking advantage of the fact that she was vulnerable, barely dressed and at the mercy of the weather.

Now he really felt ashamed.

"If you could only come to the house," she implored, "there's a window open on the first floor. If you could climb in for me and unlock the front door, I would be immensely grateful."

Another shiver ran through his body.

Why the thought of following her to her house should suddenly cause him to feel afraid, Darren could not rationalise.

But he still experienced an overwhelming feeling of trepidation at the very moment she mentioned it.

He hesitated for a second or two, before replying.

Darren still felt the full weight of his embarrassment at being caught out gawping at the woman's breasts, so denying her now, seemed more than just churlish.

"Okay," he agreed, reluctantly. "Lead the way."

"Oh, thank you," the woman replied. "You really are most kind."

As they walked, they introduced each other. The woman's name was Edith Mannering, and she and her husband lived alone in the old house. She explained that he was away on business and would not be home for a couple of days.

Edith further went on the explain that she always had trouble sleeping while her husband was away, which was why she had taken to wandering through the graveyard late at night, as a way of tiring herself out.

"It may seem a trifle morbid to some," she explained, "but really they are only stones."

"It's what's underneath them that terrifies me," Darren half-joked.

"Well, when you consider how many plague pits we still

9

have in this country, you might argue that you are more likely to be stepping over someone's final resting place than not, if you take my drift."

Darren had never considered such an argument, and the sudden thought of it made his skin feel squirmy.

He shrugged it off as they approached the house.

The only light available was what shone over the graveyard from the adjacent street. But by the time the arc reached the house, it was mostly in shadow.

Edith opened the gate which led to the private garden in front of the house. The iron hinges creaked their opposition as she did so. "Sorry," she apologised. "My husband keeps promising to oil them."

As they approached the front of the house, Darren squinted up through the darkness, and sure enough, he could see one of the upper windows was open.

He had never been much of a climber. Even as a child he had always struggled to scale trees, even when his friends seemed to be able to shoot up them without any problem.

Other than the old lead wastepipe which ran down one side of the building, Darren could not see any vantage point he could use to access the open window.

As if reading his mind, Edith said. "There's a ladder round the back of the house, I'm sure it's long enough to reach. I could give you a hand to bring it around."

Darren nodded. It seemed the best, if not only option and was a good deal safer than trying to shimmy up the pipe.

He followed Edith around to the garden. The ladder was a large metallic one, with a telescopic shaft, and three layers. Darren was sure it would do the trick.

Once they had carried it back around the front, Edith stood back as Darren hoisted it to a standing position, before moving in front of him to help him support its weight while he negotiated the release catches on each side.

They managed between them to extend the ladder until the top of it sat just under the open window.

The ground beneath the bottom prongs was soft and pliable, and as soon as Darren mounted the first rung, he felt the contraption sink into the mud.

He waited until he was sure it would not go down any further, before beginning his ascent.

Edith waited at the bottom, and once he had passed the fifth rung, she held the frame in place, bracing her bodyweight against both sides so as not to let it slip.

Halfway up, a sudden rush of wind caused Darren to cling to the ladder for fear of being blown off. By now the perspiration he had built up while jogging had dried on his skin, and his present lack of exertion left him feeling cold, and vulnerable.

Once the breeze died down, he continued on his way, desperately trying to avoid the temptation to glance down to where Edith stood, for fear that the experience might unbalance him, and send him crashing to the ground.

As he placed his hands on the ledge of the open window, Darren stayed still for a moment to catch his breath. Now that he was holding onto something solid, he felt a rush of relief sweep over him. Even so, he reminded himself that he was not out of the woods yet, and that he was in no position to be cocky.

Taking another rung up, Darren dipped his head inside the window, and arched his upper body so that he was across the threshold.

With the moon being at the back of the property, the room he was about to enter was still very much in shadow, but his eyes adjusted quickly to the lack of light, and he saw that there was nothing below the window for him to fall into, save a dozen or so pairs of ladies' shoes, which had all been neatly arrayed side-by-side.

Not having the skill or the confidence to swing his body round and enter feet-first, Darren leaned all the way over and reached down for the floor. Bracing himself with his hands just in front of the shoes, he lunged forward and managed to complete a forward-roll on the floor.

As his legs came down, his feet hit the side of the king-sized bed which dominated the room, and as he fought to regain his balance, he managed to scatter several of the shoes with his hand as he groped for purchase.

He sat there for a moment, breathing hard, and feeling quite proud of himself for having completed the first part of his task.

Now all he had to do was go downstairs and let Edith in, and he could feel the real hero of the piece.

Darren navigated himself out onto the landing and felt along the wall for a light switch. To his dismay, when he flicked the button, nothing happened. He flipped it on and off several times in frustration, then gave up.

Feeling his way along the banister, he walked towards the top of the stairs.

There was another switch on the wall opposite, but alas, this one too failed to bring forth any light.

Keeping a firm hold on the railing, Darren made his way downstairs. As he reached the bottom, he could just about make out a dim shadowy figure through the frosted glass of the front door.

He walked across the hallway, careful not to bump into anything along the way, and opened the door to reveal a very shivery Edith, standing on the welcome mat.

Before he had a chance to take a step back, Edith flung herself at him, wrapping her arms around his neck, and burying her face against his chest. "Oh, you absolute star," she cried, excitedly, squeezing him for all she was worth.

Although taken-aback by her sudden display of affection, Darren enjoyed the feeling of having Edith's lythe, supple body so close to his. Especially as there was only a couple of flimsy pieces of fabric to separate them.

Feeling a little foolish, Darren returned the hug, lifting his arms up so that they could envelope Edith's head, as he gently stroked her hair.

Darren could feel that she was absolutely freezing from the cold night air, and decided that, even if she were only doing it to garner some heat, he would wait for her to release her hold first.

He was certainly in no hurry.

It even crossed his mind that when Edith had made a point of going into detail about her husband being away, was she perhaps coming onto him?

He had heard of stories of much stranger encounters than this, which ended up with the couple in bed, spending the night in passionate, sweaty lovemaking. So, the fact it had never happened to him before, might mean that it was finally his turn.

The thought of their naked bodies writhing and twisting beneath the sweaty sheets of her king-sized bed as they took their time pleasuring each other until the sun came up virtually blew his mind.

Darren kissed the top of Edith's head and began stroking it with the palm of his hand.

Before he could stop himself, Darren felt his ardour rising.

His bulge protruded through his jogging pants, and he could feel it pushing against Edith's belly.

He was sure that she would push him away, disgusted with him for trying to take advantage of the situation. But, to his surprise and delight, she merely held him tighter, pushing him against her. He even felt a slight swivel in her hips which caused him to release a low, pleasurable moan.

After a few moments, Edith released her hold, and moved back slightly. Darren felt her loss, and his facial expression must have exposed his disappointment.

Smiling, Edith lifted herself up on tiptoes and planted a gentle kiss directly on his lips.

Even though his stomach was churning inside with anticipation, Darren knew that women preferred men who were cool, and always in control. He could not let her know how nervous and anxious he was at the prospect of spending the night with her.

Taking a breath to calm himself, Darren asked. "Are you sure your husband isn't coming back just yet?"

Edith nodded.

"I can't believe he'd leave you alone in a big house like this." It sounded like a ridiculous thing to say, and Darren realised it the second the words left his lips, but it was too late now.

To his relief, Edith laughed. "Well," she purred, "I'm not alone anymore, am I?"

Darren leaned back in for another kiss, but Edith placed the palm of her hand gently on his chest to hold him back. "I think we need to throw a little light on the subject," she suggested. "Don't you?"

Darren looked up at the darkened bulbs above their heads. "I tried several of the switches on the way down here," he explained, "but none of them seemed to work."

Edith sighed. "It's just the fuse box, again," she said. "The electrics in this place are a complete joke. There's a switch in the basement which will bring them all back to life again, would you mind?"

She tilted her head to indicate towards the other end of the hallway.

The thought of venturing down into a creepy basement in the dark was hardly an enticing prospect. However, Darren felt he was in no position to start acting like a scaredy-cat now that he was so sure that he and Edith were going to spend the night together.

"No problem," he assured her.

Edith led him by the hand towards the wooden door at the far end of the hallway.

Once there, she opened it and holding onto him for balance, she reached inside along a shelf until her fingers found what she was looking for. She pulled herself back out, using Darren's arm as a safe hold.

"Here you are," she said, offering him a torch.

Darren took it gratefully and tried the knob. To his relief, it worked first time.

He shone the torch into the basement and saw a rough-hewn wooden staircase leading down into darkness. The beam from his torch was not able to penetrate the gloom further down, but he was satisfied it was strong enough for him to see where to put his feet.

"Would you like me to come down with you?" Edith asked, cheerfully.

Darren shook his head. "No, don't worry, those steps look like they might have splinters, and you're in your bare feet."

Edith reached up and kissed him again. "My hero," she said, smiling.

Darren felt his cheeks blush but hoped in the dim light that Edith had not noticed.

As he began to descend the staircase, Edith called after him. "The fuse box is just at the bottom of the stairs to the left of that old freezer, all you have to do is flick the big switch back down, and we're sorted."

"Okay," Darren called back, concentrating on where he was putting his feet.

When he reached the bottom step, Darren shone the torch around the room. The basement had a much higher ceiling than he had anticipated, as the only other cellar he had ever been in belonged to his Auntie Joan, and that was so low he had to crouch down inside it whenever he ventured in to fetch something for her.

He scanned the walls with the beam. It looked to him as thought Edith and her husband used the cellar as a convenient place to dump items which they either did not want or did not need on a regular basis.

There were several crates piled up on one side, many with shipping marks etched into them. There were several suitcases lined up, and what appeared to be an old-fashioned trunk like the ones you saw people using in old films, when they went abroad.

There were a couple of ladders, much smaller than the one Darren had used to gain entry, stacked against each other in the corner, and to one side a small utility area with shelving, on which there were several rolls of green disposal bags for garden waste, some gardening tools, gloves, and a medium-sized chainsaw.

"Have you found it yet?" Edith's voice drifted down from above.

Darren swung the torch around to his other side. There he saw the large chest freezer Edith had mentioned, and directly above it, attached to the wall, was the fuse box.

"Got it," he assured her.

Darren made his way over and pulled down the front cover of the box.

Seeing the switch, he carefully pulled it down, and immediately he could see light shining through the open doorway above him.

"Brilliant," called Edith. "Now if you could do me one more small favour, can you fetch up the joint of meat from the freezer? I need to let it thaw overnight."

"Will do." Darren tucked the torch under his arm so that the beam shone ahead and lifted the lid of the chest freezer up.

It took a moment for his brain to register what he was seeing.

Inside the deep freezer was Edith's dead body. Lying on her back, frozen solid, with her eyes open and staring straight up at him.

Darren could not move.

His breathing came in huge gasps as his mind desperately tried to make sense of what he was staring at.

"He killed me before he left on his trip." The voice echoed down the flight of stairs. It was still Edith's voice, but now it sounded somewhat distant and ethereal.

Darren managed to tear his eyes away from Edith's corpse, long enough to glance up the wooden staircase.

To his horror, he saw the figure of Edith, floating down the stairs towards him, her arms outstretched as if she wanted to embrace him. Her head tilted slightly to one side, and on her face, a look of wistful longing.

"He plans to cut me up and bury me in the graveyard, when he gets back." The voice filtered through, but Edith's lips no longer moved as she spoke. "You won't let him do that to me, will you?"

# CASTLE DE'ATH

Conrad Vorst slammed the door of his cottage shut with such force it caused the wood to shudder within its frame.

His poor young wife Inga sat up with a start. As was her habit, she had fallen asleep by the fire waiting for her husband to return from his meeting. Whenever Conrad and the Brotherhood met, she knew that there was a good chance he would not return home until way past dinner time.

Conrad was a Town Elder, and much respected throughout the community by those of a certain persuasion. At sixty-five he still had a straight back and an air of authority which garnered him, if not respect, then at least fear from those whose paths he crossed.

His position gave him immense power which, if truth be known, he secretly relished, although he would be the first to deny it if ever anyone had the temerity to ask him.

For above all else, Conrad considered himself to be a pious individual. Staunchly religious to the point of fervour, and able to quote the bible far better than even their parish priest.

Conrad's first wife had died in mysterious circumstances while he was away on business for the state. It was alleged that he returned home to find her lifeless body lying prostrate at the bottom of the stairs.

Upon further examination, it was discovered that her throat had been cut.

No suspicion was ever cast towards Conrad, at least not by anyone who cared to voice it, and eventually a local man of limited intelligence and a propensity for overindulgence in alcohol, was convicted and hanged for the crime, albeit on flimsy and unsubstantiated evidence.

Rumours that Conrad had only married her for her family money were never substantiated, nor mentioned amongst those who knew better than to incur his displeasure.

After a brief period of mourning, Conrad married the daughter of one of his fellow elders. Inga was nearly half his age, but willing to accede to her father's wishes that she should marry the aging widow.

Although Conrad made a habit of lecturing on the sin of fleshly love, he took his young bride whenever the urge took control. Afterwards, there naturally followed a session of prayer, where he would drag his wife to her knees and beg God's forgiveness for their transgression.

If, after a suitable time on bended knee, Conrad felt that they had not been absolved, he would always blame his wife for acting in a seductive or alluring manner in order to entice him to debauchery and beat her across her naked buttocks with a birch, until he was satisfied that their souls had been cleansed.

Over time, Inga had grown used to such flagellation, until the point of accepting it as a follow-on, or even a pre-requisite, from their union.

Inga rose from her seat and rubbed the sleep from her eyes. "Husband," she enquired, respectfully. "Whatever is the matter?"

Without answering, Conrad began pacing up and down their narrow entrance, his hands clasped firmly against his ears as if to shut out some noise which only he could hear.

Such histrionics were not at all unusual in his case, especially when having just returned from a meeting. The root cause, Inga suspected, was the Baroness De Courtney who resided in a castle which sat above the town. As the evening sun began to set, the castle cast a long shadow over the area which, Conrad had decreed to anyone who would listen, demonstrated that the baroness had conjured up the Devil to join her in her nightly round of debauched depravity.

Conrad, much to his chagrin, was unable to exude any authority over the baroness, though not from want of trying. He had made a spectacle of himself in the town square the first time he confronted the baroness concerning his suspicions of the ungodly wickedness which she and her entourage indulged in within the walls of her castle, during the hours of darkness.

It was obvious from his reaction that Conrad had not been prepared for the ridicule and scorn which the baroness proceeded to pour on his assertions, leaving Conrad red-faced and humiliated in front of the very crowd he was hoping to impress.

From that day forth, the baroness had become the target of his constant rage.

However, as she was a distant cousin of the King, to all intents and purposes she was untouchable.

Such a circumstance did not however, stop Conrad in his quest to rid the vicinity of those reprobates which he believed were the cause of any and all misfortune which might befall the God-fearing people of the town. In his quest, Conrad had made it public that he intended to ride to London to elicit an order from the King himself, permitting him to take direct action against the baroness.

Gossip had it that the King had sent him on his way with a flea in his ear, and the promise that if any harm befell the baroness, he would hold Conrad personally responsible.

The truth of the matter was that Conrad had no actual proof of any depraved behaviour taking place within the castle walls, and to the majority of the townspeople-whether or not they admitted it to Conrad's face-the baroness offered them protection as the King's representative. But in his mind, the sheer decadence of someone in her position, meant that *something* had to be happening during her nightly banquets.

Some speculated that his insistence of nefarious activities at such affairs stemmed from the fact that he had never received an invite to one, nor was he ever likely to.

"Is something wrong, husband?" Inga asked, again, having received no answer from her first enquiry.

Conrad turned to face her. His eyes burning. "Wickedness!" he spat. "Wickedness and debauchery in that place of sheer evil." He raised his hand and pointed behind him in the general direction of the castle.

Inga had been expecting such a response, so she merely nodded, and averted her gaze to demonstrate her modesty.

The gesture was not lost on her husband. "I am sorry my dear that you have to hear such harsh language from me," he apologised. "But we cannot turn our eyes away while acts of such depravity and iniquity are happening right under our noses."

He began to pace the floor once more, rubbing his hands together as if to keep out the cold, all the time muttering under his breath.

"Let me fetch you your supper," Inga suggested. "You must be starving."

Conrad turned on her. "You cannot expect me to eat at a time like this," he taunted. "I must remain alert and focussed at all times. There is work to be done. God's work."

Inga sighed. "But husband, you've only just returned home, surely you have time to stop for some bread and stew before you set off again."

Conrad raised his hand as if about to slap her across the face.

Inga turned her head to one side and closed her eyes, anticipating the blow.

But instead, Conrad slowly lowered his hand without striking. "Nothing must come between me and my work for God. Nothing!"

"But you have no evidence," Inga offered, bravely. "If you approach the King again without solid proof, you might end up in the tower, or worse."

Conrad spun round his face flushed with excitement. "Oh, but we have proof, oh yes we do. Three worthless girls caught leaving the confines of the castle earlier this day. Laughing and drinking, and acting in ways that are completely unrepentant, having previously satisfied their lustful ways along with that evil woman, the baroness. Yes, this is what we've been waiting for, now we will have all the proof we need," he turned to look at his wife. "I go now to ensure a fair trial ensues, after which, we will finally have our justice."

Inga knew better than to argue, so she merely nodded her understanding.

Conrad rode through the countryside on his way to the town hall. The sky was starting to turn dark as dusk began to settle. By now, the rest of the elders should have been summoned to order. Their work tonight would be arduous and taxing on their bodies as well as their spirits and minds, but it was nothing they had not been compelled to do before, and Conrad felt confident that they would not let him down.

Since the king had passed the new act, there was no longer a need for the elders to prove that death had resulted from the evil practice of witchcraft. So long as he could show that the suspects had indeed been in league with the Devil, Conrad could justify putting them to death.

The only burden now was having to prepare the gallows for their hanging. Although he had personally preferred the old system of burning them, the new law stated that hanging was now the appropriate punishment for these vile creatures.

So be it. Conrad was not one to snub the law as it stood. However, for the sake of their wretched souls, Conrad ensured that once their life had been extinguished, and they had hung there for all to see for at least half a day, their earthly remains would be burned on a pyre until nothing remained but ashes.

Conrad brought his horse to heel and dismounted, tying his animal off on one of the posts leading up to the hall's entrance. He could tell from the other beats tethered already, that the rest of the brotherhood were already in situ.

Conrad entered the hall, and as he did so, the rest of those gathered rose to their feet and waited for him to take his place at the head of the gathering.

Conrad climbed the stage in silence and took his seat in the middle of the bench. Seated on either side of him were two elders, making the requisite number of five to sit in judgment and pass sentence.

Once he was seated, everyone else in the hall did likewise.

"Bring in the prisoners," Conrad called out, loud enough so that everyone could hear.

Immediately, the door which led to the cells was opened, and three young women, bound to each other by a length of stout rope, were dragged in by their jailer and deposited in the makeshift dock area.

The three girls shivered and trembled as they stood, awaiting their fate.

The dresses they wore had all been torn and shredded, so that now they barely covered their modesty. Each had long hair, which was matted and caked with dirt, as if they had been dragged across the floor backwards. Their feet were bare of shoes or stockings, and they shuffled from one foot to the other on the cold wooden floor.

From their faces it was plain that they had been crying, and fresh tears spilled from each of their cheeks as they surveyed the crowd before them.

After a moment, Conrad called out. "Elisabeth Broom, Abigail Adams, Anne Barrow, you have all been accused of practicing the dark arts for the purpose of serving your one true master, Satan."

The crowd gasped, as one.

Several chants of: 'Hang-em' and 'Witches' ran through the crowd until Conrad raised his arm, calling for silence.

Conrad waited another moment before continuing. "How do you all plead?"

The girls all turned to each other, and nodded, before saying in unison, "Not guilty, sir."

A general grumbling ran through the crowd, followed by more calls similar to those shouted earlier.

Conrad waited for the cries to die down, before turning to the jailer who had frog-marched the girls in. "Master Vile, you have been assigned to interrogate these three women, have you not?"

The jailer shuffled forward, removed his cap, and nodded. "Yes, sir, that I have," he replied.

"And what have you learnt during this time?" Conrad continued.

The jailer glanced at the three girls, then quickly turned back to face his questioner, before answering. "They all admitted to me that they have had indecent dealings with the Devil, sir." The man made the sign of the cross as he spoke.

A roar came from the crowd.

"It's a lie, sir," one of the girls called out.

"Silence!" shouted the elder immediately to Conrad's right.

The girl who had spoken, shrivelled back in her place.

"It's perfectly true, sir," one of the other girls confirmed. "That man tortured us until we made up lies, just to make him stop."

"Silence!" another of the elders barked. "You will not speak such slander against this good man." He pointed directly at Vile. "He is a servant of the state, and as such, is authorised to carry out such an interrogation in order to arrive at the truth."

Vile bowed his head, reverently, so that no one in attendance could see his cheeks flush.

Abigail Adams, the only girl not to have spoken thus far, stretched out her arm and pointed directly at Vile. "Put this man on oath," she demanded, "and let him swear on the Bible that he did not coax an answer out of us by whipping and applying brands to our skin." She parted a torn piece of her dress and, turning to face the crowd, she revealed a large brown mark on her skin.

The crowd gasped once more.

The other two girls began to reveal similar marks to their friend, which elicited further expressions of shock and surprise from those gathered.

Conrad shot to his feet. "Wait!" he demanded. The crowd quietened down. "I will inspect these allegations myself."

With that, he pushed back his chair, letting it scrape along the stage, and climbed down before walking over to the dock.

"Be careful, sir," Vile warned him. "It might not be safe to get too close to them, you never know what spells of wickedness and evil they may cast on you."

Conrad smiled at the man. "Thank you for your concern," he said, "but I have the power of the Lord to protect me, these wretches will not have their wicked way with me."

Satisfied, the jailer stood back, allowing Conrad to enter the dock.

He walked right up to the women, close enough to rub noses with them if he had a mind to. Conrad stared at each one in turn, holding their gaze for several seconds before he began to speak. "If any, or all of you will confess to this gathering that you have been involved in licentious behaviour with the baroness in Castel De'ath, I can guarantee you all a fair and merciful trial, especially if you admit that you were led astray by that wicked woman." He kept his voice down so low that even the women in front of him could barely hear what the was saying.

The three girls exchanged confused glances. Finally, Abigail spoke up. "But that would be a lie," she stated. "We haven't

25

done anything up at the castle other than clean it, which is what we're paid for."

Conrad closed his eyes and pursed his lips together in an attempt to staunch the rising anger he could feel in his chest.

When he opened his eyes again, there was a look of pure malice in them, focussed directly at the three girls. "This is your final chance," he whispered, almost spitting the words out. "Confess all here and now, and you will receive more mercy than you deserve. Now confess!"

This time the three girls all answered in unison, desperately trying to explain that they only confessed earlier because their jailer had tortured them.

Conrad had heard enough. He shot up his hands to staunch their torrent of objections, and the girls all pulled back, convinced that he was about to strike them.

Conrad's face was flushed red, and perspiration trickled down his cheeks. The girls could tell from the expression on his face that he was far from happy with their protestations and would not be satisfied with anything short of a full confession.

After a moment, without speaking, Conrad began inspecting the marks on the three girls. He pulled their torn garments aside and felt along their skin with the palm of his hand, pressing and squeezing at will, causing the girls to gasp in pain as he kneaded their tender flesh.

He made a point of feeling them all over. Cupping their breasts in his palm, he fondled their soft flesh, and rubbed their nipples vigorously with the inside of his thumb.

When he was done, Conrad turned to Vile and nodded, before making his way back to his seat. "I have made a proper inspection," Conrad informed the gathering. "And it is my opinion that the marks these women bear, are in fact scars caused by the Devil's touch.

Another loud gasp, accompanied by more calls for the girls' demise, ensued.

The three girls huddled together as if by doing so, they might be able to protect each other from the venom being aimed at them from the crowd.

Standing in the middle, Abigail Adams put her arms around the shoulders of her fellow prisoners and pulled them in close.

Conrad raised both arms into the air and called for silence.

By now, the crowd were growing fevered, and several began crossing themselves and uttering silent prayers for protection.

Once silence was restored, Conrad conferred with his fellow judges, before passing sentence. "It is the decision of this learned gathering, that the three prisoners in the dock are all guilty of practicing the dark arts, and as such, they will be hanged at dusk tomorrow."

The crowd roared their approval.

"And may the Lord have mercy on their souls." Conrad made his final announcement without bothering to wait for the crowd to die down.

On his way back home, Conrad could not stop thinking about the feel of Abigail's breast. In truth, Conrad had always been attracted to the girl, and had he discovered her before marrying Inga, she would now be his wife, instead of her.

The other two girls had perfectly adequate bosoms, but Abigail's were by far the plumpest and comeliest he had ever come across, and he wished that there had been some way he could have taken them between his teeth during his inspection, without causing suspicion as to his true motive.

He could not help wondering whether Vile had taken full advantage of his position and helped himself to whatever the women had on offer. He would not put it past the town blacksmith, who also acted as town jailer and executioner when needed.

Conrad wondered if he could enact some form of subterfuge which would allow him to gain access to Abigail the following day. Then he could do more than just fondle her breasts, he could take his time with her and enjoy himself until he was satisfied.

He chided himself for such a wicked thought. He knew that God was watching him and knew his mind. It was one thing to dispose of those who had been in collusion with the Devil, their souls were already damned. But if he were to take advantage of his position of authority and commit adultery, that was a different matter altogether.

He had a wife of his own, and God allowed him to do as he pleased with her, it was his right. So, he would just have to satisfy himself with his present situation and leave it at that.

When he threw open his front door, Inga jumped up with a start.

She had stayed up like a dutiful wife, waiting for his return, stirring the stew to keep it moist and tender. "You startled me," she said, catching her breath. She could tell from the expression on Conrad's face that he was in the mood for more than just stew. But she acted as if she suspected nothing of the sort.

Conrad expected his wife to remain demure and coy, at all times.

Inga made her way over to the pot and continued to stir the contents.

"Shall I pour you some wine?" she asked, casually.

"Yes," Conrad replied, removing his shoes before plonking himself down at the table.

Inga poured him a large cupful and brought it over to him.

Conrad glugged it back, then slammed the empty cup back on the table. "More," he demanded.

Inga did as she was told, and fetched him another full cup, along with some bread and butter for her husband to have with his supper. She placed them before him, then returned to the pot and filled him a steaming bowl of stew.

Conrad ate in silence, draining his second cup in one long swallow, before pushing the empty cup back across the table towards his wife.

The stew was hot, but he did not care. Conrad slurped it down, mopping up the gravy with some buttered bread. As he ate, he watched the way his wife's hips swayed from side to side as she walked over to fetch him more wine. He had warned her before about the way she carried herself. Moving her hips in such a provocative manner was not becoming to a wife of a Town Elder.

Conrad knew that he would have to administer discipline tonight. But it was her fault for not obeying her husband's strict command.

By the time Inga returned with Conrad's third cup of wine, he had finished his meal.

"Would you care for some more, husband?" Inga asked, sweetly. "There's plenty more in the pot."

Conrad shook his head, his eyes fixed on his wife's face.

Inga recognised the signs and accepted them.

She waited patiently by his side while Conrad threw back his third cup of wine.

When he was finished, Conrad wiped his mouth with the back of his hand, and let out a deep, guttural belch which echoed in the tiny kitchen.

As he stood up from the table, his chair fell back, landing on the floor.

As Inga reached down to retrieve it, Conrad grabbed her by the wrist, and squeezed it, hard. Inga yelped in pain and surprise, but she did not try to resist. She knew that to do so would make things all the worse for her.

Conrad dragged his wife up the wooden stairs to their bedroom.

Once inside, he threw Inga on the bed, face down with her legs dangling over the edge. She stayed put while Conrad removed his coat to allow him more freedom of movement.

Casting the garment aside, Conrad moved towards the far wall and took down the birch he kept there on a hook. He swished the wooden rod through the air twice, before striding back over to Inga's prone body.

With one hand he pulled up her dress, exposing her under-

29

garments, before ripping them down her legs, leaving her bare flesh on display.

Raising the birch high above his head, Conrad brought it down hard on his wife's naked posterior. Inga's whole body shifted with the force of the blow, and she let out a tiny cry, which only seemed to excite her husband.

As a cruel smile stretched across Conrad's lips, he lifted the birch and smacked it down again on his poor wife's behind. Again, and again he beat her, until his arm ached. All the while Inga stayed as still as she could, suffering the beating with as much dignity as she could muster.

When he was finished, Conrad threw the birch onto the floor, and removed his trousers. He entered Inga from behind without warning.

As always, she was compliant, and did not resist as her husband shoved himself deep within her, forcing himself back and forth, grunting with the effort.

He grabbed hold of her hair with both hands and began to pull it.

After a while, he began to hiss in his wife's ear as he took her. "You evil bitch, you slut. You are little more than a common whore, parading yourself around the town for all to see. You fucking witch, I'll have you dangling from a rope before the sun sets on another day."

Conrad continued spewing out bile until he finally managed to ejaculate.

After he was spent, Conrad lay on top of Inga, breathing heavily from the exertion.

Inga waited patiently for him to climb off her. Once she was free, Inga undressed in silence, and pulled on her nightgown. Once Conrad had donned his own nightshirt, the two of them knelt on the floor across the bed from each other, with their palms clasped together in prayer.

Conrad led them in prayer, begging God for forgiveness for the evil deed they had committed, assuring him that they had acted within their marriage vows and not in any way as a result of lust of wicked thoughts.

They prayed for more than an hour before Conrad finally decided that they were done.

Soon after, he fell asleep.

Upon waking the following morning, Conrad rode straight to the castle to confront the baroness, once more. Although he knew that he could not bring her to justice, he could at least revel in the fact that he had three of her disciples under lock and key and witness the smug look on her face dissipate when he informed her that they were to be strung up at sundown.

As Conrad approached the castle his eagerness to confront the baroness began to wane. The monolithic towers of the mighty structure actually appeared to glare down at him, like the malevolent eyes of some mythical beast.

There was no reason for him to feel threatened, in fact, the baroness had never been anything but courteous and respectful to him, other than when she was admonishing him, or making fun of his calling.

But even so, Conrad now wished that he had brought along other members of the brotherhood to assist him in his task. He considered returning for them, but from this distance he was aware that the baroness could see his approach, and the last thing he wanted was for her to feel superior to him as a result of watching him turn tail and run.

Puffing out his chest, Conrad rode on to the front arch. The two guards on duty recognised the Town Elder as he approached and turned to each other and grinned.

"Halt," shouted one, as Conrad pulled back on the reins to steady his steed.

"I have come to see the baroness," Conrad barked, keeping his voice steady. "She will see me."

The guards looked at each other. "Wait there," ordered one, as he turned and walked back into the courtyard.

Conrad *huffed*, loudly. Someone in his position should not be left loitering by the entrance like some travelling merchant. He knew that the guards were being particularly obtuse as they had witnessed the baroness bringing his temper to the boil on his last visit.

If he remembered, he would report them to her when he was finally granted an audience.

After a few moments, the guard returned. "Inside," he said, indicating behind him with his thumb.

Conrad did not bother to thank the man, but rode past both guards, not caring if he should knock them over on his way.

He was met at the main door by one of the baroness's servants, who led him to the grand chamber, where he found her having breakfast with several guests.

"My dear, Mr Vorst," the baroness called out when she saw him. "What an unexpected pleasure, will you partake of some breakfast?"

Conrad bowed his head just low enough to show he knew the order of form, but not low enough to demonstrate due respect. "Thank you no, Baroness," he replied, standing up. "I'm afraid that I come here with a most serious purpose. Could we have a moment alone?"

The baroness turned to the rest of her guests. Sweeping her hand across the table, she said, "My guests have no secrets from me, personal or otherwise, pray continue with this most intriguing matter."

Conrad bit his bottom lip. He recognised several Barons and their wives amongst the guests, and he knew that in such company he had to watch his tongue for fear of being accused of insolence, or disrespect.

"Come, come my dear Conrad, you have us all sitting on the edge of our seats in anticipation." The baroness mocked.

There was a general laughing and hand-slapping on the table from those around it.

"Very well," Conrad seethed. "If you insist. I must inform you that we held a trial last evening, after which no less than three of your...associates were found guilty of immoral conduct and incitement to conjure up the Devil." He noticed the baroness taking notice and had to prevent a smile from crossing his lips as he continued. "As a result, they are all to be hanged at sunset, in the town square. I thought it only proper to inform you should you wish to attend the ceremony."

The baroness placed her cup on the table. "And who are these 'associates' as you put it?" she demanded.

As Conrad spoke their names, he could see the expression of hatred and loathing on the baroness's face and smiled to himself as he had been the cause of such anguish to her. For he knew that although she was protected by the King, he was still the one who had the commission for conducting such trials, and once judgment had been passed, there was little, if anything, that she could do about it.

The baroness pursed her lips and took in a deep breath before she spoke again. "I presume that this trial you mention was held before a full court, and in the presence of witnesses?"

Conrad smiled broadly. "Naturally, Baroness," he assured her. "I myself was the lead judge, so you may rest assured that all proper formalities were adhered to."

"I'm sure," she agreed. "And the hangings will take place at sundown, you say."

"Yes, Baroness. May I reserve a place for you and your guests?"

The baroness smiled, although the expression did not reach her eyes. "That is most thoughtful of you, a hanging might prove most amusing, but it will not be necessary. My guests and I have a previous engagement."

"I see," Conrad smiled, openly. "Forgive me, I just presumed that as they were friends of yours..."

"Friends!" the baroness snapped. "I believe I paid them to clean the castle on a few occasions, I would hardly call them *friends*. Or do you suppose that I make a habit of intimately associating with all of my servants?"

"I apologise, Baroness, I did not mean to intimate that these creatures were close to you in any meaningful way. But they had been witnessed leaving your castle in somewhat merry spirits."

"So, because my servants appear cheerful, that is an excuse to put them on trial for witchcraft?"

"I can assure you, Baroness, that the trial was conducted with every propriety. They were given ample chance to make a defence."

"I'm sure," the baroness replied, lifting her cup to her lips, and draining it in one long swallow. A servant nearby hurried over to replenish her cup. "Well, thank you for choosing to bring this situation to my attention, Mr Vorst. I trust you will have an enjoyable evening. Good day to you."

Conrad's face flushed at the disrespectful manner in which the baroness dismissed him from her presence. But he held back and bowed once more, before being ushered out of the castle by another servant.

Conrad rode straight to the jail where he found Mr Vile busily constructing the gallows for the triple hanging.

Conrad dismounted and stood with his hands on his hips, inspecting the man's handiwork. "You are sure that this will be ready in time, Mr Vile?" he asked, his voice stern, and demanding.

Vile stopped what he was doing and turned to face the elder. It was clear to Conrad that the jailer had not heard him approaching. His face was covered in perspiration from his labours, and his clothes stuck close to his skin. "Oh, yes indeed, sir, you can rely on me. Everything will be ready in time for sunset, no question about it."

The jailer nodded his head repeatedly as he spoke.

Conrad smiled. "That is well. Did you have any trouble with the three of them during the night?"

"Not a sound, sir." Vile assured him.

"I need to inspect them one more time," Conrad informed him. "Please give me your keys."

Vile fumbled with the large ring on his belt which housed the keys for the jail cells, as well as those for his workshop, and the hall. "Do you want me to be with you, sir?" he asked, hopefully. "Just in case they try anything with you in their company."

"I should be fine, thank you for your concern, Mr Vile," Conrad assured him, holding his hand out for the ring of keys.

Inside the jail the air stank of putrefaction and faeces. It was obvious to Conrad that Vile had not bothered to clean out the cells in a while.

He lifted his hanky to his nose to help mask the pungent odours as he made his way towards the cells which housed the three women.

Conrad found them all huddled in one corner of their respective cells.

Making his way to Abigail's cell, he opened the door and entered, locking it behind him. Once inside, Conrad walked over until he was standing directly over the slumped figure of the pathetic woman.

"Stand up," he demanded.

She did not move. Though he could tell from her breathing that she was still alive, with her eyes shut, Conrad could not be sure whether she was asleep or not.

"I said stand up!" he repeated, more harshly this time.

Abigail still did not stir.

One of her bare feet was poking out underneath her shredded skirt. Conrad moved forward and placed his foot on top of it, pressing down with all his weight.

"Ow, get off me," Abigail squealed. "You're hurting me."

"I'll do a darn sight more if you refuse my command," Conrad informed her, pressing his foot down one more time before removing it from hers. "Now, get up."

Abigail rubbed her sore foot with her hands then stumbled to her feet.

The other two convicts turned and gazed in their direction through their bars.

Conrad noticed their movement. "Turn away, this is nothing to do with either of you," he shouted. Both girls looked up at their friend before turning their faces away.

Conrad looked down at Abigail and smiled. He was a good deal taller than her, and as she had her head down, he could not see the expression on her face.

He moved forward. Fearing that he was attempting to tread on her toes again, Abigail scurried backwards until her shoulders hit the cell wall behind her.

Smiling to himself, Conrad took another step forward until they were so close together, that their bodies were barely an inch apart.

He crooked his index finger and placed it below her chin, lifting it up until she was staring into his eyes. Conrad grinned. "I've just left the baroness," he informed her. "I asked her if she wanted to vouch for you three, perhaps make a recommendation for leniency," he paused for effect. "But she declined my kind offer. It seems as if she has abandoned all of you to your fate. And yet, you still refuse to tell me what her involvement was in your sordid little affair."

Abigail sighed. "There was no sordid affair, we already told you."

Conrad moved closer so that now his body was literally pressing against hers. He could feel the soft compliance of her bosoms against his onslaught. Conrad felt himself growing harder.

Abigail tried desperately to move back, but there was nowhere left for her to go.

Conrad grinned down at her, pleased with himself for having his victim powerless, and at his mercy.

He shoved forward until his hardened member crushed against the girl's belly, then he began to rub himself back and forth, up and down, moaning softly at the sensation.

"Why don't you let me pleasure you?" Abigail suddenly asked him. The shock of her question took Conrad by surprise, and he stopped in his tracks and pulled away so that he could look upon her face once more. He needed to see if she was in earnest, or merely attempting a ploy to take him off guard.

When he gazed into her eyes, Abigail nodded her head, answering his unasked question.

Without a word, she slipped her hand down between his legs, and began massaging his stiffness with her hand.

Conrad was completely taken aback, and a gasp of sheer shock and surprise escaped his lips before he had a chance to react.

Abigail continued to rub her hand along his shaft, whispering to him of his size and how much she longed to have him inside her.

Conrad could feel himself losing control.

He bent his head and buried his face in her neck, kissing it, frantically.

Just then, Conrad began to hear the distant sound of singing. The music was soft and beautiful, like a heavenly choir had just alighted on the ground outside.

God had sent them.

Sent them to watch over Conrad and celebrate his noble work.

God was watching him.

*Watching him in union with a witch!*

Conrad let out a cry and pushed himself away from Abigail. He stood in front of her, panting and perspiring profusely. She had a sly smile on her face, and for a moment, her eyes appeared to him as if they were on fire.

In their dark pools, Conrad could see his own reflection with horns growing out of his head, and a maniacal look on his face.

Conrad screamed and turned to leave the cell. He knew had to get away from the witch before she had a chance to trap him, forever. He fumbled with the ring of keys, unable to find the correct one to unlock the door.

From behind, he could hear Abigail Adams laughing.

The other two convicts rose from their seated positions and walked across their cells until they were as close to him as their confinement allowed.

Their laughter joined in with that of their friend, until the noise became unbearable in Conrad's ears. Their laughter metamorphosised into that of a single voice, which then changed from the joyful laughter of a young girl into the cackling sound of an old hag.

As he fought with the lock, he dropped the ring.

Bending down to retrieve it, he could sense Abigail creeping up behind him.

With shaking hands, he finally managed to find the correct key, and threw open the cell door. Charging outside, he slammed it shut behind him to prevent the witch from escaping. But to his surprise, when he turned around Abigail was sitting down at the back of her cell, where he had left her.

The sound of laughter had stopped.

Glancing over at the other cells, Conrad saw that both other girls were also sitting huddled up in the corner, where they had been originally.

*Had he imagined the whole thing?*

Conrad locked the door with his eyes fixed firmly on Abigail.

Once he was sure the door was locked, he took out his handkerchief and wiped the perspiration from his face.

None of the girls moved while he stood there.

Back outside, Conrad mounted his steed and shouted out to Vile. "Your keys, sir."

Vile turned just in time to catch the weighted ring as it came hurling towards him.

"And make sure that everything is ready in good time," Conrad commanded. "I will brook no delay, am I understood?"

Vile tugged his forelock. "Yes sir, everything will be ready, as expected," he assured the elder.

Conrad rode home as if his tail were on fire.

His mind was tortured by visions of the reflection in Abigail's eyes.

*The Devil, with his face, looking back at him.*

*What did it mean?*

Obviously, the witch had cast a spell on him. Forced him to see things which could not possibly be true. He was a man of God. His soul was safe. His work was the work of God, and surely his place in heaven was assured.

But still, he could not shake that image from his mind.

He felt stained. Dirty. Tainted by the evil which emanated from the witch.

He needed to cleanse himself. Not just his body, but his mind, and his soul.

Entering his cottage, Conrad ran up the stairs without bothering to acknowledge the presence of his wife standing at the tub, washing his clothes. He took the stairs two at a time until he reached their bedroom. Once inside he slammed the door and fell to his knees in prayer.

There he stayed for the rest of the day. He ignored the frequent pleas from Inga to come down and take some food or wine. She did not enter the room, for she knew better than to disturb her husband when he was lost in prayer.

Eventually, the sun began to slowly set in the western sky.

The time had come.

Conrad forced himself back up to a standing position. His old knees *creaked* and *groaned* with the effort, having been locked into the same position for so long. Ignoring the discomfort, Conrad settled himself and marched downstairs.

Inga was waiting obediently for him, a concerned look on her face.

Conrad did not acknowledge her presence, offering only a slight nod of thanks when she passed him his hat.

"Husband," she said, softly. "Will you not stay to take a bite before you go out? You have not eaten all day; it will make you weak."

Conrad stopped in his tracks, staring directly in front of him towards the front door. In a rare moment of tenderness, he reached to his right and squeezed his wife's hand.

Surprised by the gesture, Inga almost snatched her hand away, but managed to keep it steady when she realised what he was doing.

"I don't need food to nourish my soul," he announced. "God will keep me strong for the duty I must perform. He will not allow me to falter."

With that, he left the cottage.

Conrad rode out to the jail to meet the rest of the elders whom he presumed would already be there to greet him.

To his chagrin, when he rode into the clearing, he noticed that Vile had not completed work on the gallows. In fact, it appeared as if he had not made any progress since Conrad had left him earlier.

Annoyed, Conrad dismounted and tied up his mount. He called out for the man, but there was no answer. Again, he shouted his name, but to no avail.

Conrad marched up the wooden steps to the hall's main entrance and threw open the doors. Inside, the hall was empty. Conrad had expected the rest of the elders, plus the townsfolk who would make up the majority of the onlookers, to be eagerly awaiting his arrival, but not a soul had turned out.

He began to wonder if he himself was too early, but the sun had waned far enough to turn the sky dark, so he knew that he was not the one at fault.

Bemused by the lack of attendees, Conrad made his way over to the jail.

To his surprise the door was unlocked. He made his way through expecting to find Vile asleep in a corner having consumed too much wine with his lunch, but the man was nowhere to be seen. What was more concerning was that all the cells were empty. The girls had gone.

Conrad stood there for a moment to think.

His mind could not fathom what was going on.

Where was everyone?

Conrad walked over and checked each cell door, individually. There was no mistake, they were all unlocked, and there was no sign of the keys.

A sudden feeling of unease began to descend over him, and he realised that he was standing directly outside the cell which had earlier housed Abigail. The combined sound of the women's laughter began to echo through his mind.

Louder and louder, it grew, until eventually Conrad had to slap his hands against his ears in an attempt to block it out.

Conrad ran from the empty jail out into the street, his hands still glued to his ears. Several children who were passing saw him and began to laugh and point at him. "Get back to your homes, at once," he bellowed. "Or I'll fetch you all a beating."

The children ran off, laughing to each other.

Nothing made any sense to him: the lack of a gathering, the unfinished gallows, the missing witches, nothing.

The baroness must be responsible for all this. He knew it as well as he knew his own name. He should never have informed her about the hangings. While he prayed for strength, that woman had obviously used her influence to sabotage the proceedings.

In his mind, Conrad could hear the woman laughing at him with her consorts.

She had probably even arranged to have the three witches transported back to her castle, and right now they must all be drinking and cavorting and laughing at his expense, wondering at the expression on his face when he discovered what she had done.

Doubtless she had used gold coin to bribe Vile, that stupid incompetent.

But what she had done to influence the rest of his peers, he had no idea. They were men of means in their own right, and as dedicated in carrying out God's good work as he was.

Either way, he had to find out and bring that evil woman to justice.

Regardless of the King's warning, Conrad was sure that if he showed sufficient proof of her sinful ways, he would have no option other than to support Conrad in carrying out God's work.

Conrad mounted his horse and raced off into the night.

As he rode on, the sky above him grew black, and lightning streaked across it, followed by a sudden peal of thunder.

Galloping through the forest, lightning struck several trees along his path, sending huge branches crashing to the floor, some missing him by mere inches.

Unperturbed, Conrad raced on.

When he arrived at the castle, he saw the same two guards who had been on duty earlier, blocking his way. But this time they both moved aside as if they could tell that he was on a mission which they dare not try to impede.

The main door to the castle stood open and gathered around it were a cluster of household staff, looking troubled. Conrad removed his copy of the Bible from his saddle bag and held it up, as if challenging them to move aside.

Upon seeing his book, they complied and made a gangway, inviting him to enter.

Conrad surmised that they too had witnessed enough ungodly happenings within the castle and were now willing to see their mistress taken into custody and punished for her evil doings.

As Conrad jumped down from his horse, he stopped to remove his crucifix from the saddle bag, along with a small bottle of holy water which he had had blessed by the Cardinal on his last visit to London.

Armed with his holy relics, Conrad stood tall and marched into the castle.

The group of servants followed a little way behind him as he marched from room to room, demanding that the baroness show herself and surrender to his authority.

But she was nowhere to be found.

Finally, Conrad turned to the servants who had been tailing him and shouted at them to reveal their mistress's location. A rather timid-looking young maid stepped forward and pointed with a shaky finger towards a blood-red curtain which was draped across a far wall.

Conrad strode over with great purpose and flung the material cover aside, revealing an oak door which, once opened, led to a passageway which took Conrad to the top of a flight of stone steps.

The walls held lit torches which allowed Conrad to navigate his way down, but even so, he kept one hand against the wall to his right just in case there might be a trapdoor waiting to swallow him up.

As he descended, he could hear the sound of wailing and chanting emanating from somewhere below.

Conrad felt a surge of satisfaction that he was finally about to catch the baroness in the middle of practising the black arts. This was the moment he had been waiting for, and he could not wait to see the look of shock and surprise on her face when he confronted her.

Finally, Conrad reached the bottom of the stairs.

He turned back to see the servants still huddled behind him, watching his every move.

Along the passage stood another large wooden door, from behind which Conrad could hear the voice of the baroness instructing her minions.

Taking a deep breath, Conrad flung open the door, holding up his Bible and crucifix in one hand, and the bottle of holy water in the other. "Stop!" he demanded, raising his voice so that it could be heard above the chanting. "Creatures of darkness, I come here to…"

His words trailed off as he saw his young wife Inga, naked, cavorting around the room along with several of his fellow elders, and a myriad of nubile young females in various forms of undress.

Once his presence had been registered, everyone stopped what they were doing and turned in his direction.

Conrad was so taken aback by the sight of his wife, not to mention his peers, that for a moment he was unable to make any sound, whatsoever. He merely stood there with his mouth open, in shock.

Eventually the baroness appeared through the crowd and walked over to him.

She too was naked, and moved as if unaware, or at the very least unconcerned, by her exposure.

The baroness carried a golden goblet in one hand, and when she reached him, she offered it to Conrad, smiling. The gesture broke the spell, and Conrad pushed the cup away, sending it flying across the room, spilling the red liquid it contained out onto the floor.

The baroness frowned. "That was impolite, Mr Vorst. And very disrespectful of your host."

Conrad turned to face her. "You are no host of mine," he seethed. "How dare you think to involve me in this debauched heresy."

The baroness smiled. "I'm sure that your lovely wife does not find it so," she replied, turning, and holding out her hand towards Inga. Conrad's wife dutifully accepted the gesture and walked over to where they stood. Ignoring her husband, Inga went straight to the baroness and laid her head on the woman's shoulder.

Conrad could feel his face flush red. Reaching forward, he grabbed Inga by the wrist and wrenched her away from the baroness, slamming her against the wall behind him.

He pointed down at his wife, as the force of the blow had left her sprawled on the floor. "I will deal with you when we reach home," he said, threateningly.

Suddenly, he was seized from behind by several of the group, his own fellow elders included. Conrad fought to regain control, but he was easily overpowered by the sheer numbers involved. Losing his grip on his holy relics, he heard the sound of the bottle of holy water smashing as it hit the stone floor.

Through the crowd, he saw the faces of the three women who had been due to hang that evening, making their way through the crowd. Together they came over to Inga and helped her back up to her feet. The four women stood there watching him in defiance as Conrad struggled against his captors.

The baroness clapped her hands and signalled to those holding Conrad to drag him to the middle of the room.

As he emerged through the gathering, Conrad saw the stone altar which dominated the floor. He immediately began to drag his feet whilst simultaneously attempting to wrench his arms free. But the hold on him was far too great, and he soon realised how futile his struggle was.

Without warning, Conrad was hoisted into the air and carried over to the altar.

Once there, he was slammed down on his back against the stone slab. The wind was knocked out of him, and Conrad lay there, gasping for air, while members of the crowd secured him to the slab with silk sashes.

Before long, both his wrists and ankles were tightly bound to the altar, and Conrad could feel the restraints tighten the more he pulled against them.

Inga and the three naked witches moved in around him.

Conrad gazed up at his wife, his eyes pleading. "Inga, release me at once. What are you doing?" But his wife merely smiled down at him as the other girls removed his neck-scarf, and unbuttoned his shirt, revealing his naked chest.

The crowd gathered round, their faces staring down at the hapless man as he continued to try and seek help from those amongst them whom he had, until now, considered his friends.

The baroness appeared at the head of the altar, and when

Conrad looked up at her he saw at once the large, curved blade which she held with both hands above her head.

The crowd began to chant in a language which Conrad did not understand.

As one, they began to sway from side to side, all eyes still fixed on him.

The longer they continued, the more frenzied their mantra became, until they seemed lost in spell which controlled their every movement.

Louder and louder, they grew, until the combined unison of their voices echoed around the vast chamber.

Conrad struggled with what little strength he had left, but it was to no avail.

"Our master thanks you for your sacrifice," The baroness shouted above the deafening noise from the gathering. "He has been waiting for you."

Conrad released a scream which became lost in the company, as the baroness brought the blade down.

# DOMINIC

"I'm bored," Steph whined, extending her leg from its bent position so that she could kick Darren, who was leaning against the bonnet of his dad's car. "I said we should go clubbing."

"Get off," Darren snapped. "I spent fifty quid on you last night going to that posh restaurant you wanted. Fucking waste of money that was, as well. I was still hungry when I got in."

"That's because you're a gannet," Molly laughed. "Nothing but a trough full of baked beans will satisfy you."

"It'd be a darn sight cheaper than the rubbish we ate last night," Darren agreed. "I mean, who in their right mind would fork out all that dosh just to eat raw fish? It doesn't make any bleedin' sense."

"That's because you're a philistine," Steph mocked, swinging her leg back for another swat. "I am trying to educate your jaded palate."

"Nothing jaded about my palate," Darren replied, moving just enough to avoid Steph's fast-approaching foot. "I just knows what I likes, and that's that."

"And what he doesn't like is spending a fortune on poncy

food that rich people only eat so they can show off to their friends," Greg observed.

"Exactly," Darren agreed, raising his hand in the air for his friend to 'high-five' him.

Darren, Greg, and Andy tilted back their heads and drained the last gulp from their cans of beer, before crushing them and hurling them in the direction of the litter bin, a couple of feet away.

All three missed. The cans clattered against the side of the bin, before falling to the floor and rolling to a stop on the tarmac.

"Almost," announced Andy, proudly, before releasing a massive belch which seemed to fill the night air.

"Pig." Steph called out.

Darren and Greg then expelled air from their mouths in a similar vein.

Darren moved, again, this time to avoid his girlfriend's swinging handbag.

"Are you just going to leave those there, like that?" Evelyn asked, sarcastically, not attempting to disguise the distain in her voice.

The three men all looked at each other, and shrugged, before Darren reached into the car for more beers. He passed the cans onto his friends.

Sighing loudly, Evelyn walked over to the bin and retrieved the three crumpled cans, placing each one inside the receptacle, along with her own empty paper cup.

"I don't know why you bother, Eve," Molly called out. "Not with these three wastrels around."

"It's not a question of bothering," Evelyn stated, making her way back over to the car. "It's a question of preserving our planet, before it is too late."

"Again," said Molly, "I don't know why you bother when you're around these three." She reached inside the car's open window and grabbed her friend another paper cup from the stack on the seat.

Evelyn shook her head, refusing the offer. "I've had enough, thanks anyway."

"Oh, come on, Eve, it's Saturday night, let your hair down a little," Steph chimed in, extending her own empty cup towards Molly, who was busy refilling hers with wine.

"She's right," Molly agreed. "Just because we're stuck out here with these three losers, doesn't mean we can't enjoy ourselves a little."

"I've had enough, thanks," Evelyn confirmed. "I've got church in the morning."

The three men laughed. "What?" asked Andy. "You afraid the priest might smell it on your breath, and know that you did not spend the evening locked away in your bedroom, praying for him to save your soul?"

Evelyn glared at him, keeping her lips tightly pressed together. She did not wish to lower herself to his level, so thought it best to say nothing.

"Leave her alone, twat-features," Steph shouted. "At least she has a soul worth saving."

Andy pulled a face, before knocking back another swig from his can.

"Well, isn't this a fine how-do-you-do?" observed Molly. The six of us, out here in the park on a Saturday night, same as always. God we must be a pathetic bunch."

"I don't see the problem," Greg responded, smirking. "It's a lovely summer's night. The stars are out, and so are we. We have the park to ourselves, and all the beer and wine we can drink. Who needs anything more?"

"Me, for one," Molly retorted.

"Me too," Steph chipped in. "We've been hanging out in this place since we were kids. Aren't we a bit too old for this? We're eighteen, we should be doing something more sophisticated with our time."

"Such as what?" Darren demanded. "I'd hardly call clubbing sophisticated."

"At least it's an excuse to get dressed up, and go out," Steph reminded him. "Even if we only went for a drink, at our age we should be making more of an effort on a Saturday night, that's all I'm saying."

Darren shook his head and gulped another swallow.

He didn't wish to antagonise his girlfriend too much. After all, it was Saturday night, and once they had ditched the others they had planned to go back to Steph's place. With her mum working the night shift at the local hospital, they would have the place to themselves.

"At least when we were younger, we used to dream about adventure," Molly added. "Back then, this was as far as we were allowed to come from home. But now we can go wherever we want, within reason, and we're still stuck here drinking cheap plonk from paper cups."

Greg held up his hand. "I'll have you know that stuff was a fiver a bottle down at the off-licence," he protested.

Molly gave him one of her *looks*, which automatically made him shut up.

Greg knew when his girlfriend was growing pissed with him, and that *look* meant that she was almost there. If he pushed it, he knew he would pay later.

"So, what would you have us do?" demanded Andy, free from any restraints which a girlfriend might impose.

Steph shrugged. "I dunno, something."

The group had all known each other since kindergarten. Over the years, some of them had drifted apart, meeting new friends, and joining other groups connected with clubs or associations they had become members of.

But, somehow, they always seemed to end up back together.

Out of all of them, Evelyn was probably the outsider. She had never really invested too much in their relationship, preferring her own company to any of them. After a while, they stopped bothering to invite her to tag along with them. But both Steph and Molly began to feel bad when they saw that their friend was always alone, so eventually they contrived a chance meeting as an excuse to bring her back into the gang.

The boys did not seem bothered either way, but both Steph and Molly knew that they had done the right thing.

Over time, Darren and Steph had become an item, and subsequently, Greg and Molly followed suit. No one ever expected Andy and Evelyn to get together, and for good reason. Evelyn had always been extremely religious, and very studious. Whereas the older he became the more Andy seemed to regress into ever deeper realms of immaturity. A direct result, the others presumed, of him trying to live up to the reputation of his elder brother, a local thug, who was presently serving time for a smash-and-grab raid which had resulted in an old lady being very badly hurt.

Andy was extremely defensive of his older brother, and everyone knew not to mention the incident, unless they wanted an argument.

"I think I'll head home," Evelyn announced, clearly fed-up with the lack of imagination amongst the group. In truth, Evelyn still preferred reading alone in her room to spending the evening watching her friends become drunk. But she often tagged along so as not to cause offence.

"No," Molly called, "you can't leave just yet, it's still early."

Evelyn gazed at her friend and shrugged she shoulders. "Well, it doesn't look as if any of us has any specific plans, except maybe to get drunk and throw up." She glanced over towards Andy who was presently draining his latest can.

"That's why we need to come up with a plan," Steph chimed in. "Come on, we're young, we're free, we've got booze and the use of a car, we should be doing something fun." She looked at the others as if in expectation of someone having an idea.

"I know," Andy suddenly blurted, stopping mid-sentence to let out a huge belch. "Why don't we head over to the old loony bin? I hear they're planning on sending in the wreckers any day now. It might be our last chance to have a nose around."

Both girls screwed their faces.

"Hey," answered Greg. "The boy has a plan. What about it?"

"Cool with me," Darren agreed. "It was in the local paper the other day that the security firm who had the contract have pulled out their team due to a dispute over pay, so no one is there guarding the place."

"That place has been condemned since forever," Steph added. "There's a reason why no one is supposed to go near that place."

"Yeah," agreed Molly. "After that fire they had there years ago, the whole place is ready to fall into the ground. We'd be idiots to even venture inside."

"You wanted something fun. Different. Exciting," Andy shot back. "What could be more adventurous than a last farewell to the town's one and only nuthouse?"

"That place gives me the creeps," Evelyn replied. "They did a documentary on it a few years back. The things they did to the patients. Those experiments they carried out on those who had no living relatives. It was awful."

"Most of them were out of their skulls anyway," Greg stated. "They probably didn't even know what was happening. I'll bet some of them even liked it." He grinned at the other two men for support.

"Greg's right," offered Darren, taking up the batten. "No one died as a result of those experiments. And who better to use as guinea pigs?"

"That's outrageous," Evelyn yelled. "How would you like it if they experimented on you like that?"

Darren looked flustered, taken aback by Evelyn's sudden uncharacteristic outburst.

He turned to his mates for reassurance that he had not crossed a line.

The other two raised their eyes to heaven.

"Darren!" demanded Steph.

He turned back to see the look of disappointment on her face, and shrugged his shoulders, apologetically.

"Ignore him, Eve," said Molly. "You know what these three are like when they get together and drink too much."

"The more they drink, the smaller their brains get," Steph agreed.

"Charmin'," said Andy, keeping his gaze lowered.

Determined not to let the moment ruin the mood, Molly drained her cup and stood up, straight. "Well, I for one am willing to confess that, tasteless jokes aside, I have always wanted to go and see that place. I've heard some really creepy things about it, and if they are planning on razing the place anytime soon, this might be our last chance."

"Are you serious?" asked Steph, incredulously.

Molly nodded, excitedly. "Come on, it'll be an adventure. Better than sitting around here all night. And we've got three beefy blokes to protect us in case any of the inmates happen to be wandering around."

"Yeah, atta girl," said Greg, moving in to put his arm around his girlfriend.

Andy tossed his empty can. It hit the rim of the bin, then jumped in.

He held his hands up in triumph.

"So, are we game?" asked Darren. Not wishing to risk the shot, he took a few steps forward and only let go of his can once he was sure it would make its target.

Steph looked over at Evelyn, who now had her head down.

"Come on," ushered Molly. "It'll be a gas."

"Eve, are you in?" Steph asked her friend. Part of her was hoping that Evelyn might object. Steph was not comfortable with the idea, although, she would never admit it to the others.

Evelyn finally looked up. "I suppose so," she muttered, under her breath.

"Woo-hoo," shouted Andy, skipping towards the back door of the car. "Let's go see how the other half live."

"You know," Evelyn announced, "there have been rumours

that *he* might still be living there. There was a report on the news last year. Didn't any of you see it?"

The others all exchanged curious glances.

Suddenly, Molly slapped her hand against her mouth, as if to stifle a scream. "Oh my god," she exclaimed. "I had forgotten all about that." She turned to look at Evelyn. "But didn't they say that they had the place searched from top to bottom, and there was no sign of him?"

"Who?" demanded Andy, starting to feel the enthusiasm amongst his friends dissipate.

"Dominic Craven!" Evelyn announced.

The name sent a shiver throughout the group. Although the boys pretended not to be fazed by it.

"Oh shit," spluttered Steph. "I'd forgotten about him. You don't really think after all this time that he might still be there, do you?"

"Yeah," Darren offered. "They only said that on the news because they couldn't find him after he escaped en route to that other place, after the fire."

"I still shudder when I think of what he did," confessed Steph. "And to think, he used to go to our school. He even lived around the corner from you, didn't he?" She looked towards Evelyn.

"Not too far away," Evelyn replied. "I could see his backyard from my bedroom window."

"He's probably long gone by now," suggested Andy. "That place they took 'em to was miles away. How would he have managed to get back here? He wasn't exactly hard to miss, the big lunk."

"That's a point," agreed Greg. "I know the old asylum was large, but after the fire, there couldn't have been enough room left to hide a monster the size of him."

"Do you remember when he walked down the street?" Darren asked. "He virtually blocked out the sun."

"I just keep remembering what he did to his poor family," Steph said, shivering.

"I know," replied Andy. "Strangled them all with his bare hands, then ripped them apart. When the police were called, they reckon they found bits of bodies all over the place. And our man Dominic was just sitting there, in the kitchen, eating one of his old man's legs. Gives you the creeps."

"Well, he probably needed to build back his strength after all that activity," Darren joked. "I heard he washed it down with a pint of his own piss." He received a well-aimed elbow in the ribs from Steph for his trouble.

"I wonder why he killed them?" Mused Molly. "I mean, at his trial he never spoke, other than to confirm his name. You would have thought if there was a reason behind his actions, then would have been the perfect opportunity to mention it."

"I dunno," Greg chipped in. "There are times when I've wanted to strangle my lot."

"That's not funny!" scowled Evelyn.

Greg held his hands up in submission.

"Ignore him E," said Molly. "It was just a turn of phrase. I'm afraid tact and diplomacy are alien terms to him."

"It was obvious why he killed them all," quipped Andy. The others all turned to look at him. "It's because he was a nutjob. Why do you think they sent him to the loony bin in the first place?"

"That was just his brief's defence tactic," suggested Darren. "It's well known that the more evil and wicked the crime, the more likely it is that people will presume the perpetrator is insane. No one wants to think someone like that could be normal, like them."

"Hark at you," said Steph, raising her eyebrows. "A sensible comment for once in your life."

"Don't worry, I won't let it go to my head," replied Darren, smirking.

"I remember the day they moved him to the new asylum," offered Andy. "They had a separate van just for him, with four guards all chained to him. Everyone was out in the street watching it go by. You would have thought he was royalty, or something."

"I just remember the huge feeling of relief everyone had when they took him away," said Steph.

"Until the news that evening, when they reported that the van carrying him had been found abandoned outside of town, with no sign of him, or the guards anywhere to be seen," added Darren. "They never did find those bodies."

"Do you think he did for them?" asked Molly.

"Well, they searched the area for ages without finding any sign of them," Darren confirmed.

"That's when they started speculating that he must have made his way back to the old asylum," said Andy. "The papers reckoned it was the only place he ever felt at home."

"That's sad," said Steph.

"And creepy," added Molly.

"Maybe, we should go and check the place out to see if we can find any evidence that he's still living there," offered Andy.

Darren turned and gave his friend a stern look.

Andy held his arms out. "What?" he asked, evidently unaware of his faux pas.

"Forget it," announced Steph. "I've changed my mind about going there now."

"That's what," stated Darren. He slid over to his girlfriend and placed a comforting arm around her shoulder. "Come on, babe, ignore him. It'll be a gas, you'll see."

Clicking on, Andy said. "Yeah, Steph, I was only kidding. Come on, it might be our last chance to see inside the place before they pull it down."

"It would be more appropriate if this were Halloween," Evelyn pointed out.

"Well, we can't leave it until then," said Greg. "It'll probably be nothing more than a pile of rubble by then."

"And an awful lot colder," Andy pointed out.

Steph turned to Molly. "Are you sure about this?" she asked, tentatively.

Molly nodded, excitedly. "Yeah, come on, it'll be a laugh. And an adventure. Come on, we'll all be together."

Reluctantly, Steph nodded.

They all piled into Darren's father's car. In reality it was only designed to seat five, so Molly always sat on Greg's lap whenever they went out in it.

Not wanting to be stopped by the police, Darren made a point of sticking to back roads. He knew that if he was caught it would mean a fine at the very least. But fortunately, Molly was quite small and managed to duck down whenever another car passed, just in case.

The drive took them fifteen minutes. Now that there were no security guards patrolling, no one had bothered to report the outside lights which had been either smashed by kids or had just fused, so the few remaining lights cast an eerie shadow over the property.

Despite the fire, the building was still enormous, and looked capable of housing several dozen inmates should the need arise. But no doubt due to health and safety such an idea was probably scrapped which was why all the existing patients had been moved.

The wrought iron railings which surrounded the perimeter were still intact, so Darren parked the car on the nearest street, and they walked the rest of the way.

The main gate stood at well over six feet, so when they arrived at it, Evelyn was the first to point out that there was no way she was going to able to scale it.

The other girls agreed, although, Steph could tell that Molly was game.

"Let's try round the other side," suggested Andy.

The wind began to pick up as they rounded the next corner. The street to their right was reasonably well-lit, so the group stayed close to the railings to keep them in shadow. The last thing any of them wanted was some nosey neighbour alerting the police to their nocturnal activities.

Once they reached the far end of the street, they turned left, and followed the railings by the side of the railway tracks. From this angle, they were protected from the wind by the building, except for when a train passed at speed, whipping up the air around them.

Halfway down the path, Greg, who had taken the lead, held up his hand.

The others stopped in their tracks and waited.

They could see him moving closer to the railing and peering through the bars.

After a few moments, Greg pulled back and came over to join the others.

"What was that all about?" whispered Darren.

"I thought for a moment that I could see someone at one of the upper windows, walking around. It was hard to tell because of the darkness. I think it must have just been a shadow, or something."

"What if the security team have been called back in," ventured Steph. "Or perhaps they have a contract with a different bunch. They might be patrolling right now, watching us from the windows."

"I doubt it," offered Darren. "For a start there used to be a security van parked out front while the other lot were there."

"Well, maybe they just dropped the guards off and drove away," suggested Steph, feeling more and more as if she wished she had never agreed to this jaunt in the first place.

"Nah, it was nothing," Greg assured her. "Like I said, it was probably just a shadow from the building."

"Are you positive?" Evelyn demanded. "Because adventure aside, I do not wish to be caught on private property and risk being arrested."

Greg held out his hands. "I'm positive. There was no one

there. Look, I wouldn't want to get caught either, you know. So, if I did see someone, I would have said so."

The girls all exchanged glances.

Molly nodded, as if to assure them that her boyfriend was telling the truth.

They continued on their way along the path. After a few hundred yards, Greg suddenly held up his hand again.

They all stopped.

The he turned to face them with a huge grin spread across his face. "Here we are," he announced, indicating to a point just beyond where he was standing.

They huddled round to see what he was alluding to.

A few feet in front of where they stood, there was a sizeable gap in the railings, where it appeared that something like a car, or a lorry had crashed into them, dislodging a portion of the barrier from its holding.

The gap was by no means large, and it tapered off as it rose. But the space at the bottom looked just big enough to allow a person to crawl through.

"Is that it?" asked Steph, incredulously.

"It's big enough," replied Andy, moving in closer for a better look.

"Do you think we could carry on a little further?" suggested Steph. "There might be a larger gap further up."

"There's plenty of room here," insisted Greg. "And what's more, we're shielded her by the railway, so no one can see us."

Steph turned to Molly. "What do you think?" she asked, hopefully.

Molly shrugged. "Go on," she said to Andy. "You're the biggest. If you can get through without any trouble, I suppose the rest of us can too."

Rising to the challenge, Andy fell down on all fours and slid through the gap without too much effort. Once on the other side, he sprang to his feet and took a bow as if expecting applause which did not come.

"How was it?" asked Greg.

"Lemon squeezy," Andy responded, smiling.

"Okay, who's next?" asked Darren.

Before anyone else could move, Molly crouched down and eased her way through the gap. Andy helped her back to her feet once she was on the other side.

"Come on," she said, ushering the others on. "It's no problem."

One-by-one, they followed, with Darren bringing up the rear.

Once they were all through, they stood in place for a while, looking up at the back of the old asylum.

Greg had been right about the shadows. Besides the couple of outside lights which were still in action, there appeared to be some emergency lights inside the building, which illuminated some of the rooms on the upper, and lower floors.

The group realised that if they stared at them for too long, the shadows created by the beams did appear as if someone was watching them.

After a moment, Darren announced. "Well, come on then. Fortune favours the brave and all that." He linked his arm through Steph's to urge her to start walking.

Once they moved off, the others followed.

As they began to approach the rear of the old asylum, Steph and Molly both shivered in unison. It was almost as if the breeze was somehow stronger on this side of the railings. Greg and Darren only had on shirts, which, if they gallantly took them off for their girlfriends, would leave them bare backed. So, neither offered.

The asylum was built on four levels, and as they approached, the group began to feel the unnerving sense of surrender which they suspected the inmates must have felt when they were being marched inside. In some cases, for the rest of their days.

The main car park was at the rear of the building, and there still appeared to be a couple of white trucks nearest the back entrance. From the outward appearance of them, they had not been used in ages. They both had flat tyres and broken windows, so the group presumed that they had been left behind during the migration as they were not worth the effort of moving.

The main light above the ramped entrance was out. But as the friends fell in line between the two dilapidated vehicles, they could see a light at the far end of the entrance corridor, lighting their way.

Darren and Steph were the first to reach the doors.

Darren left her at the bottom of the ramp, and walked up, stopping just out of reach of the handles. He had half-expected to see chains keeping the doors together, but he was pleasantly surprised when there were none in place.

Darren twisted back to look over his shoulder at the others. He could tell by the expressions on Andy and Greg's faces that they were both eager for him to check the doors.

Moving ahead, Darren grabbed hold of both handles and pulled.

They did not give.

Bending down, Darren could just make out a bar of some sort crossing between the jambs. He stuck his finger between the gap and was just able to feel the touch of metal. The bar was obviously on the inside which should mean, he surmised, that the doors swung open, when unlocked.

Taking hold of both handles firmly, Darren heaved for all he was worth.

When nothing happened, he began to jerk the handles violently, grunting with the effort.

After a while, Evelyn called out. "Let's leave it, they're obviously locked."

Darren stopped pulling and turned around, breathing heavily. "No," he protested. "I can feel them starting to give. A few more tugs, and I think we'll be in." He looked over towards Greg and Andy. "Come on one of you, give me a hand."

Greg stepped forward and together the two men took hold of one handle each.

"Maybe we'd have better luck around the front," offered Molly.

"Yeah," agreed Steph. "Before one of you do yourself a mischief."

The men ignored the comments and Darren counted down from three for them to start their endeavour.

After the first two pulls, the doors began to give.

Both men let go of their respective handles and rubbed their palms on their jeans before taking up their grip.

The metal rod screamed and whined against the force from the exertion the two men inflicted. It seemed intent on preventing them entrance, as if it were under some form of sacred vow to the rest of the building.

Suddenly, there was a sound of something clanking on the linoleum floor beyond the doors, and the two men looked at each other with great satisfaction.

The bolt had held fast, but one of the casings for the lock had evidently come away.

Another joint effort and the doors swung open.

Darren and Greg high-fived each other, and stood in place, sucking in air as they tried to gather their composure.

Andy edged around the girls for a better look.

Inside, the corridor was dimly lit by the few remaining overhead strips that still worked. In between the lit sections there were areas of complete pitch, which gave him an uneasy feeling that something might be lurking in those areas. Forgotten patients, crouching in the safety of the darkness, wating for unsuspecting victims to enter their domain.

Andy shook the feeling free and chided himself for letting his imagination run riot.

The three girls were now all huddled together in a group, peering in through the newly opened doorway.

Having caught his breath. Darren turned to them. "What d'yer think?" he asked, expectantly. "Ready for an adventure?"

The girls exchanged worried glances.

"I'm not so sure about this," ventured Steph.

"Me neither," agreed Evelyn.

"What, after all our efforts?" whined Greg. "Come on, it'll be an adventure. Who knows what we might find inside? Maybe there's some old equipment we could nick. Or maybe there's a stack of medication just waiting for us to help ourselves. Those things sell for a fortune on the net."

"Are you being serious?" Molly demanded. "What the hell do we know about selling drugs? You know that the police can trace the source of those things, don't you?"

Greg looked embarrassed. "I didn't mean heroin or anything like that. I was thinking maybe anti-depressants or happy pills, you know. That sort of thing."

Molly shook her head in despair.

Turning to the other girls, she said. "Well, what's it to be? Are we going in?"

"Come on," called Darren. "Don't you want to see where Dominic Craven was held? Greg's right. There could be all sorts of equipment they left behind. Perhaps there's even some digital evidence of the things they did to the inmates back then. The papers are always willing to pay for that sort of thing. Come on."

He walked down the ramp and held out his hand towards Steph.

Reluctantly, she took it, and allowed him to lead her in through the open doorway.

As they passed him, Greg took the initiative and went to fetch Molly. She at least appeared more eager to join her boyfriend, and he suspected that she had only appeared to be unwilling to show unity with her friends.

Taking his hint from the others, Andy held out his arm for Evelyn to link with.

Ignoring the offering, Evelyn marched in behind the others, followed by Andy.

Once inside, they all stood in the foyer to acclimatise them-selves with the ambiance of the place. As with most medical facilities there was a cloying clinical odour about the place, which immediately assailed their nostrils. It was a cross between antiseptic and cleaning fluid. Although, judging by the state of the place, it had not been cleaned in an age.

"Isn't this neat?" said Greg, not sounding too convinced by his own announcement.

"Whatever," replied Steph.

"So, where to first?" asked Darren, desperate to keep the mood light. Despite what the girls had said earlier, he was intent on finding something of value inside the place which he could make a profit from.

"Let's start checking out the rooms," suggested Andy.

Slowly, they moved off. Darren led the way, still gripping Steph by the hand.

They began to check out the rooms on the ground floor. Most were abandoned operating theatres, judging by their size and viewing platforms.

Other than the odd broken chair, all the furniture had been removed. There were a few discarded cardboard boxes which, according to their labels, had once contained bandages, or syringes, but nothing worth growing excited about.

Once they had checked all the downstairs rooms, Greg stopped outside the lift at the far end of the corridor. By now they had reached what would have been the main entrance, and just above the reception desk there was a large sign which informed them what was on each floor.

The fourth floor advertised the 'Sleeping Quarters'. When he saw it, Greg turned to the others. "Who wants to go see where our man Dom was tucked up at night?" he asked, excitedly.

"Good one," agreed Darren.

Looking above the lift, Greg could see from the light that it was apparently on the fourth floor. "Looks as though someone beat us to it," he announced, smiling.

He pressed the call button, and it lit up, immediately.

"Don't tell me that thing is still working?" asked Steph, timidly.

"Why not?" answered Greg. "You can't expect the ghosts to have to use the stairs, can you?"

Molly hit him hard on his arm. "Wise guy."

"I don't think it's such a good idea for us to use it, even if it does appear to be working." Suggested Evelyn.

"Why not?" asked Andy, watching the counter descend to their level.

"Well for one thing, if it breaks down with us inside it, who the hell are we going to call to come and rescue us?"

Molly instinctively took out her mobile. She barely had one bar. "Does anyone else have a signal?" she enquired.

One-by-one, the others checked their phones.

They were all dead.

"What's that all about?" asked Greg, rhetorically.

"I think it must have something to do with the construction of the facility," Evelyn offered. "A lot of these places were still built with lead linings because of the sensitive instruments they used. I doubt anything as advanced as Wi-Fi ever crossed their minds at the time."

Darren lifted his mobile above his head and swung around several times, eventually giving up.

Just then, the lift *pinged* as it arrived at their destination.

As the doors slowly began to slide open, Steph felt an unnatural shiver run through her body. She was sure that as the doors opened, there would be some axe-wielding maniac waiting for them on the other side.

She cuddled up to Darren but did not reveal her fear.

The doors finally opened, revealing an empty left.

Greg turned to the others. "So, what do we say? Up, up and away?"

Andy took a tentative step inside and examined the interior, before turning back and shrugging his shoulders. "No congealed blood splayed across the walls," he announced. "I say let's give it a whirl."

"Not me," insisted Evelyn. "I'm far too claustrophobic to trust something which hasn't been in daily use for so long. Especially as, like I said, there's no one to come and get us if it conks out."

"You wanna walk up eight flights of stairs?" asked Andy, blocking the aisle of the lift door, just in case it began to close on him.

"I'd rather that than trust this," Evelyn replied.

"Anyone else wanna take the stairs?" asked Andy.

They all looked at each other.

Steph and Molly exchanged a glance between them. They both knew that the other felt bad for abandoning their friend. But, by the same token, neither of them fancied an eight- flight climb.

Molly turned to Evelyn. "Come on Eve, it'll be fine, we're all together," she said, soothingly.

Evelyn shook her head, vehemently. "No thank you," she replied. "I'd rather take my chances on the stairs if it's all the same to the rest of you."

"By yourself?" asked Steph, concern showing in her voice.

"Fine by me," Evelyn responded, sharply.

Finally, Andy gave in. "All right," announced, loudly. "I'll accompany you, don't worry."

Feeling obviously extremely proud of his valiant gesture, Andy puffed out his chest and marched over to stand next to Evelyn.

"Thanks, but I'd rather go by myself," she explained, moving away from him.

"Well, that's just charmin' that is," said Andy, clearly hurt by Evelyn's rejection.

"Don't take it to heart," Evelyn told him. "I don't need anyone to come with me, that's all. I'm quite capable of climbing a few stairs unaided, thank you."

"Are you sure?" Steph asked, still feeling guilty at not volunteering to stay with her friend. She knew how much Evelyn disliked Andy, which was probably her reason for refusing his help. But if Steph or Molly offered, it might have been a different answer altogether.

That said. Now that Evelyn had refused Andy, if she then accepted help from one of the girls, it would prove, in front of everyone, her dislike of him.

"Don't worry about me," Evelyn assured Steph. "I'll feel much safer moving at my own pace than in one of those things," she pointed at the lift.

There was a moment's pause, before Greg said. "Okay then troops, let the venture continue." He walked in through the open doors with Molly by his side.

Andy followed.

Steph gave Evelyn's arm a gentle squeeze before she and Darren entered.

Evelyn stood in front of the lift door and watched it close on her friends, before making her way to the staircase.

The doorway to the staircase was over to the left of the lift, and when she opened it, the door creaked loudly on rusty hinges, echoing through the vertical tunnel before her.

Unlike the rest of the lobby, the staircase was in complete darkness. Reaching along the wall, Evelyn managed to locate a switch. But, to her dismay, after flicking it up and down a couple of times, there was still no light.

She sighed, deeply.

Moving towards the nearest banister, Evelyn put her hand out so that she could feel the metal top of the rail. Once there, she gripped it to ensure her balance, before moving closer until she could feel the bottom of the rail with her feet.

Evelyn gazed up into the darkness. With no windows on the staircase, she was robbed of any natural light which may have assisted her in her plight.

Once the door to the staircase had finally closed on its rusty hinge, Evelyn could barely make out her hand in front of her face. Now for the first time, she was starting to regret not considering travelling with her companions. Or, as a lesser option, allowing Andy to come with her.

Evelyn edged her way around the side of the bend in the banister rail and felt for the first step. As she lifted her foot and placed it on top, she heard a distant *shuddering* like the sound of an old lift gate being drawn across.

She waited, listening just to make sure it was not her imagination.

The noise still echoed in her ears.

It was then that she realised that the noise was emanating from below her.

She remembered just catching sight of a flight of stairs leading down, when she first entered the stairwell, but it was not part of the flight she was about to ascend, but a separate set, just inside the entrance.

Evelyn stayed put for a moment and strained to hear more.

Again, she heard the noise. But this time it sounded further away, but one thing she could be positive about was that it was definitely coming from somewhere below.

On the way up, the lift creaked and groaned as if struggling under the weight of the five occupants. At one point, the light inside flickered, catching Molly unawares, and before she could stop herself, she had released a tiny *squeak* of fear.

The strip spluttered a couple of times before returning to strength.

There was a general feeling of relief amongst the friends, although Andy felt entitled to laugh as if he had been the only one not to be concerned by the event.

When the doors finally rattled open, both Molly and Steph were the first to leave, breathing a sigh of relief once they were in the corridor.

As the men joined them, Molly said. "I suppose we'd better wait her for E before carrying on."

Steph nodded. "Yeah, let's go and wait in the stairwell, that way we can all be together before venturing any further."

"Come on then," agreed Darren. "Stairwell's over here." He pointed at the door, and they all piled through.

It was only once they were in the stairwell that they realised they were in darkness.

Greg reached along the wall for a switch, but as with the one Evelyn had tried downstairs, there was no change when he flicked it.

"Oh, well, that's just great," muttered Molly.

Darren moved back and blocked the door from swinging shut, thereby allowing a faint glimmer of light from the lobby to penetrate the darkness.

Greg walked over to the edge of the banister rail and peered down into the gloom.

"Can you see her?" asked Steph, hopefully.

Greg shook his head. "Not yet."

They waited.

After a few minutes, Andy asked. "Any sign?"

"Nope," Greg replied.

"You must be able to see something by now," Molly whined.

"Do you wanna come and take a look?" Greg offered.

Molly walked over and grabbed hold of the waistband of his jeans for support. Peering around her boyfriend, she looked down into the dwindling darkness, and listened.

Not only was there no sign of their friend, but she could not hear her making progress, either. "Eee," she called down, her voice echoing back at her.

She waited for the sound of Evelyn's voice to shout up in her usual tone of frustration that they needed to be patient.

But nothing came.

Molly turned back to look at Steph, unable to hide the worried look on her face.

Taking the cue, Steph moved in and stood beside her. She screamed into the darkness.

"Eeeee. Are you there?"

She waited for her voice to dissipate.

Still there was no response.

The two women looked at each other. Then Steph turned to Darren. "We should be able to see her by now, and there's no way she did not hear us scream. What are we going to do?"

Reluctant to leave the door to shut, robbing them of what little light they had, Darren scratched his head and thought for a moment. He had a feeling what was coming next, and he knew that if Steph asked him, he would feel obliged to climb down and look for Evelyn.

Finally, he asked. "Do you want me to go down and look for her?"

The words made Steph go cold. As much as she was concerned for her friend, she did not relish her boyfriend leaving her side and venturing down into the darkness, to encounter, heaven knows what.

"Let's give her a few more minutes," suggested Molly. "It might be further down than we thought. Perhaps she's taking a rest and is too puffed to answer."

"Or perhaps Dominic has caught her!" suggested Andy, doing his best impression of Boris Karloff.

"You're not helping," said Darren.

"Yeah, stick a sock in it, mate," Greg chided.

Andy held his hands up. "Oh, come on you lot, I was just trying to lighten the mood. Evelyn opted to take the stairs, no one forced her. I'll bet she got tired and decided to go back down and wait for us on the ground floor. That's why she can't hear you shoutin' for her."

Aside from his genuine knack to rub people up the wrong way, Andy often had pearls of wisdom which made sense. This, possibly, being one of those occasions.

The others considered his suggestion.

Then, Steph said. "She wouldn't just turn back without letting us know."

"But how would she do that?" offered Andy, feeling as if he was winning the argument. "None of our phones have any bars."

"He's right," offered Darren. "It was probably more of a climb than she anticipated, and when she grew tired, she just turned back. Let's face it, I doubt she wanted to wait in the darkness for us to call down to her. There's no way of knowing if she would have heard us, anyway."

Molly and Steph both peered back over the railing.

Neither could see, or hear, any evidence of their friend's approach.

They looked back at each other. "What d'yer think?" Molly asked.

Steph shrugged. "They're probably right, but I feel awful about leaving her alone down there. She must be creeped out."

"Then I'm sure she would just leave and go back outside," said Andy. "She knows we'll be out again before long."

"Do you want me to go downstairs and check on her?" asked Darren, sensing that his girlfriend was still not convinced.

Steph thought for a moment. "Tell you what," she said, "we'll take the lift back down and make sure she's alright, then come straight back up. You lot can start exploring, we'll catch you up. Okay?"

"Are you sure?" asked Molly.

"Yeah," replied Steph, making her way back over towards Darren. "No point in all of us going back. We won't be long."

Seemingly satisfied with her offer, the others all made their way back out into the corridor.

The lift was still there with its door wide open, so Darren and Steph climbed back in and hit the ground floor button.

Molly waved to her friend as the doors began to close. A sudden feeling like someone was walking over her grave, made her shiver, and an eerie thought entered her subconscious that she would never see her friend again.

Realising the others had not noticed, she shrugged it off.

Once the doors were closed and they could hear the lift starting to descend, Molly linked arms with Greg, and they turned to look along the corridor which led to the sleeping quarters.

"Follow me, gang," announced Andy, clapping his hands, and rubbing them together, before striding off in front of them.

The lift's lights spluttered and blinked on the way back down, just as they had on the way up. Steph clung to Darren, who did his best to try and convey his confidence that they would reach the ground in one piece.

Once they back at reception, they scanned the corridor in both directions, but could find no sign of Evelyn.

Darren called out several times, but to no avail.

Reluctantly, they made their way back towards the back entrance to see if Andy had in fact been right about where their friend had gone.

The night air was cool and refreshing, blowing away the stuffiness from inside the building. They both searched the surrounding area from the entrance, but still there was no sign of their friend.

Darren could sense that his girlfriend was not at comfortable with the situation.

He placed his arm around her and hugged her close. "You know what she's like?" he offered. "I'll bet you anything she just got hacked off and went back to wait at the car. She'll be safe, you'll see."

Steph released a long breath through her teeth. "I wish we could see the car from here," she said. "Just to be sure."

Darren sighed. "It's too far to be bothered to walk, or we might as well go back ourselves and wait for the others in the car. Come on, nothing's happened to her. I don't think she even intended to climb those stairs."

Steph looked at him. "What do you mean?" she demanded.

"Come on, you know she was not exactly keen on the idea of

coming here in the first place, so I reckon once she saw the inside, she decided enough was enough."

"Then why didn't she say something?"

Darren shrugged. "Probably didn't want to let you and Molly down."

Steph gawped at him. "Me? I was hardly enamoured by the idea, myself."

"I know," replied Darren, controlling his voice in an attempt to calm Steph down. "But Molly was, and once she had convinced you, Evelyn probably just thought it was easier to tag along, rather than act like a wet blanket, that's all."

Steph did not look completely convinced, but she seemed to accept his explanation, all the same. She gazed out into the night, still hoping for a sign that her friend was safe and well. But there was nothing to see except trees, and the railway on the other side of the railings.

After a moment, Darren convinced her to go back inside.

As they approached the lift, Steph suddenly had an idea. "Let's quickly check the stairwell," she suggested. "Just in case she fell over. She might be lying there with a sprained ankle or something."

Darren agreed, although in truth he knew that if Steph was right, there was no reason why Evelyn would not have returned their call earlier.

They entered the stairwell and made their way over to the main flight.

They both stared up into the darkness for a moment, then Darren called up.

As expected, there was no response.

He could tell that Steph was still not happy with the situation, so after a moment he said. "Listen, you wait here a second, I won't be long."

Steph grabbed him by the arm. "Where are you going?" she said, her voice trembling.

"I'm just going to run up a couple of flights, just in case she's passed out on the stairs."

"I'm coming with you," Steph insisted.

Darren placed his hand on top of hers. "It'll be far quicker if I run alone," he reasoned. "I'll only be out of sight for a couple of seconds and be back here before you know it. I won't go far."

Steph was far from convinced, but she had to admit it was a good idea. At least then it would allay any fears she had about Evelyn being slumped over the staircase, unconscious and in need of help.

She let go of his arm and nodded.

Darren pecked her cheek and began taking two stairs at a time on his way up.

Steph clung onto the banister rail for support as she stared up into the gloom after him. By the time Darren had topped the first flight he was out of sight of her, but at least she could still hear his footfalls on the concrete.

As the echo of Darren's feet grew more faint, Steph began to wish that she had refused to let him go up alone. At least together, she would not be afraid.

She chided herself for ever allowing the others to talk her into this.

Just then she heard a *scraping* sound echoing up from below.

She spun round. In the darkness, she could not see the other staircase which led to the basement, but she knew it was there, having noticed it when they entered the stairwell.

Frozen to the spot, Steph listened intently.

She had no idea what could have possibly made the noise, but whatever it was, if it came any closer, she was prepared to scream the place down, and run for her life if necessary.

Darren would hear her scream and know that something was up. Hopefully, he would make it down before whatever was in the basement reached the landing.

As much as she loved him, Steph felt far too vulnerable to

stay where she was alone while something crept towards her out of the shadows.

She gripped the banister post until her knuckles hurt. Straining to hear, her mind raced with all manner of grotesque creatures which might have made the noise she heard.

Steph desperately wanted to call up for Darren, but she was frozen with fear at the prospect of alerting whatever was lurking below.

Finally, she heard the sound of Darren descending the stairs.

Steph waited and did not turn around until he was back on her landing. As soon as he was within reach, she grabbed his arm and pulled him close. Keeping her voice to a whisper, she told him about the sound she had heard emanating from the staircase which presumably led to the building's basement.

Darren's expression mirrored her concern. "What kind of noise was it?" he asked, looking over her toward the other staircase.

"I dunno, it was like something being dragged along the ground. I only heard it for a second."

Darren considered their situation. Being so close to the entrance they had first used to come in from outside, meant that they could be out of there in a matter of moments. But then they had the problem of how to alert the others. With none of their phones receiving a signal, the only way to communicate with them was to return to the upper floor.

They waited in the darkness.

After a minute or so, Darren said. "Well, whatever you heard, it hasn't made any sound since."

Steph turned on him. "What, do you think I imagined it? Perhaps you'd care to go down there and see for yourself?"

Darren tried to pull her close, but Steph resisted him.

Eventually, he gave up, realising that it was just making the situation worse.

"Look," he said, frustration creeping into his voice. "All I meant was that whatever you heard could have been a door swinging in the breeze, or a rat dragging something across the floor, that's all. I mean, whatever it was, it has stopped now, so chances are it was a one-off."

Steph relaxed. His explanation made sense, and it was not the case that he just did not believe that she had heard anything to begin with.

She eased herself against him and Darren gave her a comforting hug.

After a while, he said. "Listen, we'd better get back upstairs, the others will wonder what happened to us."

Steph trembled. She knew he was right. As much as she wanted to leave the wretched place, there was no way they could just abandon their friends.

"Come on," Darren coaxed, leading her from the stairwell. "The sooner we get back up there the sooner we can all call it a night."

They made their way to the lift and were both surprised to see that the doors were shut. Steph looked up at the indicator, which stated that the car was presently in the basement.

"Oh, my God," she gasped, "look." She pointed up.

Darren followed her gaze. He knew immediately what she was thinking because he was thinking the very same thing.

Whatever Steph had heard earlier, had now called the lift down to the basement.

Before either of them had a chance to say anything more, the indicator showed the car was rising.

On the fourth floor, Andy checked out the third room along the corridor.

So far there was nothing of any great interest in either of the first two, other than a couple of old metallic bed frames, and a couple of broken chairs. It was clear that the asylum had been stripped of any useable assets after the fire, which made their treasure hunt a bit of a damp squib.

The third room Andy inspected was completely bare, with

not so much as a discarded cup lying on the floor. "This is pants," Andy observed.

"Why?" asked Molly, "what were you expecting to find, an escaped lunatic?"

Andy turned back, grinning. "Well, you never know, do you?"

"I'm willing to bet the other rooms along here are all the same," said Greg, glancing down the rest of the corridor.

At the far end the access was blocked by scaffolding with hazard warning tape criss-crossing the gaps. A sign ordered people to 'Keep Out'.

"I expect that is as a result of the fire," Greg remarked, pointing towards the sign.

Andy stepped past his two friends and glanced down to where Greg had indicated.

Sighing, he said. "I reckon we should go down and try some of the rooms on the next floor. This floor is a bust."

"We can't go down without the others," Molly pointed out. "How would they know where we are?"

Andy thought for a moment, then replied. "Alright, tell you what, you two remain up here, I'll go down and start the exploration alone until the others arrive."

"Are you nuts?" Molly blurted. "You want to venture down alone?"

Andy shrugged. "What's the big deal? I'm a big boy now, I can take care of myself," he replied, cockily.

Molly turned to Greg and gave him one of her *looks*.

"They'll be back in a minute," he suggested, "what's your hurry?"

Andy knew that Greg was only agreeing to wait because that was what Molly wanted. If it had been just the two of them up here, he would have followed Andy downstairs without waiting. "This place is turning into a complete let-down," he stated, despondently. "If there's nothing of any worth on the next level, we might as well leave."

Andy began to make his way back along the corridor towards the lift.

"Seriously!" exclaimed Molly.

"You two love-birds wait here, I'll see you both downstairs."

He depressed the call button and waited.

"Come on Andy, you're being a dick," Greg called after him. "It's better if we stick together."

"It'll be fine," Andy shouted back, turning towards his friend. "As soon as the others get here, just follow me down." He heard the lift *ping*, as the doors began to slide open. "Don't worry," he assured them, "I won't try and keep the loot to myself."

Before he had a chance to turn back and face the open lift, a large arm shot out and grabbed him by the neck, yanking him inside the car.

From down the corridor, Greg and Molly looked on in shock.

At their angle, neither of them had been able to see who was in the lift, only a quick glance at the massive arm which protruded and grabbed their friend.

For a moment, neither of them could move.

Then they heard the sound of the lift door closing.

Spurred on by the sound, Greg left Molly and ran down the corridor towards the lift, calling out for Andy. But by the time he reached it, the door had already closed, and the lift was making its way back down.

Greg hit the call button several times, frantically hoping that it might change direction. But it continued on to its primary destination.

Molly walked slowly down the corridor towards him, her hands up at her mouth as if trying to prevent a scream escaping. When she reached her boyfriend, she grabbed him roughly by the shirt. "What the hell was that?" she stammered. "Did you see who it was?"

Greg shook his head slowly, still looking at the blank metal screen. "No, by the time I got here the door had already shut."

Molly pulled against his shirt. "What the fuck was that?" she demanded. "Do you think it was…" her words tapered off, almost as if she were afraid to utter his name for fear that he might here her.

Greg turned back to her. "It can't be, that's ridiculous." He reasoned. "How could it be?"

"They never found him," Molly stated. "He could be anywhere, why not here? He spent enough time here. This was probably as much as a home for him as his own. It makes sense that he would come back if he got the chance."

Greg looked at her. As much as he hated to admit it, everything she said made sense.

The truth was, he did not want to believe it. There had to be a rational explanation for what they had just witnessed.

The question was, what?

"I want to get out of here," Molly squealed, pulling frantically on Greg's arm. "Now!"

Greg nodded. He could not fault the logic in her demand. Whatever was in that lift, whether it was Dominic or not, it was obviously a serious threat to them all, and from the size of the arm they had seen, too big to argue with.

"Let's go downstairs and try and find the others," he suggested. "We'll take the stairs."

Molly pulled against him. "But what if there are more of… that?" she stammered. "What if they're waiting for us downstairs? What if there're a whole bunch of those freaks hanging back in the shadows just hoping we'll barge straight into them?"

Greg grabbed hold of her by her elbows and shook her once, to calm her down.

By now, there were tears streaming down Molly's cheeks, and the look she gave Greg was one of desperation and fear.

He held her close to him. "Look," he said, trying to keep his voice calm and reassuring. "If that thing was Dominic, we know there was only ever one of him, right. And if the tales are true…

well we know what he'll be doing to Andy right now, so he'll be busy for a while, at least."

His words, although intended to reassure Molly, were making her gag.

The fear in her eyes intensified.

"What I mean is," Greg continued, softly. "This is the perfect chance to get away, but we need to move, now."

Molly considered his idea, then nodded.

Greg guided her back towards the stairwell, all the time glancing over his shoulder, just in case. He could feel the blood in his veins thundering in his ears, and for a moment he was afraid that he might pass out. But realising that would be the end of them both, he shook the feeling away and continued down the corridor.

Molly beside him blubbered with her hand covering her mouth in a vain effort to staunch the noise.

As they reached the door to the stairwell, Greg turned back for one final look, just to ensure that the creature from the lift had not somehow managed to make its way back up to them, without being heard.

Fortunately, the way was clear, so he opened the door ahead of Molly, and the two of them entered the darkened stairwell.

They made their way to the top of the first flight, shuffling their feet along the stone floor for fear of tripping over something in the darkness.

Once they reached their goal, Greg gripped the handrail and guided Molly towards it.

"Okay," Greg announced, "here we go then."

Molly grabbed his shirt. "I'm frightened," she squealed. "What about Steph and the others. Shouldn't we wait here for them?"

Greg pulled her towards him and hugged her. "They went down to find Eve, so they're probably already waiting for us downstairs."

*If that thing hasn't got them already.*

He kept that thought to himself. Molly was already frightened enough.

"But they think we're still up here," she whispered, desperately trying to keep her voice under control. "What if they come up while we're on our way down?"

Greg shrugged. "Well, they can't use the lift, not with that *thing* in it, and if they use the stairs, we'll meet them on the way."

Molly glanced down into the darkened void below.

Suddenly, the pitch-black gloom held all manner of monsters, just waiting for anyone stupid enough to descend into their lair.

"Shouldn't there be some sort of fire exit, or at least a staircase running down the outside of the building?" Molly asked. "At least then we could see where we're going."

Greg thought for a moment, before answering. "I reckon that the doorway is probably buried behind all that scaffolding, otherwise we would have seen it down the other end. Perhaps it was destroyed by the fire."

Molly's heart dropped. Greg was probably right the entrance was doubtless out of reach now. She peeked over the edge of the banister once more. The way below looked no more inviting than it had the first time she looked.

"Come on," ushered Greg. "The quicker we set off the sooner we'll be out of this place."

Downstairs, Darren and Steph watched as the lift swept past their floor on its way down to the basement without stopping.

"That's weird," Darren remarked. "That's the second time it's done that."

"You know what that means," replied Steph.

"Stupid thing's broken."

"No, it means there's someone inside it, overriding the controls."

They looked at each other. Darren considered his girlfriend's suggestion. It made perfect sense. But who was inside the lift, controlling the buttons?

It could not be Evelyn, surely? Where would she have found the keys to override the system?

Perhaps there was security on site, after all.

"I don't like this!" Steph's announcement cut through Darren's thoughts.

"Well, that makes two of us," he agreed. "What do you wanna do?"

Steph bit her bottom lip while she thought. If she were being honest, what she really wanted was to make a dash for the exit, and not stop until they were safely back at the car. Afterall, that was doubtless where Evelyn was right now.

But what about the others? They could not just leave them upstairs waiting for her and Darren to come back. How would she feel if they had done the same to her?

The only plausible option at that moment seemed to be for them to take the stairs up to find their friends so they could all leave together.

They could, of course, try the lift one more time.

But to her mind there was something sinister about the way the car had ridden past their floor on both occasions, without stopping.

Someone had to be controlling it.

But who?

"Let's take the stairs," she announced. "It's the only sensible thing to do."

Darren turned to her, shocked. "Are you insane? The sensible thing to do is get out of here and wait for the others back at the car."

His words sounded more comforting than she dared let on. "We can't just leave the others behind," she insisted. "How would we like it if they did that to us?"

Darren shrugged. "We'd cope," he responded, unconvincingly.

"Darren!"

"Alright, alright," he gave in, reluctantly. "I suppose you're right." He looked back at the lift. "I'd still like to know who's controlling this thing, mind you."

Steph grabbed him by the arm. "Let's just put it down to a malfunction," she suggested. "I didn't like the way it *groaned* and *grumbled* on the way up, anyway."

"S'pose," Darren mumbled, staring up at the indicator. The lift car was back in the basement, once more.

Darren felt the urge to take the stairs down to see what was going on.

Whoever was controlling the car had to be down there.

But he knew that to embark on such a venture would mean a serious berating from Steph. Not to mention the fact that his bravado did not allow for such an act of foolhardiness. If Steph had insisted that he go, then he would have no option, he reassured himself. But in truth, he knew that would never be the case.

"Come on then," he said. "Let's go find the others and get out of this dump."

They made their way back towards the staircase entrance.

Once inside the stairwell, Darren held onto Steph's hand as he led the way up.

Neither of them bothered to glance in the direction of the down staircase as they passed it. If they had, they might have noticed a pair of eyes staring up at them through the gloom.

Above them, Greg and Molly had already reached the third-floor landing.

Breathing heavily, as if the task had been particularly exhausting, they huddled together on the landing gathering their strength in preparation for the next stage of their journey.

The faint glimmer of light which shafted in through the tiny window in the door leading to the floor outside, offered them little comfort as it barely illuminated the area a couple of centimetres in front of the door.

Even so, the thought of rushing out through the door so that they could at least have some form of light around them, even if it was only the meagre glare from the emergency bulbs, crossed both their minds.

Though neither admitted it.

Greg made sure he had a tight hold on Molly's sleeve, before taking his first tentative step towards the next flight.

Molly resisted, momentarily, before following on.

In the gloom, they continued to shuffle along the flat surface of the landing for fear of stepping on something which might cause one of the to lose their balance and take the other along with them.

The going was slow, but at least it was steady, and they were making progress.

"Okay," announced Greg. "Here we are, next flight. Are you ready?"

"Yep," Molly replied, not sounding in the least bit convincing.

They began their descent. Greg had made a point of sliding his foot down the side of each step until he felt the solid level beneath him. In the darkness he feared that they might come across some vast cavity where the staircase had been destroyed in the fire, leaving nothing beneath them but emptiness, into which they would plunge headlong, never to be heard from again.

As ridiculous as his thesis sounded to himself, Greg could not help but fear the worst, so every precaution became an absolute necessity.

The deathly silence made things worse.

They had decided not to speak so that they could hone their concentration on making their descent as safe as possible.

But, even so, Greg could not help wondering if some animated conversation might not help to alleviate the overwhelming sense of dread he felt with each step.

From out of nowhere, they both heard a distant *rumbling* sound.

They both stopped and listened.

After a moment, Molly whispered. "What's that?"

"I think it's the lift." Greg replied, straining to hear.

"Do you think it's the others coming to get us?" Molly asked, hopefully.

Greg thought for a moment. "Could be. Perhaps they've only just found Eve so they're on their way back for us."

"We have to warn them," Molly urged. "About...that thing in the lift."

Greg turned to her, but even from this distance, in the dark, he could not make out the expression on her face. "If they're in the lift," he whispered, "then that thing isn't."

"Oh yeah," answered Molly, feeling a little ridiculous that she had not thought about that before speaking. "Perhaps we should go back up, then. They'll be heading for the fourth floor, after all."

"No way," Greg insisted. "By the time we made it back up there in the dark, they'll probably be on their way back down to find us. And besides, it might not be them in the lift."

Molly squeezed his arm. "Oh my God, you don't think?"

"I don't know what to think right now," Greg hissed. "All I want is to get you outside and safe, then we can think about what to do next."

Feeling guilty about their friends, Molly could not help but find comfort in Greg's words. She certainly did not relish the idea of spending any more time in the asylum than was absolutely necessary. Besides, Greg was right, their best hope of helping the others was to go outside and phone the police, and to hell with the consequences.

She suspected that Andy might be dead already, and if not, he was certainly being held captive by whatever owned that enormous arm they had seen emerge from the lift. So, either way, the police would have more on their plate than bothering about some minor breaking and entering.

"Come on," Greg urged. "Let's keep moving."

At the turn of the next flight, they both stopped again as they heard a noise coming from below.

Instinctively, Greg slapped his hand over Molly's mouth, afraid that she might say something and alert whoever was below them.

He turned to face her in the gloom and placed his index finger against his lips. He could just make out her head nodding. Removing his hand, he turned back and leant over the banister railing to see if he could catch a glimpse of anything through the darkness.

Greg waited for close to a minute, but it was impossible for him to ascertain anything in the darkness.

The pair of them huddled together and strained to hear whatever it was that had made the noise.

Then it came again.

The frustration of not being able to tell what it was, or how far away it might be, was beginning to take a toll on Greg. He gripped the side of the rail, until the whites of his knuckles began to show.

From behind, Molly tugged at his shirt.

Greg spun round. Even through the darkness he could see that she was terrified.

Surrounded by darkness, and now with their way ahead cut off, they had no option left but to retrace their steps and go back upstairs.

Just then, Greg remembered the sound of the lift motor. They had no way of knowing where the car was at that moment, and if it was above them, then whatever had taken their friend might be waiting for them, upstairs.

Another sound from below echoed up through the staircase.

Greg was just about to drag Molly back up the stairs to face whatever might be there when he heard a familiar voice in the distance.

For a moment, he could not be sure, and reasoned that it might be the result of his imagination playing tricks on his. But he stayed where he was and cocked his head to one side in an effort to hear more clearly.

After a while, he heard it again. There was no doubt this time, it was Darren.

Greg leaned over the banister once more and waited until he could hear the distinct sound of footsteps on the stairs. Once he had, he called down, keeping his voice low, but loud enough to be heard.

"Greg, is that you?" Darren shouted back, seemingly oblivious to any kind of danger which might be lurking in the shadows.

"Darren," Greg called out, taking Molly by the hand, and pulling her along after him.

"We're coming," Steph called up, clearly out of breath from the exertion.

"No," urged Greg. "Stay where you are, we're coming to you."

Steph and Darren turned to each other. They both heard the urgency in Greg's voice, and suddenly they were in no hurry to climb any further. They decided to retrace their last few steps so that they were at least on the solid ground provided by the landing between floors.

There they waited while Greg and Molly made their way down to them.

When they met, Molly almost launched herself into Steph's arms, blubbering like a child.

Greg was happy to see his friends again, he almost hugged Darren, but stopped himself in time and merely slapped him on the shoulder.

"Where's Andy?" Darren asked, looking behind hid friend.

Greg caught his breath. "He's gone, mate, something grabbed him, something huge."

Darren looked puzzled. He was not used to his mate playing practical jokes, and in fairness to him, he did not sound as if he was doing so now.

"What do you mean, *something*?" Darren asked, perplexed. "Grabbed him from where?"

Greg moved back a step and held his arms out in front of him. "We were in the corridor, up there," he indicated above, "when Andy decides he wants to go off exploring on his own. While he's waiting for the lift, we're still standing at the other end, so we can't see the lift doors when they open. Suddenly, this bloody great arm shoots out from the lift and grabs Andy by the throat, dragging him inside. By the time we got there the doors had shut."

Darren turned back to see Steph's reaction to what they were being told.

Before they had a chance to decide, Molly pulled away from Steph, and started blubbering through her tears. "It's true, it's true, it's all true. Something huge and hideous grabbed Andy and yanked him onto the lift. It was horrible."

Steph pulled her friend back and continued to comfort her.

The two men looked at each other. "We need to get out of here, fast!" Greg said, trying to keep his own voice from cracking.

Darren turned to Steph, and in the gloom, he could just make out her nodding her head. "Right, we're out of here," he confirmed. "Back to the ground floor, the doors are still open where we came in."

Together the four of them bundled their way down the stairs, each trying desperately not to trip over in the darkness. It did not matter who took charge, or who went first or last. Their one and only aim was to reach the bottom in one piece and leave the wretched place.

By the time they reached the final flight, Greg was in the lead, with Molly directly behind him.

Just as they rounded the final bend, Steph let out a scream as her foot missed the stair and she tumbled forward. Darren, who had been bringing up the rear, reached out to grab her, but only managed to clamp his fingers around air.

Greg yanked Molly out of the way so that she would not receive the brunt of Steph's fall, but in doing so, he sent his girl-friend spinning towards the stairwell entrance.

Turning just in time, Greg managed to buffer some of Steph's weight as she fell towards him, but he was not in time to save her foot from sliding between two of the railings or twisting itself as her weight carried her forward.

Steph screamed out, in agony.

Greg had at least managed to save her head from hitting the concrete, so he eased himself back, laying her gently on the floor while Darren joined him.

Steph's foot was still stuck, so Darren concentrated on freeing it to relieve the pressure. Behind them they could hear Molly crying, so Greg left Steph in his mate's capable hands and made his way across the landing to find his girlfriend.

When he reached her, Molly was sitting on the concrete floor, leaning against the railing for the basement stairs. She was sobbing and holding her arm at the elbow. "Are you alright, babe?" Greg asked, crouching down beside her.

"No," she snapped. "You pushed me over and I landed on my elbow, I think my arm might be broken."

Greg kissed the side of her head. "Come on now," he soothed, "it can't be as bad as all that." He took her hand and held it, gently. "Can you squeeze my finger?" he asked.

Molly complied. The movement hurt, but not too much.

"And again," Greg urged, "do it a couple of times. Tell me how it feels."

Molly did as she was asked. "It hurts a little up my arm when I squeeze, but not too much."

"Good," replied Greg, "then you can still give me a hand job later."

Using her good arm, Molly swung a roundhouse which caught Greg on the shoulder.

"What was that for?" he asked, feigning surprise.

Before Molly had a chance to answer, the pair of them were

grabbed from behind and yanked roughly down the stairs before either had a chance to defend themselves.

Darren and Steph heard their friends cry out, which was followed by the sound of a door slamming, after which, their voices grew more distant until they finally stopped altogether.

Without thinking, Darren ran to the top of the basement staircase and screamed out their names. His call echoed down the dark corridor but was not answered.

Seconds later, he heard a blood-curdling scream emanate from somewhere below. But it was cut-off by a sickening *thud*.

In panic, Darren took the first two steps down, then stopped when he heard Steph calling to him. "Darren, no," she yelled. "Don't you go, too. You can't leave me here on my own, I need you."

She was right, of course, and he knew it.

Whatever had grabbed their friends had done so with an ease and swiftness which defied logic. Nothing on earth could be that fast and strong.

*Nothing human at least!*

"Darren," Steph called, desperation streaming from her voice.

Darren slapped the railing twice, hard enough to make his hand sting. Even if Steph was not disabled right now, he knew deep down that there was no way he would dare to venture down to the basement alone. Not after what Greg and Molly had told him about Andy.

He knew that whatever had taken him, was probably the same thing which had just snatched his other two friends, and whatever it was, it was too much for him to handle alone.

Darren ran back up the stairs and made his way over to his girlfriend. Steph was now crying openly and holding the ankle which had earlier been caught in the railing.

Darren moved behind her and placed his hands under her armpits. "Okay, on three," he instructed.

Steph braced herself with one hand on the floor and the other gripping one of the railings. On his count, Steph shoved herself away from the floor. The second she put weight on her foot, her ankle gave way.

The pain which shot through her lower leg was excruciating, and Steph *yelped* loudly from the effort.

Darren held her weight as Steph lifted her injured foot off the ground.

"I take it that was a bad idea?" he offered, jokingly.

"I can't put any weight on it," Steph replied. "Even a tiny bit of pressure is agony."

Darren sighed. "Okay, so plan B." With that, he made sure Steph was supported on her good leg, while he moved to her side and brought her arm around his shoulders. "Now just lean on me, and I'll support your weight," he instructed. "If that fails, I'll have to carry you out over my shoulder."

Together they limped out past the staircase entrance, where their friends had been captured moments before, and out into the main corridor.

The dull gleam from the emergency lighting was like a blessing compared to the pitch-black of the stairwell.

They looked both ways before Darren manoeuvred Steph around to face the back entrance where they had originally come in. "Not far to go, now," he assured her. "Once we're outside I'll call the police, okay?"

Steph nodded.

They made their way at a shuffling pace towards the back doors. All the time listening out for any sound which might indicate the presence of whatever had taken their friends.

The emergency lights *hummed* above them as if threatening to burst and go out at any moment.

As they neared the doors, Steph suddenly stopped in her tracks.

"What's wrong, babe?" Greg asked, concerned.

"Look." Steph pointed ahead of them towards the entrance doors.

Greg followed her lead and saw at once that the doors had been pulled to, and that there was now something crossing between the handles of each one.

He strained to see what it was, but in the poor light he could not make it out.

"What's that?" he asked, annoyed.

"It looks like a bicycle chain," Steph answered. "Someone's locked the doors."

"Impossible," Greg snapped. "We're the only ones here..." His words trailed off as he remembered his friends had not disappeared by their own accord.

They stayed in place for a moment, wondering what to do next.

After a while, Greg said. "Come on, we need to check it out, it might not be locked. Someone might be having a joke with us."

He did not sound too reassuring, but Steph knew that they had few, if any, other options. They continued towards the entrance, but the closer they came, the more they both realised that the chain was in fact locked in place.

Greg left Steph leaning against an old cabinet while he went to inspect the chain.

The links were covered by a thick plastic coating, and when he grabbed at it, he discovered the thick padlock binding the two ends together.

Greg pulled and yanked at the chain with all he had, although he knew it would never budge. But then he had heard stories of people under stress suddenly becoming so strong they were able to lift cars off the ground, so he thought it might be worth a try, on the off chance.

After a few moments, Greg stepped back and began kicking at the doors. Due to the damage he and his friends had caused when they broke in, earlier, the doors would not close completely, but with the chain on the gap was far too small to allow either of them to pass through.

He turned to Steph, defeated.

Steph could see that their situation was hopeless.

This was their only way out as far as she could tell. Even if there was another option, there was only so far that she could travel on her bad foot, and as strong as he thought he was, there was no way that Greg could carry her, indefinitely.

The cool breeze that rushed in between the gap in the doors, only served to tempt and tantalise her, like some selfish tall child dangling something just out of reach of their smaller peer.

Eventually, Greg gave up. He came back to Steph and put his arms around her.

They held each other while trying to figure out a solution to their predicament.

Greg kissed Steph on the lips, then said. "Listen babe, there's nothing else for it, I'm going to have to try and find something to smash those doors open."

Steph pulled back, shaking her head. "You're not leaving me here alone, no!" she demanded. "I'm coming with you."

Greg held her gaze. "You know that's a rubbish idea, you're in too much pain. Just wait here for me, I won't leave this floor, I promise. If you see or hear anything just yell, I'll be here in seconds."

Steph hated the thought of being abandoned, but she knew that Greg was right, it was the only way, and she would just have to tough it out in order for them to have any chance of escape.

Holding back a fresh batch of tears, Steph nodded.

Greg hugged her again, and then turned away and started making his way back down the corridor. He wracked his brains trying to think of something he might have seen when they first arrived which might do the job. But he could not think of anything even remotely suitable.

Every time he was about to enter another room to check, he turned and waved back at Steph, just to assure her that he was nearby.

Steph waited, patiently, cursing herself for ever agreeing to come to the hospital in the first place. She knew that if she had said no, the others would have fallen in line without too much fuss. They were her little gang, and she had always been in charge, whatever the blokes might have thought.

As Greg moved further down the corridor, it became harder for her to see more than his outline in the poor visibility afforded by the emergency lights. But she still took comfort in the sound of him opening and closing doors.

Staying in place, Steph attempted to place some weight on her bad foot. But the moment she did so, the pain shot up through her ankle, so she released it, and continued to stand on one leg, while the pain subsided.

A sudden rush of wind from outside caused the entrance doors to bend in as far as the chain would allow.

*Who the fucking hell put that bloody chain on the doors?*

She knew that there were only a couple of viable answers to that, and of those, the only one that made sense was whoever, or whatever, had taken their friends.

Steph heard another door-latch *click* somewhere further along the corridor.

Then suddenly the lights went out, altogether.

Steph held back a scream.

The entire corridor was now in total darkness.

She desperately wanted to call out to Greg, but she knew that if she did then she would be alerting whatever was in the basement to their situation.

She had to remain calm. It was probably just the lights on a timer, shutting down as it was programmed to do.

Nothing more.

Steph listened for the sound of Greg's approaching footsteps. He would realise at once how shaken she would be in the darkness and would leave his task to come and check on her.

The waiting was agony.

Steph strained to listen, but there was nothing.

Her heart began to rise in her chest. Her mind began to conjure up all manner of creatures lurking in the shadows, slowly making their way towards her under the cover of darkness.

Steph looked around for some place to hide, suddenly feeling overly exposed in the corridor. But there was nowhere for her to hide. At least, nowhere that she could safely reach with her injured foot.

She needed a crutch.

She needed Greg back by her side to support her weight.

Just then, she heard something. The sound of another door closing.

Greg must have been inside a room when the lights went out, so now he was back out in the corridor. Perhaps he did not even realise they were out if they only did so in the corridor and not in the individual rooms. Who could guess what sort of programme they used in such a dump?

Then she heard the footsteps.

Slow, even treads, making their way along the corridor towards her.

Steph bit down on her fist to stop herself from calling out. She knew that it had to be Greg on his way back to check on her. But in the darkness, she needed reassurance.

The footsteps echoed down the empty hall as they grew louder with each step.

Steph squinted through the darkness, hoping to catch even a tiny glimpse of her boyfriend approaching, but it was still too dark.

Finally, a figure came into view, close enough, even in such poor light, for Steph to see who it was. "Eve!" she cried. "Oh my God, you're still alive, we thought it had got you."

Evelyn strode up to Steph and hugged her.

Pulling back, she asked. "Thought what had got me?"

Steph shook her head. "I don't know, we didn't see it, but it

95

grabbed Andy and the others. There's only Greg and me left now."

"And me," Evelyn corrected her.

Steph grinned. "It's so good to see you, where have you been?"

Evelyn shrugged. "Oh, you know, just wandering around, exploring. This is quite a place."

"Eve listen, Greg's somewhere back there looking for a crowbar or something to break us out of here, can you go and check on him for me? I can't go anywhere because I've busted up my ankle, and it really hurts."

Evelyn gazed down at Steph's foot. "Oh, poor you, that won't do."

"Can you go and find Greg for me? We need to get out of here before…Whatever it is, finds us."

"You mean, Dominic." Evelyn chided. "He has a name, why don't you use it?"

Steph stared at her friend, open-mouthed. "What are you saying? You mean, you know who's been doing all this to us?"

Evelyn smiled. "Of course, I do. Why do you think I brought you all here in the first place?"

Steph could not believe what she was hearing. "But you never brought us, you didn't even want to come."

"That's what I wanted you all to think. But I had to do something, Dominic has been getting awfully hungry, lately." She turned around and looked off into the darkness. "Haven't you baby?"

# HAUNTING

The first night was the worst. Or, at least, the most unsettling.

I had reached that time in life where I could no longer go through an entire night without at least two bathroom visits. As I dried my hands off afterwards, I suddenly became aware of a sense of foreboding. It was hard to describe, there was nothing specific that I could put my finger on, it was just a feeling that something was *different*.

As I was staying in a rented cottage far off the beaten track, my imagination was apt to run away with me from time to time. Being a writer of horror fiction, my mind was forever exploring new and more twisted ways of telling a story, and as such, it did not usually take much to plant such a seed in my thoughts.

For a second, in my half-asleep state I had to remind myself that I was awake and not in the middle of one of my more gory tales. But as I switched off the light and began to make my way along the corridor back to bed, that original feeling of unease refused to release its hold on me.

I stopped in my tracks and listened.

At first, there was nothing. But then, just as I was about to continue towards my bedroom, I heard what sounded like a faint *clink*. It was the sound of a china cup being placed back in its saucer.

I rubbed my eyes and tried to feel more awake and in touch with my senses. The sound had been faint, and had lasted all of a spilt-second but, nonetheless, it was still discernible.

I must have stayed in that same spot, holding my breath as best I could, for at least five minutes. Whenever I was forced to expel the air, I tried to do so by making the least sound possible.

After five minutes I decided I must go downstairs and investigate.

There was no way of descending the stairs without announcing my presence. Each and every stair made its own unique sound when you placed any weight on it. Ironically, when I first viewed the property, I saw that as a bonus, thinking that at least if someone tried to break in, I would be able to hear them before they reached me.

As I made my way down, I half expected to hear the sound of someone running out the door, bumping into tables, and knocking over chairs in their haste to escape detection.

But there was none of that.

This in turn made me presume that the perpetrator was instead lying in wait to pounce the moment I came into view. I had heard that some burglars were brazen enough to face their victims when discovered, rather than escape without their booty.

Though, to be honest, what treasure the thief might hope to find was a mystery to me. The cottage was rented out with the bare minimum of furniture in situ, and as I was on a travelling holiday, the only possessions I had with me were what I could comfortably hold in my rucksack, and sports bag.

Even so, perhaps the mere sight of the chimney being used was enough to inspire some local thief to decide to investigate the lay of the land.

I say *local*. The nearest property to me belonged to the owners of the cottage, and that was almost a mile away. After that, I think they said the next closest was at least a mile further. Therefore, this intrepid burglar, if he existed, would have had to have made quite a trek on the off chance that I had something worth the effort.

There was of course my fold-up bike, which at the time was probably the most expensive item I had with me. But that was safely tucked away under lock and key in one of the outhouses.

Once I reached the bottom of the stairs, I paused and strained to listen for any indication that I was not alone.

I heard nothing, save the sound of the wind outside, when it picked up speed.

I was standing in the main reception room which housed the fireplace, a sofa with matching armchair, and an occasional table festooned with magazines and books on the shelf underneath. There was a television and old-fashioned stereo unit in one corner, and the walls were adorned with paintings courtesy of the lady owner, who had informed me, proudly, that if I was interested in any of them, she would consider all serious offers.

I could see the main door for the cottage just to the right of the television unit, and even from here I could see that the chain was still on.

On the other side of the room was a stone wall which separated this room from the kitchen/diner. Because of the angle of my view from where I was standing, I could not see the back door which was tucked away at the far end of the kitchen.

Once I was convinced that whatever I had heard was not in fact an intruder, I strode purposely into the kitchen so that I could double-check the kitchen door was locked.

As I turned the corner to enter the kitchen, my blood froze in my veins.

There, sitting at the table, a cup and saucer before her, was a beautiful woman.

I had never seen her before, nor had any idea who she was. I would estimate that she was probably in her early to mid-thirties, with beautiful chestnut-coloured hair which she kept tied back in a loose ponytail.

99

She turned to face me when she heard me enter and smiled.

My heart was still thumping ninety to the dozen in my chest at this point, however, I found myself smiling back as if everything was just as it should be.

After a while I found my voice and said, "Hello."

"Hello," she responded, as if it were the most natural thing in the world.

My mind was racing. Due to my profession, I had conjured up all sorts of scenarios similar to the one I now found myself in, where the hero of the piece kept his cool and toughed it out, even when there was a macabre ending to look forward to. But now that I was actually in the middle of the story, I found myself completely stripped of all bravado.

The woman turned away and gazed out of the window, into the night.

I, meanwhile, looked around to see if there was any evidence of an accomplice waiting to pounce the minute she took my attention away. But it appeared as if we were alone, after all.

I watched her for a moment longer before speaking again. "Sorry," I began, keeping my tone gentle and non-confrontational, "but may I ask what you are doing here?"

The lady turned back to face me and lifted her cup. "Just enjoying a cup of tea," she replied, nonchalantly. She had a strong French accent, and if I'm honest, I have always found French ladies to be incredibly seductive. It was not just their accents but more a 'total-package' kind of aura they seemed to exude.

Stuck for something else to say, and not wanting to appear rude, regardless of the circumstance, I muttered, "You're French, how exciting."

She relaced her cup and held out her hand. "Chantelle," she offered.

I walked over and took it in mine. Her skin felt so soft and light, it was almost as if her hand were not there. "Simon," I replied, shaking it gently.

Her smile was captivating, her eyes alluring, and right then and there I knew somehow that I had nothing to fear from her. But that still did not explain her presence in my kitchen.

Even so, I took the chair opposite her and sat down.

She looked so small and petite I felt as if I could lift her up with one hand.

After taking another sip from her cup, she asked, "Do you like it here?"

By 'here' I presumed she meant the cottage, so I replied, "It's my first time being here, but so far it seems very pleasant. Have you been here before?"

"Oh yes, I stay here all the time when I'm in Ireland. There is nowhere else like it in the world. The people are so kind and friendly, they really make you feel like you're at home."

Well, that at least told me something about her, unless she was making it all up.

My mind continued to try and fathom what was happening. I knew that there were two other bedrooms in the property, so I wondered if perhaps the owners rented them out separately. But if that were the case, then surely, they would have mentioned it to me when I booked? It was possible that they forgotten that they had already sub-let one of the other rooms. Or perhaps they each thought their partner had informed me.

Either way, it seemed a very rum arrangement to me.

"Are you planning on staying long?" I asked, casually.

She shook her head. "Not long, I just really fancied a cup of tea. I think it is the water here that makes it taste so lovely. Back home I stick to coffee."

I nodded as if everything was just fine. Meanwhile, inside my stomach was churning.

I considered making an excuse and going back to my room to call the owners to try and find out what was going on. The fact that it was the middle of the night did not bother me in the slightest. After all, if they had sub-let the property without telling me, then they deserved to be woken up to explain themselves.

But there was something purely captivating about this lady which prevented me from wanting to leave her. Regardless of her reason for being there.

The horror writer in me continued to flood my mind with ideas about her having escaped from a mental institution for the criminally insane and making her way out here to the place where, years ago, she tore her husband to pieces with a carving knife, before devouring his entrails.

But one glance at her sweet smile eradicated all such thoughts.

It was hard to decide what topic of conversation to embark on, under the circumstances, so as she drained her cup, I offered to make her another one, stating that I would join her.

She thanked me, so I stood up and went over to the kettle.

Switching it on, I turned to ask her how she took her tea…but she was gone!

I looked around the room, astonished by the fact that she had managed to move so quickly and quietly. Even her cup and saucer were gone.

I called out to her, but there was no reply.

I honestly do not know if I searched the cottage for her before going back to bed, because the next thing I remember was waking up in the morning, with the sunlight shining in through my window.

My early hours encounter seemed more like a dream than anything else, and for a while I tried to convince myself that I had imagined the entire episode.

Yet, it felt so real.

This time I did make a search of the other bedrooms, just in case, but as I expected, they were all empty with no sign of anyone having stayed in them recently.

After breakfast I cycled down to the owner's cottage on my way to town. I pondered whether or not to say anything to them,

after all, what was there to say other than the fact that I had had
a vivid dream.

I decided in the end not to say anything and to keep on
heading into town, but just as I rounded the corner towards their
abode, the lady of the house appeared at the gate and waved
to me.

It would have been churlish not to stop and wish her for the
day. After all, this was not London, and such rudeness would
not leave a good impression. So, I braked and pulled over
beside her.

"And how was your first night then?" she asked brightly. The
owner was about the same age as me, that is to say mid-forties,
and aside from a couple of silver hairs her features appeared
unaffected by the strains and stresses one usually associates with
people of our age, certainly those who live in the city.

The easy, laid-back approach to country life clearly
suited her.

"Just fine," I lied, "I slept like a baby."

She smiled and nodded. "It is so lovely and peaceful out
here, isn't it? And none of that awful noise or light pollution you
get in the towns."

"Have you and your family lived her long?" I enquired.

"Let's see now, we arrived her almost twenty years ago, now.
Fell in love with the place as soon as we saw it. Couldn't wait to
move here from stuffy old London."

I had not detected much of an accent when I first spoke to her
the day before, and now I knew why. "So, you moved her from
London? Not a native as such?"

"Good heavens, no, we're both a couple of blow-ins. But the
people in town accepted us right from the start. They're very
nice people in the main, one or two oddballs, but that is to be
expected anywhere." She laughed at her own joke.

Part of me was adamant that I was not going to mention the
previous night. For one thing, I did not want my landlady to
think that I was odd, or strange in any way. Also, she seemed so

genuinely happy that I was enjoying my stay, that I did not want to bring her down by asking her if any of her previous clients had ever spoken about suffering from nightmares, or hallucinations.

For what else could it have been? My mind had obviously projected the woman onto my subconscious because the cottage seemed the ideal place to have a romantic adventure. My previous girlfriend and I had split up over six months earlier, and whether or not I admitted it to my friends, I was lonely.

What better than to meet a mysterious lady with a sultry foreign accent in the middle of nowhere?

In the end, I decided against saying anything and potentially ruining her morning.

Once in town, I took a ride out to the coast and spent a very pleasant morning sitting on the beach, watching the waves and the children playing in the sand. The sea had always had a calming effect one me, but also it inspired me to motivate my creative juices. After all, I had taken this holiday to escape the mad hustle and bustle of London and my hectic social life, and to try and begin writing my latest novel.

I had already accepted a commission from a new publisher which, if things went well, could land me a three-book deal, so my incentive was well and truly in place. Now all I needed was a story.

By early afternoon I had managed to jot down a couple of ideas, though nothing specific, so decided to take myself back into town to find somewhere for lunch.

I stopped by at a pub I had passed on my way out to the sea, and chained up my bike outside, much to the hilarity of some drinkers sitting at a table near the entrance.

When I glanced over to see what all the excitement was about, one of them waved at me and called over, "You needn't bother with that here, no one will try and take your bike."

I waved back my thanks, and heard them muttering something about me not being local as I went in.

Inside the pub there were a smattering of drinkers dotted around the place, most of whom turned when I entered, so I offered a smile to break the ice. I went up to the bar and waited patiently while the only man serving finished his conversation with one of the patrons.

Finally, he came over to me. "Good afternoon, sir," he said, brightly, "and what would you be having today?"

There was no evidence of a lunch menu to be seen, so I asked tentatively if they did sandwiches. To my surprise, as well as delight, the barman placed a menu in front of me which he had grabbed from beneath the bar. It seemed odd to me that they did not leave them out, but I thanked him without question and ordered a pint of Guinness while I perused their fare.

My pint was prepared with a perfect shamrock on the surface, and I grinned openly while I ordered myself a ploughman's lunch.

When the barman brought my meal over to my table, instead of placing my plate down in front of me and leaving, he sat down opposite me. "So, I take it you're over here on holiday?" he asked.

It occurred to me that, judging by the rest of the clientele, I stuck out like the proverbial sore thumb as an outsider, or a *blow-in* as my landlady had explained.

The idea of a member of waiting staff sitting down at your table when they brought your meal would have seemed completely bonkers back in London. But I presumed that such behaviour was considered normal in quaint quiet places such as this. In fact, it would have probably been deemed *rude* in such a place for the man not to.

Without going into too many details I explained to the man where I was from and the reason for my little holiday, such as it was. He seemed genuinely interested and not merely making conversation for the sake of it. When I told him where I was staying, he suddenly sat back in his chair with a strange faraway look in his eyes.

Before leaning back in, he quickly scanned the bar area as if afraid that someone might be listening in on our conversation. When he was satisfied that they were not, he moved forward and whispered, "Have you seen our Chantelle yet?"

His words struck me like an ice-cold slap of water.

He must have realised from my reaction that he had hit a nerve, so held up his hand before I had a chance to answer. "I suspect Mrs Moss has not explained to you about your guest?" he stated, shaking his head. "What it is with these people I'll never know. Perhaps she thought you wouldn't see her and be none the wiser. But I take it from your expression that that's not the case?"

Unconsciously mimicking his earlier action, I too had a quick look around me before replying. "I thought it was a dream," I confessed. "How on earth did you know…" I trailed off, not sure where the conversation was going to next. It was completely surreal to me that this complete stranger could possibly know something which I had not shared with anyone else.

It felt almost as if he could see inside my mind, and the sensation unnerved me to the extent that I no longer wanted to be there.

The man must have seen my discomfort, as he stood up and told me to enjoy my meal, before making his way back over to the bar.

I picked at my lunch but finished my Guinness. Paid, and left.

That night I sat in the kitchen until almost midnight before sleep claimed me.

I took myself off to bed but woke at roughly the same time as the previous night. Without thinking, I immediately went back downstairs to the kitchen.

As I entered the room, I was not exactly sure what I expected to find, but when I saw Chantelle sitting at the table with her tea in front of her, I was no more surprised than if the room had been empty.

She looked up as I walked in and smiled that same disarming smile which she had given me the night before. "Hello," she said, as if it was the most natural thing in the world.

"Hello," I replied. "What happened to you last night? I turned around and you were gone."

She simply shrugged her shoulders as if that was all the answer I needed.

I took the chair opposite her and laid my hands on the table. Chantelle turned to gaze out of the window.

"I met a friend of yours this afternoon," I said, "old chap, works in a pub in the town, The White Horse I think it was called."

She turned back to face me. "Jed?" she asked.

I shook my head. "Sorry, I didn't get his name. Friendly sort of bloke. As soon as I mentioned where I was staying, he asked if I'd seen you. It appears that your reputation proceeds you."

"He's a very nice man," she replied. "Makes the most delicious seed cake."

"I'll have to try some next time I'm there."

It was so easy for me to forget that I was talking to a ghost. Chantelle seemed as real to me as anyone I had ever met before. The fact that her presence was obviously known by some of the locals, made the situation feel almost normal. After all, it was not as if Jed had warned me against her.

Before coming out to this part of Ireland, I had read a story about a mystical white lady who drifted upon the surface of a lake, nearby. The story said that people were afraid to go there because if they saw her, they would not live to see another day.

Evidently, this was not the case with Chantelle.

To be honest, even if Jed, or my landlady Mrs Moss, or anyone else in town for that matter had warned me against her, I'm not sure I would have heeded the warning.

I could not get over the feeling of tranquillity her presence seemed to have over me. It was as if she exuded some inner sense of compassion which made you forget all the horror and suffering that was carrying on around you.

I wanted to take her hand in mine again, just as I had done last night. I desperately wanted to feel the softness of her touch, the gentleness of her skin on mine. But it was too late now to offer mine in friendship without it looking clumsy and awkward.

So instead, I just sat there and gazed upon her. I watched her sip her tea until my eyes grew heavy and I must have fallen asleep.

To my shock and surprise, I woke up in bed once more, unaware of having made my way up the stairs. For a brief moment, I wondered if Chantelle had somehow managed to transport me up, lifting me with heavenly arms as if I weighed no more than a baby.

Could such things be possible?

I spent the next day at the cottage, desperately trying to set out a format for my novel. I was already three days into my refuge, and thus far I did not have a single word to show for it.

But, as I should have expected, my mind kept drifting back to Chantelle, my very own ghost. It is odd how the word 'ghost' always seems to conjure up negative feelings. When most people hear that word, their thoughts immediately turn to stories of dusty, old mansions, and ruined graveyards. Headless corpses and phantom riders charging through the darkened countryside. Yet here I was looking forward to my next encounter with great anticipation.

Of course, there was nothing remotely frightening or threatening about Chantelle. Even so, had you have told me before this trip that I would be so calm in the presence of a visitor from the other side, I would have called you insane.

Only goes to show.

Then an idea burst out of the blue. Perhaps I should plan my latest novel around Chantelle. After all, ghost stories are very in fashion at the moment.

To be honest, my readers are quite particular in their tastes, and, according to their posts on-line, they enjoy my work because of the amount of blood and gore I fill the pages with. They expect a certain amount of violence and more than a smattering of sex, so I was not altogether sure how they, or my publisher for that matter, would take to me writing a ghost story, rather than a straightforward horror novel.

It might be a unique twist for me. Alternatively, I could spend the best part of six months finishing it, only to discover that my publisher was not interested. It would not be the first time.

Plus I doubted there was anything gory or blood-curdling about Chantelle's life or death. I imagined that she probably passed away peacefully in her sleep of some previously undiagnosed medical condition, and the only reason she was haunting my cottage was because she loved staying here.

I wondered how much she would tell me if I asked her that evening. Presuming that she planned to visit me, that is.

A sudden wave of melancholy wafted over me just then as I sat at my laptop. I realised it was at the possibility of her not coming to visit me that night.

It was a very odd sensation. After all, it was not as if she was some local girl who had caught my eye, with whom I was hoping to start a relationship with.

Yet, even so, I could not deny the feeling of despair which grew in the pit of my stomach as I considered the possibility of never seeing her again.

That night, I made a point of going overboard with the coffee and stayed downstairs on the sofa until I fell asleep. I did not want to miss the chance of waking up, and decided it was more likely if I was closer to the kitchen when Chantelle appeared.

As before, I woke in the early hours, and almost turned over and went back to sleep before I remembered what I was doing there.

Chantelle was waiting for me. That same sweet smile, those

same gorgeous eyes and perfect skin. She always looked as if she had just come in from outside with her slightly lop-sided pony-tail which gave her a *windswept* look.

We talked briefly, much the same as on the previous occasions. It was general chit-chat, nothing specific. At one point, during a lull in the conversation when she had her face turned away towards the window, I almost asked her to tell me the story of her life, and more to the point, her death.

But my nerve failed me, so I stayed quiet and just watched her sipping her tea.

At some point I yawned and apologised as I placed my hand over my mouth.

"You look sleepy," she observed. "Why don't you take yourself up to bed."

Before I had a chance to answer, it was morning, and I was back in bed without any knowledge of how I managed to end up there. A familiar pattern.

As I had chickened out of asking Chantelle directly about herself, specifically the manner of her death, I decided that I would try and discover the truth by some other means.

My landlady clearly knew the story, or so old Jed had intimated, so I decided to make her my first port of call that morning. To avoid putting her in an awkward position, I left it until late morning before cycling over to her cottage, presuming that by then her teenage children would have gone out for the day with their friends.

As before, Mrs Moss was standing in her front yard as I cycled into view, and when she saw me, she smiled broadly and waved. She was hanging out some washing, so I waited patiently by the wall for her to finish, before engaging her in conversation.

We chatted amicably for a while before I broached the subject of Chantelle.

The second I mentioned her name I saw the woman's face fall.

There was an awkward silence which seemed to last a lifetime but was in reality probably no more than a couple of seconds.

Then she said, "I suppose you'll be wanting your money back, now!"

Her announcement took by completely by surprise. "Why on earth would I want my money back?" I asked, bemused.

She pursed her lips together. "Has someone in the town been talking? Or did you read something on the web? We're not a freak show you know, just an honest couple trying to earn a few extra pounds by renting out our holiday cottage."

I assured her that she had no reason to reproach herself, and that I had no intention of leaving before the week was up, so there was no question of me seeking a discount, let alone a refund.

She seemed to calm down slightly upon hearing this.

"I just wondered why you did not mention her to me when I booked," I ventured. "That's all."

She shrugged, and gazed down at her feet, sheepishly.

She made a fuss about kicking a stone out of the way, although in truth, she had to dislodge it with her foot before moving it on.

Finally, she shrugged her shoulders and looked back up at me. "It all happened long before we moved here, and I don't like to talk about it. That's all." She snapped.

I nodded my understanding. "But surely you must have realised that I would have questions after meeting her?" I kept my voice low, and unchallenging. It seemed like the best way of extracting information from her.

"She doesn't always appear," she confessed. "So, it's not as if it's worth mentioning just on the off chance, is it? Besides, most of those who do see her, or think they do, usually accept that it was just a trick of the light, or as a result of them having too much to drink, so I just laugh it off with them."

"I understand, but I've seen her, and spoken to her, on the last three nights, so I know she is no figment of my imagination."

She was growing flustered again, and for a dreadful moment I was afraid she might insist on refunding me my money and demanding that I do not stay another night.

I waited a moment for the air to clear, before continuing. "When you say, it all happened a long time ago, what exactly are you referring to?"

"Her…The…Look, I said I don't like talking about it, so can you please just leave well alone? You can decide whether you want to continue staying with us, or not, it's up to you. But please do not mention this again, and especially around my children."

I could tell how upset she was becoming, so I assured her that I would continue with my stay and apologised for having asked her about Chantelle.

As far as I was concerned, I was in the right, it was her fault for not mentioning Chantelle in the first place. I mean, who rents out a property with a live-in ghost, and then does not bother to mention it to the tenant?

By the sound of it, I was not the first to have seen her, so I would have expected Mrs Moss and her hubby to realise that they would be better off coming clean with future renters. But as it was, the mere mention of her seemed to send my landlady off at the deep end, so perhaps it was more a matter of them coming to terms with their unwanted houseguest than any of their prospective clients.

It made me wonder if they knew about her before they bought the property.

If not, then surely to goodness they would have a legal claim for damages from the seller?

Either way, not my field of expertise, and besides, it was not as if Mrs Moss was likely to wish to enter in a discussion with me concerning the subject, so best left alone.

This left me with another quandary. How was I going to find

out anything about Chantelle if my landlady refused to talk about her?

Then, I remembered Jed. He seemed like the talkative type, and after all, it was he who brought up Chantelle in the first place. Furthermore, she had seemed quite fond of him when I mentioned to her that I had met him, so that too was a good indication that I was on the right track.

I took myself back to the pub. They had just opened when I arrived, so being a *blow-in*, I chained up my bike and went in. Jed was serving a couple of old boys, so I stayed in the background until he had finished.

I checked my watch and saw that it was just after eleven. As much as I love a pint, it was far too early for me to start drinking, so once Jed was free, I sidled up to the bar and asked him if it was possible to order a coffee and have a quick chat.

He raised an eyebrow when I mentioned the *chat*.

Jed joined me at my table which was on the other side of the bar from the early-morning drinkers. He obviously knew why I wanted to talk to him, and fortunately for me, he was a far more forthcoming than my landlady.

He kept his voice low while he spoke for obvious reasons. "It must be near twenty-four years ago now," he began. "Chantelle Le Grande was her name. She was a married lady with two young daughters, but from what we heard afterwards, her marriage was not the happiest. She lived and worked in Paris, but discovered us while on a walking holiday, and fell in love with the place, and who could blame her.

"She rented the cottage you're staying in from the previous owner, old Jacks, but he's long gone now too. She would come down here at least twice a year. Out of season, of course. During the summer months you can barely move around town for tourists, but during the winter months we're down to our bare bones, with the occasional blow-in." He winked at me when he said it.

"What was she like?" I asked.

His face lit up. "She was a lovely lady. Gentle, softly spoken, always with a smile on her face. I think the whole town fell in love with her, and over the years she became a regular fixture. She used to come in here every single day for tea and seed cake. She used to tell me I made the best seed cake she had ever tasted. A good thing too, as it was the only thing I could bake without ruining it." He laughed at the memory.

"She told me about your seed cake," I admitted. It felt strange to say the words out loud considering the fact that I was talking about a ghost. But Jed simply nodded and smiled his *knowing* smile.

"That's kind of her," he said. Leaning in closer he whispered, "Next time you speak to her, tell her I send my love, and tell her how much we all miss her, will you?"

I nodded.

"Yes," he continued, "she was indeed a lovely lass." I noticed a tear trickle down his cheek, and he wiped it away, clearly embarrassed. "Look at me," he said, "silly old fool."

"Not at all Jed," I tried to reassure him. "You obviously cared for her very deeply."

He nodded once more, as he took out a hanky and blew his nose.

"It was just after Christmas," he carried on. "Early January, I think, and as usual Chantelle drove into town in her rented car and stopped off here before going up to the cottage. She came in the following day, as usual. Nothing out of the ordinary. We spoke a while; she spoke perfect English but with a lovely accent. Then, the following day I didn't see her which I thought was odd as she had told me that she had booked the cottage for the entire week." He shrugged. "I presumed that she had either taken herself off for a drive somewhere, or just fancied a change, so it didn't ring any alarm bells."

He looked off into the distance, and I could see that the retelling of the story was causing him some discomfort. But I was desperate to learn the details, and he was my best shot, so I did not interrupt him, or ask if he was okay to carry on.

Though I did feel bad about that.

He took a deep breath. "Some ramblers found her later that afternoon. It was only by chance. They were lost and it was starting to grow dark when they saw her cottage and decided to ask for directions." This time he did not bother to wipe away his tears. "Someone had beaten her to death with an iron bar. They found it a few feet away from her body. Her face was smashed to a pulp, so they say…Poor darling."

Now he had to deal with his tears as they began to flow like a river.

Jed held his hanky to his eyes and sobbed, quietly, for at least a minute.

The other drinkers in the bar glanced over but did not leave their table to investigate. I suspected that they knew why he was crying, as they were probably locals, and thus knew how Jed felt about Chantelle. It was not a huge leap to imagine that being a stranger in town they also knew where I was staying.

I leaned over and patted Jed's arm. "I'm sorry old son," I said, "if it's too traumatic for you to continue then I completely understand."

But Jed shook his head, and blew his nose once more, before continuing. "No, that's the worst of it. That poor, lovely girl came to us because she trusted us, felt safe here, and we let her down in a most terrible way."

I shrugged. "Well, that's a little harsh on you," I pointed out. "There was nothing you could have done to save her."

"Not the point." He shook his index finger at me like a schoolmaster admonishing a tardy pupil. "She came to us for refuge, and we should have protected her from the monster who killed her. Simple as that!"

I waited a moment before carrying on. I still wanted to know more, but by the same token, I was starting to feel like a bully for plugging the old man for information.

After a while, I asked, "Did they catch whoever did that to her?"

Jed's face darkened. He shook his head. "No, we never did. Hard to believe in such a tight community, especially during the off-season. A stranger would stick out a mile, and none of us wanted to contemplate the thought that one of us might have done such a terrible thing. But, even so, the Garda questioned almost every man in town, checking on where we all were, and who we were with. But one by one they discarded us all."

"Were there no suspects at all?" I asked, bemused. It seemed ridiculous to me that in such a small, or relatively small, community that the local police could not find a viable suspect for such a hideous crime.

Jed looked straight at me. "There was talk, always in in such a small place as this, suspicions run rife, but nothing specific enough to point the finger. No, it's to our everlasting shame that we weren't able to bring Chantelle's murderer to justice."

"So, her case is still open?" I asked.

He nodded. "That it is, and will remain so, possibly forever, unless someone confesses, or the Garda come up with some new evidence. Not that it is likely after all this time. According to the reports in the papers, whoever killed her must have been drenched in her blood. And yet he somehow managed to vanish into thin air."

"Someone must know something?" I suggested.

"Quite possibly, but if they do, they're not saying anything. And they haven't for over twenty years."

I asked Jed if he himself suspected anyone, but he refused to say. As he put it, there was enough gossip in the town without him adding to it.

But he assured me that if he ever found out, he would happily kill them with his bare hands, even if it meant him spending his last days behind bars.

He also mentioned that he was not the only local who felt

that way. It appeared that Chantelle had left quite an impression on those she met, while she was there.

I thanked Jed and left the bar.

I cycled around town for a while, then headed out towards one of the vast open spaces which surrounded the town. I stopped at the brow of a particularly steep hill to catch my breath. From my vantage point I could look out over the sea, so I stayed there for a while to drink in the atmosphere.

The tranquillity of my surroundings could not overshadow my inner sorrow at the terrible fate which befell Chantelle. Sitting atop that hill felt a million miles from anything so destructive and evil, and yet, it had occurred only a few short miles away.

Even the splendid beauty of the scenery could not dispel the sadness in my heart, so I decided to head back to the cottage and wait for my nightly visitor.

My trepidation at the thought that Chantelle might not appear weighed more heavily on my mind than before. Now that I knew the tragic circumstances surrounding her death, I could not help wondering if she would feel the need to stay away to avoid any awkward questions I might venture to ask.

But that made no sense. She was not obliged to answer anything I asked, and there was nothing I could do about it, regardless.

To my relief, she appeared, as before.

This time I had drifted off at the kitchen table, so when I woke, her beautiful face was the first thing I saw.

I rubbed the sleep from my eyes. "Hello again," I said, somewhat bashfully.

"Hello again," she replied, with her customary smile.

I wondered if, being a spirit and all, she might already know about my conversation with Jed that morning. I have heard it said that when you die you discover the answers to everything you ever wondered about.

As it turned out, I did not have to consider the prospect for long.

"You spoke to Jed." Chantelle came straight out with it, without any prompting from me. It was almost as if she could read my mind.

I felt my face go red. "Yes," I admitted. "He sends his love."

"I know," she replied. "And did he quench your thirst for knowledge?"

There was no reproach, or bitterness in her tone. In fact, I detected a slight edge of joyfulness in her tone. Almost as if she was taking pleasure in my embarrassment at having been caught out for talking about her.

"Well, he…" I did not know where to go, and Chantelle knew it.

"There's nothing to be ashamed of," she assured me. "You are a writer and naturally inquisitive."

I could still feel my face burning, in spite of her reassurances.

I resumed by now that she knew everything. But even so I felt that I had to try and justify my inquisitiveness. "He told me about how you died," I said. "I'm so sorry, it must have been horrendous."

My words sounded inadequate to say the least, and I regretted not formulating a more appropriate sentence before wading in.

But it was too late, now.

Chantelle merely shrugged and took a sip of her tea.

I was hoping that she would say something, anything at that point, because I knew what I was burning to ask her, and I would have loved some indication from her that it was okay for me to ask.

But she tortured me with her silence.

In the end, I just came out with it. "Jed told me that they never caught the man who did that to you," I said, as if it was somehow news to her. The entire conversation was just so surreal, I decided that there was no proper way to approach the subject, so I just continued and hoped for the best. "If you tell me, I promise that I will do everything within my power to see that he is brought to justice."

I meant every word, and I believe that she knew it.

Chantelle put down her cup and placed an elbow on the table. She stared at me for the longest time with her chin resting in her palm.

For a moment I was afraid that she would just evaporate before my eyes.

But then she said, "How do you know it was a man?"

Her question really knocked me for six. Anyone hearing about the awful circumstances surrounding her death would automatically presume that her killer was a man. That was not just me being sexist, it was a natural conclusion based on the history of murderers throughout history.

The only time I had ever heard of a woman bludgeoning someone to death, it was the result of them having suffered years of abuse by their partner before finally, and understandably in my opinion, *snapping*.

Women who murdered for their own gain, generally did so with poison, surely.

Chantelle noticed the look of puzzlement on my face, and her smile returned.

Was she making fun of me?

If so, I realised that I did not care. But I had to know. "Are you telling me it was woman who did…that, to you?"

She paused a moment before answering. Then said, "No, I just wondered why you automatically thought it was a man."

"So, it was a man?" I charged in, possibly a bit too strongly. I sounded like a barrister trying to catch out a suspect in the dock, and that was never my intention. "I'm sorry," I offered, before she had a chance to answer, or take Umbridge. "I didn't mean to be so forceful, it's just that I would really like to see the man, or woman, who…did that to you, brought to justice, that's all."

"Why?" she asked, casually.

"Why, well because you're so lovely, and I don't just mean that to sound flippant, but from what I know about you, you never hurt a fly, and no one, especially someone so nice, deserves to have suffered the way you did."

As hard as I was trying to be sincere, my words sounded flat, even to my ears.

I wanted to say more to justify what I was trying to explain to her, but in the end, I just kept my mouth shut to avoid making things worse.

When she realised that I was finished, Chantelle sat back in her chair. "I appreciate your sentiment," she said, "but it is no longer important. What's done is done."

I could feel the hairs on the back of my neck rising and had to calm myself down before speaking. "No, Chantelle, that's not fair, it's not right. Whoever they are deserves to pay."

She smiled. "I'm no one to judge," she replied. "And now, you need to sleep."

I fought to stay awake, but as usual, she was right, and the next time I opened my eyes I was in bed, and it was morning.

I decided over breakfast that I would speak to my landlady concerning an extension of my stay. Chantelle had been adamant last night that she would not divulge the name of her assailant, but it occurred to me that perhaps I could at least persuade her to drop me a clue.

When I reached the Moss holding, there was the lady of the house as usual, working in the garden. Today she was washing the downstairs windows, so she did not see me approach until I was directly outside her gate.

She turned with a start, and her face immediately went red.

"Good morning," I offered, cheerily.

She waved back, somewhat dismissively, completely the opposite to her usual greeting. I watched as she placed her cloth back in the bucket of soapy water, but then, instead of turning to walk towards me, she simply picked up her bucket and went back inside her cottage.

I waited patiently for a couple of minutes, presuming that she just wanted to pour the dirty water away before coming over to talk to me. But to my surprise, she did not venture back out, and after another couple of minutes the door was closed from inside.

I must confess that I was little taken back by her rudeness, especially as she had been so pleasant and cheerful up until I had mentioned Chantelle.

Either way, I knew right then that my mission was not going to be an easy one, as the woman clearly did not wish to speak to me.

Nonetheless, I decided that this might still be my best chance to have her agree to extending my stay at her cottage, so I opened the gate and walked up to the front door.

Through the net curtains I could just make out two adult figures pacing back and forth inside the. They were clearly arguing, but it was impossible to hear what was being said from my vantage point.

I waited a moment before knocking. The door was answered by Mr Moss, a short, bespectacled man with a very obvious toupee adorning his head, the colour of which did not match his sideburns.

We introduced ourselves, and I could see his wife in the background, pretending she was preoccupied with dusting, and therefore too busy to speak to me.

I began by congratulating him on owning such a beautiful holiday let as a sly way of taking him off guard. "So much so," I told him, "That I was wondering if it might be possible for me to extend my stay for a couple of nights?"

It was almost as if I had asked him if I might spit-roast his children for dinner.

His face grew positively red with rage, and for a moment I genuinely though he might explode there and then, right in front of me.

Instead, doubtless realising from my expression that he was

over-reacting, he dropped his gaze and apologised, saying with a shaky voice that the cottage was already booked.

I did not believe him for a moment, but I was not in a position to call him a liar. After all, he could merely have refused my request without offering me any explanation, so, in his mind, it was probably more to save my embarrassment than his.

I looked over his head at his wife. Her face too turned a rather unhealthy shade of puce, and she bent down to pick something up which was not there to begin with.

They had obviously discussed the possibility that I might make such a request between them since my last conversation with Mrs Moss, and it was clear that their minds had been firmly made up.

I thanked them both, even though by then the wife had disappeared from view and asked if I might be notified should their 'tenants' decide not to come.

Mr Moss assured me that he would. He lifted his head for a split second but dropped it again the moment his eyes reached mine. He held out his hand, which I shook, and he closed the door before I even had a chance to turn away.

I took myself back into town to see my old friend Jed, but to my dismay his wife informed me that he had left early that morning for a meeting in Galway, and that he would be staying overnight.

I thanked her and set off for the hills for a last look out over the sea.

I had managed exactly zero concerning my novel that week, and I knew that unless I could pull something out of the hat over the weekend, I would be in for an earbashing come Monday morning.

Even so, at that moment in time such things seemed unimportant, almost laughable.

Every time I closed my eyes it was Chantelle's sweet face that I could see, and with it came back all the horrendous details of her murder. How could someone have done that to her? What evil monster crossed her path at just the wrong moment?

Jed had been convinced that it was not a local who was responsible for the heinous act, and he came across to me as someone who had genuinely cared for Chantelle, so I knew that he was not just saying it to protect the integrity of his fellow locals, or indeed, his precious Ireland, which he was also staunchly proud of.

Perhaps, in his heart, he just refused to associate such a vicious and unnecessarily brutal crime with the place and people he loved so much.

Either way, I believed him when he said what he would like to do with the culprit if he ever found him.

I stayed on the hillside to watch the sun slowly slip beyond the horizon before cycling back. As I passed Jed's place, I stopped in for a final Guinness.

While I drank my pint, Jed's wife came over to me with a plastic container. She explained that when Jed phoned her earlier, she mentioned my visit and he asked her to save me a couple of slices of his world-famous seed cake, just in case I popped back in.

I thanked her and asked her to pass my thanks onto her husband.

I had no real appetite for dinner that evening. The thought that it was my last chance to see Chantelle, filled me with a heartfelt sorrow which I could not explain.

Once more, I drifted off with my head resting on my hands at the kitchen table and was overjoyed when I raised my head to see her sitting opposite me, smiling, and drinking her tea.

"Hello," she said, cheerily. "I was beginning to think you weren't going to join me tonight."

I glanced at my watch, and it was almost five o'clock. "I'm sorry," I apologised. "I must have really been out of it."

"That bike ride must have really taken it out of you."

123

Her words stunned me for a moment. "You saw me?" I spluttered.

She nodded. Then asked, "Have you got something for me?"

I must have looked puzzled by her question because she laughed out loud, shaking her head from side-to-side. Her ponytail seemed to fall loose, and her beautiful silky hair fell down around her shoulders.

I shrugged, shaking my head, still unaware of what she might be referring to.

Then she indicated with a nod of her head to the counter behind me. I turned and saw the plastic carton Jed's wife had given me.

"Oh, that," I said, shocked by my own forgetfulness. I brought it over and removed the lid, displaying the two neatly sliced pieces of cake in front of her.

Chantelle removed one and held it to her nose, inhaling deeply. "Ahh," she sighed.

I watched as she took her first bite. It was clear to see that she relished every morsel.

Once she swallowed, she slid the carton over to me. "You must," she insisted.

I did as I was told, and had to admit, it was delicious. Even so, I was more entranced by watching her eat, then by what I held in my hand. She closed her eyes while she chewed, so I allowed my gaze to linger, focussing on her beautiful lips moving up and down.

She caught me watching. She had such a captivating laugh that I could not help but join in at my own embarrassment.

When she finished her cake, she washed it down with the remainder of her tea.

I offered her the rest of my slice, which was still over half its original size, but she declined, politely. "I could never manage more than one slice at a time," she explained.

She turned and gazed out of the window.

In the distance, the first signs of day began to lighten the eastern sky. Being winter, I knew that it would still be a while before it was fully daylight, but I also knew from past experience that Chantelle was usually gone by now.

I hated myself for having overslept.

"There is so much I want to ask you," I said. "So much I want to know."

She turned back to face me, her smile as enigmatic as always. "I know," she replied, understandably. "But some things in life must remain a mystery, no matter how much we would like it not to be so."

It was as if she could read my mind.

I dared not utter the words still burning in my mind.

"I think you need to go now," she said, softly.

Her words whacked me hard from inside my chest, as if someone were in there suing a hammer-drill to try and break out. "No, please," I begged. "Just a little while longer. I won't be here tomorrow."

"Neither will I," she explained. "Now go, you need your rest."

I tried to argue, but the next thing I knew there was someone knocking frantically on my front door.

I lifted myself out of bed and went downstairs, the persistent *knocking* accompanying my every move. I opened the door to find a young girl, probably no more than eight or nine, standing on the stoop.

"Hello," she said, cheerfully. "My mummy says you have to leave in an hour so she can clean the place for her next guest."

Rubbing the sleep from my eyes, I thanked her, and promised her I would be ready in good time.

I watched her make her way back down the path, and a moment later, I saw a small, red car with Mrs Moss at the wheel, driving past my gate. It was obvious that the woman could not bear to see me, just in case I called her out in her lie.

Not that I would have. But she was not to know that.

On the journey home, as well as for four days after I reached there, I trawled the internet for any and all details I could find on the life and death of Chantelle.

There was indeed a wealth of information, which I devoured for hours at a time.

The details concerning her murder were no less gruesome than Jed had stated, and I could feel my temper rising with every report that a suspect has been dismissed by the local police. There had even been a couple of mysterious sightings of strangers in the area at the time, which were followed up, but still led nowhere.

I have always prided myself that I am not one to dwell on things, especially those which we have no control over. But, in Chantelle's case I was more than prepared to make an exception.

From what I read, there was not a single person who had a bad word to say about her, and she seemed to touch the hearts of everybody she ever met.

Including mine.

# THE GLADSTONE BAG

C onnie Glass climbed down from the train and took in a deep lungful of refreshing sea air.

Having been couped up among the crowds, dirt, noise, and pollution of stuffy London all week, she always enjoyed her Sunday getaways and made a point of choosing somewhere a little way off the beaten track.

It was her first year at university where she was studying forensic medicine, and so far, academically at least, things were going reasonably well. Her tutors seemed decent enough, and her fellow students were, on the whole, quite friendly, although Connie had already managed to suss out some of those who were clearly there more to party, than to study.

Those were the ones she tried to steer clear of. Not that she did not enjoy a good party as much as the next person, but she knew that this was her big chance to make a career in an area which she found absolutely fascinating, and she did not intend to risk it all for the sake of a hectic social life.

She feared that she had already managed to gain a reputation from some of party-people for being boring, having turned down so many invites thus far. But it seemed to Connie as if there were invites flying around almost every evening, and on the couple of occasions she had ventured into the student bar, it was so crowded she had to walk straight back out again before being jostled for standing room by those clambering to gain access.

Having been brought up in the rolling abundance of the Somerset countryside, Connie was not used to crowds, and did not actually realise how affected by them she was until arriving in London. The shock to her system of standing in the middle of Victoria station with hundreds of strangers barging past her without so much as an apology, almost made Connie turn around and catch the first train back.

But eventually, she managed to steer her luggage cart over to a relatively quiet corner of the station, where she took in several deep breaths and waited for her anxiety to pass.

She knew that she had invested to much in her future education to lose the opportunity as the result of being intimidated by a bunch of rude travellers. So, she steeled herself and fought her way through to the nearest taxi rank, where she caught a cab to her university, where she had managed to secure accommodation in halls.

Connie had been brought up by her aunt Mavis since her parents were both killed in a freak accident whilst driving home from a party. Neither had been drinking, and there were no other vehicles involved, so it appeared to the police as if her father-who had been driving-had merely lost control of the car on a steep curve, sending it plummeting down an embankment, killing both of them instantly.

Mavis was Connie's father's younger sister, and although she did the best she could for the girl, the bond which connects a child to their parent had already been severed by the accident, and Connie never felt completely at home with her aunt.

Although she never married, Mavis had a string of boyfriends over the years, many of whom Connie never took to. Therefore, she often spent her spare time locked in her room reading or listening to music through her headphones to help drown out the strange noises which would permeate the thin plaster wall which separated her room from her aunts.

Her aunt was never unkind or cruel to her, but Connie always felt as if she were more in the way than anything else. So, when the chance to enter university came along, she decided to make a fresh start and follow her dreams to study at the best university in the country, for her chosen subject.

Connie's mindset towards her studies was simple. As well as attending all her lectures, seminars and tutorials, Connie ensured she always arrived early so that she could find a seat in the front row. This assured that she did not miss a single word of each class, which in itself was not always easy, as some of her lecturer's had an annoying tendency to move away from the lectern as they spoke, which in consequence meant that they also moved away from the microphone attached to it.

Her positioning also mean that she was as far away as possible from those annoying individuals who seemed to treat the lecture hall as another excuse for a social catch-up. They were the ones who talked consistently throughout classes, escaping detection by holding their hands in front of their mouths.

Fortunately for Connie, those students tended to congregate toward the back of the hall in an effort to conceal their nefarious activity.

Besides her classes, Connie spent as much time as possible in the student library, always positioning herself in one of the segregated cubby-holes, as far as possible from the noisier areas with the large tables.

Out of desperation, Connie would occasionally take herself back to her room to study. But this in itself often proved an unviable prospect, as the students on either side of her made it a habit of having friends over for impromptu wine and pizza gatherings.

The one and only thing which seemed to give Connie a release from her pent-up frustration at all the distractions, was her Sunday trips out of the capital. Using her student identity card, Connie had discovered several web sites which offered discounts on return train journeys to many different parts of the country.

So it was, she had begun a routine where she would try and have an early night on Saturday, so that she could make an early start the following morning and spend the day basking in the sights and sounds of whichever part of the country she had found the cheapest ticket for.

As the weeks passed, these trips became more of a necessity than a luxury, and Connie used them as a way of clearing her mind in preparation for the following weeks study.

Whenever possible, Connie would pluck for a seaside location, preferably one which was not too touristy. Once there, her itinerary was generally the same: A walk along the beach-if one were available. A visit to any site of historic value, so long as the entry was free. Hotdogs for lunch. A gentle stroll through the lanes, nooks, and crannies, which each town offered, browsing through some of the quaint antique shops she discovered while exploring. Afternoon tea, or perhaps an ice cream on the beach if weather permitted. A visit to any second-hand bookshops in the vicinity, where she often treated herself to a harmless novel which she could devour the following week to alleviate the tedium of study. Finally, a bag of chips to eat on the train back home.

Her favourite part of the day was usually her perusal of the antique shops. Even on the sunniest of days, Connie would often lose herself among the old masters, bone china, antique silver, and general bric-a-brac on display.

Although unable to afford most of what she admired in those shops, Connie occasionally came across a hidden gem that was not too pricy.

Her real passion was for antique medical equipment, which, although in keeping with her studies, often raised an eyebrow if she mentioned it to the individual serving.

But most of the time Connie was just happy just to be out of London, and away from the alcohol-infused party atmosphere of her student dormitory.

Today's jaunt had taken her to a tiny fishing village of Moreton Bay, on the east coast.

The moment Connie stepped out of the station she was immediately captivated by the picturesque scenery which greeted her. It was even more spectacular than the shots she had seen on the internet.

Although approximately a half-hour's walk from the station, she could already smell the sea air, and she stood on the platform for a couple of minutes to savour the experience.

She spent the day in her usual fashion, and after lunch, Connie ventured past the port and into the main hub of the village where the majority of the shops were located.

At the end of a rather cramped alleyway, she came upon an antique shop which, from the outside, appeared to be closed. Disappointed as she was, Connie stepped up to the main window and held her hands above her eyes so that she could have a better view of the inside.

Although the lights were off, she was still able to see that the shop was crammed full of crates and boxes, some of which were still sealed, whilst others, which had already been opened, overflowed with all manner of items waiting to take their place on display.

Connie strained her eyes to try and see how far back the shop stretched, but in the gloom, she could not make it past the second room.

A sudden *tinkle* to her right, made her look up, sharply. The door to the shop was now open, and a woman in her mid-sixties, or so Connie guessed, stood in the doorway, smiling at her.

"Oh, I am sorry," Connie began, feeling guilty for being caught, even though she had not actually done anything wrong.

"That's quite all right," the woman assured her. "I'm afraid we're not open yet, we only took possession of the premises yesterday," she explained.

"I see," Connie replied, dejectedly. "You seem to have a plethora of fascinating items already in," she continued, indicating through the window she had just been staring through. "I'll bet it will all look spectacular once you have it all organised." She moved around so that she was now standing in front of the woman in the doorway.

"Well thank you my dear, that is so nice of you to say." The woman turned to one side and purveyed the melee of assorted containers inside. "We've just taken delivery from a house clearance," the woman laughed, "or should I say, a mansion clearance, just up the way from here. The gentleman who inherited the property insisted that we evacuate everything yesterday as part of the deal. Considering that we only won the bid the previous afternoon, it was all a bit of a rush, but here we are."

"How odd," remarked Connie. "I wonder what his hurry was."

The woman shook her head. "Well, from what I gather, the gentleman had been in a long legal battle over inheritance with some of the other members of his family, and his legal bills were starting to mount up. Even so, I can't see why a week or two would have made that much difference. We had to use a local removal firm as the ones we usually use were already booked up."

"Did you manage to move everything in time?"

The woman sighed. "Of a fashion. We had all the smaller items brought here, but we have had to hire a storage facility in the next town for the larger items. My husband is there now checking the itinerary. As I say, it has all been a bit hectic, but once the dust settles, I'm sure we will have it all under control."

Connie peered around the woman. "It all looks very exciting," she exclaimed, genuinely interested.

"Perhaps you could come back and visit us next week," the woman suggested. "We hope to open on Saturday."

Connie shook her head, slowly. "Alas, I'm only here for today. I'm a student in London and Sundays are my get-a-way days. I only ended up here because they had a special student discount offer on my ticket."

"Oh, I am sorry," the woman replied, with genuine emotion in her voice. "Well, let's hope your ticket will allow you to come and visit us again someday. If there is anything specific you would like us to look out for, you can always leave me your number."

"Oh, no, that's alright," said Connie, not wanting to put the kindly woman out.

"It's really no trouble," the lady assured her. "We tend to conduct business in the old-fashioned way, my husband and I. We keep an exercise book full of names and phone numbers of clients who are on the lookout for specific items, so it will be easy enough to add you to it, no obligation, of course."

Connie thought about it for a moment. "Okay, then," she agreed, "if you're sure it won't be any trouble?"

The woman ushered her inside the shop and closed the door behind them.

"Now if you would be so kind as to wait here," she asked, "I'm afraid with everything all over the place we don't want you tripping over something and hurting yourself, that would never do."

Connie laughed. "And I'm clumsy enough to do just that," she admitted.

The woman reached down beneath the counter just off to Connie's left and flicked a switch. Seconds later they were bathed in light.

Connie took advantage of the situation and scanned the array of items which filled the shop. She was now even able to see into the two rooms further away, as the light switch appeared to control the entire ceiling stretching as far as she could see.

From behind the counter, the woman reappeared with the promised notebook.

She placed it on top of the counter. "Now then," she began, skimming through the pages until she found a blank one. "If you'll give me your name, phone number, and any specific items of interest, we'll be in business."

Connie leaned over and gave her name and mobile number. When she mentioned her fascination with antique medical implements, the woman stopped writing and looked up at her with a puzzled look on her face.

Connie smiled, reassuringly. "I know it might sound a trifle macabre, but you see, I am a student of forensic medicine, so these things have always held a fascination for me."

After a moment, the woman nodded. "I see, well yes, I suppose in your chosen field it is not unusual to have such an interest." The woman bent back down to finish writing the description in her book.

Once she was finished, she closed the book and placed it back behind the counter.

Then a thought struck her. "Now I come to think of it, we did have quite a substantial collection of medical implements at our London address, but we sold them all to a museum when we decided to move down here. We didn't think we'd have much call for such items in such a small village."

Connie's face dropped. "Oh, what a pity," she sighed, "I'd have loved to have had a look through them before you sold them on. Just my luck," she shrugged.

The woman gave her a friendly pat on the shoulder.

Suddenly, her eyes opened wide. "Just a minute," she said, eagerly. "I'm sure I saw something come in yesterday from that mansion sale I told you about. Now, what was it?" The lady gazed up into space as if hoping the answer might be displayed on the ceiling.

Connie waited, expectantly.

She hoped that whatever it was, it was something affordable. She had once found a beautifully restored doctor's chair, but the shop keeper wanted way more for it than her lowly student budget could afford. That and the fact that, once in situ, she would hardly have had room to move around in her student cubby-hole.

Even so, it broke her heart to have to refuse the sale.

"I know," the lady suddenly announced, snapping her fingers. "You just wait there a moment and I'll be right back."

Before Connie had a chance to respond, the woman scuttled off into one of the other rooms.

Connie waited, patiently. Tempted though she was to explore some of the bookshelves which lines the wall to her right, she did not wish to abuse the lady's hospitality by straying away from the spot. Afterall, if she did manage to trip over and break something, chances were that it would be an item of considerable value which she would be paying for until she graduated.

In the distance Connie could just about here the woman muttering to herself as she searched. Although it was taking longer than Connie had anticipated, there was no way she was going to just walk out, especially considering how kind and considerate the woman had been to her, first by letting her inside, and then by taking the time to rifle through, who knew how many, boxes, looking for something especially for her.

After all this effort, Connie sincerely hoped that whatever the lady finally located was something she actually wanted and could afford.

"Tah-da!"

Connie smiled to herself as she heard the lady's cry of triumph from the next room.

She held her breath in anticipation. Staring ahead of her and awaiting the woman's reappearance with her prize.

At last, the lady re-emerged into view, holding something between both hands.

As she came closer, Connie could see that it was a worn leather bag, of the type often used by doctors and surgeons during the nineteenth century.

A Gladstone bag. The name suddenly came to her just as the

woman arrived back at the counter and placed it in front of Connie. "Now then," she exclaimed, excitedly. "What do you think of that?"

Connie looked it over. It certainly appeared to have been well used by its owner. "It's beautiful," she announced, gazing up to see the expression of joy on the lady's face.

The leather was badly scuffed all over, and one of the straps which folded across the opening, was just about hanging on by a thread. The clasp, which Connie suspected, had once been so shiny it would dazzle anyone when brought into contact with light, was now dull and scratched, and barely able to complete its function.

But all the same, to someone like Connie, it would take pride of place amongst her collection.

"Do you mind if I open it?" she asked, eagerly.

"Not at all," the lady assured her, "please be my guest."

Carefully, taking into account the bag's age and condition, Connie lifted back the brass catch, and the bag sprung open before her.

A cloud of dust sprang up before either of the women had a chance to move out of the way, which resulted in them both being overtaken by a fit of coughing.

"Oh my," expressed the antiques dealer once her spluttering had subsided. "I take it that hasn't seen the light of day for a while," she observed.

"I think it's mostly leather-dust," suggested Connie. "Looks like this hasn't been treated in a long time, if at all."

Once they had both regained their composure, Connie returned to her investigation of the bag's contents.

She recognised several of the instruments within, although others appeared completely alien to her.

In amongst the usual paraphernalia, she expected to find: Scissors, forceps, syringes, etc, there was a small, flat, red velvet box. Carefully removing it from the rest of the contents, Connie placed it on to of the counter. "Would it be okay for me to see inside?" she asked, tentatively.

The woman nodded. "Of course, my dear, I found it for you."

Connie half-expected the container to be empty, but she was pleasantly surprised when she lifted it to find that it was heavier than she imagined.

Undoing the button, Connie opened the box to reveal a set of extremely slender knives, which, although showing some signs of not having been polished in years, were still in remarkable good condition.

"They look interesting," the woman observed.

"I believe they are post-mortem knives," Connie revealed, removing the largest one from its holder and lifting it up into the light. "And by the look of them, they are still as sharp as ever."

"How gruesome," the shopkeeper remarked, pulling a face. "Do you mean these were actually used to cut open dead bodies?"

Connie nodded. "Yes, I'm sure they were."

"Quite revolting." The woman responded, holding her hand against her chest.

Noticing her uneasiness, Connie replaced the knife back in the box, closing the lid, tightly. "I'm sorry," she apologised, "I did not mean to upset you. I appreciate that my chosen field of study is not everyone's cup of tea."

The woman nodded. "That's quite alright, my dear. I should be used to such things by now. You'd be amazed at some of things we had brought in when we were in London. My husband is the great expert, you know. To me, antiques are all about jewellery, paintings and china, that sort of thing. Still, each to their won, I suppose."

Connie gazed back down at the bag and ran her hand across the top of the leather.

"So, is this the sort of thing you were looking for?" the shop-keeper asked.

Connie looked up and nodded. "Yes, definitely," she admitted, "but I very much suspect that such a specimen will be out of my price range."

The woman thought for a moment. Then she asked. "So how much would you be willing to offer for it?"

The question took Connie back for a moment. She had only ever seen items such as the bag at auction before, and there they went for several hundreds of pounds.

"I don't want to insult you," Connie stated, earnestly. "Much as I would love to own this, I really do not think that I could offer you an honest price."

The woman leaned forward and nudged Connie gently with her elbow. "Go on, make me an offer, I won't be insulted," she assured her. "I'm not saying that I'll accept it, necessarily, but if you don't ask, you don't get, as my old mother used to say."

Connie turned her attention back to the PM knives. They alone would be the pride of any collection, even without the rest of the equipment inside the bag, or indeed, the bag itself.

She wondered how cheeky the antique's dealer would think her if she made an offer for them alone.

After a while, Connie shook her head. "I can't, I'm sorry, I would not want to insult you by making an offer I could afford. Especially after you've been so kind in hunting this down for me."

The woman smiled. "Such honesty should not go unrewarded," she observed. "Now listen to me, much as I'd love to give this to you because you are such a lovely, not to mention, honest young lady, I cannot, my husband would kill me. However, I have a few rules of my own, and one of them is that the first customer of a new venture can bring a great deal of luck to the vendor if they are treated well, and by buying this, you would become our official first customer, so make me an offer."

Connie felt her cheeks flush. The woman was being so kind, she hated to think that she might be fiddling her out of a small fortune by taking advantage of her sweet nature.

She decided that she would make a serious offer and, if it

were accepted, she would just have to tighten her belt for the next couple of months to make up for it, even if it meant no more trips to the sea for a while.

Connie unzipped her bag and took out her purse. Removing her credit card from the side pocket, she placed it on the counter, and was contemplating what sort of offer to make, when the woman interrupted her train of thought.

"Oh, lord no," the lady laughed. "We haven't set up the till yet, so I can't take a card payment. Haven't you got any cash on you?"

Connie hesitated. "Well, yes, but not much, I only took out enough for the day. I could go and try and find a cash machine, if..."

"Never mind all that," the woman insisted. "How much actual money do you have on you?"

Connie checked the slots within her purse, and pulled out two ten-pound notes, placing them on the counter. The others came up empty, as she feared they would. She shoved her hands inside her jean pockets and felt several coins, so she plucked them out and laid them next to the notes.

Her change included several pound coins, so in total, she presented a grand some of twenty-seven pounds, and seventy-four pence.

Connie looked back up at the woman, sheepishly, feeling embarrassed that she was making such a low offer.

To her astonishment, instead of balking at such a paltry amount, the lady slid the coins back in Connie's direction and grabbed the two notes. "There now," she said, "I think twenty pounds is a fair price, what do you think?"

Connie could not conceal her surprise. "You're not serious?" she exclaimed. "Twenty pounds, for all of this?"

The shop owner was not fazed by Connie's reaction. "That's right, now do we have a deal?" she replied, smiling warmly.

Connie opened her mouth to object some more, then realised that the lady was merely being kind, realising that she was dealing with a poor student who really appreciated the find.

Before Connie had a chance to say anything else, the woman took out a pad and began to write out a receipt for her. Handing it over, she said. "There you go, sorry it's not a proper one, but like I said, we haven't even set up our till yet."

Connie held her hand out for the receipt. "Are you really sure?" she asked again. "This is very generous of you. I feel awful."

The woman waved aside her objection. "I told you," she said, "the first customer of a new venture must be totally satisfied, otherwise the entire business could go to wrack and ruin." The woman winked at Connie. "Now let me find you a carrier bag."

As the woman disappeared into the back of the shop, Connie surveyed her new purchase. Her heart gave a little *jump* as she held it in her hands and reminded herself that it now belonged to her.

Connie checked her receipt, just to make sure she was not imagining it. But sure enough, the receipt showed the purchase for twenty pounds for a black, leather bag, plus assorted medical instruments.

When the shop keeper returned with a large carrier bag, Connie thanked her again, and promised if she was ever in the area again, she would pop in and say hello.

The lady waved her off with a cheery smile.

Checking the time, Connie realised that she needed to make a move or risk missing her train.

Once inside the carriage, Connie found a seat with a table. There was no one else sitting nearby, so she took advantage and emptied her new purchase, spreading the various instruments out in front of her.

She found it incredible that she was holding equipment which had doubtless been used on patients over a hundred years before. It was such an amazing find that Connie could still not believe her luck. She still felt terrible that the shop owner had charged her so little, but then she reconciled herself to the fact that the woman was in business and was not an old doddery pensioner who she had conned out of a family heirloom.

The lady obviously saw the excitement on Connie's face when she brought out the bag, and as such, she had decided to do something wonderful and let her have it for whatever she had in her purse. Or, not even that, as it turned out.

Connie studied the knives contained in the red velvet box, closely.

She had seen post-mortem knives before at the university, and there were even some antique ones in a glass case in their museum. But from what she remembered they did not appear to be in as good a condition as the ones she now held.

Connie led the tip of her forefinger along the sharp edge of the largest blade.

Careful not to put too much pressure on it, she still had to snatch her hand away when she felt the cold metal bite into her flesh.

Turning her hand around, Connie saw a tiny speck of blood start to appear at the top of her pad. She pressed her skin just below it, and the spot began to spread.

She was about to stick her finger in her mouth, when the thought came to her that, given the age and use of the knife, she might not wish to risk catching anything from it.

Removing a tissue from her bag, Connie wrapped her finger, and held it tightly until the blood congealed.

She carefully replaced the knife back in its shield and closed the lid of the box before putting it back inside the bag, along with the rest of the instruments.

Searching through her purse, Connie managed to find a plaster, and used it to wrap around her injured finger. She disposed of the bloody tissue in the wastepaper basket behind her seat. The knife had been a good deal sharper than she had anticipated, which after what must have been countless years since last being used, she found rather surprising.

Even so, she was not about to let a simple cut finger dampen her euphoria at making such a magnificent find.

*So long as I haven't caught tetanus or something from it!*

The sudden thought disturbed her. But then she remembered receiving a jab five years earlier when she accidently stood on a rusty nail which was poking out of a piece of wood and masked by overgrown foliage. The doctor had assured her that the jab was good for ten years, Connie heaved a great sigh of relief at the memory.

Excited as she was, Connie decided only to show her new find to a small group of fellow students on her course. Those whom she knew she could trust to keep it to themselves. The last thing she wanted was every Tom, Dick and Harry knocking on her door. Besides, her find was not to everyone's taste, so she did not wish to make a song-and-dance about it.

Most of all, she could not wait to show it to Professor Spindle, one of her lecturers.

Although happily married, and in his forties, Connie had a secret crush on him which she dared not share with anyone. It was enough for Connie just to have him within reach, such as when he would lean over to check something which she pretended not to understand.

The smell of his aftershave was intoxicating.

Connie waited behind after his next lecture, and once the other students had all filtered out, she presented the professor with her latest find.

She was overjoyed at his interest in her purchase, and even asked permission before attempting to open it and survey the insides.

He seemed particularly thrilled when he opened the red velvet case and discovered the PM knives. "Do you know what?" he asked, having spent several minutes in complete silence holding each blade up to the light. "You should take this down to our archive lab, they could run a DNA test on some of these. If there's any trace evidence, and they're in the system, I'll bet they could even give you the names the patients who were carved up with these."

"Really," replied Connie, astonished by his revelation. "Even after all this time? I mean, these knives probably haven't been used in a hundred years."

"Tut-tut," he joked, his tone mocking, but playful. "Have you not been paying attention to me in class?"

Connie's cheeks flushed. Naturally, she aimed to be a good study, but she had to admit to herself that, on occasion, she allowed her mind to wander when the dreamy professor was talking passionately about his favourite subject.

"If you show these to one my colleagues in the archive wing," he continued, not waiting for Connie to reply, "I am sure they would be most interested in running some basic tests. Trouble is," he warned, "if they get too excited you might have a hard time getting them back."

That night, Connie could hardly sleep. Not as a result of any anticipation she felt at the prospect of having her PM knives tested by the laboratory team, but more from the fact that Professor Spindle had taken such an interest in her purchase. Not to mention the fact that he had stayed back after class and chatted with her for almost half-an-hour.

It made her feel like a schoolgirl with a huge crush.

Thrilled by the prospect of discussing the lab's findings with the professor. Connie made an appointment to show them her knives.

Just as Spindle had suspected, the lab team were ecstatic at the prospect of being able to test some genuine PM knives as old as Connie's. But not as excited as she was when she heard that Professor Spindle had discussed her find with his colleagues in the department.

The mere thought that he was speaking about her, made her feel all squirmy and warm inside.

When the time came to actually hand the red velvet case of knives over, Connie remembered her professor's warning about getting them back afterwards. Therefore, she negotiated a signed contract with the head of the unit. Promising to deliver them back to her, unaltered, as soon as the tests were complete.

"Out of interest," Connie asked, "what sort of results are you hoping to achieve?"

Professor Atkins, the present head of the archive unit, scratched his head, thoughtfully, before answering. "Well, as you are no doubt aware, everyone has a unique DNA fingerprint, and in the same way the police compiled a database of all the criminals they've had in custody, here at the archive lab, we have compiled our own version where we list DNA from deceased individuals. We call it the database of the dead," he chuckled, obviously amused by his own joke.

Corrie smiled, humourlessly, not wishing to offend someone she might apply to for a job one day. "And you suspect there might be DNA traces on some of these knives left behind from some of the post-mortems they've been used on?"

"Exactly," Atkins beamed. "We have already collated several specimens from items held in New Scotland Yard's famous Black Museum. Fortunately for us, the officers who stored some of their most gruesome exhibits placed them in sealed containers, and never removed them again, until we made a request. It's absolutely fascinating."

The professor's enthusiasm was infectious, and Connie could not help but become swept away by it. "Do you hold out any real hope?" she asked. "I mean, PM knives, even as old as these, would have been cleaned thoroughly after each operation."

Atkins grinned. "Our technology is extremely advanced," he replied, evidently proud of his laboratory's equipment. "Even the slightest trace not visible to the human eye can reveal an entire DNA code for our log."

"But supposing the code doesn't match one you already have, it won't mean anything if you cannot say who it belongs to, surely?"

Atkins shook his head. Still smiling, he said, "Not at all, even if it does not correspond to a profile which we already have on the system, we submit a report of how we obtained it, from what, and whom. Your name will appear on our system as the owner of the item, and the details surrounding how it came to be in your possession. That is the purpose of our database. We have literally thousands of hits we don't have names for, but the more we add, the more likely we might find a match, even a familial one. You see, as a scientist, it saddens me to think that once a person dies, their DNA profile dies with them. So, items such as yours could give us access to a DNA lost in time, and by adding it to our database it almost feels as if a part of that person lives on. Do you see?"

Connie nodded. "Science marches on," she grinned.

"Exactly."

The tests were due to take a couple of weeks, and during that time it gave Connie an excuse to visit Professor Spindle in his office, just so she could update him with fact that no one had contacted her as yet.

There was a part of her that still felt bad that she had paid so little for the bag, and she hoped that the lady in the shop had not received a hard time from her husband when she told him how much she had sold it for.

Connie was not sure when she would revisit Moreton Bay, if at all, so the chances of 'popping in' as promised, were very slim. It had been a pleasant enough location for her Sunday jaunt, but she felt as if she had already seen everything the village had to offer, so Connie knew she would probably spend the money visiting a different port.

One evening when she was sitting alone in her room sorting through her receipts, she came across the one from the antique dealer for the bag. She was about to crumple it and throw it in the bin, when she considered that Professor Atkins might want to take a scan of it to add to his database for the PM knives.

She felt a shiver of excitement that her name was going to

appear on the database as the one who discovered the knives and brought them to the laboratory's attention.

Gazing at the receipt, Connie noticed that the shop's phone number was printed across the top, beside its name. She decided that in place of making another visit there, she would call the number the following day, and thank the lady once more for her bargain. She considered telling her about the archive unit as well, as it was purely scientific and did not enhance the value of the purchase in any way.

The last thing she wanted was to make the lady feel bad for letting it go at such a cheap price.

Connie left it until her lunch break the following day before calling the shop.

She was relieved when it was the lady who answered the phone, because not knowing the situation between them, she did not wish to listen to an irate husband ranting on about his wife's lack of business acumen.

"Hello," said Connie, "you may not remember me, but I called in at your shop last Sunday week. You weren't officially open, but you are very kindly..." Connie was not given a chance to finish her sentence before the woman cut in.

"Yes of course I remember you, you were the young lady who purchased that old leather bag, oh I am glad you called, now just wait a minute for me."

Connie heard the receiver being planted down on the counter, followed by a rustle of papers, and the distant incoherent mutterings from the antiques dealer.

"Are you still there?" the lady asked, after a moment.

"Yes, I'm here," Connie confirmed.

"Right then, do you have a pen to hand?"

"Yes," replied Connie, bemused. "Why?"

"Oh, this is fortuitous," the woman continued, "I was so hoping you might call in one day, and here you are on the phone, just as good. Now, please take this number down."

The woman relayed the telephone number, then made Connie read it back to her, just to make sure she had it.

"Who is this for?" asked Connie.

"Well, let me tell you," the lady began. "A couple of days after you dropped in, we had a lady drop in, frantic she was, bless her, most insistent that we let her in, even though we weren't officially open yet." The woman paused for breath, evidently exhausted by the haste at which she was trying to convey her story. "Anyway, it appears that the house clearance my husband had just completed was from this lady's uncle's house, but her cousin arranged everything before she had a chance to check over the contents."

"Oh, I see," said Connie, feeling her stomach gurgle at the prospect of what was about to come. She suspected that the shop keeper was going to inform her that this woman, whoever she was, had some legal claim to the Gladstone bag she had bought, and now was doubtless going to threaten her with legal action if she did not return it.

"Anyway," the woman continued. "According to her, that bag I sold you belonged to her great-great grandfather and was very precious to her. She was most distraught when I informed her that I had already sold it. She kept asking for your contact details, but I explained to her that I didn't have them."

"So, she left you her number in case I called in?" Connie surmised.

"Well, yes, I remembered you saying you might drop in next time you were in the area, so I promised her that I would keep her number to one side, and pass it onto you, should you ever drop in."

"Sounds to me like she wants the bag back." Connie surmised.

"Quite so. She asked me how much I had sold it to you for, but I informed her that such information was confidential, and she seemed to accept that."

"Was she angry?" Connie asked, feeling bad for the owner.

"Not angry as such, more upset I'd say. She seemed very dejected when she left the shop. Anyway, I promised her I would pass on her number to you if I had the chance, and I have done so. It's up to you whether or not you decide to contact her, or not."

"Thank you," replied Connie, "did she leave her name?"

"Oh, didn't I give it to you? How remis of me." There followed more shuffling of paper, and whispered mutterings, before, "Are here we go, her name was Carla Bond."

Connie scribbled the name down next to the phone number.

After a moment, she asked, "I know it isn't fair to ask you, but what do you think I should do?"

There was a pause on the other line. Then, "Well it's really not my place to say. The bag is your property, we contracted the sale quite legally, so it was mine to sell to you, so it is up to you what you decide to do with it next."

"If I call this woman and refuse to sell it back to her, do you think she might grow aggressive over the phone. I really don't want to end up in an argument and have to slam the phone down on her."

"I hardly think it will come to that," the shopkeeper advised. "I mean, she was genuinely desperate to get her hands on it, but she knows now that it is your property so she will probably offer to buy it back from you, but that is between the two of you. If you don't agree a price, no one is going to force you."

The woman's words helped calm Connie down. She was right. She had made a legal purchase, and if this other woman wanted to have it, she would have to offer Connie a reasonably price. Part of her did feel bad that it appeared to be a family heirloom which she obviously had a great affinity for. But if that were the case, then she would surely have made arrangements to remove it from the estate sale, in advance.

Either way, Connie decided whatever the circumstances, the woman deserved the courtesy of a phone call.

She thanked the antiques dealer and hurried off to her next class.

Connie toyed with the idea of calling the woman over the next couple of days. She was fairly confident from what the antiques dealer had told her, that the woman would not start making demands, or threatening legal action if Connie refused to sell her the bag.

But even so, it did sound as if the woman was desperate to get it back.

Connie weighed up options in her mind. If the woman was genuinely heartbroken at losing the family heirloom, was she happy to part with it? It was, after all, the pride of place amongst her antique medical instrument collection.

But then she considered how she would feel in the other woman's position if something she treasured so much had been given away by accident, and how grateful she would be for the chance to have it back.

In the end, Connie realised that she could not rest easy in herself if she did not at least try and discover how genuine the woman was.

Finally, she called her.

The phone was answered on the first ring. "Yes!" The voice sounded stern, almost demanding.

"Hello," Connie began, "you don't know me, but I purchased the old medical bag from the antique shop in Moreton Bay."

"Oh, yes, hello," the woman broke in, her tone now much more agreeable and polite. "Thank you so much for calling me back, I really appreciate it. Did the lady in the shop explain the circumstances to you about how I managed to lose it?"

"Yes, well, sort of," Connie replied. "She said something about your cousin selling it on without your knowledge."

"That's right. I'm afraid he and I have never been close. The bag belonged to our great-great grandfather you see, and it had been passed down to my uncle. When he died, I had hoped it would pass down to me as my cousin had no interest in it. But my uncle died intestate, so my cousin claimed everything and just wanted a quick sale."

"Didn't you ask him for it?" Connie enquired. "I mean, if he didn't really appreciate it."

The woman sighed. "I would have done, but I was abroad on work when my uncle died, and by the time I heard anything my cousin had sold the lot. Lock, stock and barrel."

"I'm presuming it has great sentimental value for you, then?"

"Yes, it does. I know it might sound silly, but I have researched my family tree for years now, and my great-great grandfather was a man of particular interest to me. He was actually quite famous in his day, and I would love to own something which he used on a regular basis. It would somehow make me feel closer to him."

Connie could feel her heart sink. Even if the woman only offered her the original purchase price, she knew in her heart that she was going to have to hand it over. The poor woman sounded genuinely distraught by the loss, and Connie would not be able to live with herself if she did not do the right thing.

"Well then," she said. "I suppose you want it back?"

"Oh yes please," the woman pleaded. "Naturally, I do not expect you to be out of pocket, so I'll happily pay you what you paid for it, plus a finder's bonus of shall we say a hundred pounds?"

Connie almost dropped her phone. "A hundred pounds!" she stammered. "There's really no need for that, I only paid twenty pounds for it."

"That's not the point," the woman insisted. "By returning it to me you will be doing me a great favour, and you don't have to. At the end of the day, you bought it in good faith, and I have no legal or moral right to demand it back, so I will most definitely be in your debt."

"Even so, there's really no need for you to pay so much for its return, I'll be happy to give it back to you for the original twenty."

"Let me ask you something Connie," the woman's tone took on a slightly stern edge when she spoke. "What do you do for a living?"

The question took her by surprise. "I, well, I'm a student."

"I thought so," she said, evidently pleased with herself. "You sound very young and intelligent. So, you tell me, what student is not short of cash, eh?"

"Well, yes, but…"

"But nothing. You are doing a very nice thing for me, and I intend to reward you for it, so let's say two hundred pounds in cash for the return of my heirloom. Do we have a deal?"

Connie felt terrible. But it was almost as if the woman was throwing money at her.

"Come on, what do you say?"

"Okay. I mean, what can I say, you're being extremely generous."

The two women exchanged details. Carla Bond lived in east London, not a million miles from Connie's university, and she was extremely anxious to have her relative's medical bag back. She asked Connie if she could bring it over to her that evening, even offering to pay for a return taxi for her.

For reasons she was not completely sure of, Connie did not want to tell the woman about allowing the archive laboratory to conduct tests on the PM knives. So, she made an excuse for that evening, promising that she would contact Carla the following day to finalise the arrangements.

After class that day, Connie made her way to the archive labs to see Professor Atkins. She felt sure that by now, even if they did not have a definitive profile, at the very least they must have had enough time to extract any viable source of DNA from the knives.

If, on the other hand they had not, then she would simply inform the professor that she needed her knives back by, at the latest, the following afternoon. That would give her enough time to take them over to Carla's and collect her reward.

As bad as she felt about the money, Connie could not help but feel the tingle of excitement which ran through her body at the thought of the profit she was making on the bag, and in such a short space of time.

The receptionist at the archive put a call out for Professor Atkins, and Connie waited nervously for him in reception. She hated the thought of a potential confrontation with the scientist. After all, she had been told how long it might take for them to extract a specimen. But circumstances had changed, and he would just have to accept that it was her property, and she wanted it back.

Moment later, a very excited and animated Atkins appeared through the glass doors which separated the reception area from the main building.

The moment he saw Connie, he began gesturing wildly with his hands for her to follow him inside. "This is so exciting," he told her. "I was on the verge of calling you. We have made a most excellent find from your knives, one of the best we've made in ages."

Connie was taken aback by his comments, but still swept along by his enthusiasm.

"That's interesting," she remarked. "I'm glad they were of some use to you."

"They were, indeed," Atkins gushed, "and I can't wait to tell you about it. Let's go up to my office, we can have some privacy there."

Connie followed him up two flights of stairs, which Atkins took two at a time. He was certainly very sprightly for a man of his age, but as there was hardly anything of him, Connie guessed that he was either a keep-fit fanatic, or just someone who was lucky enough to possess a fast metabolism.

Once inside his office, Atkins closed the door and removed a pile of papers from the only spare chair in the room, other than his own.

Connie noticed that the red velvet box which contained the

PM knives was sitting on his desk, ready for her to take away. She only hoped that they were all in situ.

Atkins plonked himself in his own chair on the other side of the desk from Connie, and began shuffling through an open file, filled with printed sheets, along with several scribblings along the side of each one.

"Where to begin?" asked Atkins, rhetorically, still sifting through the pages from the file. After a moment, he looked up at Connie. "We found a minute droplet of dried blood on the largest blade in your box," he began, excitedly. "This tiny speck, once processed, was actually already in our database, it belonged to someone who died towards the end of the nineteenth century. Can you believe that?"

Connie was surprised. "That is incredible," she agreed. "But how come they were in your database? Were they someone famous?"

"Of a sort," Atkins proposed. "Have you ever heard of a lady by the name of Marie Jeanette Kelly?" His eyes widened in anticipation.

Connie thought for a moment before shaking her head. "No, sorry," she admitted.

Atkins seemed disappointed. "Perhaps you knew her as Mary Jane Kelly, instead?"

"No, sorry, still no bells."

"Ah, well, not everyone's cup of tea I suppose. Well, the lady in question was the last known canonical victim of none other than Jack the Ripper. Now what do you think about that?"

Connie was stunned. "But, how…" she began.

Atkins cut her off in mid-sentence, bursting with excitement to explain. "Well, if you remember, I told you when you first came in that we have DNA profiles from the Yard's Black Museum, one of which we transferred from some fabric which was alleged to have been the tattered remains of the garments Miss Kelly was wearing on the night she met her fate. The specimen from your knife was a perfect match. So, we can presume that these post-mortem knives," he indicated to the velvet case in front of them, "most probably belonged to the doctor who carried out her post-mortem. Which we have discovered was Doctor Thomas Bond. So, these were probably his knives. How exciting is that?"

Connie wrinkled her nose. "I suppose *exciting* is one word to describe it," she agreed, half-heartedly. "Gruesome is probably more apt."

Atkins looked shocked. "You're a scientist," he announced, as if informing Connie for the first time, "surely you realise the benefit and necessity of a post-mortem?"

"It's not that so much," Connie replied, feeling as if she had to justify herself. "It's more the association with a serial killer that turns my stomach."

Atkins nodded his understanding. "Of course, I see what you mean. But, from a scientific point of view, this is a very exciting find." He leaned forward in his chair, placing his hand on the red velvet case. "I don't suppose you'd be willing to donate this to our little museum, here in the archive?" It's nowhere near as grand as the Yard's, but we're still very proud of it."

Connie felt a lump form in her throat. She hated to pour cold water on the professor's obvious enthusiasm, but she had already given Carla her word, and she was not prepared to go back on it now."

"I'm sorry, professor," she replied. "I'm afraid that I've already promised to sell it back to the shop where I bought it. They have had a client asking about it, and they've made me a very generous offer. Sorry."

She did not know why, exactly, but something inside her made Connie feel that Carla would not appreciate her informing Atkins that it was she, and not the shop, who had made the offer.

"How much?" asked Atkins, raising his eyebrows. "We're not without means here, too. I'm sure we can come to some sort of arrangement. After all, you are bound to be spending some of

your time in our lab as part of your studies. It always helps to
have a friend on the inside, so to speak."

There was an edge to his voice which made Connie feel that
he was giving her an ultimatum rather than making her an offer.

It was not a tone she cared for and made her all the more
adamant that she would sell the knives and bag back to Carla.

"I'm sorry, Professor," she said, politely, rising to her feet.
"But I have already promised to sell these back to the shop." She
held out her hand for the velvet case. "Now, if you'll excuse me,
I really have to go."

Atkins opened and closed his mouth without speaking. The
expression on his face conveyed his annoyance that his little ploy
had failed.

He looked down at Connie's open hand as if it were something detestable that he would rather not touch.

Realising that arguments would be futile, he reluctantly
picked up the case and handed it over to Connie. He did not
bother to thank her for lending it to him in the first place, but
instead made a strange *umph* noise, and mumbled something
below his breath which Connie could not hear and did not wish
to enquire about.

Before leaving the office, Connie opened the case to make
sure that all the knives were present. If her action offended the
professor, she no longer cared after his change in attitude toward
her. She thanked him for his time and let herself out of his office.

Once she was back in her dorm, Connie reunited the knives
with the rest of the instruments in the bag.

All the way home the thought of those knives being associ-
ated with a serial killer, even if he did not physically come into
contact with them himself, made her cringe.

The minute she had them locked securely back in the bag, she
washed her hands, twice.

Professor Atkins had been right about one thing though,
from a scientific perspective, it was intriguing to consider the
place her purchase held in history. Connie was sure that there

were certain macabre collectors in the world who would pay a small fortune for it. But as she had told Atkins, she had already given her word, so that was an end to it.

Later that evening, after dinner, it suddenly occurred to Connie that Carla's surname was the same as the doctor who had carried out the post-mortem on Mary Jane Kelly.

Now she began to piece things together.

Carla's great-great grandfather was obviously this Doctor Thomas Bond that Atkins had told her about. No wonder Carla wanted the bag back. Having a relative who conducted the post-mortem of a victim of England's most notorious serial killer, was genuinely something to be proud of. This made Connie feel even more compelled to return the bag to Carla, regardless of how much more she might have been able to make for it from either Atkins, or some other collector of such antiquities.

The following morning, as promised, Connie called Carla and made arrangements to visit her that evening, to give her back her property.

Although Carla had offered to pay for a taxi, when Connie looked up her address, she realised that it was only a short bus ride to the woman's home, so she decided to use public transport instead, as she still felt awful about the profit she was making from the exercise.

It had been a cloudy day, and by the time Connie reached the right street, the clouds had turned dark grey and looked as if they were about to let loose a downpour.

Carla's home was tucked away at the end of a back street, which was only accessible from this end via a tiny alleyway.

Most of the other properties on the street appeared to have been converted into flats, but judging by Carla's front door, and the lack of bells on show, hers was still a single dwelling. Connie surmised that it was probably worth a small fortune in the present market, and a tiny devil-voice whispered in her ear that she should have held out for more cash. But she dismissed it from thought as she rang the only bell.

Carla Bond looked older than she sounded on the phone. Connie had imagined her to be in her early to mid-thirties, but now that she was standing in front of her, Connie judged her to be late forties, to early fifties.

But, regardless of her age, she was a very striking woman.

Carla had answered the door wearing a long, black dress made of simple cotton which stretched seductively over her ample figure.

Her hair was jet-black, and hung down around her shoulders, like a veil. She had a straight fringe which fell down below her eyebrows, making her large, doleful eyes seem to *pop* from her head.

Her skin was so pale that Connie wondered if she had ever been out in the sun, and it contrasted perfectly with the deep red lipstick she wore to cover her pouting lips.

"You must be Connie?" Carla said, smiling down at her from the top stoop. "Please come in and make yourself at home."

Connie thanked her and entered through the open doorway.

Once inside the vast hallway, Connie waited for Carla to close the front door behind her, before venturing any further inside.

"Please," Carla gestured towards the open door at the far end of the hallway.

Connie walked on, with Carla following.

The flooring was solid flagstone, with a repeater pattern throughout. Connie's trainers made no sound as she walked save for an occasional *squeak*, whereas Carla's stilettoes *clacked*, echoing throughout the passageway.

Once inside the dining room, Connie handed Carla the large plastic carrier bag in which she had brought the Gladstone bag. "This is yours I believe," she offered, smiling.

Carla took the bag eagerly and placed it on a small occasional table to one side of the room. There, she opened it and took out the medical bag.

She turned to face Connie. "Don't think me rude," she

explained, "but I just want to check the contents to make sure my no-good cousin hasn't disposed of any of the instruments."

"Please, go ahead," ushered Connie. "Everything that was inside when I bought it is still in situ."

Carla smiled. "You're very understanding."

After a perfunctory inspection, Carla removed the red velvet case which held the PM knives. She carefully opened the cover and surveyed the contents.

Connie heard her breath a huge sigh of relief once she was satisfied that they were all accounted for.

Carla turned back to face Connie, and a huge smile spread across her face. "Thank you. Thank you so much. I cannot believe I almost lost them." It was at that moment that she seemed to notice that Connie was still standing. "Oh, how rude of me, please take a seat while I fetch your money. Would you like some tea, I've just boiled the kettle?"

Connie thanked her but declined the offer of refreshments.

The old house had a creepy kind of aura about it, which she suddenly found very unsettling. The furniture within the dining room looked to her as if it might have been bought when the house was first built, and the furnishings gave off a musty odour, which assailed her nostrils whenever she breathed in too heavily.

The chair she sat in was rickety and felt as if it might be on its last legs.

Connie waited patiently while Carla disappeared upstairs, returning moments later with a large brown manilla envelope, which she placed on the table in front of her.

"Please check the contents," Carla offered, "just to be sure."

Connie blushed. "I'm sure it's all there, and it's far more than I deserve."

"Nonsense," Carla assured her. "You've no idea what these instruments mean to me. I was crushed when I first found out that my stupid cousin had let them go."

"Yes, you mentioned on the phone that they had sentimental

value," replied Connie, opening the envelope, and carefully flicking through the crisp twenty-pound notes inside.

When she finished counting, she realised that there was in fact, two hundred and fifty pounds inside, rather than the two hundred they had agreed on.

Upon mentioning the discrepancy, Carla brushed it away with a flick of her hand, stating that the rest was for her taxi fare, and that she did not wish to hear anything more about it.

Connie thanked her profusely and shoved the envelope inside her handbag, ensuring that the zip was securely fastened. She could not wait to leave the old house, but she did not wish to appear rude, especially as Carla had been so generous with her.

By now, her host had returned to the PM knives, and was in the process of taking each one out of its holder and scrutinising it, in the light. "Did I tell you these once belonged to my late great-great grandfather?" she asked.

"Yes, you did," replied Connie, politely. "You said that he was quite famous in his day."

"Oh yes, he was. Infamous almost. He lived in this very house as a matter of fact."

"Really, how interesting."

"He was a doctor, I presume?" enquired Connie.

"A surgeon, actually," Carla replied, carrying the red velvet case over to a standard lamp behind Connie, where she began to re-inspect the knives, once more.

She seemed so proud to be talking about her relative, that Connie wondered if Carla already knew that he had carried out the post-mortem on Mary Jane Kelly. She presumed that she did, after all, Carla had told her over the phone that she had completed extensive research on her family tree.

Even so, it seemed like a good opportunity to drop it into the conversation, on the off chance that Carla was not aware of the fact. Furthermore, if she were aware of it, then Connie hoped it would give her the chance to feel proud, knowing that someone else knew it too.

She could see Carla from the corner of her eye, running her finger along the edge of one of the blades. She hopes that she would not suffer the same accident that had befallen her on the train.

Connie decided not to say anything about that particular incident.

"I presume that you already know," Connie began. "But your great-great grandfather was the police surgeon who carried out the post-mortem on Mary Jane Kelly."

"How on earth did you know that?" asked Carla, evidently shocked by the revelation.

Connie, realising that she had backed herself into a corner, knew that she must come clean about the archive laboratory. "Sorry, I should have said," she began, turning in her chair to face Carla. "Before I knew about you, I had agreed to allow our archive lab to inspect those knives for any traces of DNA. I'm a student of forensic medicine, you see."

"I see," replied Carla, clearly intrigued. "And what did they find exactly?"

Connie turned back in her seat, feeling awkward sitting at such a strange angle. "Well, according to the professor in charge, they found a minute trace of DNA on one of the knives which matched a sample they already had on file belonging to this Mary Jane Kelly. She was the last known victim of Jack the Ripper if you can believe it."

"I see, and from that they presumed that my great-great grandfather must have used these knives to perform her post-mortem, correct?"

"Yes, quite extraordinary," Connie continued, wishing that Carla would come back around to her side of the table. It seemed so rude to show the woman her back while they were talking, but she was afraid to move the old chair around for fear it might fall apart.

"Quite." agreed Carla.

"You must be very proud that your relative was a police surgeon, especially such a famous one?"

"Oh, he wasn't a police surgeon. He was Jack the Ripper!"

Before the realisation of Carla's words had taken hold in her brain, Connie felt the cold steel of the knife slide across her neck.

# BORDELLO OF BLOOD

Terry Stansfield gazed longingly at the clock on the wall opposite him. It was now 7:45pm, just fifteen minutes until clocking off time. At least, it would be if Polly was ever on time for her night shift.

Terry knew that his colleague hated working nights alone, but over time he had grown to have very little sympathy for her plight. To his mind, she was nothing short of greedy. She did not need to work the weekend night shift at the Botanical Plant. She was constantly boasting to him about how much money she made from her salon.

But Polly was never satisfied when it came to money. For someone who constantly bemoaned her lack of money, she drove a brand-new BMW, had more designer clothes and accessories than most A-list stars, and insisted on owning every new electronic gadget which came on the market, regardless of whether she needed it or not.

But for Polly, the night shift gave her an opportunity to earn some easy money with very little effort. No one ever worked at the plant overnight, and on weekends especially, staff had usually vacated the building by 6pm at the latest. Therefore, all Polly had to do was sign on with control when she arrived, and sleep on one of the couches in the rest room adjacent to reception, until her relief arrived in the morning. So long as she remembered to set her alarm for her two-hour check-in calls with control, no one would ever be the wiser.

Yet still she complained.

The truth was, Polly was petrified of being alone in such a large building overnight, and she threatened to quit the job every single Friday night when she arrived. But, as always, she was back again the following week, eager to make more easy money.

Eight o'clock came and went. Terry packed away his empty lunch box, newspaper, and work jumper in his sports bag, in anticipation for the start of his weekend.

Friday was the one night of the week which Terry looked forward to above all others, and not just because it signalled the beginning of his weekend.

This was the night that Terry treated himself to a visit to 'Pleasure Island,' a brothel tucked away rather discreetly on an old industrial unit, on the outskirts of town.

Since his second wife left him *in search of herself*, Terry had remained single, partly through choice, and partly through lack of it. At fifty-three he was not what most women would call a *catch*. Although he was always immaculately turned out, and prided himself on his hygiene and general appearance, since taking this job and sitting on his bum all day, five days a week, he had noticed his belly starting to protrude a little more each week, to the point where he could no longer button up his favourite jeans.

For a while now he had been promising himself that he would start a diet and exercise routine. But the truth was that, even though he did not have a physical job, he was too drained at the end of his shift to do anything other than stop off at the chippy on the way home, and slump in front of the telly with a couple of beers, until he finally dozed off.

He had attempted to join a local gym, but when he added up

the cost of the membership, added to the fact that at most he would only be going at weekends, it did not exactly prove to be cost-efficient.

So it was, his life had fallen into an unhealthy routine of junk food, beer, and general laziness.

8:15pm, and still no sign of his colleague. She was seriously starting to take the mick now, and no mistake. It would not have been so bad if he could have at least claimed for the overtime, but when she finally arrived, Polly was always full of apologies and sweet smiles, so Terry never had the heart to stay mad at her long enough to make it count.

He hoped that Jessica was on tonight. He knew, or at least suspected that Jessica was not her real name. All the girls at the brothel were Eastern European, yet all seemed to have names such as Judy and Rose or Sarah and Dawn. Terry supposed that the names they used might have been the English translation of their actual names, but he also knew that it was commonplace for prostitutes to use a pseudonym as their working name.

Jessica was by far the best in his opinion. Some of the others clearly did not wish to be there. Not that he could blame them, it was hardly a lifestyle choice that most women would make. But Jessica always greeted him with a smile, was generally cheery, and never rushed him like some of her colleagues.

The problem was, this made her particularly popular, so Terry had often had to wait for up to an hour if he wanted to see her, which in turn, seemed to tick off the other girls on duty who were obliged to keep trying to convince him to go with them instead of waiting.

It would not have been so bad if he could call ahead and book an appointment with Jessica, but the brothel did not seem to understand the concept of such an arrangement. The tough old bird who ran the reception was a mean-spirited, cantankerous sow, who chain-smoked, even though it was illegal to do so inside a workplace, and always tried to con more out of the punters than the five-pound entrance fee.

Jessica had confided in him that the woman actually owned the business, and beside the entrance fee, the girls had to give her half their earnings, including any tips they made. She also told him that terrible things happened to any girl who tried to keep back more than she was allowed.

In some extreme cases, those girls were never seen or heard from again, and Terry could not help but wonder if that had anything to do with the two rather unpleasant looking characters who always seemed to be parked across the street from the brothel.

Places like Pleasure Island did nothing for their trade if they had bouncers on the door. If anything, it put a lot of the passing trade off trying to enter. Therefore, it made perfect sense to Terry to keep a couple of beefy-looking blokes close at hand should they be needed. But not so close as to put the punters off.

Terry wondered if the girls who worked there, like Jessica, stayed by virtue of their own accord, or had been made an offer they could not refuse. Even so, he had often been tempted to ask Jessica to leave with him, and never go back.

He was not completely stupid, and he knew that there was a chance Jessica did not even like him. Most working girls put on an act for their clients to keep them coming back, and there was no reason for him to suspect that Jessica was any different. But over time, Terry had really fallen for her, and in his fantasy-mind, they would move away together and find some idyllic rural spot, far away from the hustle and bustle of city life and spend the rest of their time together running a pub, or B&B.

Then, every night, exhausted from the day's toil, Terry would climb into bed next to his adorable girlfriend, and make passionate love to her until the sun came up.

Terry shook his head and chastised himself for allowing his imagination to run wild, yet again. In truth, Terry had never made love with Jessica. Not that she did not arouse him, but it seemed wrong in that place. He knew that if he did ever manage to persuade her to leave with him, that it would be a different story, entirely. But in that place, no.

Jessica did, however, give him the best hand-job in the world.

Plus she allowed him to play with her bare feet.

Terry had had a foot fetish for as long as he could remember. As a young boy, he once found himself hiding under his elder sister's bed when she and her friends suddenly decided they had had enough of watching television in the lounge, and wanted to be alone, away from his parents, to discuss boys and fashion and any other nonsense that came into their heads.

He had only been in his sister's room because she had stolen his Action Man, and he was desperate to find it. But when he heard her and her friends running up the stairs he just panicked, and slid under her bed to hide, until they left.

His mother had just had a cream carpet laid in the lounge and hallway, so the house now had a strict 'no shoes inside the house' policy. Therefore, when his sister and her friends arrived in the bedroom, they were all in their bare feet.

While he lay quietly under her bed, trying desperately not to make a sound and be discovered, Terry found himself with his face mere inches away from a succession of painted toenails, and crinkly soles, as the girls all sat on the bed, dangling their feet over the side.

Terry was too young to understand anything about sex at the time. But he found himself being irresistibly drawn to the array of naked feet, all so tantalisingly close to his nose.

It was the first time Terry remembered feeling a stirring between his legs, and it frightened him, but excited him at the same time. He managed to edge himself as close as he dared, without being discovered, to the nearest pair of feet which belonged to a girl named Laura Colley, who lived next door.

He was so close that whenever she moved her legs, her bare soles almost caressed his face. Before that moment, the only reference to feet Terry had experienced, was when his mum used to complain about his dad's smelly socks when he kicked off his shoes in the porch. But, as he took great joy in pointing out, it was her rule he was obeying, so she would just have to lump it.

But Laura's feet seemed to exude an intoxicating odour, which Terry breathed in as deeply as he could, careful not to make any noise, while stuck under that bed.

The first time he masturbated, it was at the thought of Laura Colley's gorgeous feet.

But Jessica's were even more lovely. Or maybe it was just that, unlike Laura's, he actually had a chance to play with hers.

Finally, he saw the blue-white beams from Polly's car sweep across the forecourt.

*At last.*

He checked the time, it was almost 8:30pm. Perhaps it was a good idea after all that he was not able to book a specific time slot with Jessica. If he relied on Polly, he would always be late.

"Hey babes, sorry I'm late, give me some sugar." Polly barged through the main door, arms full of shopping bags which suggested that she had been in the west end spending more of her hard-earned cash, as usual.

She dumped the bags on one of the leather chairs to the side of the main door and came over to Terry with her arms open wide.

Dutifully, Terry stood up and came around the desk for his hug.

Polly planted a hard kiss directly on his lips, and before releasing him, slid her hands down his back until they reached his rump, which she then squeezed as if they were ripe melons. "Oh, my man has the goods," she gushed, in that fake American accent she often put on.

"What's your excuse this week?" Terry asked, not fooled for a moment by her greeting.

"Traffic baby, traffic. I left the salon early 'cos I had to do me some serious shopping for a party I've got to go to next week. An' I left the west end with plenty of time to get here, but once I drove out of the car park, I hit a wall of traffic which did not move for an eternity. You're lucky I made it in at all."

"I'll consider myself privileged," Terry replied, not bothering to mask the sarcasm in his voice. Sometimes, Polly's attitude towards him made Terry feel as if she only played up because she knew he would never take things further.

He had no qualms doing a colleague a favour, but she really took advantage of his good nature, and presumed she could get away with it by simply giving him a quick grope and a kiss.

She had even made jokes about him staying with her overnight. But Terry knew that she only wanted the company, and if he did try it on, she would probably run a mile, and start screaming that he had misread all the signs.

Hell, he would not even put it past her to scream rape, if she thought it might be an easy way of making money by threatening to sue the company for leaving her alone with a potential rapist.

Refusing her offer of staying for a coffee and a catch-up, Terry climbed into his car and checked his appearance in the rear-view mirror. As he suspected, Polly's amorous advances had left him with a huge red smudge from her lipstick, so he wiped it away with a tissue before setting off for his rendezvous with Jessica.

Pleasure Island was only about fifteen minutes away by car, and as Terry turned into the street, he saw the familiar black van parked across the road from the entrance. He did not bother to glance in the direction of the side window as he parked up, but he felt fairly sure that the occupants would be the usual men keeping an eye on the place.

He checked himself once more in the mirror, and removed a mint spray from his glove box, squirting the vapour twice on his tongue, and once underneath it.

Locking the car door and setting the immobiliser with his fob, Terry walked into the club.

The receptionist recognised him immediately, but as usual,

she did not bother to acknowledge him, other than to hold out her hand for the five-pound entrance fee.

Terry handed over the money, which the woman took without bothering to look up from her phone and made his way through the curtain which led to the waiting area. From behind, he heard the woman mutter something incoherent into the intercom

Being relatively early for a Friday night, there were only two other men seated on the long leather sofa, and they both kept their heads down when Terry arrived. He planted himself on one of the single chairs opposite to them, and aimlessly picked up one of the porn magazines from the table beside it.

A few moments later, the door to their waiting area opened, and two of the working girls entered. Terry recognised one of them as a girl called Sonia. When she saw him, she immediately turned her attention to one of the other men.

Terry had only met Sonia once, when he first started visiting the massage parlour. When he finally managed to explain to her what he wanted, she refused point blank, stating that she was not a 'weird-girl'. It was that night that he met Jessica, who came in to replace Sonia.

Sonia said something in her own tongue to the girl who was with her. The girl looked over at Terry, then immediately switched her gaze to the other man waiting. Terry pretended not to notice being snubbed. Anyway, he hoped his Jessica would be there to see to him, that evening.

The girls took hold of each man by the hand and led them back through the door they had initially entered from.

Terry waited patiently.

After a few moments, he could hear footsteps approaching from along the corridor, and seconds later Jessica appeared. As soon as she saw Terry, she smiled broadly, and held out her hand for him to follow her.

Terry stood up, dropping his magazine in his haste. He bent

down and grabbed it, replacing it on the table with the others, before walking over to Jessica.

"Hello, darrrling," she drawled, planting a kiss on the side of his cheek. She had such a beautiful accent that it was hard for Terry to believe that she spoke the same language at the crone of reception.

"Hiya," was all he could manage as a reply. Even after all this time, he still felt like a schoolboy with a crush when he saw her.

She led him down the corridor to a room at the far end. Inside there was a couple of rickety-looking chairs, a couch with some of the stuffing falling out, and a single bed. Beside the bed there stood a small table, on which were several boxes of condoms scattered about, some baby wipes, and a bottle of baby oil, the smell from which permeated the air.

The overhead bulb was a dull red, as if the punters needed to be reminded that they were in a brothel.

Once inside, Jessica closed the door behind them. "You want usual?" she asked, seductively.

Terry nodded and reached into his jacket for his wallet.

He handed her the usual fifty quid fee, and she smiled as she tucked the folded bills into the back pocket of her jean shorts. On his first couple of visits, Jessica would always leave the room with the money, returning a few minutes later, which he presumed was so she could give the money to the receptionist for safe keeping. But now Terry believed that she trusted him enough not to try and grab it back once they were done.

He often wondered why the receptionist did not just demand the money upon entry. But then he saw a documentary where the girls at another brothel somewhere up north, explained that the reason behind the working girls taking the money was so that they could negotiate as much as possible from the punters, before agreeing on a price.

It made sound sense to Terry. After all, no one was going to hand over a fortune to the hag on the desk before seeing the girls.

Jessica began to undress him, folding his clothes before placing them neatly on one of the chairs.

Once he was naked, Jessica slid her bare hands up and down his body, stopping when she reached his growing shaft. She went down on her knees before him, and gently began to kiss the underside of his penis, causing him to moan, softly.

It was at this point that Terry had to fight to stay in control for fear that he might shoot his load before the fun really began.

As if sensing his caution, Jessica laughed and stood up. She removed her vest over her head, letting her long blonde locks fall down around her shoulders.

She pressed her body against his, letting her naked breasts mash against his chest.

Jessica leaned in and began to kiss the side of his neck, before working her way up and nibbling his ear lobe.

She could feel his erection pushing hard against her tummy, and she clasped his buttocks with both hands before rubbing herself against him.

Terry groaned out loud. He could feel himself leaving a wet trail across her abdomen.

Finally, Jessica moved back. She gave him another quick kiss on the mouth before lying back on the bed. With her feet dangling over the edge.

She was wearing white gym pumps, and no socks.

Terry knelt down on the floor and carefully untied the laces to both of Jessica's shoes, before removing them, altogether. Before placing them on the ground, Terry held each shoe over his nose and mouth, and breathed in, heavily.

The aroma from the girl's feet was like nectar to him.

He looked up and say Jessica smiling down on him, clearly enjoying the display.

It reminded Terry of how his second wife used to act when they first went out. Back when she considered his fetish as nothing more than harmless fun. But that was before things turned nasty. Two years into married life and she began referring to his fetish as 'perverted' and 'disgusting'.

Their marriage continued to slide downhill from there, until eventually ending up in the divorce courts, where she sited 'horrendous sexual demands' as part of her case.

Terry knew that he was well out of it now.

Especially as he now had the pleasure of enjoying Jessica's gorgeous feet.

Once he had finished with her shoes, Terry put them on the floor, and began work on her bare feet. He spent the next fifteen minutes kissing and licking them, all over, before sucking her perfectly manicured toes.

While he went to work on her second foot, Jessica eased her other one down between his legs, and began to play with him. She was able to make a *spanner* between her big and second toe, and she used this to clasp around his throbbing member, and stroke it until he felt sure he would explode.

Eventually, Terry could take no more, so he lay beside Jessica on the bed, where she began to rub his penis back and forth with the soft palm of her hand.

Terry could feel his ejaculation rising. A hand-job from Jessica always felt to him like slipping into a warm bath. He closed his eyes for a moment, then opened them back up to see her smiling face gazing down at him, mere inches away. Her long golden hair tickled the sides of his cheeks as she moved her hand up and down.

He tried to lift himself off the bed, desperate for one more kiss from those oh-so-perfect lips, but Jessica held him down, still smiling at him, until he exploded all over her hand.

Once he was spent, Jessica reached over and pulled out a couple of wipes from the packet nearest her. She used one to wipe Terry's seed off her hand, and the other to clean up what was left from around his groin area.

The wipe was freezing cold, and always made Terry shudder when it first made contact with his skin. But he did not complain. Jessica was so caring and gently as she applied herself to her task.

Once they were both dressed, Jessica led Terry by the hand back out to the waiting area. As they stepped through the door, they were met by the crone from reception, who shoved something in Terry's hand before he had a chance to realise what was happening.

He looked down at it. It was a flyer promoting a special event at the brothel.

As Terry studied the poorly written words, he heard Jessica speaking to the receptionist in her own tongue. Jessica sounded cross with the woman, as if she had done something wrong, though he could not imagine what.

The woman replied by shouting over Jessica in a threatening manner. She began gastrulating with her hands, waving them around in the air as if she were actually threatening to strike the prostitute.

A couple of the other girls, who had doubtless heard the commotion, rushed out to where Jessica and the crone were arguing, and gently began to coax Jessica back inside.

Terry looked up, just in time to see Jessica being whisked away, back through the door.

"You come tomorrow, ten o'clock," the crone began. "Ten pounds, one price, all service, plus drink." She pointed at the flyer in his hand. "You bring this, or no come."

It certainly sounded to him like the deal of the century, and a far better option than spending Saturday evening in the launderette as was his usual routine, before heading to the pub for a couple of pints.

But he could not understand why Jessica had seemed so alarmed when the old women had given him the flyer. Perhaps, she was not on duty for the event, and was afraid that Terry might hit it off with one of the other girls, and so stop being her client.

It made no sense to him. Surely Jessica knew how he felt

about her by now. No one else would offer him the same level of service, and besides, he was in love with her. As futile as that love might be.

He nodded his thanks to the receptionist and left.

It was not his custom to visit the brothel more than once a week, but for this price, how could he refuse?

Terry spent Saturday going through his usual routine, but he could not get the thought of visiting the brothel that night, out of his mind. In truth, he did not know why he was so excited. There was no guarantee that he would even see Jessica, especially after the way she behaved yesterday. Terry presumed that she would not be there, so did not low himself to become too over excited at the prospect.

After his visit to the laundry, Terry went home and showered. He had already enjoyed his traditional Saturday morning bath that day, but with all the running around he had done since then, he felt a shower was in order.

He dressed smartly in a sports jacket, and black trousers. He even decided to put on a tie. There was no dress code from what he could tell but considering he could not make a single word from the writing, he did not want to turn up and be refused admission due to being improperly dressed.

When he arrived at the brothel it was a little before ten.

He saw the ubiquitous van parked across the road, so as usual he ignored it and made his way towards the entrance.

It was then that he noticed the four men loitering in the door-way. Terry stopped in his tracks. For a moment he thought they might be police about to make a raid on the brothel but judging by their marching bomber jackets and general demeanour, he soon realised that they must have been hired as bouncers for the evening's festivities.

Even so, Terry approached them slowly, not wishing to raise any suspicions on the off chance that they were in fact coppers.

When he was a couple of feet from the entrance, one of the men turned around and looked directly at him. Before Terry had a chance to react, the man called to him. "You got voucher?"

Terry took out his voucher and held it up. The man waved him in, and the others moved to one side to allow him access.

The old crone on the reception took his voucher and the ten-pound note Terry held next to it. He presumed that under the circumstances she would be collecting all the money tonight. The woman threw the voucher into a wastepaper bin next to her desk and shoved the money into her usual drawer.

Without bothering to look up, she waved him through to the waiting area.

Once through the curtain, one of the girls was waiting beside a cabinet laden with bottles of vodka and beer, and cans of coke. "What you like?" she asked, pleasantly.

"Beer is fine," Terry replied.

The girl flipped off the top of one of the bottles with a bottle-opener and handed it to him. Terry took a sip. As he expected, the beer was warm, but he smiled at her anyway and raised the bottle as if in salute.

The girl opened the door which led to the rooms. "Party down here," she informed him. "Enjoy."

Terry smiled and stepped through the door. At the far end of the corridor, he could hear the sound of music thundering through the air. He followed the sound, passing the rooms on either side which the girls usually took their clients to.

He noticed there was a spyhole in the door at the end, and just as he was about to knock, the door opened, and another of the girls, this one naked, welcomed him in.

Terry had never been in this room before, and he was surprised by how large it was compared to the individual ones on either side.

The main lights were off, and there were disco balls shooting swirling beams around the room.

There were chairs spread out around the circumference, on which sat around twenty men, each with a young naked girl on his lap. At the far end of the room was a bar area, with two more naked girls serving. The music was being blasted out of a set of six speakers attached to the wall, just below ceiling level, but there was no sign of a DJ inside the room.

Terry stood just inside the door and surveyed the set-up of the room.

He glanced around casually, trying to see if Jessica was anywhere to be seen, but she did not appear to be there.

Terry felt his heart sink. But he had suspected from her reaction the previous night that she might not be attending this function.

Suddenly, her felt someone take hold of his elbow. He turned to see the girl who had opened the door for him, smiling, and gesturing for him to go with her.

She was stunningly pretty, small, very petite, with shoulder-length dark hair, but she still was no Jessica.

Even so, resigned to the fact that she was not on duty that evening, Terry allowed himself to be escorted to one of the vacant chairs dotted around the room. As he sat down as instructed, the girl immediately sat on his lap, and, taking the bottle from his hand, she tipped her head back and emptied the contents down her throat.

Holding up the empty bottle, the girl signalled to the girls behind the bar, and one of them trotted over with a replacement beer, which she handed to Terry.

Not sure what else to do, Terry took a shot. At least this one is almost cold, he thought. As he drank, the girl on his lap swung her legs around so that she was straddling him, with her legs wrapped behind the chair.

Terry offered his bottle to her, and she took another swig, before placing it on the floor next to the chair. She began to unbutton Terry's shirt. Once it was open to the waist, the girl slid her hands inside, and began to rub his torso, sensually.

Terry closed his eyes.

A weird part of him felt guilty, as if he was cheating on

Jessica. But he reasoned with himself that if she were there, he would naturally choose to be with her, and what's more, she knew that he was coming, so it was her choice not to attend.

The girl eased his shirt down over his shoulders, exposing his bare flesh. She leaned in closer and started rubbing her lips against his neck, her soft breath tickling his nape.

Terry could feel himself starting to go hard beneath her bottom, and so could she.

The girls rubbed herself against his stiffening member, as she continued to nuzzle his neck. Terry wondered if they were going to adjourn to somewhere a little more discreet, or if this was all part of the itinerary.

Terry had never had sex in front of an audience before, and he was not altogether sure that he wished to start now, regardless of how hot the girl was making him.

The girl however, appeared lost in her work, running her fingers through his hair, and gripping onto it while she explored his neck and ears with her tongue.

Terry closed his eyes and leaned back, exposing himself to her.

His own moans mingled with those from the men around him, each of them experiencing a similar erotic performance to his.

Terry did not notice when the music suddenly rose in volume, making it loud enough to cause the floor to shake. He was too engrossed in what was being done to him by the young prostitute.

Another twinge of guilt suddenly struck him. Although he had never felt like having sex in this place, even with his beloved Jessica, Terry knew that if the young girl led him away to one of the bedrooms, he would not be able to resist.

Terry opened his eyes.

His partner pulled her head back and smiled down at him.

As her lips parted, Terry saw the elongated incisor teeth protruding over her bottom lip.

Just then, Terry could hear blood-curdling screams as all the men seated around the room began thrashing and struggling to break free from their concubines.

He was not given time to react.

The girl on his lap threw her arms around him, pinning him back against his chair.

Her smile was replaced with a hungry leer, as she focussed her attention on the side of his neck. Leaning closer, he could feel her breath against his skin.

The girl licked him once more below his ear, as if to make ready her point of attack.

Terry knew it was futile to struggle. She was far too strong.

He closed his eyes in anticipation of the bite which would doubtless end his life.

From nowhere, the girl was wrenched from the chair, and thrown across the floor.

Terry felt the sudden release, and opened his eyes, not knowing what to expect.

He looked up to see Jessica standing over him, her twisted to one side as she stared down at the naked woman she had just attacked. The girl was now lying on her back, on the floor, staring up at Jessica with malicious intent behind her eyes.

Jessica shouted something to her, which Terry could not understand. But it was obvious from her reaction that the girl did. She lifted herself up, slowly, to a standing position, all the time keeping her eyes fixed directly on Jessica.

Terry continued to watch in stunned amazement, as the girl circled towards Jessica until they were no more than a foot apart.

Jessica stood her ground, unflinching, as the girl began to spit words which, even if he did not know their meaning, Terry could guess the sentiment.

Jessica made her reply in far less vicious tone than the girl had used, but still menacing enough to convey her intent.

The two women stared directly into each other's eyes for what seemed to Terry, an eternity.

Finally, the young girl ran her tongue across her bared fangs and turned away.

Terry looked past Jessica's form as the young prostitute who moments before had been about to end his life, fell to her knees and sunk her teeth into the thigh of a man who was lying on the floor, convulsing as another of the prostitutes drank from his neck.

When Jessica turned to look down at him, Terry felt his legs go from beneath him. He was glad to be sitting down, otherwise he felt sure he would just crumble before her.

Instinctively he knew that she was angry with him for attending the event, and especially for allowing himself to be set upon by one of the other girls.

Jessica wanted him for herself.

If anyone was going to drain his life blood away, it was going to be the girl who had pandered to his weird sexual desires all this time, and no one else.

Unlike the other girl, Jessica had no fangs on display. It was still the same sweet face that he always looked forward to seeing when he visited the brothel.

He attempted a weak smile of apology.

Jessica held out her hand to him. Terry took it, without hesitation. Any thoughts of escape did not even enter his mind. For a start, there were those four burly blokes at the main entrance, and Terry felt sure that, under the circumstances, there would probably be the same welcome waiting at the back.

Managing to stand on shaky legs, Terry let Jessica guide him out of the blood-soaked room, and along the corridor to one of the bedrooms.

Once inside, she undressed him the way she always did, and began to rub herself up against him. She was already naked, just like all the other girls on duty tonight, and even with the impending doom which he knew was coming, Terry could not help but grow aroused by her touch.

He desperately wanted to whisper to her that he was sorry

for what he had done. But he felt that apologies were too long overdue.

Terry winced as he felt the sharp point of Jessica's fangs pierce the skin on his neck. But he did not resist. Instead, he held her tightly, as if he welcomed what was to come.

Jessica drank, deeply. Sucking the blood from his veins.

Terry felt himself starting to drift away. He was no longer sure if he were still standing, and he did not care.

After a while, Jessica pulled back from him.

Terry opened his eyes and saw a single trickle of blood snake down from the corner of her mouth. He resisted the urge to wipe it away as if it were a piece of food gone overboard, and just stared back at her beautiful face, instead.

Leading him to the bed, Jessica gently pushed him back, then climbed on top of him.

Using her hand, she clasped her fingers around his throbbing penis, and stroked it up and down a few times before effortlessly sliding it inside her.

She rode him until he exploded inside her.

When he was spent, Jessica slid off him, and leaned down to take him inside her mouth, using her moist lips and tongue, to clean away any remaining cum.

Terry was ready to die. He felt a strange pulsating throb in his neck where Jessica had fed, moments earlier. He imagined it was what was left of his life blood ebbing away.

But he really did not care, anymore.

Jessica lay down beside him, and began kissing his chest, working her way up to his face, before parting his lips with her fingers, and thrusting her tongue inside his mouth.

Afterwards, Terry finally felt the strength to ask. "Am I dying now?"

Jessica lifted herself up on one arm. "What you mean, dying?"

Terry gazed up into her eyes. "You're a vampire, aren't you? I don't mind. You've bitten into my neck and drunk my blood, so doesn't that mean I am going to die now?"

Jessica laughed, and bent down, kissing the end of his nose. "No, silly man, I did not drink deep enough for that." She wagged her index finger at him. "But Zana would not have thought twice about it. If I had left you to her, then you would be dead by now, yes."

Terry felt a flush of heat hit his cheeks. "I'm so sorry about that. I thought you weren't working tonight; I did look for you when I arrived."

"And when you see I'm not there, you go with her? I see."

Terry opened his mouth automatically to defend his position, then closed it without speaking.

"Very wise," Jessica cautioned him. "It better not to lie to a vampire, we are not very forgiving."

"I love you," he replied, keeping his gaze fixed on her eyes.

She stared at him. After a moment, she said. "I believe you are. What am I to do with you, eh? Love between a human and a vampire is never easy. Always ends in tragedy."

"I don't care," Terry stammered, sincerely. "I want to be with you, forever."

Jessica smiled. "Forever, is a very long time for a vampire."

"Then make me one of you," Terry pleaded. "Just so long as I can be with you, I don't care about anything else."

Jessica stroked his brow with her fingernail. "If I turn you," she cautioned, "you will be my slave. There is no other way."

Terry lifted himself up, and grabbed her hand, kissing it. "Good," he replied. "I want to be your slave."

Jessica furrowed her brow, as if she were about to impart something serious.

For a moment Terry felt a tingle of trepidation.

Then she said. "If you are my slave, I'll make you kiss my smelly feet every day, as punishment, even when you're good, and do everything I say."

Terry fell back laughing. "Then I'm already yours to command."

Jessica waged her finger again. "Don't say later on that I did not warn you, slave."

With that, she lowered herself back on top of him, and continued to drink from his open wound.

# THE PORTRAIT

It was in early spring when I received the letter from Brathwaite and Hewson Esq, Solicitors, concerning their client, my distant cousin, Felicia Winthrop.

In truth, we had never been a close family and I had not seen my cousin since my parent's funeral some ten years earlier, so I was somewhat intrigued to receive the said communication, requesting that I contact them as a matter of urgency.

I wrote back immediately, and within a few days, received their reply, which stated that my cousin had not been seen in the village in over a month, and that the local squire had launched an investigation into her disappearance, and as part of that investigation, Messrs Brathwaite and Hewson were making enquiries as to whether I had any knowledge of my cousin's whereabouts.

Although born in London, my cousin Felicia had become something of a 'country mouse' having inherited a property from her late father in Wiltshire, many years earlier. The house in question was set on a large estate which had belonged to the Sommerville family since the time of the reformation.

I had only visited the property on one occasion, that being for my uncle's funeral, and remembered it as being a very sturdy, stone-built structure, with a slate roof, set in a charming, picturesque village, a few miles from the nearest station.

Being a man of business, I naturally lived and worked in London, and had precious little free time for jaunts into the countryside, which is one of the reasons my cousin and I had rather lost touch since she moved.

I replied to the letter immediately, assuring them that I had, in fact, not heard from my cousin for some considerable time, and asked there was anything I could do to assist in the search.

It was suggested, by return post, that as my cousin's nearest relative, I might consider travelling down to add weight to the ongoing inquiry.

The proposition could not have come at a more inconvenient time so far as work was concerned. But having explained the situation to my employer, I was granted a fortnight's leave of absence on compassionate grounds.

I travelled down to Wiltshire the following day by train. Before leaving, I forwarded a telegram to the solicitors, informing them of my plans, and was delighted to be met at the station, upon my arrival, by the squire's carriage.

The driver was a surly individual named Haskins, who, although not one for conversation, was polite and professional enough for his position.

I was taken directly to the offices of Brathwaite and Hewson, where I was introduced to the latter, the former being away on some business concerning one of their clients.

Mr Hewson was a rather sour-faced individual, whose monotone voice matched his countenance perfectly.

"You might find it a little odd for a solicitor to become involved in these circumstances," he explained. "But we have been asked by the squire to lend our assistance in any way we can, and as he, as well as your dear cousin," he corrected himself, flushing slightly, "are both valued clients, we are naturally only too pleased to acquiesce."

"Thank you," I replied, politely. "Yes, I would be grateful for any assistance under the circumstances. I presume the local constabulary have been informed?"

"Indeed," I was assured, "the squire is also our local magistrate, so he quite naturally has connections with our local police and has volunteered to spearhead the investigation himself, due to the lack of any senior officers in the district."

"That is very good of him," I observed.

Hewson, much to my astonishment, almost released a smile. "Squire Sommerville is a great man," he enthused. "Without him, I'm not altogether sure our little community would have thrived the way it has, over the years."

I listened as the solicitor continued to expound on the virtues of the squire, pretending as best I could to be interested. It was clear to me that Hewson held the man in very high regard, doubtless as a result of the amount of work he put their way.

After what seemed like an eternity, there was a knock at the door, and one of the clerks put his head in to enquire if we wanted tea. By now, I was gasping, but I could tell at once from the expression on the solicitor's face that he was annoyed by the interruption, so before he had a chance to dismiss his clerk, I turned in my chair and graciously accepted his kind offer.

The refreshment certainly helped me through the next half hour, during which Hewson droned on about how busy they were dealing with some conveyancing details on behalf of his precious squire.

The man spoke so slowly, and deliberately, it made me wonder if they earned much of their keep by charging their clients by the hour. At times I felt compelled to jump in and finish his sentence for him before giving him the opportunity to take another roundabout route, before finally arriving at his destination.

By the time he had brought me up to speed, the spring sun was already on the wane.

As I walked down the stone steps which led to the street, I was pleasantly surprised to see that Haskins was still parked in the same spot I had left him, hours earlier. I had presumed that he would have left immediately upon dropping me off at the solicitors. Otherwise, I would have left my overnight things in the carriage. But he explained to me-with his usual dour expression-that the squire had instructed him to take me to my cousin's house, where he would be waiting to greet me.

The journey took less than half-an-hour, and when we arrived at my cousin's home, I could see through the curtains that the gas lamps were already lit. Haskins waited in his carriage-doubtless to take the squire home after our meeting-as I alighted and knocked on the door.

The door was opened by a young girl, possibly no older than eighteen, smartly turned out in a maid's outfit. She curtsied upon seeing me, and stood back to allow me in. Before closing the door, she excused herself, and ran to the carriage to speak to Haskins.

At the end of their brief conversation, Haskins slapped the reins and the horses set off back down the lane.

When the girl returned, she introduced herself as Stella, and explained that she was employed by my cousin as her daily help, and that the Squire had asked her to wait at the house to meet me, as he had been called away unexpectedly.

According to Stella, the squire had promised to call back the following morning.

She took me upstairs to what would be my bedroom during my stay, where a cosy fire was already blazing in the hearth.

Without any urging from me, Stella placed my overnight bag on the bed, and began to place the contents in the wardrobe, and the chest of drawers.

"I'll clean your shoes for you in the morning, if that's alright," she offered, placing my spare pair by the door.

After showing me around the rest of the house, all except my cousin's bedroom, naturally, Stella led me back downstairs, and informed me that she had prepared a meat pie for my supper, and that it would be ready in about ten minutes.

In the meantime, she showed me into the parlour where another inviting fire had been lit, and poured me a large glass of whiskey, placing it on a table next to a sumptuous armchair.

I sat back and savoured the first taste of my drink, while listening to the logs crackling on the hearth.

The room itself was immaculately presented, with not so much as an ornament out of place. This, I surmised, was a credit to Stella's industriousness, and my cousin's discerning eye.

All the furniture was made of dark wood, possibly mahogany, although I could not claim to be any sort of expert. Most of my own furniture back at my flat in London consisted of hand-me-downs from my late parents, as well as a few pieces I managed to pick up at auction, none of which seemed to actually match once I had them in situ.

As my aperitif slid a warming path through my upper body, banishing the cold from my journey, I gazed around the room to take in the décor.

My eye suddenly caught sight of a portrait which was hung above the mantlepiece.

The gas lamps on either side of it were down low, which cast most of it in shadow, but as I strained to look, there was something immediately familiar about the subject.

I drained my glass and walked over to it for a closer look.

Having stared at it for a few moments, I realised that it was a painting of my missing cousin. She had naturally aged slightly since my last visit, which was why it had taken me a while to recognise her, but she was still an incredibly handsome woman by any accounts.

I turned up the gas lamps adjacent to her portrait for a better look.

In the picture, she was glancing to her left, as if her attention had just been caught by a noise, or someone entering the room, and in her lap, lay a small dog, a terrier, with its head resting on her arm.

I stared at it for quite some time. The artist was obviously very adept at his profession, and he had managed to capture my cousin's countenance perfectly.

I did not hear Stella enter the room until she cleared her throat, politely, to announce her presence.

I turned and smiled. "This is a painting of my cousin, is it not?" I asked.

"Yes sir," she replied. "The squire commissioned it as a present for the mistress for her last birthday."

"It's marvellous," I said, admiringly, "and what a lovely thought." Then an idea occurred to me. "Were they courting, do you know?"

Stella blushed. "Well," she replied, clearly unsure of how to proceed. "I would not wish to speak out of turn, sir."

"Not at all," I assured her, smiling. "Anything you tell me shall remain between us."

She smiled, nervously. "Well, I have no actual confirmation you understand, but there was gossip in the village a while back that the squire had proposed to her."

"So, they were to be married, after all?"

Stella glanced at her feet for a moment, before looking up, sheepishly. "From what I heard the mistress refused his advances. But as I say, sir, this is only what I've heard. Not that I listen to common gossip, you understand."

I nodded my appreciation for her candour. "And even after such a rejection, the squire still went ahead and paid for this commission?" I asked, signalling to the portrait.

Stella nodded. "I believe the squire still presented the mistress with the odd little trinket of his affection. But from what I gleaned, she remained steadfast in her resolve."

Stella did not sleepover once her duties for the day were concluded. She informed me that she still resided with her parents in the village and was grateful to the squire for continuing to pay her wages, since my cousin's disappearance.

As time was getting on, and it was clear that Stella wished to leave, having remained in the house past her usual time, I decided to make further enquiries concerning my cousin from her the following day.

After dinner, I took myself back into the parlour for an after-dinner glass of port.

Stella had been good enough to stoke the fire for me, so the room was still lovely and warm when I entered.

I sat myself back down in the same comfortable chair I had used before dinner.

Whether it was the wine I had consumed during my meal, or the general hustle and bustle of the day, I was finding it hard to keep my eyes open. Train travel had always taken a toll on me, so I decided that once I had finished my drink, I would take myself upstairs to bed.

Without realising it, I fell asleep where I was sitting, and woke up several hours later in the same position. The fire had burnt itself down to its last embers, and I could feel a chill seeping into my bones as I sat up and shrugged myself off. My half-finished glass of port still sat on the table beside me, so I knocked it back to fend off the cold.

It was as I stood to stretch, that my eyes were suddenly drawn back to my cousin's portrait. Something had changed about it, I was sure, but at that moment I could not discern what it was.

Rubbing the sleep from my eyes, I went over and stood directly before it, scrutinising the picture for anything which seemed out of place.

I had almost given up and decided that any such difference was merely in my sleep-addled mind when it struck me.

My cousin was no longer looking directly off to her left in the portrait, but was now glancing more towards the front, directly at me.

Everything else in the portrait seemed just as before. Even the little dog was still in the same position. But there was no denying that my cousin's head had turned-albeit slightly- since I had first seen her picture.

Although I had dozed for what must have been the best part of a couple of hours, the lure of my bed began to outweigh my curiosity. Therefore, I took one last look at the painting to confirm my suspicions, before turning off the gas, and going to bed.

I slept incredibly well for the rest of the night and did not wake until I heard the sound of Stella pottering around downstairs.

After a while, there was a knock on my door, and Stella arrived with a piping hot cup of tea. While I drank, she made up the fire for me, and began to fill a tin bath with hot water.

After my bath, I made my way downstairs, where the smell of bacon cooking assailed my nostrils. Stella had the table set, and I sat down to eat: porridge, followed by eggs and bacon, toast and home-made thick orange marmalade, all washed down with several cusps of Stella's delicious-tasting tea.

By now, all thoughts regarding my cousin's portrait had quite slipped my mind, and it was not until later that morning when the squire called round and we adjourned to the parlour, that I was reminded of the occurrence from the previous evening.

As I was now in company, I decided not to draw attention to my suspicions. However, as I passed by my cousin's portrait, I glanced towards it quite casually, and was taken aback when I saw that it was now as it had been when I first laid eyes on it.

My cousin had moved back to her original position, so that she was now, once again, gazing to her left.

I blinked and shook the matter from my mind so that I could concentrate on my guest.

Before I had the chance to offer the squire some refreshment, Stella appeared with a silver tray, upon which sat two glasses of sherry. It appeared that she was already familiar with the squire's tastes, doubtless I presumed from his previous visits.

The squire was a quite a large man, both in height, and in girth, with a great bushy moustache which curled up at the sides almost to the rim of his glasses.

His cheeks were ruddy from his walk, and before sitting down to partake of his sherry, he removed his gloves and splayed his hands in front of the fire, as if to rejuvenate his circulation.

He wore a thick black overcoat over his tweeds, which had the most ornate-looking gold buttons fastening it together. As he slipped off his coat for Stella to hang up for him, I could not help but notice that one of his magnificent buttons was missing.

I decided not to mention this to him just in case he became embarrassed at my noticing it.

We talked for the beat part of an hour, during which time, Stella replenished the squire's glass three times. I on the other hand, made mine last throughout our conversation.

He seemed genuinely upset by my cousin's disappearance and assured me that he intended to do everything in his power to find out what had happened to her, as he was convinced that she had not merely packed up one night and left the area.

"I'll level with you, young sir," he said, leaning in a little closer as if afraid someone else might hear our conversation. "Your cousin was a mighty fine tenant, and the least trouble of all the others I have around here. I will be truly sorry if she has decided to leave us for good. Especially, as she never said a word to me, or any of my groundskeepers before leaving."

I smiled. "Yes, Stella informed me that you had a great affection for my cousin."

At this statement, the squire flushed red, and I could see that I had made him feel somewhat uncomfortable, which had not been my intention.

I pretended not to notice his discomfort and turned in my

chair to point to my cousin's portrait. "Stella informed me that you had this commissioned for my cousin, as a present."

I waited a few moments longer than necessary before turning back to face him, in the hope that it would allow him a chance to recover himself.

"Oh that, yes indeed," he replied cheerfully. "Not a famous artist as yet, but a local man who I have great faith will one day be a master. I've commissioned several landscapes from him in the past and am fast building up a fine collection of his works. Your cousin admired some of them when she visited the manor once for tea, so I thought it was a fitting present for her."

"Very generous I'm sure," I assured him. "And not the sort of thing she would leave behind."

"Exactly," he agreed. "And that is my point. Why, if she had decided to move on, would she leave without taking anything with her? Young Stella assures me that your cousin did not take so much as a stitch of clothing with her, other than what she was wearing when she last saw her."

"That is very odd," I agreed. "So, what, if you don't mind me asking, do you think has happened to her?"

He shook his great head and peered at me over his glasses. "I cannot believe that foul play was involved, that's for certain. Everybody around here only ever had good things to say about her, and she kept herself to herself."

"So, if it is foul play, you suspect someone from outside the village?"

"Well, I cannot believe it is a local, but strangers around here are few and far between. And what's more, when one of them appears, everybody knows about it, and there were no strangers reported in the area around the time of her disappearance."

I thought for a moment. "So, what do you suggest we do?" I asked, hopefully.

The squire drained his glass. "You can rest assured that I have instigated the most thorough investigation. As the local magistrate, naturally I have connections at the highest level with law enforcement, and I'm having every inch of the countryside searched for miles around, just in case."

"That's very kind, and much appreciated," I assured him. "But what can I do?"

"Well, I was thinking that perhaps you could contact any other members of your family whom your cousin might have decided to visit, for whatever reason, just in case."

"You think she might have suddenly decided to drop everything and go on holiday?" I asked, quizzically.

He shook his head once more. "Not holiday, as such," he ventured. "I was thinking more along the lines that she received word that someone was ill or needed her assistance in a hurry. I thought that perhaps you might know who that might be."

I thought for a moment, then shook my head. "If I'm honest, we were not really that close," I admitted. "Which was as much my fault as anything. I work in London and business keeps me extremely busy, so over the years we have manged to lose touch."

He nodded his understanding. "Of course, I can appreciate how business can take over one's life."

Just then, the old grandfather clock in the hall struck the hour.

The squire pulled out his pocket watch and flipped open the cover.

"Good heavens," he exclaimed, forcing his bulk out of the chair with some difficulty. "I hadn't realised the time. I have a luncheon appointment in the village. Please excuse me, I really must dash."

Without being summoned, Stella appeared with his coat, and helped him on with it.

I stood and we shook hands, and the squire promised to keep me abreast of any developments concerning my cousin.

Once he had left, I asked Stella to join me in the parlour.

I could tell immediately by the concerned look on her face, that she presumed I had some bad news to convey, so I attempted to put her mind at ease by smiling and insisting that she take a seat opposite me, to be comfortable.

Before speaking, I glanced over at my cousin's portrait once more.

As I suspected, she was still facing off to her left.

As much as I wished to share my experience of the previous evening with someone, I did not wish to appear foolish or unstable in front of Stella, so I decided for the moment to keep the incident to myself.

I asked her to inform me of the exact order of circumstances surrounding the last time she saw my cousin.

"Well sir," she began, gazing around the room as if for inspiration. "I remember it was a Tuesday, and after lunch the mistress went for her daily stroll into the village. I remember thinking at the time that she was gone longer than usual, but I presumed she had met someone and had grown lost in conversation.

"I must confess, that when she had not returned by teatime, I was starting to panic a little, as it was most out of character for her to miss her afternoon tea without first giving me fair warning. Anyway, I kept the pot on the stove, and continued with my usual duties. When she finally returned, it was almost 5 o'clock, and I rushed to meet her when I heard the door go."

Stella looked me straight in the eye before she continued.

"I must confess sir, the second I set eyes on the mistress I knew that something was up."

"How do you mean?" I asked, curiously.

Stella blushed, slightly. "Well, if you'll forgive me for saying so, the mistress looked dishevelled, which was completely at odds with her usual appearance. Her coat was mis-buttoned as if she had dressed in haste, her bonnet was untied, and one of her stockings had lost its garter and was all wrinkled up. I had seen the mistress when she left, and I can assure you now that she was immaculate as usual when I closed the door behind her."

"Did she say what had happened to leave her in such disarray?"

Stella shook her head. "I'm sorry sir, but she didn't, and it was not my place to ask. But I could tell at once from the look on her face that something was troubling her."

"What happened next?" I enquired, fascinated by the maid's revelations.

Stella leaned in as if she were afraid someone might overhear our conversation.

"She asked me to run her a bath," she said. "Even though she had had one that very morning. It was most odd, sir. I had never known her to bathe in the afternoon before. Anyway, I did as I was told and lit the fire in her bedroom before filling the tub. Then when she called me back to empty the water, the mistress was already dressed for bed."

"That was a little early," I observed. "Was she in the habit of retiring at that time?"

"No sir, never in all the time I worked for her. I thought at first that perhaps she just needed a little nap after being out for so long, so I asked her what time she wanted her supper. But she just climbed into her bed and pulled the covers over her, and told me she wasn't hungry, and that I could leave for the day once I had emptied the bath."

"So then, what did you do next?" I asked.

Stella shrugged. "I didn't know what to do, so I just did as the mistress had instructed me. I emptied her bath, took little Toby out for his evening walk, put another couple of logs on her fire, turned off the gas lamps, and went home."

"Toby is the dog from the portrait, I presume?"

"That's right sir. When I brought him back, he ran straight up to the mistress's room, he used to sleep on the bed with her, you see."

"And the next morning?"

This time she sat back in her seat, and looked at me, sheepishly.

"She was gone, sir. I arrived at my usual time, took the mistress up her morning tea, but she was not in bed. I searched the house from top to bottom, calling out to her, but she was nowhere to be seen. Little Toby was jumping up and down in this room as if he were possessed, bless him. He knew something was up, even if I didn't."

"So, then what did you do?"

"I went about my usual duties, sir. Not realising of course that there was anything wrong. I just thought the mistress had gone for an early morning walk, having gone to bed so early and all."

"So then when did you inform the authorities about her disappearance?"

She thought for a moment. "It must have been around three that afternoon. By then, I had made up the mistress's bed, and noticed that her nightdress was not hanging up in the usual place. I knew she would not go out wearing it, even under a big coat it would not make any sense. So, then I took Toby for a walk because he was still racing around creating merry hell and called in on the squire to tell him what had happened."

"I see, and what did he do?"

"Well, at first he seemed uninterested, and dismissed me out of hand. Which I found a little odd as he had always been so fond of the mistress."

"So, what did you do then?" I asked, perturbed at the squire's initial reaction to Stella's information.

"Well, sir, as I say, I was quite taken aback by the squire's lack of concern, so I thought to myself that perhaps I was overreacting. So, then I took Toby down into the village with me and made my own enquiries, but no one had seen the mistress since the previous afternoon."

"Did you not think to inform the police?" My words came out a trifle harsher than I had intended, but my frustration at the lack of the squire's interest was starting to infuriate me.

Even so, I apologised to Stella, and asked her to continue.

"As it happens, I did see the village constable while I was down there. But when I told him what the squire had said, he shrugged it off as well, and told me just to keep the squire informed, in case he wanted to lodge an official missing person's report."

"And, later, after she didn't show up? How long did you leave it before you reported back to the squire again?"

Stella thought before answering. "It was exactly at the same time the following day." She said, finally. "I had stayed on the previous evening way past my usual time, in the hopes that the mistress would come back. I didn't know what to think, but I wanted to make sure that the house was warm and cosy, and that there was a hot stew to welcome her." She looked down at her hands. "But by ten that night, I knew that my folks would be growing concerned as to why I was not home, so I made sure the fireguards were in place, and turned off the lamps. I wasn't sure what else to do, sir." She looked up at me, almost pleadingly.

"That's okay," I assured her. "No one could expect you to have stayed any longer."

She smiled. Looking relieved. "Thank you, sir. Anyway, I made a point of arriving all the earlier the next morning, but there was still no sign of the mistress. So, when I took Toby out for his morning walk, I stopped off at the squire's, but he was over in the next village on business, or so his man told me."

"What, you had reason to think he was lying?" I enquired.

She shook her head. "Not really," she admitted. "It was just that I could see his carriage was still in the courtyard, and a groom was walking the squire's favourite horse in the grounds. I had never known him to go out further than the estate other than in his carriage, or on Lightning before. So, it just seemed a little odd."

"I understand."

"So then, I came back here, and continued with my duties, until the afternoon. Then, just as I was about to set out to see the squire again, he arrived at the door. His man had told him I had called earlier, so he said he thought he'd save me the trip."

"What did he have to say when you informed him that my cousin still hadn't returned?" I asked.

Stella shrugged. "He just said that perhaps she had gone to visit a sick relative or friend and would be back soon enough."

I was slightly taken aback by her explanation. "So, he wasn't even going to begin a formal inquiry at that point?" I asked, incredulously.

"No, sir, but then I insisted that had the mistress have left to go on such an errand of mercy, she would have surely left a note at the very least. Not to mention, by then I had taken the liberty of checking through the mistress's wardrobe, and none of her clothes were missing, save what she had been wearing the last night I saw her."

"What did he have to say about that?" I pressed.

"That was when he reconsidered about starting an investigation," Stella replied, triumphantly. I could tell that she was quite proud of herself, under the circumstances, for insisting that the squire take action, and good for her, I thought.

"And since then?" I asked. Fearing I already knew the answer.

"Nothing, sir," she responded, dejectedly. "I still come here every day in the hope that the mistress might return. I go about my duties as always, and make sure that everything is left spick and span should the mistress return after I've gone, but that's all. The only other thing I did was to take Toby home to my house, as the poor little thing was fretting terribly here by himself, and I couldn't bear leaving him alone, night after night."

"That was very kind of you," I acknowledged. "I hope he is not a burden on your poor parents?"

"Oh, no sir, my mother dotes on him. My father even jokes that when the mistress returns, he will have to buy mother a replacement to stop her getting down."

I thanked Stella for her candour and dismissed her so that she could continue with her duties.

That evening, after dinner, once Stella had left, I retired back to the parlour to ponder over Stella's reconstruction of the events leading up to my cousin's disappearance.

From the sound of it, something must have taken place while she was out on her walk which upset her greatly. But whatever it was, could it be so distressing so as to cause her to up-sticks in the middle of the night, and leave the house dressed only in her nightclothes?

Had that been the case, as ludicrous as it sounded, where would she be going in such a state of undress?

If she had suddenly decided to leave the village, for whatever reason, then surely, she would have taken the time to dress, and pack. My cousin, from what I knew of her, had always been a reasonable, down-to-earth, intelligent woman, and not one prone to irrational flights of fancy.

It was with these thoughts spinning around in my mind, that I dozed off, once again, against the sumptuously soft leather of the armchair, buy the crackling fire.

I woke with a start.

The last of the embers were emitting a vague orange hue from the hearth, and the room had grown a good deal colder due to the lack of heat.

Rubbing my eyes, I stretched out the cramp in my joints, and was about to lift myself out of the chair, when I caught sight of my cousin's portrait, once more.

There was no mistaking it this time. Her figure in the frame had moved to the extent that she was actually looking in the opposite direction to that of the original picture.

I froze to my seat. A sudden chill ran through my body, as if icy fingers were stroking my skin, from within.

I shook any remnants of sleep from my head, before standing up and moving closer to the picture.

For the sake of my own sanity, I stood there for an age, just staring, unblinking, at my cousin's face. There was no movement in the picture, no subtle hint of a wind blowing from one side or the other which might cause some slight distortion to the view before me. I even found myself concentrating on Toby's fur coat, to see if there was even the tiniest of movements perceptible.

But soon I came to the conclusion that the only difference was that my cousin had turned her head, so that she was now glancing towards the other side of the parlour, towards my left.

Tearing my eyes away, I too looked in that direction for any trace of what she might be staring at. But everything was the same as I remembered it from earlier.

None of the furniture had been moved, and the curtains were still drawn shut, as Stella had left them. At my request, she had turned down the gas lamps at that end of the room, so that majority of it was in shadow as I peered through the darkness. But there was still a sufficient glow from the lamps nearest me to offer enough light to assure me that there was no one crouching in the half-light, waiting for an opportunity to launch an attack.

I steadied my nerves and reached down for the brandy glass I had left on the side table before dozing off. I threw back the remnants of the brown liquid and shuddered as it slipped down.

I turned back to my cousin's portrait.

"What is it you are trying to tell me, dear cousin?" My words echoed throughout the empty room, and I must admit, I felt foolish the moment they left my lips.

Talking to inanimate objects in such a way that made it sound to someone else who might be listening as if you were expecting a reply, was not the behaviour of a man of business, who had cultivated an air of respect and authority in our great city.

Yet, here I was, doing that exact same thing, and feeling all the more desperate for a reply.

I stared at the picture for the best part of an hour, until the fire had burnt itself out, completely, and my bones had grown tired and stiff from standing in one place.

Turning off the gas, I took myself to bed.

The following morning, I was awoken by the sound of *yapping* coming from downstairs. This was quickly followed by the scurrying sound of tiny claws on wood, as something rushed up the stairs.

I heard whatever it was scamper along the corridor, yelping in a high-pitched squeak of excitement, as it did so.

There followed an excitable scratching against one of the doors further along the corridor, in combination with more yelping, and whining.

Bemused as I was by all the comings and goings outside, I stayed put as I heard Stella marching up the stairs, calling after Toby in a stern, though hushed, tone.

There were further kafuffles as Stella presumably reached the landing, and I could hear the dog race back across the landing, past my room. It then seemed to screech to a sudden halt, back-pedalling its claws frantically against the polished wooden floor, followed by the sound of something much heavier crashing to the ground, which I imagined was Stella making a desperate grasp for it, and missing.

As I slept with my bedroom door open, seconds later, a tiny terrier, not much bigger than a sewer rat, raced into my room, and jumped up on the bed, wagging its tail and barking at me, as if I were the one who was out of place in the room.

I watched, bemused by the little dog's antics, as it ran from one end of the blanket to the other, crouching down on all fours with its tail wagging furiously, before launching itself at a space a few inches in front of it, then repeating the process all over again.

Stella knocked and entered the room looking sheepish and full of apologies.

"I'm sorry sir," she announced. "My parents have gone away for a few days to see my aunt, so I hoped you would not mind if I brought little Toby in with me. He gets very boisterous if left alone for too long."

"So I see," I remarked. "He's certainly an energetic little fellow."

After my bath I went downstairs for breakfast and was astonished to find little Toby jumping up at the parlour door and barking at it.

Stella explained that, since the day she came in to find my cousin missing, Toby had seemed obsessed with the room, especially a cabinet at the far end, just by the window.

She took him out for a walk while I ate, and when she returned, I opened the parlour door to go inside and read the morning paper which Stella had brought me.

As I unlocked the catch, Toby made a bolt for the door, his lead still around his neck, dragging behind him along the floor.

Just as Stella had said, he made a beeline for the cabinet, and immediately began jumping up at it, and barking loudly. The cabinet was of a stout wooden construction, and about three feet high, so the little chap had no chance of gaining any height on it, no matter how hard he tried.

"What's in there?" I asked Stella, who was still busy removing her coat and scarf.

"Just some china plates and accessories which the mistress brought out whenever she was entertaining," Stella replied.

I went over to the cabinet and Toby moved aside to allow me to open it.

As Stella had said, there was nothing untoward about the contents of the cabinet, although our little friend seemed intent on telling us otherwise.

Having inspected the inside, I closed the door, much to the chagrin of Toby, who immediately ran to one side of the cabinet and began frantically sniffing and scratching the floor at one end of it.

Stella came over and grabbed his lead. "I'm sorry sir, I'll keep him in the kitchen with me, he won't bother you."

As the weather was particularly pleasant, I took a stroll into the village after lunch.

Whilst browsing along the main road, I happened to come across a constable on his beat. I introduced myself and made enquiries as to any update concerning my cousin.

The officer assured me that the squire was overseeing the investigation personally, and he seemed to think that such a statement should quell any concerns I might have that not enough was being done.

On the way back home, I stopped off at the local church, which was conveniently situated a short walk from my cousin's dwelling.

The door was open, so I ventured inside and lit a candle for her, before kneeling in one of the stalls to say a quick prayer for her safe return.

As I walked back home along the path, with the gravestones on either side of me, I suddenly had the impression that I was being watched.

I stopped, and spun round.

Off to my left, towards the far end of the cemetery, I saw an old priest standing beside what appeared to be a freshly dug grave. He was not actually looking in my direction, but more so down towards the pile of earth which lay to one side of the hole.

I thought for a moment, then decided to make my way over to him and introduce myself. He was obviously deep in thought, or prayer, as my sudden arrival beside him seemed to stir him from his reverie, and he almost jumped when he realised that I was there.

"I'm so sorry," I offered, apologetically. "I did not mean to startle you."

He eyed me up suspiciously, then reluctantly accepted my offered hand.

After introductions, I explained my connection to the locale, and asked if he knew of my cousin, or could shed any light on her disappearance.

The old priest shook his head, slowly. "I am very sorry," he replied, "I'm afraid I have no idea where your cousin might be, she certainly never confided in me of any plans to go away. But then, if I'm honest, she was never one to stop and talk after Sunday service, so we really only know each other to nod and smile to."

When he finished speaking, he immediately turned his attention back to the empty grave in front of him. I took that to mean that he had no wish to continue our conversation, so I made my excuses and walked away.

In truth, I do not know if he stared after me as I walked away. But I must confess, I felt a shiver at my back as I left the courtyard which I could not explain.

That evening, after Stella and Toby had left, I settled myself once more in the parlour, taking the chair opposite my cousin's portrait.

For a while, I watched it intently, waiting for some sign of movement to convince myself that I had not been hallucinating the previous two evenings.

After a while, with no change whatsoever, it occurred to me that perhaps the picture would not change whilst being observed so closely, and might only do so, if at all, when the watcher was elsewhere engaged. Therefore, I recharged my glass and took a book down from one of shelves to read.

Over the course of the next few hours, I glanced up periodically at the portrait, hoping to witness some change in my cousin's appearance. But I was disappointed on each occasion.

Eventually, I dozed off to sleep.

I awoke with my book on my chest. The fire was still burning brightly, so I fancied that I must have only dozed for a moment or so.

I looked straight ahead of me at the portrait, and true to form, my cousin's image had once more turned as if she were looking in the opposite direction to that which she had been painted.

I glanced over to follow her gaze, and for a moment, I could swear I saw a figure loitering in the corner, next to the cabinet Toby had been so obsessed with earlier.

I strained to see through the half-gloom cast by the gas lamps nearest me.

The figure appeared somewhat blurred, as if I were looking at it through a frosted glass. It was relatively short, and willowy, and the more I stared the less it appeared to be standing there, as hovering.

It was almost as if the apparition was some form of reflection rather than a solid object, and as I watched, it began to float, gracefully, from one end of the cabinet to the other.

I blinked, and tried to re-focus my gaze, fearing for a moment that perhaps the sensation of waking, plus the brandy, might be causing my eyes to play tricks on me. But, when I opened my eyes again, it was still there.

The shadowy figure seemed to be dressed in a long flowing gown, which billowed behind it as if drawn by an unseen draught.

From this distance I could not make out any specific features of the face, but I was certain that the figure was crowned with flowing locks, which cascaded around its shoulders.

I must confess, at that moment I found myself shrinking back into my chair, terrified that whatever I was watching might suddenly begin to levitate towards me until our faces were mere inches apart.

Something inside told me that should I look upon that face from such close quarters, I would instantly go insane and spend the rest of my life as a babbling lunatic, confined to Bedlam.

But it appeared I had nothing to fear, for no sooner had such thoughts entered my mind the apparition began to drift towards the sturdy wooden cabinet, and then I watched in utter disbelief as it seemed to merge with the piece of furniture, before disappearing through the wall behind it.

I sat there, stunned, for several minutes before I was once again able to move.

Once I could feel my legs again, I stood up from my chair and poured myself a large glass of whiskey, knocking it back neat, in one swallow.

Wiping my mouth, I looked back over at my cousin's portrait.

Her head was still inclined towards where the figure had hovered, moment before. But now her arm too had moved, and it was pointing in that same direction as if willing me to investigate the place where the apparition had vanished before my eyes.

Fortified by the liquor, or perhaps afraid of what might become of me should I fail to act, I strode over to the cabinet and turned up the gas lamps above it.

The item was, as before, just sitting there, unmoved, with no sign of tampering.

I inspected the wall behind it where the figure had melted into the plaster, but there was no sign of anything untoward. Again, I opened the doors and inspected the china within. All appeared as it had done earlier in the day.

I went back over to the portrait.

My cousin was still pointing in the same direction, but now, I was sure I could see a change in her expression as well. Her eyebrows had knitted together somewhat, in a look of defiant consternation, and I must confess that upon seeing it for the first time I recoiled in shock.

I had no idea what she wanted from me.

There was nothing else in that corner of the room where the cabinet stood.

I was about to ask her picture once more to explain her erratic behaviour, but I managed to stop myself before any words left my mouth, afraid that if she answered me, my senses would leave me, as I feared, never to return.

In frustration I strode back over to the cabinet, and carefully began to remove the delicate china, one piece at a time, placing each item safely on the floor at the other side of the window.

Once the cabinet was empty, I felt inside for any sign of tampering.

But there were none.

As I was about to start replacing everything back inside, an idea struck me. Crouching down, I grabbed hold of the underneath of the cabinet and, pushing with my legs, lifted one end so that I could move it away from the wall.

Now that it was empty, it moved easily enough, so I went to the other side and repeated the process until the cabinet stood several feet away from the wall.

I studied the wooden panelling in great detail, before running my hands over it, pressing and pushing against every edge and corner that jutted out.

Suddenly, a panel which had previously been hidden behind the cabinet gave way.

There followed a grinding of metal and chains, and a scraping as a piece of the wall began to move backwards like a door being opened from within.

I stood there in stunned silence looking at the opening which, at full stretch, was big enough for a man to climb through.

After a moment, I went back over to the sideboard which sat beneath my cousin's portrait and hunted for a candle. Having found one, I looked up to see my cousin's face before me, with her lips curled up at the end of her mouth in a gentle smile.

I shoved my candle into a holder and forced it down until it took hold.

Lighting it, I shielded the flame with my hand as I walked back over to the opening which I had discovered in the wall.

Taking a deep breath, I ventured inside.

A few steps in, I found myself at the top of a stone staircase. My candle only illuminated the first three of four steps, so there was no way of telling what was below from my position. Therefore, I felt along the wall for balance, and slowly began to descent the steps, into the darkness.

I counted ten in total before I settled on flat ground.

Holding out my candle, I moved it slowly from one side to the other so as to ascertain what sort of space I was in.

Confident that there were no vast holes ahead of me into which I might plummet never to be seen again, I ventured forward, sliding my foot along the floor just to be on the safe side.

After a few more paces, I came upon the body of my poor cousin.

She was lying in a crumpled heap, almost as if she had been dumped unceremoniously without regard or respect.

Although I am no doctor, I quickly ascertained that life was extinct, and stayed there for a few moments with my head bowed in sacred prayer for the sake of her poor soul.

Having recovered, I placed my candle on the ground and lifted my cousin's body off the cold ground and carried her back up the stairs and into the parlour where I laid her gently on the floor.

I had no way of knowing exactly how long she had been in that awful place. But I was able to hazard a guess, based on the amount of time she had been missing.

At first, I feared that she had somehow managed to become trapped in what I imagined must have been an old priest hole from the dark days when the king had outlawed the catholic mass. I wondered if she had discovered the hiding place, and ventured inside, only to have the doorway slam shut behind her, trapping her inside until she eventually ran out of air.

Then I considered that if that had been the case, how did the cabinet manage to manoeuvre its way back into position?

For that matter, how did all the china manage to find its way back inside the cabinet, before being put back. Surely, if Stella had seen the cabinet out of place when she arrived the following morning, she would not have merely replaced everything without investigating further.

Not to mention, once empty the cabinet was easy enough for me to move, but my cousin had only been a slight woman, and even empty, I considered that item of furniture would still have been too heavy for her to even drag across the floor, let alone lift into position.

No, it did not make sense. If my poor cousin had known about the secret hiding place, and, for some reason, wished to enter it, I doubt very much that she would have done so in the middle of the night, and without assistance.

So how did she meet such a grisly end?

It was at that moment that I noticed the bruising around her neck.

I squatted down beside her body, and carefully lifted aside her nightdress to reveal more of her neck. The bruises were unmistakable.

Clear evidence, I believed, that someone had ended her life by strangulation.

Horrified by the prospect, I stood up, intent on rousing the squire from his slumber with my findings and demanding that he do all in his power to apprehend the culprit and bring them to justice.

It was at that moment that my eye caught something peering out through my cousin's fingers, which were closed in a clenched fist.

Rigor had already taken hold, so I gently managed to ease the item out without the indignity of having to break her fingers in the process.

I sat back, stunned by what I had found.

I recognised it immediately.

It was a button, identical to the ones I had noticed on the squire's winter coat.

My mind reeled with possibilities.

How had such an item managed to find its way into my poor dead cousin's hand?

Unless…No, surely not. Could it be possible that the squire had something to do with her demise?

Had he in fact been the one who left those awful marks around her neck?

Did he attack my cousin, and lose his button in the process, not realising until it was too late, where it had gone to?

Then I remembered noticing the missing button on his coat when he called round.

It had to be.

I carried myself back to my chair, and poured myself another drink, knocking it back too quickly and almost choking in the process.

I turned to see my cousin's picture on the wall.

Once more she was gazing off to her left, as she had been initially.

Was her task complete?

She had shown me where to look for her body, and sure enough, I had found it.

Now I understood that my task had only just begun.

My initial instinct was to inform the authorities and have the squire arrested on suspicion of wilful murder. He would pay for his actions at the end of a rope if I had anything to do about it.

Fuelled by a sudden desire for justice, I leaped out of my chair, and strode out of the room to fetch my overcoat.

Then a thought struck me.

I had only been in the village a short time, but the overriding impression I had been given, was that the squire held a great position of authority in the vicinity, not to mention the fact that he was the local magistrate, and as such, had considerable sway with the local constabulary.

It occurred to me that if I were to go running into the village, alerting all and sundry of what I had found behind the wall in the parlour, there was every chance that the tables could be turned against me.

After all, I had no witnesses to prove my story, and the production of the squire's coat button meant nothing in itself, other than I had found it inside the house.

Even if I had left it in situ, it could still have been claimed that I forced it between my cousin's dead fingers myself to try and plant suspicion on the squire.

But she had been missing since before I arrived, I consoled myself. Surely that was proof enough of my innocence.

Or did I sneak down from London one night and kill my dear cousin, bury her behind the wall, and sneak back to London to await news of her disappearance?

It was far too easy to twist the truth against me.

I sat back in my chair to think.

I had to do something before the morning and Stella's arrival. I could not just leave my poor cousin's body lying on the floor. Even if I Stella believed my tale, what good would that do? They could say that we were in it together, secret lovers who contrived to murder my cousin for her inheritance.

It sounded completely ridiculous to me, but how easy would it be to convince a jury?

Especially one consisting of men who considered the squire to be a pillar of their community.

I sat there for what seemed an age, listening to the sound of the clock *tick*.

At one point, I even considered placing my cousin back in her makeshift grave and pretending I had not found her. But, as the thought entered my brain, I caught a glance of her portrait, and knew that I could not just leave her there for who knew how many years.

It was not until the small hours that something clicked in my mind.

I remembered the freshly dug grave in the cemetery. It certainly would not be the most dignified of burials, but at least my cousin would be in consecrated ground, and hopefully she would finally be able to rest in peace.

Racing up the stairs, I rummaged around in a trunk in a spare room and managed to find a large blanket which I decided would be, if not ideal, at least suitable for the purpose.

I carefully wrapped my cousin's corpse in the blanket,

tucking it in at the edges to ensure that none of her limbs were protruding just in case someone happened to see me outside. What story I would give, however, was something I decided not to dwell on until the need arose.

Outside was as black as pitch. The only gas lamps in the street were down towards the entrance to the estate, and their glare did not even reach my cousin's house.

I looked up at the sky. Fortunately, there was no moon, and low clouds scudded across the stars, blocking them from view, and preventing their light from penetrating the gloom.

Hoisting my cousin's body onto my shoulder, I made my way towards the churchyard. I prayed that God smiled upon my enterprise, appreciating that it was being carried out with the very best of intentions, and the utmost respect. Even if he did not approve, I at least hoped that he would not allow my venture to be uncovered.

The open grave was as I had seen it earlier, doubtless in preparation for a ceremony the following day. The gravediggers had even done me the courtesy of leaving their shovels nearby, which was a blessing as I had not thought to bring one with me.

I placed my cousin's wrapped body beside the open grave, and climbed inside, taking one of the shovels with me.

The drop seemed further than I had imagined, and for a moment I was struck by the thought that if I could not claw my way out, I would be found there the next day, with an awful lot of explaining to do.

Fortunately, however, the side walls were still pliable enough for me to make purchase, so, once I had dug down a little deeper, I hoisted myself up and carefully pulled my cousin's corpse towards me, before gently lowering it into the hole.

Having covered it with the soil I had loosened, I climbed out of the grave, and stood above it, looking down to see if there were any indication that it had been tampered with.

Now I wished for some light, but there was none. I stared

down into the black maw but no matter how hard I strained I could not see the bottom.

Before leaving, I shovelled some of the freshly removed dirt from the mound at the side, just to be on the safe side.

Filthy, and covered in perspiration from my endeavours, I made my way back to my cousin's property, and through drooping eyes, put the cabinet back in situ, and replaced all the china as I had found it.

Aching, and craving sleep, I took myself upstairs and fell asleep on top of my covers.

The next morning little Toby woke me up again with his excitable *yapping* as he scurried up the stairs and jumped on top of me.

We played around for a few moments until Stella came in to retrieve him.

Clearly shocked by my appearance, and the fact that I had obviously slept in my clothes, I held up my hands and came up with a tale that I had decided to take a stroll before bed, and foolishly managed to slip and fall into a ditch.

I made light of the situation, and Stella too saw the funny side.

She made me up a bath, and promised to brush down my evening suit, later.

After breakfast, I decided to take another look at the grave where my cousin was now-I hoped-resting in peace. I must confess, I had a nagging thought that I had not covered her sufficiently, and needed to check one more time, just for my own peace of mind.

I had not heard the church bell toll as yet, so I thought it safe to presume that the funeral had not started.

As I neared the entrance to the cemetery, my heart skipped a beat at the first toll of the church bell.

I was too late!

I cursed myself for not setting out before breakfast, instead of after.

Even so, I had to see my mission through. If my task from the early hours were to be discovered, I felt compelled to be there to see my life unravel. For I knew that upon discovery of my cousin's body, no amount of explanation or finger-pointing from me was ever going to wash with the local constabulary. I would be hauled away to trail and, doubtless, strung-up in double-quick time if the squire had anything to say about it.

Once I entered the cemetery, I could see the procession leading from the church to the graveside. The two gravediggers stood to one side of the hole, shovels at the ready. In a strange way I almost felt comforted by the sight of them, for I presumed that they must have inspected the plot, even if only a cursory glance, before the service commenced.

If that were the case, then I felt it safe to presume that my interference had not been discovered.

Even so, I trembled inside while I watched the grave-side ceremony take place.

I bowed my head in reverence along with the rest of the mourners, all the time raising my eyes so that I could see every-thing that was taking place, still afraid that at any moment my deed would be revealed.

The service seemed to take forever, but eventually I saw the priest signal to the gravediggers to lower the casket on top of my poor cousin.

I said a silent prayer, both for her eternal soul, and as a thank you to the Almighty for not allowing my desecration-for that was how it felt-to be exposed.

Once the service had concluded and the mourners dispersed, I waited behind until I saw the gravediggers flatten down the top layer of soil, before turning to leave.

Back at the house, I was met at the door by the ever-excited Toby, who literally jumped up into my arms before I even had a chance to take my overcoat off.

Stella came rushing out of the kitchen when she heard the little chap barking and apologised for his behaviour. I assured her that it was completely fine and encouraged the dog to follow me into the parlour, where he jumped up onto my lap as soon as I took my seat.

I had often heard it said that animals possessed a sixth sense, and when he looked up at me from behind his over-grown fur, I felt sure that I saw in his eyes a sympathetic look, almost as if he understood what I had done, and why I felt I had to do it.

When Stella brought in a strong coffee a few moments later, she remarked at how surprised she was that Toby no longer seemed intent on scratching the wooden panel at the end of the room. "That was why I was keeping him out of here," she informed me. "I was afraid he might do some damage to the mistress's cabinet, or the panel behind."

I brushed her comment away and put his behaviour down to nothing more than canine mischief.

As I sat there gazing at my cousin's portrait opposite me, my mind turned towards the problem of how I was going to force the squire to admit his guilt about the death of my poor cousin.

I knew right away that there was no point in confronting him, as he would only deny it, and what is more, he would then be on to me, and who knew what he might cook up in order to take revenge.

I had to bear in mind that he carried a great deal of weight locally, and from what I had gathered thus far, the local police would not hear a word against him. They would, in fact, be far more likely to believe that a stranger like me was up to no good, so I knew I had to tread lightly.

Oddly enough, fate took a hand, as it often does.

That very afternoon I received a message from the squire inviting me to dine with him at his house.

I accepted his offer, and that evening, found myself in his huge dining room, around a table which could easily seat twenty. I spent the majority of the evening listening to the squire as he regaled me with tales of his ancestors, which he could date back to the Norman conquest.

I found him to be a very boastful individual, exceedingly full of his own importance, not to mention a drunken bore of the first water. At first, I tried to keep up with is excesses, but by the main course, I had begun to only allow my glass to be replenished once to every third one of his.

He gave me a complete rendition of how one of his ancestors had received favour from King Henry Vlll, for being one of the first noblemen in the vicinity to sign the act recognising the king as head of the church in England.

The squire went on to say that, with a broad smirk, that if the king had ever discovered that his ancestor remained a staunch catholic who used to keep his own priest hidden inside his house, so that he could hear mass, and take confession, in secret, he would doubtless have stripped him of all his assets and thrown him in the Tower for good measure.

Feeling bold, probably as a result of all the wine, I feigned surprise, and interest, stating that I had never seen an actual priest-hole before, in the hope that I might see a spark of guilt in the squire's eyes.

But there was none.

Instead, he invited me to survey the one he had been speaking of, which was situated in his library.

He instructed his butler that we would take dessert after a short break, and excitedly ushered me through to the library, which was at the back of the house, several rooms down.

Naturally, I played ignorant, and went along demonstrating mock interest, and curiosity.

The squire teased me at first by betting me five Guinee's that I could not find the entrance by myself. I played along, pushing and pulling at different panels along both sides of the library, and reaching for certain volumes which I suggested might have been placed there specifically to disguise the lever which opened the secret passage.

After ten minutes or so I held my arms out in defeat. The squire boomed with raucous laughter. "I knew you'd never guess it," he proclaimed, victoriously. "I'll have that five guineas off you before you leave tonight."

Still laughing to himself in triumph, he walked over to a shelf which housed a fine set of collected works by Dickens, and spreading his fingers out, pressed against ten individual volumes. There followed a creaking and a grinding of metal and stone-not unlike the sound the priest-hole at my cousin's made-and sure enough, the entrance revealed itself.

The squire retrieved a candlestick from the table in the middle of the room, and lit each of the three candles it held, before carrying them over to where I stood, before the darkened entrance. "Come on," he said, enthusiastically, "let's have an adventure. It's cost you five guineas so you might as well get some value for your money."

I followed him inside, his candles illuminating the inside of the structure just in front of him. The air inside as we ventured in, was dank and heavy, and a musty odour assailed my nostrils, causing me to almost gag.

As with the passage in my cousin's house, there was a short landing which eventually led to a steep flight of stone steps. "Now watch your footing here," the squire warned. "Some of these stones steps have worn down over the years."

As he began his descent, I followed closely behind.

It occurred to me how easy it would be to simply reach out and give him a hard shove, sending him head-first down into the darkness to meet his fate. A much kinder end than he had afforded my poor cousin. But, as I stood there, I knew that my own religious beliefs would not allow me to commit such a mortal sin, no matter how much I felt he deserved it.

I prayed silently to God to keep me strong, and resist performing such a vile act.

Suddenly, the squire let out an almighty cry, and before I had a chance to react, he pitched forward and disappeared from sight.

I stood there, frozen to the spot.

As he had fallen, the squire naturally dropped his candle-stick, plunging the area into immediate darkness so that I could not even see my hand should I hold it up in front of my face.

Apart from his initial scream of shock, the squire had not made another sound. But I could not help but hear the awful squelching noises made by his body as if slammed against the stone steps on its way down.

After a moment, I called down into the darkness, but received no response.

Carefully, I edged my way back up the stairs and emerged into the library.

I summoned his staff, who soon came running, and within seconds his butler and coach driver took it upon themselves to venture down into the priest-hole to check on their master.

I stayed in the library, suffering from shock, while one of his serving staff fixed me a stiff drink.

Several minutes later, the butler and driver re-emerged from the entrance to the secret

passage, their ashen expressions told us what we had already guessed.

Their master was dead.

Naturally, there was a full investigation, and my statement was taken by a senior ranking officer from the nearest town. I did not need to lie, and told everything exactly as it had played out, several times, in fact, before the officer was completely satisfied.

The staff confirmed my story to the extent that I had spent the evening in congenial company with the squire, having been invited to dine with him, and they confirmed that there was nothing which they either saw or heard, that might indicate that we were anything other than on friendly terms.

At the inquest, the coroner decreed that the squire's death was an accidental one, due in no small part to the amount of alcohol he had consumed that evening.

I attended his funeral, as I believed it might look odd if I did not.

Over time, as her only next of kin, I took over my cousin's house, and used it mainly as a summer retreat, although I did visit there on several bank holidays when I felt the need to get out of London and leave the smog behind.

I kept Stella on at her usual salary, and she made a splendid job of keeping the house spic and span, and always treated me to a warm welcome when I came down.

I often left flowers at the grave of Mrs Hilda Swift, the unwitting accomplice in my little subterfuge. I made sure that I split each bunch in two, one for her, and one for my dear cousin.

They are both still remembered in my prayers.

# THE SLITHERING FLESH

The welcoming party from the Chimera Scientific Research unit huddled together in a tight group as they awaited the arrival of their test subjects.

The assembled group included Professor Donald Hemp, esteemed world expert in radiation, and the founding member of the unit. Next to him stood Dr Terrence White, who, at thirty-five, was one of the youngest recipients of the much-prized Albert Einstein award for physics in enhancing medical breakthroughs. His research had led to advances in prostrate radiation therapy, which thus far had saved an estimated ten thousand lives.

The others assembled were all notable experts in their chosen fields of research and had been gathered together under the official secrets act to assist Professor Hemp with his latest breakthrough.

Although the majority of the distinguished gathering preferred the solitude and isolation which accompanied their individual endeavours, they had each been offered a full lifetime research grant in consideration of putting their own primary research on hold in order to take part in this latest experiment.

The result of which, if Professor Hemp's invention proved fruit-ful, would revolutionise the field of nuclear power in weaponry.

"I thought you said they were only minutes away?" Dr Wayne Nicholson shouted out against the biting wind, the force of which whipped up flurries of the deep snow which covered the surrounding mountains.

"That's what the Brigadier told me over the radio," replied Dr Harold Clarke, shrugging his shoulders. "Do you think I would have dragged us all out here just to admire the view, otherwise?"

"Well, where the bloody hell are they?" demanded the professor, furiously rubbing his

upper arms with his hands to try and improve his circulation.

The sun had already slipped beneath the highest peak on the horizon, and the sky above was fast turning from white to a leaden grey in the east.

The outside lights which circled the facility's perimeter, cast an eerie shadow outside the circle of illumination it provided for those gathered.

Just then, there was a low rumbling noise emanating from behind the nearest peak.

The group all turned in unison towards the sound, and waited until the headlights from the lead vehicle came into view.

"At last!" shouted another member of the group.

They watched as the two unmarked rough-terrain trucks cut a swathe through the freshly fallen snow to their door.

Once all three had stopped, a tall man dressed in an army uniform under an unzipped parka jumped from his seat and made his way over to the gathered scientists.

"Professor Hemp?" he asked, surveying those before him.

The professor came forward and held out his hand. "Brigadier Hampton, I presume?"

The two men shook hands.

"I take it your team have all been briefed?" The brigadier

enquired, his voice loud enough to carry against the biting wind, without him having to shout.

The professor nodded. "You can rest assured brigadier, each and every member of my team has been fully prepared, I can vouch for that myself."

The brigadier scanned the faces present, as if attempting to sniff out a potential traitor amongst the pack. His steely glare surveyed each scientist in turn, holding their gaze for several seconds, before moving on to the next.

Finally, he nodded his head.

Turning back to his vehicle, the brigadier held up the baton he had wedged under his left arm and nodded a signal to the men in the cab.

Two soldiers who had shared the cab with him, emerged into the snow, and trudged around to the back of the truck. Within seconds, the scientists watched as a dozen squaddies, all dressed in military fatigues with balaclavas covering their faces, jumped from the back of the vehicle and made their way around to the one behind.

Each soldier carried an automatic pistol in a side holster, as well as a machine gun held tightly in position under their arm, secured by a leather strap around their shoulder.

Upon command from the brigadier, one of the soldiers rapped forcefully against the back door of the second truck with his fist.

The platoon all took a few paces back and waited patiently for the doors to swing open.

As they did, each soldier appeared to grip their weapons tighter, and the scientists heard a faint *click-clack* as safety catches were removed before the weapons were aimed directly at the opening doors of the truck.

A shout went out. "Disembark, one at a time, do not attempt to run or you will be shot!"

The scientific group had all been briefed as the professor had assured the bombardier. However, the reality of the situation now that they were actually watching the scene unfold before them, brought an uneasy feeling of concern to those in attendance.

They watched as one-by one, ten men emerged from the truck, and jumped down onto the thick blanket of white beneath them.

The soldiers used their weapons to signal to the prisoners that they must move along the side of the vehicle and stand in a line, until the last man was out.

Each man was handcuffed, and wore thick metal bracelets around their ankles, secured by a chunky solid-looking chain. They were still wearing their prison issue uniforms, and some of them could clearly be seen to be shivering in the extreme cold.

Once the last of the prisoners joined the line, more orders were barked out from one of the soldiers, and the prisoners all turned to their left, facing the scientists.

Even from this distance, several of the scientific group shuffled uneasily as they noticed the venomous stares the prisoners gave them.

Terrence White turned to the professor. "You did tell us that these men had all volunteered for this experiment, didn't you?" He tried to keep his voice down, but loud enough to be heard, nonetheless.

Before the professor had a chance to answer, the brigadier spun round to face him.

"You needn't concern yourself with the fate of these individuals, doctor." His expression was hard and menacing, with his brows furrowed beneath his military cap of office. "Each man you see before you have been deemed by law to spend the rest of their natural life in incarceration, as a result of committing some of the most heinous crimes against mankind."

The brigadier's stare was unwavering as he spoke.

Dr White presumed that the man, for whatever reason, felt that such explanations were unnecessary, and he felt it beneath his dignity to have to explain himself to non-military personnel.

"That may be," replied White, unperturbed by the senior officer's demeanour. "But whatever their crimes, they are still human beings, and as such I just wished to confirm that they were fully aware of the risks involved. They have a right to know what they have signed up for…"

"RIGHT!" the brigadier broke in. "RIGHT!" He took a few paces towards the group. Some of the other scientists shuffled back, instinctively. But Dr White held his ground as the officer approached him.

The brigadier stopped when he was within a foot of White.

The two men locked eyes. In the freezing cold, there were visible plumes of air emanating from the officer's nostrils as his breathing laboured. The look in his eyes told those gathered that he was desperately trying to control his anger before he continued to speak.

"Er, perhaps we should get everyone below ground and into the warm," Professor Hemp took a tentative step towards the two men, although he was obviously addressing the brigadier rather than his colleague. "After all," he continued, in his most diplomatic tone, "we don't want our test subjects to catch pneumonia just before the trial begins."

The brigadier kept his focus on Dr White for a moment more, before turning on his heel and barking his next set of orders to his troops.

Upon instruction, one soldier led the way towards the entrance of the complex, with another bringing up the rear. In between the remaining soldiers strategically placed themselves between the prisoners, ensuring that they were under no illusion that if needs be, the soldiers were willing to shoot to kill.

"Dr Cribbing, perhaps you might like to lead the way?" The professor asked.

The scientist jumped, as if being woken from a midday snooze.

"Of course, professor, it'll be my pleasure." Dr Cribbing

attempted a smile as the first soldier approached but received no such pleasantry in return.

Once inside the complex, the scientist led the group down a winding corridor which eventually brought them to a large set of lift doors.

While they waited for the car to reach their floor, the rest of the scientists, along with the brigadier, followed on.

No one spoke during the expedition, except for a few mumblings from some of the prisoners, which were immediately shouted down by the nearest soldier.

The corridor along which they had made their way to the lift lobby was encased in dull grey steel, and immediately made some of the prisoners wish for the relative comfort of their cells.

Although the brigadier was being honest when he informed Dr White that the prisoners had been fully briefed as to what they were signing up for, the fact remained that once they entered the facility, the reality of their situation became all too actual for some of them to accept without questioning their acceptance.

Like the scientists, each prisoner had been made to sign the official secrets act. But, as the brigadier had expressed to his superiors at the time of being selected to lead the operation, men such as those chosen were hardly likely to adhere to the rules and norms of those in society.

In order to encourage the assistance of those chosen, certain inducements had been allowed which, under normal circumstances, the prisoners could only have dreamed of.

After they had agreed to acting as test-subjects, the prisoners were removed from their present confines and transported to a military prison where their actions could not be witnessed by their fellow inmates.

Once there, they had been treated to a full week of meals provided by a local restaurant, where they could order anything they wished from the extensive menu, including alcohol. Those among them who smoked, were given fine Havana cigars to enjoy, instead of their usual roll-ups, and the army even shipped in a dozen high class escorts and paid for them to spend the entire night with the prisoners.

Although under strict instructions, one of the escorts almost became the next victim of her client, who allowed his particular penchant for strangling young women to get the better of him. Fortunately for her, the prisoner's antics were all being monitored by close circuit cameras, so the soldiers on duty were able to intercede and save her before it was too late.

The lady was given twice the agreed sum for her services, which seemed to have the desired effect.

The lift doors opened, and Dr Cribbing stood to one side to allow the soldiers to enter with their charges. The lift was designed to hold over twenty persons, but as that made the confinement a little too close for comfort, the brigadier suggested that the platoon made the journey in two lots, with six prisoners in each group.

Dr Cribbing heaved a sigh of relief when it was suggested that a couple of his colleagues should accompany him in the first car.

The lift descended for several minutes, taking the occupants deep below the surface to the purpose-built laboratory below ground.

Once at the bottom, there was another lengthy walk along a similar uniform grey corridor before they reached the electronic doors which led into the facility's main theatres.

The rest of the research staff who had all been too busy with their preparations for today's experiment to join the welcoming party outside, stopped what they were doing and looked up, the moment the first group arrived.

It was plain from their demeanour that some of them were not altogether comfortable with the circumstances surrounding the events about to take place. The mere sight of the soldier's weapons was enough to put some of them on edge. But they were all too committed to the process to consider backing out now.

Likewise, as soon as they laid eyes on the enormous experiment chamber at the far end of the room, some of the prisoners grew restless and began to back away from their guards. The soldiers used their guns to cajole the convicts into a corner of the laboratory, where they used their own bodies to coral them in to await their confederates.

A bank of chairs had been set up, and each prisoner was pointed towards one.

Dr Cribbing and his colleagues who had travelled down with him, quickly dispersed, and mingled with the rest of the scientists, looking over their results and ensuring that all necessary preparations were in order.

After a short while, the rest of the group emerged through the doors which led to the lift corridor. Again, some of the prisoners reacted badly to the sight of the test chamber, and a couple even attempted to turn and run back towards the lift. But the sight of the guards who were bringing up the rear, pointing their weapons directly at them, caused the two men to stop dead in their tracks, before reluctantly turning back towards the laboratory.

Once the prisoners were all gathered together in a tight pattern, the brigadier gave his platoon the order to remove their hoods.

As Dr White and his colleagues removed their outer clothing and hung them up, he glanced over and was taken aback when one of the soldiers turned out to be a woman.

He was not exactly sure why he was so surprised, as he knew that women made up a good proportion of today's military might. But there was something unsettling about the procedure they were about to conduct, which made him think that, given the choice, female soldiers might wish to be excused from such operations.

He chided himself for his chauvinistic impulse.

Even though White was still a young man, he had been raised by his elderly grandparents after his own parents had been tragically killed in a boating accident, when he was five. His grandfather especially, was a man very set in his ways, and brought young Terrence up to believe that there were certain areas of industry, into which a woman should not venture. The military being one of them.

His grandfather had seen action during the second world war and scoffed at the idea of having women fighting alongside him.

White often wondered how his grandmother put up with the old man. But then, she was cut from the same cloth, and accepted her lot with grace and dignity. Although, she did have a thirst for knowledge and science especially.

Terence had her to thank for his initial interest in the subject, without which, he believed he would not be where he was today. His grandfather was in banking, and insisted that his grandson joined him, but for once his grandmother stood up to her husband and insisted that Terrence should be allowed to follow his passion.

White could not help but stare in the direction of the female soldier, although, he did so discreetly so as not to appear too obvious. She was still side-on to him, so he could not see her face. Her attention was firmly fixed on her charges, so White allowed himself to let his gaze linger.

Without warning, the officer spun around and looked directly at him.

It was almost as if she had caught him staring and wanted to confront him for his impudence.

White wanted to look away, but he felt that that too would just make him appear guilty, so instead he offered a slight smile in admission of being caught out.

To his surprise, the soldier returned his smile.

Her beautiful face, ruddy from the cold, was in stark contrast to the severity of her position, and for a second, White almost forgot what they were there for.

A sudden barked order from the brigadier caused the young soldier to stand smartly to attention, along with her colleagues, and face her senior officer.

White and the others joined their colleagues in checking over the results of the tests conducted earlier with the experimental chamber.

The laboratory looked to those uninitiated, like something out of an old science fiction movie, with wall-to-wall computer banks, and everyone else in attendance decked out in white coats.

The preparations took several hours to complete, and although while they waited, refreshments were provided, the prisoners grew more restless as the time for their experiment grew nearer, and with their unease, their objections grew in volume.

Several of the scientists turned as the noise level grew, to see what the commotion was about. The scene of unrest before them did nothing to allay the concerns of those already with feelings of trepidation.

Suddenly, one of the prisoners stood up and managed to knock the nearest soldier to him off his balance. As the officer fell, the prisoner reached out and grabbed his gun, turning it towards the rest of the troops before him.

"Stay where you are," he screamed, "no one move, or I'll take you all out."

The other soldiers trained their weapons directly at him.

Several of the scientists were rivetted to the spot, by fear.

Others ran around to hide behind some of the larger pieces of apparatus.

The brigadier calmly moved forward, holding up his hand.

"Now listen to me, Bates," he said, his voice steady, and in control. "You know as well as I do that you will not make it two paces out of this room before my soldiers will shoot you where you stand."

The prisoner turned his weapon to face the brigadier. "I don't care, this whole business is fuckin' shit. I ain't getting' into that bloody thing." He signalled towards the chamber behind them with a nod of his head. "I've 'ad enough of this bollocks, and I'm getting' out of 'ere."

There was the sound of weapons being readied to fire.

The brigadier held up his hand to staunch the reaction.

After a moment, he continued. "Now then Bates, you knew full well what you were getting into when you agreed to take part in this trial. You've already received the majority of what was promised in advance, this is no time to be changing your mind."

Bates moved forward and aimed his gun at the senior officer's head.

The movement seemed to have little effect on the officer, who stayed perfectly still.

"You can't fuckin' make me get into that thing if I don't want to." Bates yelled, turning to his fellow prisoners. "None of us 'ave to, don't matter what they promised us or what we've already 'ad."

The other prisoners looked to each other for encouragement.

Several of them began to chime in with their fellow inmates

A couple of them rose to their feet, and immediately they found a soldier's weapon aimed in their direction.

The prisoner Bates, encouraged by the support from his comrades, grinned at the brigadier, and held his weapon more tightly under his arm.

"This is your last chance, Bates." The brigadier warned him. "Put down that weapon and move back to your seat!"

The finality of the order caused several of the prisoners to reconsider their actions.

Confined as they all were, underground with a dozen trained

firearms officers focussed on them, they suddenly realised the futility of their actions.

Even so, some of them refused to budge. The prisoners unwritten code did not allow for disloyalty. It was them against those in charge, and as such, the present circumstances were no different to a prison riot.

"Captain!" the brigadier ordered.

Without needing further instruction, the young female officer whom Terrence had been admiring, moved forward to stand beside her commanding officer, her weapon trained directly on Bates.

"If this prisoner does not lower his weapon by the time I count to three, kill him!"

The captain did not respond, but merely held her station.

"One…"

Bates looked around, nervously. He kept his gun in front of him, although he took a half-step backwards before he felt a chair behind his knees.

"Two…"

Bates did not notice the captain lean down closer so that her right eye was directly in front of the weapon's sight bracket.

She waited, holding her breath.

Bates, refused to give up the ghost.

He knew that the brigadier was bluffing.

You cannot shoot a man in cold blood, there was not a war on.

"Three!"

The echo of the shot rang out as a whole suddenly appeared in the middle of the prisoner's forehead.

There were gasps and screams from the scientists behind them as a trickle of blood oozed from the hole before Bates slumped to the ground, his weapon clenched in his dead fingers.

The soldiers immediately trained their guns on the remaining prisoners, who one by one shuffled back to their seats, without objection.

The captain kept her weapon trained on the dead Bates as she moved in closer to his prone form. She placed her boot on the hand which still held the weapon, and pressing down hard, slid it back a few inches across the floor, until it released its hold.

When she removed her foot, the imprint of her boot was visible on the dead man's hand.

Once she was sure that it was safe to do so, she bent down and retrieved the gun, before moving back to stand beside her senior officer.

"Well done, Captain," stated Hampton.

"Thank you, sir," replied the captain. She turned and stared at the soldier who had originally lost his weapon to the prisoner. She held it out to him, and he sheepishly moved forward to recover it.

As his trembling hand grasped the weapon, the captain kept her hold on it.

The soldier looked at her.

"We'll discuss this later," she informed him, before releasing her grip.

Upon instruction, two of the soldiers lifted the dead body off the floor and carried it towards the double doors they had entered by.

The brigadier turned to face the scientists.

The scene before him caused a smirk to brush his lips.

Several of them emerged from behind apparatus, their faces reflecting the terror churning within. A couple of the females were holding each other in an embrace of empathy, as they came to terms with what they had just witnessed.

They all looked as if they needed a stiff drink.

"Professor," the brigadier called out, "do you think you could ask one of your colleagues to escort my men back out to the vehicles to dispose of the body?"

Hemp took a pocket handkerchief from his white coat and wiped away the beads of perspiration which had formed on his forehead.

Before he had a chance to answer, White moved forward. "I'll do it," he exclaimed, staring at the brigadier with nothing short of contempt.

The senior officer held the scientist's gaze for a moment but did not offer a reply.

As White walked past the military posse, the captain turned to look at him.

The expression on her face was almost that of regret, blended with resignation.

She offered a half-smile.

In spite of himself, White returned it. His inner feelings of abhorrence at what she had just done, could not compete with the fact that she was so beautiful, White felt powerless to resist her.

Professor Hemp was obviously still in a state of shock, as he and his team watched their colleague escort the soldiers back into the lift corridor.

Harold Clarke stood forward. "Was that absolutely necessary?" he demanded, looking directly at the captain, rather than her senior officer who gave the order.

The brigadier strode purposefully towards where the scientists were huddled.

He waited until he was directly in front of Dr Clarke before he responded.

"Please do not question my authority, sir. These prisoners are my responsibility, not yours. They have signed up, voluntarily, to this vital work, and it is my job to see that they see it through to the end."

Dr Clarke sighed and shook his head, wearily. He could see there was no point arguing with the man, he was a machine, void of all human emotions.

Professor Hemp cleared his throat. "Come on everyone, let's get started, it's already late."

The other scientists returned to their work.

The door to the experimental chamber opened upon the press

of a button, and two of the scientists went inside to check that all the remote monitors were responding.

They spoke to each other before deciding to remove the one they no longer needed for the tenth test subject, who was by now being wrapped in a thick rubber matting by the two soldiers tasked with the duty.

After a while, Dr White returned with the two soldiers.

He purposely did not glance in the direction of the other soldiers as he made his way to join his colleagues.

A short while later, Hemp called over to the brigadier.

"We are ready for you now," he announced.

The prisoners immediately stiffened in their seats.

Upon command, the soldiers goaded each man to his feet, and proceeded to march them towards the chamber.

As they, somewhat reluctantly entered the glass chamber, they were met by a member of the science team who guided them to a seat and explained the procedure to them, while attaching wires from the monitors with sticky tape to their chest and arms.

Once all the men were in place, the scientists and soldiers left the chamber, and the large glass door was swung back into place. It gave off a *hissing* sound as the rubber seal slotted into place.

Everyone directly involved in the process took their place behind their computers.

Those who had already completed their tasks, stood outside the chamber, staring in at the nine men.

The professor counted down from five, at which point, the apparatus which controlled the radiation was set into motion.

For a few moments, nothing seemed to be happening to the men inside, who each stayed seated and looked around them as if they could hear something approaching.

"Half power," instructed Hemp, and several of his team responded.

Still the men inside did not move but remained seated. By

now, some of them had visibly relaxed as there was no physical reaction to cause them alarm because of what was happening to them.

After a few moments, Hemp called for full power.

Some of the scientists looked nervously at each other but obeyed, nonetheless.

They all watched the chamber.

The men inside looked calm and in control.

The professor smiled to himself, confident in the knowledge that if there were going to be some sort of adverse reaction to the radiation rays, by his calculations it would have manifested itself by now.

As the minutes passed by, some of the prisoners began to hold their shirts away from their skin and shake them.

"That's to be expected," explained the professor, to anyone who cared to listen. "The heat from the radiation will cause the men to feel a little hot, but I can assure you the intensity will not rise above that of a sunny day at the beach."

Several of his fellow scientists laughed at his explanation.

"Professor, something's wrong!" One of the scientists controlling the equipment, turned in her chair and looked sheepishly at the professor.

Everyone stopped laughing and focussed on the woman.

"What are you talking about?" Hemp demanded. "Everything is going exactly to plan.

The scientist turned back to face her screen as if she doubted her original assertion.

Several colleagues crowded around her monitor.

"She's right," Dr Nicholson announced, "look at the eV readings, the chemical bonds are separating too quickly."

The professor barged his way through his colleagues.

He studied the screen, intently.

His colleague was right, the separation of the bonds was to be expected with this level of intensity, but according to his calculations, their departure should be at half the speed they were presently indicating.

"We need to shut down!" another scientist stated, from the back. "We can't leave those men in there a moment longer."

The professor held up his hand, he needed silence to think.

"Professor!" an exasperated colleague next to him called out.

Hemp ignored their cries and shoved the female scientist out of her seat so he could try and temper the situation with the bonds.

"Oh my god, look!" this time it was one of the soldiers who called out.

Everyone turned their gaze towards the chamber.

Inside, the men had all leapt out of their chairs and ripped the monitor wires from their bodies.

Some of them were stripping off their clothing, while others were banging on the glass demanding to be released.

Their cries went unheard through the sound-proof glass, but the expression of sheer terror on their faces left no one outside in doubt that they wanted to be set free.

"Professor Hemp," cried Dr White, "what are you waiting for?"

"Give me a second!" the professor yelled back. He began frantically hammering on the keypad before him, gazing up momentarily at the screen, as he did so.

Some of the men inside the chamber began to hurl themselves against the glass in a vain attempted to break out.

"Sir," said the captain, turning to her senior commander. "I really think we need to pull the plug on this."

The brigadier did not turn his eyes away from what was happening inside the chamber.

"You know your orders, captain." The brigadier said, steadily.

"But sir," she insisted.

"Captain, do not make me repeat myself!"

There was a scream from one of the female scientists.

Inside the chamber, it appeared as if the flesh was starting to melt from the prisoner's bones.

Several of them desperately clawed at their skin as if trying to relieve an aggravating itch, and in doing so, huge clumps of flesh were coming away in their hands.

White had seen enough.

He leaned over the professor and began to shut the operation down.

"No!" Hemp cried out, trying desperately to ward off his colleague.

Eventually, White had to push the professor off his chair in order to complete the procedure.

The countdown on the screen began to descend from ten to one, ensuring that every last drop of radiation would be sucked from the chamber before the door opened.

Everyone had their eyes fixed on the chamber, as the horrific scene inside continued to unfold.

By now, some of the men inside had slumped to the ground and lay there in forms that more closely resembled lumps of clay, than human beings.

When the countdown reached zero, the rubber seal on the chamber door *hissed* once more, this time to release the door.

As the huge glass door began to swing open, the putrid stench of burning flesh from within the chamber, permeated the air, causing everyone to hold their noses against the awful reek.

It became too much for some of them, and there followed the sound of retching as scientists and soldiers alike, grabbed waste bins, buckets, or anything suitable in which to vomit.

Dr White held his breath and ran inside the chamber.

Several of his colleagues followed, though some had to back out when the smell from inside grew too pungent.

What was left of the prisoners inside was clearly beyond help.

The stodgy masses which lay scattered around the chamber did not even offer an option to check for a pulse.

As the rotting stench dissipated through the laboratory's ventilation system, several of the other scientists ventured into the chamber to survey the remains.

Professor Hemp sat at his desk with his head in his hands. Without warning, he grabbed the keypad in front of him and began smashing it against everything in sight, in frustration.

Sparks and smoke emerged from some of the apparatus he abused, but he continued until the keyboard was nothing more than a fragment of plastic in his hand.

After a moment, he looked up at the startled expressions on the faces of his colleagues, as they stood inside the chamber.

Finally, Professor Hemp stood up and made his way to join them, inside.

He gazed upon the devastation without emotion, oblivious to the looks from some of his colleagues.

A female scientist in the far corner of the chamber, bend down and placed a thermometer against one of the rotting mounds on the floor.

As she checked the reading, a hand suddenly shot out from the mess and grabbed her by the wrist.

The woman screamed as she tried to wrench her hand free, but the thing had a tight hold and refused to release her.

Several of her colleagues ran to her aid, some attempted to pull her away from the putrid mass, but it appeared to grow in size until it eventually stood the hight of its original form.

"Sir, look!" The captain pointed to the chamber.

The brigadier, who had been content to stay out of the chamber while the scientists made their investigation, looked up and stared in disbelief.

By now, several of the lumps had started to take on a human shape of sorts, and one by one, they started to converge on the scientists within.

The captain did not wait for her commander to respond.

"Men," she yelled, "grab your weapons."

The soldiers who had been sick, wiped their mouths and reassembled behind their captain, awaiting further orders.

Inside the chamber, Dr White was attempting to barge past some of the lumbering masses to assist his colleagues, but it was impossible. Every time he tried to push or shove one of them out of the way, his hand was swallowed up within their mass, and he was beginning to find it harder to extract himself with each attempt.

Several of his colleagues appeared to have already succumbed to the raging blobs, whose strength seemed to have developed beyond human rationale.

White watched in disgust as one of the blobs ripped a colleague's arm clean out of its socket with effortless ease.

He turned towards the soldiers out of desperation.

The captain immediately ordered her men to attack the chamber.

In trying to move out of their way, White accidently collided with the professor, sending the older man flying across the floor and straight into the arms of one of the blobs.

Before White could regain his own balance sufficiently to go and help, the blob wrapped its enormous arms around the professor and squeezed until his spine cracked.

The first soldier appeared by White's side a moment later.

He looked no more than a teenager, and the expression on his face was one of fear rather than courage.

The young soldier took careful aim and fired several rounds into the nearest mass.

The bullets were immediately swallowed up by the gungy mass, causing no more reaction that if it had been tapped with a feather.

The sound of the soldier's machine gun caused several of the other blobs to turn towards him. One by one, they quickly despatched whichever scientist they had been working on and moved as one towards him.

By now, several of the soldier's colleagues had made their

way through the opening. Each realising the situation, immediately opened fire on the moving blobs.

The noise within the chamber was deafening, and White held his hands tightly against his ears.

The bullets appeared to be having no effect on the blobs, but several of them penetrated the chamber, leaving a spider's web of cracked glass behind.

As the blobs continued to advance, White turned and saw the captain standing behind him. Without thinking, he grabbed her by the arm and dragged her outside the chamber.

Once outside, they were confronted by the brigadier, who held his revolver levelled at White's head.

"Get me out of here, Doctor, now!" he ordered.

The captain, still being clutched by White, looked back inside the chamber, and saw her men being attacked by the slithering blobs.

They continued to fire off round after round, but it was all to no effect.

Once their guns were depleted, some of them tried to use them to batter the blobs, swinging them in huge arcs above their heads before making contact with a sickening, *thunk!*

But it was all to no avail.

The captain turned to her senior officer. "Sir, we need to get my men out before it's too late!"

The brigadier ignored her.

With his revolver still aimed at White, he demanded. "Get me out of here!"

White released his grip on the captain's arm, and looked at her with an almost pleading expression, conveying, 'please don't go back in there'.

He turned to the brigadier. "You know the way out, just open the doors."

The brigadier lifted back the hammer on his weapon.

"Sir!" the captain objected.

"I've already tried that," he continued, "the doors won't open!"

White gave the captain a gentle squeeze on the arm and ran over to the electronic doors. He hit the buttons several times, but the brigadier was right, they did not respond.

For a moment he thought. Then he remembered the professor's outburst when he slammed the keyboard into the console.

White raced over to survey the devastation left behind.

To his horror, he saw that the professor had indeed smashed the override panel for the doors.

They were trapped!

He turned back to the brigadier and stared down the barrel of the man's gun.

"We're trapped," he explained. "The override has been destroyed."

The brigadier moved towards him, his weapon still held at eye level.

White steeled himself, waiting for the shot that would end his life.

There was no point in him trying to reason with a man like this.

He was clearly not thinking straight.

From behind, they both heard the sound of another hammer being pulled back.

White looked beyond the brigadier, and saw that the captain had drawn her sidearm, and was pointing it at the back of her superior's head.

"Leave him alone, brigadier," she said, sternly. "Don't make me shoot you!"

The brigadier remained in position for a moment, before lowering his gun.

He turned to the captain. "This is mutiny, you realise I can have you court marshalled for this!" He almost spat out the words.

"Suits me," replied the captain, keeping her gun levelled at him.

Inside the chamber, White suddenly realised that the blobs had laid waste to the last man standing. A couple of the soldiers were crawling along the floor in a bid to escape, but before they made any headway the blobs were upon them.

White looked to his side.

The panel next to him appeared undamaged.

He calibrated the mechanism, and the chamber door began to close.

The sound made the captain turn around. She looked on helplessly as the glass door swung shut, locking in what was left of her platoon, along with those hideous creatures.

Her one saving grace was that her men were already dead, and beyond pain.

The blobs, seeing what was taking place, began to shuffle towards the closing door, but they were too late.

White heaved a sigh of relief as the rubber seal set in place.

The blobs began to beat against their glass confinement, but as strong as they were, they could not penetrate the eight-inch-thick glass.

Once he could see they could not get out, the brigadier too seemed to relax, and holstered his weapon.

The captain followed suite.

"So, now what?" she asked, looking over at White.

"I suppose I'll have to try and fix this stupid release mechanism," he replied.

For the next couple of hours, White stripped the broken unit and attempted to make the necessary repairs.

The brigadier took himself away to a quiet corner and sat there in silence.

Captain Stella Borders spent much of the time looking at what remained of her platoon within the chamber. She had known some of those men since they first joined the army, and she was not ashamed of her tears when they came.

The blobs inside the chamber did not rest. Instead, they continued to try and smash through the glass, stopping only to stare down at the three humans left in the laboratory.

White's frustration was starting to show as every attempt he made to reconnect the system, ended in failure.

Stella made them all a coffee, which the brigadier curtly refused.

White took his gratefully, welcoming the assistance to stay awake.

It had been a long day, and looking at his watch, he saw that it was almost four in the morning.

"I don't suppose there's another crew of scientists making their way here to relieve you, is there?" asked Stella, hopefully.

White smiled. "I'm afraid not. This lab was purposely built in this isolated spot, and to my knowledge, no one outside who knows we're here would even think to come down here. This entire experiment was on a very lean 'need to know' basis."

Stella sighed. "Yeah, same with us. I'm not sure how far up the chain this goes, but I suspect no one will come looking for us anytime soon."

White blew on his coffee. "You can't even get a signal down here, the only communication we have is by radio, and that only works when you're on the surface."

"What will we do if you can't fix that thing?" Stella nodded towards the apparatus White was working on.

"Pray," White offered, "sleep, drink coffee, make love."

Stella stifled a laugh. "Keep your mind on the task at hand, buster," she scolded.

Suddenly, there was a shattering of glass, and they both looked up to see that one of the blobs had managed to break through the chamber at a spot where the soldier's machine gun fire had weakened the glass.

White stood up, placing his cup down.

The brigadier ran forward from his resting place.

The three of them watched as the blobs all converged at the area surrounding the broken glass and began hammering at it.

The main structure still held, but with each onslaught they could all see that the glass was beginning to crumble on impact.

"Do something!" demanded the brigadier.

White just looked at Stella and raised his eyes.

Just then, he had a thought.

He carried some tools over to the main doors and began to unscrew the cover on the panel.

While he worked, Stella and the brigadier trained their guns on the blobs inside the chamber, although both realised that their ammunition was useless against such creatures.

The glass held fast for over an hour, while White continued tinkering with the door panel.

Eventually, the first of the blobs managed to create a hole large enough for it to slither through.

The brigadier emptied his revolver into the mass as it emerged through the hole, but to no avail.

Once the blob was outside, it reformed into a grotesque similarity of human shape, and began to shuffle towards Stella.

From behind it, several of the other blobs were fighting to make their way through the space provided by their colleague.

Stella ran over to White. "They've broken through," she told him, as if he were unaware, "any suggestions?"

Before White could answer, the brigadier ran over to them, and without speaking, he grabbed Stella around the waist and threw her in the direction of the approaching blob.

Stella screamed as she slid across the floor.

"What the hell..." White demanded, but the brigadier had already re-loaded his revolver.

Pointing it at White he demanded he continue with his task.

White watched as Stella regained her feet and managed to dodge the blob.

"Look out!" White screamed.

The brigadier spun around to see what was behind him, just

then White kicked the soldier hard in the middle of the back, sending him flying forward into the arms of the nearest blob.

As the brigadier screamed and shouted, Stella made her way back around to White's side.

White tore his eyes away from the brigadier's plight and continued to work on the panel.

Stella looked back to see that another two of the blobs had made their way out of the chamber.

She turned back to White. "D'yer think there's still time to make love?" she asked, hopefully.

White could not control his laughter.

He looked over his shoulder to see the other escaped blobs helping their comrade in tearing the brigadier limb from limb.

Suddenly, the doors parted.

The gap was only a few inches wide, but spurred on by his success, White continued with his task.

Stella turned back to see that the blobs had finished in their endeavour and were now focussed on the two of them.

Another couple of blobs had forced their way out of the chamber and were busy reforming themselves on the laboratory floor.

"Any time now would be good," she urged.

The doors nudged apart another couple of inches, then stuck fast.

White stood up from his crouched position and tried to pry the doors apart with his hands. Stella joined him by grabbing one of them and heaving with all she had, but it was to no avail.

White turned to see the blobs advancing.

They had seconds left.

"Come on," he cried, "let's try one more time, you try and slide between the gap and see if it will help."

"Help how?" enquired, frowning.

"There's no time to explain, trust me."

White forced Stella to stand sideways against the gap.

He wedged her tiny frame between the steel doors, but it was a very tight fit, and she screamed out in agony as he pushed against her with all his weight.

With the blobs directly behind him, White mashed his body against Stella's and shoved with all he was worth, ignoring her cries.

Finally, Stella fell through the gap, and stumbled, landing on her rump on the hard floor.

She looked back to see White beaming at her.

"Now run," he yelled.

"Not without you," Stella screamed back, forcing herself off the floor.

But before she could reach him, she saw the blobs converge from behind and pull White away, back into the laboratory.

She watched in horror as they tore him apart, the same way they had the brigadier.

Stella screamed out in frustration.

Her cry caused one of the blobs to notice her, and it began to shuffle its way to towards the doors.

Stella was in no doubt that the blob could squeeze through the gap without even trying.

She turned and ran along the corridor, towards the lift.

A terrifying thought hit her.

What if the lift controls were damaged along with the others?

There was nothing left to lose.

The corridor felt far longer than it had on the way in, but she put that down to her own panic.

When she finally reached the lift, she frantically pressed the call button.

By the time the lift arrived, three of the blobs were barely a few feet away.

Stella kept her finger on the upper-level button, until the doors closed.

She could hear the blobs thumping on the closed doors in frustration as the lift rose to safety.

Up top, Stella used her gun to disarm the controls.

She did not want those creatures to escape!

Once outside, Stella saw that dawn had broken, the sun warmed her face as she made her way to one of the army vehicles.

She drove away, in tears.

# ALLHALLOWS'S EVE

"**T**rick or treat!" the children called out in unison as the door swung open.

Standing in the open doorway was a middle-aged man, with a half-eaten Milky Way bar in his hand. He gazed down at the gathered ensemble of costumed little ones, eagerly holding out their brightly coloured buckets.

"Yeah. Whaddya want?" he snarled, taking another chunk out of his chocolate, and chewing with his mouth open.

The younger three kiddies all moved back, nervously, bumping into their elder accomplices.

"Trick or treat," Kerry called back, completely unfazed by the man's rudeness.

"Sod off," he snapped.

At this, the twins and their younger sibling all turned away and buried their heads in their older sister's costume.

"There's no need to be like that," Jan called back. "You've scared my brother and sisters."

"So, what," the man replied, harshly. "Serves you right for disturbing me." He slipped the last of his chocolate bar into his mouth and scrunched up the wrapper in his fist.

"But it's Halloween," Kerry argued, defiantly, positioning

herself between the man and her friends. "And you've got your lights on."

The man shrugged. "So, what does that 'ave to do with anything?"

"If you have your lights on tonight, it means you have treats for the kids who dress up and knock on your door," explained Kerry, lifting up her bucket to demonstrate.

The man sneered. "No, it means that hard-working people like me have reports to finish before tomorrow. Now get lost all of you before I turn my dog on you."

"Come on, let's go," Jan whispered from behind, still comforting her siblings.

Kerry released a pent-up sigh.

She was not done yet. "Have you got any more of those left?" she asked, pointing at the crumpled wrapper in the man's hand.

"Loads," he replied, harshly. "What's it to you?"

"Well can't you at least give us some for the little ones? You've frightened them half to death with your bad manners."

The man threw the screwed-up wrapper at her, just missing her head. "Take this, it's all yer gonna get from me. Now get lost, all of you."

The man turned away to close the door on them.

"I bet you haven't even got a dog," Kerry yelled.

The man began to bark as he slammed the door.

"Come on," said Jan, ruffling the hair of her charges. "The nasty man has gone now. Let's try and find you lot some more treats before we head home."

Kerry stared at the closed door for a moment longer, before turning and escorting the others out. At thirteen she was the eldest of the bunch, and officially in charge. Her best friend Jan was still only twelve, although her birthday was only a few short weeks away.

Ordinarily, Jan's mother would have brought them out. But a twisted ankle had her laid up back on the couch, so Kerry had volunteered to assist Jan with her three younger siblings, so that they did not have to miss out on all the fun.

Jan's younger sisters were twins: Gemma and Charlotte, or Charley, as she preferred being called at the moment. Their little brother, Joey, had just turned five, and on his first Halloween jaunt where he was allowed out without a harness.

The twins were dressed in matching nurses' outfits, with fake blood smeared across them, and their faces painted to give them both a sinister smile. Joey had come as his favourite superhero, Batman, and he had some sponges discreetly stitched into his costume to represent his muscles.

Jan and Kerry had both opted for witches' costumes. They wore pointy hats with fake scraggly hair cascading down form the brim, and they had each painted the other's face green, for effect.

Their dresses were old party ones which their parents had allowed them to rip up to give the impression that they had both just flown their broomsticks through a forest, escaping the irate townsfolk.

So far, they had been pretty lucky. The nasty man at number fifteen was the first to refuse them any treats, so all their buckets were over half full.

They made their way along the street to the next house with lights on.

This time, the door was answered by an old lady, with a tin of sweets in her trembling hands. "Oh, don't you all look grand," she cooed, surveying their costumes. "I'm afraid I don't have many sweets left," she admitted, apologetically. "There were far more of you this year, than last."

"That's okay," replied Kerry. "Do you have enough to give the little ones some?"

The old lady dipped her tin so that Kerry, who was in the lead, could see inside.

There were about a dozen assorted sweets left. Kerry turned

to the others. "Come on you three, take one each," she instructed.

After the last house, the three youngest needed a little encouragement to step forward, especially Joey who still clung to his sister's torn dress for dear life.

Kerry reached back and ushered the twins forward. "Say thank you to the nice lady," she instructed, as they claimed their prize. Jan had to bring Joey along and held him up so that he could see inside the tin.

The little boy did not reach out for any. Instead, he just gazed up at the old woman, still unsure as whether or not it was safe to make a move.

In the end, Kerry reached in a grabbed a purple one for him, as they had ascertained earlier in the evening that it was his favourite colour. "Say thank you," Jan instructed him.

Joey continued to stare at the woman, who smiled down at him, and nodded.

Obviously reassured by the gesture, Joey gave the woman his biggest, cheesiest grin, and watched with great interest as Kerry dropped the sweet into his bucket.

"You're all very welcome," said the old lady.

"Happy Halloween," the girls replied.

Kerry and Jan had promised her mother that they would stick to the houses directly within their estate. It was a very well-lit area, and there were still loads of parents and children doing the rounds, so it was perfectly safe for them to be out.

Even so, Jan's mother had insisted that the eldest girls kept their mobiles on them, just so she could check on them, if the need arose.

Kerry also had a rape-alarm, which her mother had insisted she carry at all times, ever since she had started walking to and from school on her own. To be fair, as Jan lived across the road, the two girls used to walk together, which Jan's mum seemed happy enough to allow, especially as both Kerry and her daughter were sensible, level-headed girls, not prone to running off on a whim.

Added to which, the school was only two streets away, and Cheryl the kindly lollipop lady, was positioned half-way between the two locations, so the journey was by no means hazardous. But, even so, Kerry's mum still waited in their front garden until she saw her daughter turning the corner to their house.

Then she would rush indoors before Kerry saw her. Or so she thought.

Kerry never could understand her mother's concern about her safety. After all, she could take care of herself.

The troop visited another four houses before they reached the end of the estate, and by now their little baskets were almost to the brim.

As they left the final house on their round, Kerry stopped and looked across the street, to single dwelling which was, technically, still part of the estate, although it had been built years before the rest of the houses.

Realising what her friend was thinking, Jan grabbed Kerry's sleeve.

Kerry knew why, immediately.

There had been rumours flying around the estate concerning the old man who lived in that house, long before either Kerry or Jan had been born. Years earlier, some teenage girls had gone missing from the area, and local gossip speculated that the man who lived in that house had something to do with it.

The police had searched his house as part of their investigation and found no evidence of anything untoward. But such details were of no comfort to the parents of the missing girls, all of whom were convinced that the old man had something to do with their daughters' disappearance.

One night, full of booze and conspiracy theories, the three fathers of the missing girls ganged up, and broke into the house while the old man was asleep.

Their intention, or so they later revealed in court, had been to merely force him to admit his guilt, and inform them of where their girls were now.

But fuelled by alcohol, they allowed their emotions to get the better of them, and between them, they nearly beat the old man to a pulp.

The three men were considered lucky to receive only suspended sentences. But, as the old man did not receive any fatal injuries, and the three fathers were of previous good character, the Crown requested leniency, which the jury accepted.

The old man spent the best part of two weeks in the local hospital, and it was reported by the newspapers that he received a hefty sum in compensation from the Criminal Compensation Board.

All three families of the missing girls moved away from the area within six months.

"Don't tell me you're thinking of going there?" Jan asked, cautiously. Not wanting to alarm her siblings.

"His lights are on," Kerry observed. "I'll bet he's got a mountain of sweets 'cos everyone's too afraid to knock on his door."

"With good reason," Jan insisted.

Kerry sighed. "You think so?"

Jan nodded.

"That was years ago, and besides, nothing was ever proven. I reckon the stories have been exaggerated over time, and now, they are more like folklore form the Middle Ages, than actual fact."

"Either way," whispered Jan, "there's no smoke without fire, and my parents have always told me not to go near there, so can we go now, please?"

Kerry shrugged her shoulders. "Okay, scaredy-cat, only if, you're sure."

They walked back along the road towards Jan's house. The three little ones walked in front, the twins on either side of their young brother, each with a protective hand on his shoulder.

As they passed number fifteen, the man who had refused to give them any sweets earlier, was now in the process of threatening a couple of zombies with the police, if they did not leave his property right away.

"He's nasty," Jan observed.

"Mmm," Kerry agreed. "If anyone deserves a trick tonight, it's definitely him."

Jan laughed. "And you're just the one to give it to him."

"Too damn right."

Once inside Jan's house, the three little ones excitedly took their buckets to show their mother. She thanked Kerry for helping Jan with the kids and told her to give her love to her mother for her.

At the front door, Kerry and Jan hugged goodbye. "Promise me you're not going to do anything silly with that bloke at number fifteen." Jan demanded, of her friend. "I know you, Kerry Dain."

"Moi!" Kerry exclaimed, mocking the accent of their French teacher, Madame Zou.

Jan frowned. "I'm serious. I didn't like him, one bit. Best not to piss him off, he'll know it was one of us."

"You worry too much," Kerry noted. "You'll have frown lines before your time. Now go in and enjoy your sweets. And don't forget to brush your teeth afterwards," she wagged a playful finger.

Once Jan had closed the door, Kerry crossed the street towards her own house.

At the gate, she stopped and looked back to make sure her friend was not watching her from one of the downstairs windows to make she made it home in one piece.

Jan was such a worrier.

When she was sure the coast was clear, Kerry entered through the gate, opening it as slowly as she could for fear that the *squeak* it usually made might alert her mother to the fact that she was home.

Once inside her yard, Kerry crept over to the small potting shed behind the hedge. There was nothing of any value inside it, so her mum had not bothered to change the padlock when the old one rusted. Kerry lifted the lock off the catch and opened the door.

Inside the shed, she grabbed one of the myriads of old Tupperware containers littered about the floor and placed it to one side. Lifting her dress, she pulled down her knickers, and squatted over it.

Her pee came out in a huge gush. She knew that she had been holding it in for too long. Once she was finished, she settled herself, and, careful not to spill any, she lifted the container, and carried it outside.

In the darkness she suspected that no one would notice what she was carrying, and if needs be, she could always cross the street to avoid detection.

There were still several groups of children going door to door, so she blended in perfectly with the crowds.

Kerry walked along the road until she was outside number fifteen. The light was still on inside, so she was careful not to make any noise. She glanced up and down the street to make sure that there was no one else close enough to see what she was doing.

Silently, she crept up to the front door, and holding the container as far away from her as possible, she tipped the contents of her bladder over the front door.

The stench from her pee seemed far more potent now, than it had while she was carrying it in the Tupperware, which was all to the good as far as she was concerned.

Once her task was complete, Kerry crept out of the yard, and disposed of the empty container in a waste bin at the end of the street, before carrying on down towards the far side of the estate.

At the end of the estate road, Kerry stopped and looked over at the old house.

The lights were still on, but there was nobody in sight. As she suspected, the local kids had probably been warned by their parents not to go anywhere near the house, especially after dark.

But Kerry was no ordinary girl!

Checking that no one was watching, she crossed the street and entered through the gate. The hedges on either side were so overgrown that even she, as small as she was, could not pass through without being attacked by straggling branches.

Once inside the forecourt, Kerry turned back. The hedges virtually obliterated the rest of the street from view to the extent that even someone passing by would not be able to see her.

Steeling herself, Kerry took in a deep breath and walked up to the front door.

From this angle, she could see that the man had a pumpkin light inside the alcove to the left of the door. So, he was a celebrant of Halloween after all. Her original assertion had been right. Kerry could just imagine the mountain of sweets the old man must have had, due to the lack of children willing to chance ringing his doorbell.

The more she thought about it, the more Kerry began to believe that all the stories she had heard about him since she was a child, were just the result of embellishment and paranoia after those girls went missing.

After all, if the police had searched his house, then surely, they would have found some evidence if he had been guilty?

Even so, she found herself checking her pockets, making sure that her alarm and mobile were still to hand. She had them both shoved into the same pocket because she had inadvertently cut a hole in her other one when she was fashioning her costume.

Kerry checked over her shoulder one last time to make sure the coast was clear before she rang the bell.

At first, there was no response. She waited patiently for a couple of minutes, then tried it again, deciding to herself that if he did not answer after the second ring, she would just leave well alone, and go home.

She was just about to turn to leave, when she heard a distant voice echoing behind the door. "Coming."

A sudden shiver spread through Kerry's body. There was nothing spooky, or particularly menacing about the voice. In fact, he sounded like a normal, everyday sort of person, just like a thousand others.

Therefore, Kerry put her unwarranted reaction down to the fact that she had managed to, albeit unintentionally, build-up a mental picture of some deformed, deranged serial killer, lurking behind the door.

She took a step back as she heard the approach of footsteps.

"Coming," he called again, almost as if afraid that his caller might give up on him and leave before he had a chance to answer the door.

Kerry heard the sound of at least three bolts being shifted back, before the door finally opened.

As she expected, the man who stood in the doorway looked no more threatening than her own grandfather. He was wearing a long dressing gown, which reached down past his knees, and house slippers.

Kerry wondered if, tired of waiting, he had decided to call it a night, and she had disturbed him just as he was climbing into bed.

But then, if he had decided not to wait for trick-or-treaters any longer, he should really have switched off his pumpkin-light.

"Trick or treat," Kerry called, holding up her basket.

The old man stared down at her. "My," he replied, "haven't you done well, already?"

Kerry nodded. "Yes, thank you, you're my last call."

The man smiled. "Well, I am very honoured indeed that you saved the best till last, and I love your costume."

Kerry looked down at herself. As witches went, she was quite proud of the way she was turned out, right down to her eigh-teen-hole, steel-toe capped Dr Martin boots her mum had bought her for her birthday, after much pleading, begging, and sulking. They seemed the perfect accompaniment to her raggedy dress, and ripped tights. Especially after, much to her mum's chagrin, she dotted skull stickers all over them.

"Thank you," she replied. "Have you had many callers tonight?"

The old man eyes clouded over. "Just one," he admitted, dejectedly. "Earlier this evening. I was beginning to think that she would be my only caller this year. But now, here you are."

Kerry held out the sides of her dress and curtsied.

The man laughed, good humouredly. "Well, as you're probably my last caller of the evening, I think that you can help yourself to whatever you want," he said, stepping back to reveal a table in his hallway, laden down with tins of various sweets, toffees, and chocolates.

Kerry opened her eyes wide. She had never seen such an assortment, other than in a sweet shop, or the supermarket.

Just then, they both heard the sound of a whistle blowing.

The old man looked round. "Oh, that'll be my kettle, I was just making myself a hot something to take to bed when you knocked."

"Sorry," Kerry apologised.

"No, no, don't be silly," the man replied, "I'm so glad someone else came." He held the door open a little wider. "Now you just help yourself, young lady, I'm going to turn off the gas. I won't be a minute."

Kerry felt obliged to step over the threshold so that the door would not slam shut when the old man left to sort out his kettle.

He waited until she had hold of it before turning away and scuttling off towards the kitchen at the far end of the hallway.

Kerry watched him go, until he disappeared behind the kitchen door.

She ogled the mountain of goodies stacked high on the table. She wished now that she had been more insistent with Jan when they were standing across the road. Her siblings could have filled their baskets to overflowing here, and the old man would probably have been far happier to have a few more visitors.

Kerry could not help but feel sorry for the old boy.

It was obvious to her that he was still being shunned all these years after the rumours of his abduction of those girls. She wondered if he had any family, or friends who came to visit him, or did he spend every day staring out of his window, wishing he had someone to talk to.

Was Halloween in fact, his one chance a year to prove to everyone that he was just a nice old guy, who wanted to treat the local children to some goodies, as befitted the time of year?

If so, how sad was it that when there were miserable sods like the bloke down the road, who refused to take part, this old guy was not only willing, but went to the effort and expense of buying enough sweets to feed the entire estate, without having so much as a handful of grateful kids knock on his door, to show for it.

Kerry could hear him in the kitchen making his drink.

She wondered if she should ask for one herself, just as an excuse to stay for a while and chat to him. The more she thought about the misery of his lonely existence, the more she wanted to do something about it.

Perhaps, she thought, if she stayed for a while and got to know him, she could tell everyone at school about what a nice guy he was, and finally dispel those awful rumours everybody was always spreading about him.

Then, maybe, she and a select group of friends could make a point of visiting the old guy once a week or so, for tea after school. Give the old man something to look forward to.

"Won't be long," the old man called. "Help yourself to whatever you want."

"Thank you," Kerry called back.

Taking a final glance outside, Kerry let the door close on the latch.

She stood alone in the large hallway, with only a single

working bulb dangling from the ceiling, which illuminated only a fraction of the area, leaving the rest in shadow.

She walked over to the table and placed her bucket down. Prizing off the lid of a tin of her favourite chocolates, Kerry grabbed a handful and dropped them into her bucket. She took a second handful which almost filled her bucket to the brim.

Satisfied, she stood there, wating for the old man to come back out.

She did not feel right about letting herself out and leaving, after he had been so kind and generous to her.

Finally, he stuck his head around the door. "I don't suppose I can tempt you to a cup of tea, or something?" he asked, hopefully. "I've got some juice, if you prefer?"

Kerry took a deep breath. This was her chance to make good on all her ideas about showing the old boy some kindness, in return.

"Yes please," she answered. "Some juice would be lovely."

Clearly surprised by her response, the man raised his eyebrows in shock, but soon recovered his composure, and beckoned her towards him. "Come on then," he said, "there's no need to stand on ceremony."

Leaving her bucket on the table, Kerry began walking towards the kitchen.

She could not dispel the feeling of trepidation which began to form in her tummy, lying there like a lump of concrete.

Kerry knew that she could turn on her heel and be out of the door before the old man knew what was happening. But the closer she edged towards the kitchen door, the further that avenue of escape seemed to be.

The lighting in the kitchen was no better than that in the hallway. A single bulb dangled from the ceiling, leaving the periphery of the room in shadow.

There was a large wooden table which dominated the centre of the room, and at one end sat a cup and saucer, with steaming liquid in it. Obviously, the old man's drink, Kerry thought.

The old man had his head buried in the fridge. "Here we go," he said, reaching in and producing a bottle of orange squash. "Is this okay for you?" he asked, hopefully.

Kerry nodded. "Fine thank you, all this trick-or-treating leaves you with a real thirst."

"Sit down, please," the man intoned, as he retrieved a glass from a cupboard above the sink and proceeded to pour a generous helping of squash into the glass, before filling the rest of it up with tap water.

Kerry took the seat nearest to the door, and the old man brought over her glass and set it down in front of her. "There," he said, triumphantly. "Now, would you care for a biscuit to go with it?"

"No thank you," Kerry smiled. She patted her tummy. "Too many sweets already."

The man moved over to his seat. "Did you help yourself to plenty of sweets?" he asked.

"Yes, thank you, my bucket is full now." Kerry took a sip from her drink. It was still quite watery as the man had not stirred in the squash, but it was still palatable.

The man blew on his tea, before taking a sip. Deciding the temperature was just right, he drank down half the amount, before replacing his cup in the saucer.

"Speaking of your bucket," he said, "I couldn't help but notice how small it is. You can barely fit anything into it."

"I know," agreed Kerry. "But my mum said it looks too presumptuous if you carry a bigger one. Plus, I think she's afraid I'll be eating sweets for breakfast if I bring too many home. Not that she'd let me, even if I wanted to."

The man laughed. "Quite so. I hope you don't mind my inquisitiveness, but how come you are out on your own? Don't you youngsters normally walk around in groups?"

Kerry finished a large swallow of her drink. "There were five of us, but my friends had to go back home, so I thought I'd finish off by myself." Kerry did not want to let slip that Jan and her siblings had been too afraid of the old man to knock on his door. Right now, he seemed very happy to have someone to talk to, and she was feeling rightfully proud of herself for making the effort.

"Well, in that case," he continued, "you must take some more home for them, as well." He lifted his cup to his lips and drained what was left of the contents.

"Oh, that's okay," Kerry responded, feeling guilty now that she was taking advantage of the old man's good nature.

"No, no," the man insisted. "I'll hear no more of it. Now let me fetch you a good strong carrier bag." The man stood up in a hurry, then caught the side of the table with one hand, as if to stop himself from toppling over.

"Are you okay?" Kerry asked, concerned for his wellbeing.

She began to rise from her seat, but the man held out his hand as if to stop her.

"It's alright," he assured her. "Just my blood pressure. If I stand up too fast it makes me dizzy. You think I'd be used to it by now."

He waited for a moment before moving.

Kerry watched as he made his way over to a built-in larder, by the outside window. Opening the door, he disappeared inside, and Kerry could hear him muttering to himself as he searched for a bag.

She took another long swig from her glass, tasting more of the squash this time.

"Tah-Dah," the old man announced, triumphantly, holding up a large carrier bag as he stepped out of the larder. "This should do the job, nicely."

Kerry laughed. "You could fit an entire tin into that," she observed.

"Then that's exactly what we'll do," the man replied. "Plenty to go around, that's the ticket."

The man walked past her, and Kerry went to stand up, but he placed a gentle hand on her shoulder to keep her in place. "No, no, you stay there," he instructed. "Finish your drink, I'll go and fetch one of the tins from the table. Won't be a sec."

Kerry did as she was told and took another swallow.

From behind she heard the old man whistling to himself as she made his way towards the table in the hall. On his way back to her, Kerry thought she heard him open a door, then close it almost immediately.

She suspected that he was checking on his pumpkin-light, to see if it was still burning. Now that she had paid him a visit, perhaps he was hopeful that other children might follow suite. Although it was growing a little late for many more to be out, Kerry did not wish to dampen the old boy's enthusiasm, by telling him, so.

Seconds later, he reappeared behind her. "Here we are," he said, cheerfully, placing a full tin of chocolates down on the table in front of her. "Now you pop those inside your carrier bag, and you're all set for the night."

"This is really far too generous of you," Kerry said, accepting the tin, graciously.

She placed the tin inside the carrier bag and twisted the top to make it easier to hold.

"Now then," said the man, looming over her. "What about another glass of squash?"

Kerry shook her head. "No thank you, that one really hit the spot. Otherwise, I'll be busting all the way home." She laughed to herself thinking about the pee-soaked door at number fifteen.

The man seemed disappointed at her answer, but he shrugged it off. "Okay then, if you're sure I can't tempt you."

Kerry stood up. Expecting the man to take a step back when she did, she was surprised when he stayed put, almost causing her to topple backwards.

Even so, his beaming smile made her feel warm inside as a result of bringing him some much-needed joy.

Instinctively, Kerry put her arms around him and gave him a

tight hug. He was a fair bit taller than Kerry, so, even on tiptoe, she only managed to come up to his chest.

The old man held on for a moment, before letting her go, and she could not help but wonder when the last time was that he had felt any form of physical tenderness.

"What was that for?" he asked once they had parted.

Kerry shrugged. "Just my way of saying thank you," she responded.

The old man smiled, again, this time even broader than before. "Well, I must make a point of deserving such thanks again, some time," he winked.

He led Kerry back along the hallway towards the front door.

Kerry felt a numbing sensation along the side of her thigh. She suddenly remembered her mobile phone was on silent, and the vibrating was probably her mother wondering where she was.

She reached into her pocket to retrieve it with her other hand still clamped around the carrier bag. As she pulled the mobile out, something else slipped out and fell to the floor.

Realising it had to be her alarm, Kerry put her foot out in an attempt to stop it crashing against the stone tiles and setting itself off. She knew that the noise it made would probably cause the poor old guy to have a heart attack on the spot.

Kerry felt the alarm bounce off her DM and roll away. She looked down, whilst simultaneously trying to check her screen to see who was calling. The alarm rolled under the bottom of the door to her right, which she presumed would either lead to the old man's dining room or lounge.

The old guy seemed oblivious to what was taking place behind him and continued walking towards the front door.

Trying to juggle the phone and the bag, Kerry attempted to switch hands to make it easier for her to answer her mobile. As she did so, the phone slipped from her hand and fell into the bag, slamming off the tin inside.

In frustration, Kerry reached for the door handle to retrieve her alarm.

The door was unlocked. She pushed it open, and there inside she saw the figure of a petrified girl, dressed as a schoolgirl zombie, bound, gagged, and strapped to a chair.

For a brief second, her mind could not formulate the scene before her.

The girl looked up at her, her eyes wide in fear. Tears streaked her face, causing her zombie eye make-up to run into her face-paint, smearing it, and actually helping to enhance the overall effect.

The girl tried to scream, but the ball-gag strapped to her mouth prevented any audible noise from escaping.

Before Kerry had a chance to react, she felt a hand clamp around her mouth from behind. Suddenly, there was a large carving knife at her throat.

"You stupid little bitch!" The words came from the old man but gone were the soothing tones and loveable character.

Kerry felt herself being dragged backwards off balance. She dropped the carrier bag without realising it, and the heavy tin bounced off her steel toecap and rolled away until the plastic bag halted its course.

The old man pressed the sharp edge of the knife against her throat.

Kerry could feel the cold steel biting into her soft flesh.

"Now," the man breathed into her ear, "am I going to have any trouble from you, or would you rather live to tell the tale?"

Kerry nodded her head as much as his grip would allow.

"Good!" With that, he began to pull her backwards, out of the room.

Kerry could see her own fear reflected in the eyes of her fellow captive, as she was dragged away, back down the hall towards the kitchen.

Her mind raced, but with the knife being held so tightly against her neck, Kerry knew that any sudden movement might end in her own demise. She had seen people on the telly when they had their throats cut, and how they writhed and squirmed on the floor as their life blood ebbed away. She knew it was not for real, but even so these dramas liked to demonstrate reality as much as possible.

That was certainly not the way she wished to have her life end.

Nor, for that matter, did she want it to end tonight, regardless.

Hoping that she would have time to formulate a plan, before it was too late, Kerry allowed herself to be carried along by the old man, without offering any resistance.

He was far stronger than she would have suspected him to be, and she could not help but wonder, how many times he had performed this same ritual with other victims.

The girl tied to the chair in the other room was presumably the one he said had called earlier. Kerry wondered if she had disturbed him when she arrived, forcing him to make a quick alteration to his plan of action. It would certainly explain why he took so long to answer the door.

The old man dragged her through the kitchen, and for a moment, Kerry believed that he was about to take her out through the back door.

Perhaps he had an outbuilding where he took his captives before...Kerry stopped herself from thinking of what might happen if he managed to trap her in his secret den.

The point was, once he took her outside, it would be her one and only chance to make a move. At least in his garden, if she screamed, there was a good chance one of the neighbours might hear her and call the police.

Kerry prepared herself.

But, instead of going outside, the old man dragged her into his larder where he had retrieved the carrier bag, earlier.

The walk-in cupboard was barely big enough for one, and

once they were through the door, Kerry could feel the shelving on either side of her, pressing against her shoulders.

This made no sense. If she was feeling cramped inside the tiny space, how was the old man going to fit in, and close the door behind him?

He would need privacy for whatever he had planned, surely?

Once inside, the old man shoved his body up against Kerry's, until she could feel the disgusting poke from his erection against her back.

Whatever else, this was certainly exciting him.

She tried to brace herself against the shelving, but in such a confined environment, Kerry was unsure what exactly she could manage to formulate her escape.

"Now then," the old man sneered, "you're going to like this, missy." With that, he took away the hand he had wrapped across her mouth and reached above the highest shelf.

Kerry heard a *creaking* sound, as the old man pulled against something hidden from view. As he did so, the panel in front of Kerry opened, revealing a wooden staircase which descended into the darkness below.

"Even the coppers couldn't find this," the man boasted. "It's where I do all my best work. He pressed the edge of the blade even harder against Kerry's neck. She instinctively tried to back away from it, but the man's body stopped her from making any progress.

She blinked down into the darkened pit before her.

The old man shoved himself up against her terrified body, the blade attacking her from the front, and his hardened member doing so from behind.

"I was going to work on that other little bitch tonight, but I think I'll save her, now I have you." With that, he leaned in and snaked his tongue along the side of Kerry's bare neck.

She had to fight to stop the bile rising in her throat.

Kerry felt him adjust his position from behind, doubtless so that he could shove her down the staircase.

She felt his right foot slide up alongside hers.

Lifting her boot, Kerry slammed it down hard onto the old man's toes.

He screamed in agony, and Kerry felt the knife edge ease away from her neck.

Without stopping to think, she lifted her other leg, and brought the heel of her DM crashing down on his other foot. This time she actually felt the crunch of bones beneath her heel. She kept it there, twisting it from side to side, until the old man shoved her off him.

The force of his push almost sent Kerry through the open doorway, but she managed in the nick of time to stop herself by grabbing hold of the ledge on either side.

The old man backed away, until he reached the wall behind him.

Kerry spun around to face him.

She could see that he still had hold of the carving knife, however, he seemed more interested in his damaged toes, than her right now.

During the struggle, the old man's dressing gown had fallen open, and Kerry was confronted by the sight of his wrinkly, naked body.

Swinging her leg back, Kerry landed a beautiful kick straight to his groin.

This time he dropped the knife, and it clattered on the hard floor.

The old man bent over, holding his groin with both hands.

Kerry, still conscious of the drop behind her, steadied herself and held her ground.

The man looked up, his eyes burning with pure hatred, as he stared up at her from his bent position.

Reaching out, he lunged forward, though somewhat lopsided due to the fact that he seemed reluctant to let go of his privates.

Kerry took her chance. She ducked under his arm and slid around him, until she had her back to the wall. Bracing herself against it, she planted her foot directly between his bum cheeks, and shoved forward with all she had.

The old man screamed as he sprang forward through the opening, and down the flight of wooden stairs, landing at the bottom with a sickening *thud!*

Kerry moved forward. For a moment, she stood at the top of the stairs, listening for any sound which might give an indication of the old man's situation.

After a moment, she heard him groaning in the darkness. This was followed by the sound of him shuffling around on the floor, but she could tell, even from up here, that he did not have the strength, or the mobility to climb back up to her.

She waited a while longer, just to be sure.

Eventually, she called down. "Are you alright down there, you old git?"

"Fuck you, cunt. You wait until I get my hands on you, you fucking little bitch!"

"Charming," Kerry said, rhetorically.

Just to be sure, she pulled the panel back until it locked into place. She could not be sure if there was a release latch on the other side, so, taking no chances, she carried through some of the kitchen chairs and jammed them against the shelving which lined the panel.

Retrieving the knife, Kerry ran back to the room where the girl was trussed up.

Once she had released her and assured her that everything was going to be alright, Kerry found her phone and dialled 999.

The police arrived within minutes, after she told them where she was and the circumstances which had led to her call.

The police led the old man away in handcuffs, still screaming his lungs out.

The fall had cracked a few bones, but nothing too serious. He was considered fit to stand trial a few months later, and after the police excavated his secret cellar, they found the remains of sixteen girls, all in various stages of decomposition, including the original three he had been suspected of kidnapping.

Most of the other victims were later identified as either runaways or prostitutes.

The old man received a life sentence, with a minimum tariff of thirty years, ensuring that he would never leave prison alive.

The girl Kerry had saved, Paula, became a firm friend, and over time, as she was a few years older than Kerry, she became more of a big sister.

Kerry was hailed a hero in the press and was even invited to Buckingham Palace to receive an award for bravery.

She never went trick-or-treating again.

# NURSE NANCY

"Come on, Gerry, wake up for me."
    Gerry Spicer could hear the voice in the distance. Sweet, tuneful, encouraging. It was the kind of voice most men would do anything for, and right now, it was focused directly on him.

Gerry attempted a reply, but the tube which protruded from his mouth prevented him from answering.

He tried to lift his head, but even that seemed beyond his ability.

Finally, he managed to open his eyes. Only slightly at first, his lids feeling as if they had been stuck down with superglue.

They flickered open for a second, and for that brief moment Gerry caught a glimpse of the gorgeous face that voice belonged to.

It hovered above him, close enough that he felt that he could almost reach up and kiss those sensuous lips.

He wanted to see more, but his lids were heavy. Too heavy to allow him to keep them open long enough to enjoy the view.

For a brief moment, he was aware of others around him. Men and women in white coats and face masks, peering down at his lifeless body, talking over each other, none of them making any sense.

He could hear the distant *hum* of machinery in the background, and an annoying *beeping* noise which wailed intermittently, growing louder in his ear with each passing second like some form of ancient water torture.

But all of that paled away into insignificance when he heard that beautiful voice, egging him on to come back to life.

He wanted to obey, if only to be able to see her face in all its heavenly glory. To smell her scent, to kiss those lips, to feel the radiance of her smile warm him from the inside.

Gerry attempted another go at opening his eyes.

As his tired lids began to lift, he could see her face once again, hovering just above him. Gerry was sure he could feel the touch of her breath on his face.

One more supreme effort, and he could reach up and press those luscious lips against his own.

Gerry steeled himself with determined fortitude.

Then he fell back into oblivion.

The next time he opened his eyes, Gerry was in a hospital room, surrounded by a dull shower curtain which stretched across three of the four sides of his bed.

He could feel a mask covering his nose and mouth, which clamped itself against him whenever he took a breath. Gerry glanced around him, but there was nothing on display save the machine he was connected up to via a set of wires and tubes, and the small bedside table, upon which sat a plastic jug full of water, and a couple of plastic cups.

He waited for a while, his brain trying desperately to remember why he was there to begin with.

Had he been involved in an accident?

Was he the victim of a random terrorist attack?

Did one of his car tyres suddenly explode underneath him while he was bombing it down the motorway?

For now, he had no precise recollection. Other than the

distant memory of that beautiful face peering down at him, encouraging him to survive whatever procedure was being practised upon him.

Well, whatever it was, it seemed to have done the trick, because here he was awake, and alive.

Gerry flexed his fingers. The tubes protruding from his hands moved with him. The plasters which kept them in place, tugged against the hairs on the back of his hands, irritating him with their mild discomfort.

He made an effort to move his body, just enough to assure him that everything was there. No amputations, no missing limbs, everything intact and fully functioning.

Satisfied that he was still in one piece, Gerry lay back and tried to concentrate on his breathing. The face mask still bothered him, and try as he might, it felt as if it was restricting his breathing rather than assisting it.

Fed up, he lifted his arm, pulling against the myriad of attachments, and grabbed hold of the most prominent part of the mask. As he pulled, he realised that there were elasticated straps around his head, keeping the annoying cone in place. He managed to slip it off, eventually, but was annoyed when one of the restraints pinged back and slapped him on the back of his hand.

Immediately, an alarm began to sound.

Gerry lay back down and took in a few deep breaths.

The curtain was swept back, and a middle-aged black nurse appeared at the side of his bed. Without speaking, she attempted to re-attach the mask, but Gerry grabbed her wrist, and shook his head just enough to convey his displeasure.

"It's better to keep it on, Mr Spicer," the nurse announced, in a thick, African accent.

Gerry opened his mouth to speak. "Can't breathe in that." His throat was extremely sore and talking did not help. When he swallowed, it felt as if the lining of his mouth was coated with sandpaper.

The nurse noticed him wince. "I'm sorry, it will be sore for a little while, but it will soon pass." She lifted the jug of water and poured some into one of the cups. Bringing it over towards his mouth, she said. "Just a few sips, drinking water will help ease the discomfort."

Gerry complied. The cold water felt good slipping down his throat.

Once he was done, the nurse placed the cup back on the table, and attempted to reattach his mask. Gerry groaned, loudly, and gave her a menacing look.

"Okay, then," she replied, placing the mask to one side. "I'll get you something to stop you feeling sick. But if you start coughing or spluttering, we will have to use the mask, okay?"

Gerry waited. From the angle she had left the curtain open, Gerry could see that he was not alone in his room. Across from his bed was another where a man lay motionless.

When he turned to his right, Gerry could just catch a glimpse of another bed beside his. There was a bulge beneath the covers at the end of the bed, which signalled that it was occupied. But from this angle, he could not see who was in it.

The nurse returned with an injection, which she promptly fed directly into one of the tubes protruding from his body. "There now," she said. "That should help you with your nausea. The doctor will be around soon to check on your progress. You had a lucky escape, you know? Someone up there must be looking out for you."

Gerry frowned. "What happened?" he croaked. "Can't remember."

"You had a massive heart attack," she announced, gleefully. "Apparently, you were driving down the high street when you suddenly keeled over at the wheel. Luckily, you were only doing about five miles an hour, so when you hit that lamppost, your airbags didn't even inflate."

Gerry raised his eyebrows. Now it was starting to come back to him.

He had been on his way to Pete Gregson's place with a sawn-off shotgun in the boot. Pete had not been paying his dues lately, and Tommy Morven, the head of the Morven clan, had called Gerry in to sort him out.

Gerry remembered he had the shotgun stored in the secret compartment he had built under the wheel well in his boot. He only hoped that whoever towed his car away had not discovered it and reported him to the police.

"It was a miracle," the nurse continued, excitedly, "just where you were driving an ambulance was coming in the opposite direction. If they had not have been there, well, we might not be having this conversation right now."

She recapped the syringe she had used on his tube, and placed it in a small plastic bag for disposal.

As Gerry's memory recovered, he wondered if Tommy had heard about the accident.

If not, he would be wondering by now why Gerry had not returned to him with Pete's money. Gerry always managed to make his marks cough up, even if he had to be a little heavy-handed with them to loosen their grip on their purse strings.

His reputation had always paved the way for him.

In his younger days, he had no qualms about killing someone, especially if there was a large payday in it for him. Fortunately for him, he had never been caught, which was usually more down to happenstance than skill.

Not that he had managed to get away scot-free with everything. He had spent his share of time in and out of borstal, and then prison, when he was older. But never for murder.

The longest stretch he had ever received was for a smash-and-grab at a local warehouse. He had cased the job for over two months and knew exactly when the wage deliveries took place. He had even managed to suss out the location of the safe while posing as a buyer.

Then, on the night of the raid, the security guard had fallen asleep on duty, and instead of being on patrol at the far end of the lot, he was dozing in the main office when Gerry burst in.

The guard was an old geezer in his sixties, so he was not any trouble. Gerry hit him with the butt of his shotgun, and he went down like a sack of spuds.

Foolishly, while setting the timer for the explosive, Gerry removed his balaclava, not realising that the old boy had come round. Gerry gave him another smack for good measure, but the old man was still able to identify him when Gerry was dragged in for a line-up.

That had cost him three years of a six-year sentence, and a considerable loss of street cred among some of the local thugs.

Working for the Morven's was a real game-changer, as far as he was concerned.

They were a proper professional bunch, who looked after their people. If Gerry for some reason could not get his mark to hand over their loot, all he had to do was kill them as a warning to anyone else who might have the same idea.

He did not even have to worry about disposing of the body. The Morven's had another crew for that, so all evidence of Gerry's presence was taken care of for him.

All he had to do was bask in the glory and appreciation of Tommy and the clan, for a job well done.

But right now, he needed to let Tommy know what had happened before he reached any ideas that Gerry had gone into business for himself with Pete's money.

"Phone," he whispered. "I need to make a call."

The nurse smiled. "All in good time Mr Spicer. The doctor will bring your possessions with him when he comes round."

Gerry grabbed her arm, squeezing it tightly.

The nurse looked down at him, clearly shocked by his sudden movement.

"You're hurting me, please Mr Spicer."

"I want my phone!" He almost spat the words out, ignoring the pain in his throat.

The nurse tried to twist her hand free from his grasp, but he refused to let go.

"I don't have it," she cried. "The doctor does, he'll be here soon. If you need to make a call urgently, I can get you the pay phone."

Gerry released his grip.

He considered her offer, but the problem there was he had no idea what Tommy's number was. He only knew that it was No.4 in his phone book.

By the expression on the nurse's face, Gerry knew that she had not been lying when she told him she did not have access to his mobile. Over the years he had come to recognise the look of fear in the eyes of others, and hers was genuine.

The nurse took a step back from the side of his bed. Just enough to ensure that she was out of harm's way should he try another grab at her.

She rubbed her wrist with her other hand. "Would you like me to fetch the pay phone for you?" she asked, unable to hide the trepidation in her tone.

Gerry shook his head.

"Okay then," she replied, sounding relieved. "I'll just go and see what's taking the doctor so long." Before setting off, the nurse drew back the rest of the shower curtain to reveal the whole room, including the windows to Gerry's left, which opened up onto a dull, cloudy day.

As she walked away, Gerry watched the way her uniform clung to her behind. She looked in good shape for a woman of her age, he thought. But not a patch on the nurse who had appeared to him while he was still on the operating table.

Knowing his luck, she was probably already off duty.

Gerry would have to look forward to receiving her bedside manner, tomorrow.

As he glanced around, he noticed that there were in fact three other beds in the room, all of which were occupied.

The patient in each bed was asleep, or at least appeared to be.

Each had their own machine beside them, with tubes and wires snaking out like wild tentacles preparing to attack their prey.

Gerry relaxed his head back on his pillow.

'A heart attack'. He supposed he should not be too surprised after a lifetime of too much booze, junk food and no exercise. Even so, he was not in bad shape for a man of his age. He had noticed his trousers growing a little tighter recently, but he put that down to getting on. No one could accuse him of being fat.

However, now he came to think about it, his old man had died of a heart attack back when Gerry was a child. So, it could just be a hereditary thing, and not his fault after all.

Mind you, if Tommy got hold of him before he had a chance to explain himself, his days might still be numbered.

He needed to get to his phone.

The thought played on his mind as he slowly slipped back into oblivion.

The next voice he heard was that of the doctor, standing over him.

Gerry opened his eyes and saw several men and women in white coats peering over his bed. The one with the clipboard seemed to be in charge and was doing most of the talking.

As Gerry came round, the doctor smiled down at him. "Good afternoon, Mr Spicer, I'm Dr Johnson, and I had the privilege of conducting your operation this morning. How are you feeling?"

Gerry attempted a half-smile and shuffled in an attempt to sit up.

The doctor held out his hand. "Please don't exert yourself, you're still in quite a delicate condition. I hear the nurse informed you that we lost you for a while on the table. But not to worry, there's no reason now that you cannot make a full recovery. You just need plenty of rest. Now, if you have any questions you'd like me to answer."

Ignoring the advice, Gerry managed to manoeuvre himself into a more upright position. "My phone," he gasped. "Where are my things?"

The doctor looked perplexed. "Er, oh yes, we bagged up your clothes and things," he looked around him, before addressing one of the young doctors in the group. "Could you go and see where they've put Mr Spicer's things, they should have brought them by now?"

The young woman smiled and left the room.

"She won't be long," Dr Johnson assured him. "Now is there anything you'd like to ask me about your operation?"

Gerry shook his head. "I just need my phone," he repeated, evidently frustrated.

"Alright then," the Dr nodded, "Dr Samson will be back shortly with your things. But do try and get some rest, won't you? Your throat may be a little tender for a while longer, but it will soon soothe."

Gerry nodded his understanding and watched while the troop of medics moved off to one of the other beds.

The young female doctor returned soon after, carrying a large plastic bag full of Gerry's clothes.

He tried to prop himself up a little higher, shaking his head when the young doctor tried to assist him.

Gerry grabbed the bag from her, without acknowledging her assistance, and began rummaging through the contents. The young doctor raised her eyebrows but did not make any comment at his rudeness. Instead, she merely said, "You're welcome," with a tinge of sarcasm in her tone, and moved off to join the others.

Gerry emptied the contents of the bag onto his bed. There was no sign of his phone, or his wallet. He searched through the pockets of his coat and found them zipped into the inside pouch.

Suspicious of everyone, Gerry first checked his wallet to ensure his money had not been touched. He remembered collecting three hundred sovs for a drop off for Tommy that morning, on his way to Pete's.

Relieved, he saw it was all still there.

279

He dialled Tommy's number. It was answered on the first ring.

"Well, well, I was wonderin' when I'd hear from you. What's the matter, you got lost or sumink?"

Gerry cleared his throat, then regretted the action. "I've been in an accident," he rasped. "I'm in hospital. They said I had a heart attack."

"Are you 'avin' me on?" Tommy, who was used to hearing feeble excuses from members of his crew, sounding suspicious at Gerry's explanation.

"Straight up," Gerry assured him. "I was on me way to Dozy Pete's when I had a heart attack at the wheel."

There was silence on the other end.

Gerry could hear Tommy's breathing coming through. Tommy always took several deep breaths whenever he was considering whether or not to believe someone's story.

"Come on, Tommy," Gerry, gasped. "You know me better than that."

Tommy waited a few more seconds before responding. "I suppose," he admitted, reluctantly. "Did you drop the gear off like I told you?" he demanded.

Gerry could feel himself relaxing. "Yeah, got your money here with me."

There followed another pause before Tommy spoke again. "You keep 'old of it for me, I'll expect to see you when you get out, okay?"

"Yep, no probs."

The line went dead.

Gerry fell back against his pillow, his breathing coming in great heaves. He could feel his heart racing inside his chest, and for a moment he feared that he might have over-exerted himself as a result of being stressed out, trying to convince Tommy of his sincerity.

He could hear the machine beside him starting to *beep* louder.

The doctors had finished their rounds and had moved on to another room.

Gerry pressed a hand against his chest and tried to stay calm. Slowly he began to relax, and his heartbeat returned to normal.

He slid his mobile and wallet under his pillow and dropped the bag with the rest of his stuff on the floor beside his bed. It seemed now that there was nothing that he could do but stay where he was and try to make a full recovery.

Later than evening, the African nurse returned with a plate of soup, which Gerry refused. He was not hungry, and even if he was, soup would not be on his menu, he hated the stuff.

The nurse tried her best to explain that for a couple of days he needed to stick to simple food, but Gerry merely dismissed her with a wave of his hand.

Not wishing to aggravate him again after that afternoon's performance, the nurse eventually left with the soup.

The next time Gerry opened his eyes, he was both surprised, and delighted to see the nurse from the operating theatre leaning over him. She appeared to be checking that one of the wires from the machine was still in place, and in doing so, her breasts were directly above Gerry's face.

Gerry was tempted to stick his tongue out to see if he could reach them. Even through the fabric of her uniform, it was still a turn-on for him.

But, before he had a chance to put his scheme into operation, the nurse moved back.

She looked down at him. "Ah, you're awake," she smiled. Gerry could smell the freshness of her breath through her perfectly white teeth.

He nodded his response and swallowed. His throat felt a little easier.

"How are you feeling?" she asked. "Or is that a stupid question?"

"Better for seeing you," he said, grinning.

"Flatterer." She noticed him staring at the nametag she had pinned above her left breast. Tilting it, slightly, so that Gerry could see it, she announced, "Nancy."

"Lovely, what do you call the other one?"

Nancy slapped him playfully on his hand. "Naughty," she said, giggling, before realising she was being too loud, and slapping her hand across her mouth.

She glanced over at the residents in the other three beds, to make sure that she had not disturbed them. Each patient was still sound asleep, so she turned her attention back to Gerry.

Nancy began fiddling with some of the wires and tubes which were attached to his machine.

Gerry watched, bemused. After a while, he asked, "What are you up to?"

Nancy finished tightening a protruding knob which appeared to have worked itself loose. "Well, believe it or not," she began, "we're expected to maintain these babies as part of our night-shift. This place is run more like a charity these days."

Gerry frowned. "How do you know what to do? I mean, are you trained for this stuff?"

Nancy nodded. "Oh yeah, they give us training. I mean, it's not as if we have to build or repair them, it's really just a matter of keeping everything screwed tightly in place, so the wires don't fall out and set the alarms off. They manage to work themselves loose when they are being trundled from one floor to the other."

"You good at screwing?" Gerry asked, leeringly.

Nancy smacked him again, harder this time. "Stop it, you flirt, I'm on duty."

"Yeah, but I love a girl in uniform."

Nancy shook her head. "I don't know, what am I going to do with you?"

"I could give you a few ideas."

Nancy's grin suddenly faded as she noticed something to one side on Gerry's monitor.

Noticing her change of expression. "What's up?" he asked.

Nancy sighed. "Would you believe it, there's an amp plug fallen loose. I hate those things, they're so fiddly. Now I'm going to have to go and try to find a screwdriver, what a bore."

Gerry had an idea. "Hang on a sec, pass me up my stuff."

Nancy did as she was asked, and looked on, curious, while Gerry rummaged through his clothing.

After a moment, he produced a small, grey, plastic cube from his trouser pocket.

He handed it to Nancy.

She took it and turned it over in her hands. "What's this for?" she asked, bemused.

Gerry reached up and took it back, then opened the lid, revealing a tiny set of screwdrivers within. "Tah-da," he beamed.

Nancy took them back. "Oh, you are a genius," she gushed. "It takes ages trying to find anything in this place."

"Well, now you can spend more time with me, seeing to my medical needs, and things."

Nancy bent over and pecked Gerry on the lips.

"I feel better already," he admitted, beaming.

Gerry watched as Nancy went from bed-to-bed in the room, checking on both the sleeping patients, and the connections of the machines they were wired up to.

As she moved around the room, Gerry could feel himself starting to grow at the sight of her tight little behind, and the way she sashayed across the floor.

He wondered if she was doing it for his gratification.

Gerry had enjoyed the company of many women during his life. But he had never settled down, nor even come close to it. Most women he found to be a nuisance after the first six months, or so, which was usually when he decided to call it quits.

Other times he had used prostitutes, if he was desperate. The Morven's ran a couple of brothels throughout town, but Gerry stayed away from them. Tommy was very protective of his girls, and when Gerry paid for the privilege, he wanted his money's worth, which, in his language, meant being able to do whatever he wanted to the woman, without worrying about Tommy being on his back for hurting them.

Sometimes, if the opportunity presented itself, Gerry would just kill the bitch afterwards. It had not happened often, and Gerry was very careful to cover his tracks. He knew that he had to be especially thorough these days, what with DNA coming on the way it was.

The more Nancy moved in front of him, the harder he grew.

Gerry was thankful that at least *that* part of him was still in good working order.

He wondered what his chances were with Nancy, right now.

She was bound to know the hospital like the back of her hand, and everybody knew how randy nurses were. Perhaps she could sneak him into an unused private room, and they could have some fun together. She certainly seemed up for it, the way she had been acting up to him.

Besides, she owed him a favour for lending her his emergency toolkit.

Gerry closed his eyes and tried to imagine what Nancy would look like out of her uniform.

The next thing he knew, there were people in white coats buzzing all around the room.

Gerry propped himself up.

Nobody seemed to be paying him any attention, as they rushed from bed to bed, checking in on his fellow lodgers. A couple of the nurses were crying, quite openly, and comforting each other. One of them was the African nurse who had been there when he first woke up.

"'ere, what's going on?" Gerry called out.

They all ignored him.

Gerry looked for Nancy, but she was not among the rest of the medical staff in attendance.

"Will someone tell me what's goin' on?" he called out, louder this time. His throat seemed to have recovered, as the sandpaper feeling was now completely gone.

A female doctor came over to his bed. "If you could please remain calm," she instructed, her tone haughty and impersonal. "We will be out of your way soon."

"I wanna know what's happenin'," Gerry demanded, feeling his temper rising. Doctor, or no doctor, he was not going to stand for being fobbed off.

The doctor sighed. "It's really nothing for you to worry about," she assured him. "Now please, just let us carry on with our work."

Without waiting for a reply, the doctor turned on her heel and walked back over to one of the other beds. Once there, she said something to one of her colleagues, who turned around and looked over towards Gerry.

After a minute, he nodded, and the female doctor left the room.

Gerry continued to watch the scene unfold before him with great interest, and he did not notice the female doctor re-enter the room, until she was beside him.

"Are you goin' to tell me what all the fuss is about?" he demanded.

But, ignoring his request, the doctor removed a syringe from her pocket, and before he had a chance to object, she slipped the needle into one of the tubes protruding from Gerry's arm.

"What's that?" he demanded.

"Just something to calm you down," she replied, emptying the contents into the tube.

"I don't need calming down," Gerry spat, attempting to lift himself up, once more. But before he could find the strength, he felt his eyes growing heavy. He opened his mouth to speak, but the words never came.

The last thing he remembered was the screen being pulled back around his bed.

When he next opened his eyes, the screen had been pulled back, and daylight streamed in through the far window.

Instead of doctors and nurses, there was a man and a woman sitting to one side of his bed. Both were dressed in formal office wear, and Gerry knew exactly what they were.

*Filth!* They all looked, and smelt, the same.

They could see by his expression that Gerry had already sussed out who they were.

The man leaned in and retrieved Gerry's notes from the end of his bed.

"That's private," Gerry spat. "Leave 'em alone."

The male detective ignored his objection and continued to thumb through the papers attached to the clip.

"I'm DS Carlisle," the woman announced, not rising to shake hands. "And we have some rather formal questions we'd like to put to you Mr Spicer, if you're up to it."

"I'm not. I've just had heart surgery didn't anyone tell yer?"

"Yes, we've spoken to your surgeon, he was extremely helpful. Apparently, your vital signs are looking incredibly strong, so we can have you out of here and down the station to answer our questions, if you prefer?"

Gerry frowned. "What questions?" he demanded. "I haven't done nothing, so you two can just piss off, alright."

His mind raced, desperately trying to think of what possible reason they were here. He had not had to work anybody over badly for ages, and the rest coughed up their money with a slap, or two. He had not even made it to Slippery Pete's gaff, so if Tommy sent someone else to work on him, that was nothing to do with him.

Besides, he would have been in the hospital when it happened, with a full staff of alibis.

The woman flicked open her notebook. Tell me, Gerry, do you recognise any of these names: Cyril Peacock?"

Gerry squinted. "Do I look like the kind of bloke who would go around with a geezer called Cecil? Do me a favour."

Unperturbed, the DS continued. "How about, Donald Crust, ring any bells?"

Gerry shook his head. "No," he snapped.

"Well, what about John Salmon?"

"No, never heard of 'im, now is that all?"

"You've never heard of any of them," the DS repeated, well, allow me to enlighten you, they were the three blokes sharing this room with you last night, and now, they are all dead!"

Gerry shuffled himself into a seated position. It was then he felt the cold steel of the handcuff attached to his left hand. The other cuff was secured around the metal bed post.

Instinctively, he began pulling against the cuff, rattling it against the metal frame of the bed, trying to squeeze his wrist through the opening.

Finally, he gave up, exhausted. "Get this thing off me," he screamed. "You can't do this to me, I haven't done anything."

"Then you've got nothing to be concerned about, have you?" said the male officer, leaning back in his seat. "So, why don't you just answer our questions, and we can be on our way. I'm sure there's a reasonable explanation as to why all their life-sustaining machines were tampered with last night, including disarming the alarms so no-one would come and save them."

"And, oh look," added DS Carlisle, lifting something in a small plastic bag. "We found your little toolkit tucked away underneath your pillow. Now, I'm willing to bet my retirement pension our forensics can match the scratches on them, with those on the machinery at just the points where they were messed with."

Gerry's mind raced.

He tried to think back to the previous night. Before all mayhem broke loose.

His night nurse. He had lent her his tools to try and adjust the machines.

She would vouch for him.

"Where's Nancy?" he demanded, shifting his gaze from one officer to the other. "Get 'er hear, now. She'll back me up."

"And who might she be exactly?" asked the DS.

Gerry stared at her. "She was the nurse on duty last night. She borrowed my tools to fix the machines, so I know you'll find a match for them. Just get 'er in here and she will tell you herself. Go on?"

The two officers looked at each other, then DS Carlisle nodded to her partner, and he scraped his chair back and left the room.

While he was gone, the female detective scanned through her notes, once more.

"Where did you go to school, Gerry?"

The question caught him off-guard. "What?"

"Your secondary school," she repeated, "where was it?"

Gerry looked perplexed. "What d'yer want to know that for?" he asked.

"Just humour me. What was it called?"

"St Joseph's, why?"

"And when did you leave?"

"When the bastards kicked me out, so what?"

"So, you were expelled?"

"Yeah, big deal. So what? And what's this got to do with anything?" Gerry could feel his anger rising. Under normal circumstances, when questioned by the law, he always tried to maintain his cool so as not to cause any unwanted suspicion.

But this was something else.

He had not done anything, so why were the police hounding him?

"When you were expelled, you were taken straight to a specialist school for young offenders, weren't you?"

"So?"

"Your headmaster at St Joseph's gave evidence against you at the time. The result of which was you being institutionalised, rather than being returned to school. "Do you remember what you threatened at the time?"

Gerry thought. "No, what?"

Carlisle sighed and checked her notes. "You threatened to get your own back on him, one day. Now do you remember?"

"So what?" Gerry made to sit up, forgetting about the restraint. The action jolted his shoulder, sending a searing pain through his arm. "Ow, fuck!"

Carlisle ignored his discomfort. "Do you remember your ex-headmaster's name?"

Gerry massaged his tender arm with his other hand. "No."

"Well, let me remind you. It was Cecil Peacock."

Gerry remembered the blast from his past. "Oh, yeah. So, what? Old bastard's probably dead by now, anyway."

"And you know that for a fact, do you?"

Gerry shook his head. "How would I know?"

The DS turned in her seat. "Because he was sleeping in that bed last night, until someone cut off his life-support."

"What!" Gerry was genuinely shocked. As coincidences went, that was a doozy. But still, it had nothing to do with him, so why should he care what happened to the old git.

"So, in answer to my original question, you do know who Cecil Peacock is. Or was?"

Gerry opened his mouth, but his usual quick wit had abandoned him.

Instead, he sank back against his pillow.

He began to feel as if the wind had been knocked out of him.

The DS continued. "Therefore, I'll ask you again about Donald Crust. Do you know him?"

Gerry took a moment to realise the DS had put another question to him.

The shock of the coincidence was still taking hold.

"Mr Spicer?" the officer pressed.

"No!" he replied, letting his anger get the better of him.

"No, what?" she insisted.

"I don't know any geezer by the name of Donald Crisp, alright?"

"Crust," she corrected him. "Donald Crust. And you're quite positive you have never known anyone with that name?"

"Yesss!" Gerry hissed, letting the 's' slip through his teeth as if he were impersonating a snake. "Unless you're going to tell me he was my primary school maths teacher, or something equally stupid."

DS Carlisle ignored him and continued to check over her notes.

Looking up, she asked. "I see you spent three years inside, for armed robbery, and aggravated assault."

Gerry began to think back.

What were the names of his cell mates?

What were the guards called?

He was sure that none of them had the surname of Crust. Although now that he thought about it, the name did ring a faint bell.

"Yea, I was inside. So, big deal."

"So, you don't remember the name of the security guard you almost killed during the raid? The same one who identified you from a line-up, and cost you three years of your life?"

Gerry sat back up. She was right. Now he remembered the old git's name was something like 'Crust'.

He looked back over at the DS.

She was nodding her head, slowly. "That's right, Gerry," she signalled with her thumb over her shoulder. "Donald Crust. He was your victim in that bed over there."

Gerry could feel the perspiration starting to ooze from his pores.

This could not be happening.

How was it possible that two people from his past happened to end up in hospital, in the same ward as him, and suddenly die during the night?

Where was Nancy?

She was his alibi. She would tell them that he had nothing to do with tampering with their medical equipment.

If anything, she might have done it, by accident. But, even so, that would let him off the hook.

She would speak up for him. After all, she definitely fancied him.

"So then," the officer cut in on his train of thought. "Shall we agree that's two out of three?"

Gerry shifted his position, again forgetting about the handcuff. But his concern for his own welfare blocked out the pain, this time. "Look, this is fuckin' madness. Just get that nurse in here, and she'll tell you it was her that played around with their equipment, not me."

"And what would she want to do that?" Carlisle asked, sarcastically. "Did they have some connection to her past, as well?"

"How the fuck would I know, I only met her last night."

"And she just happened to borrow your little toolkit to kill off three perfect strangers? Is that what you want me to believe?"

"I leant her me tools because she said she had to make some adjustments to the machines. Including mine."

"And you don't suppose in a hospital the size of this one, they might just have the odd maintenance crew hanging around, for that sort of thing?"

Gerry was visibly shaking. "She said she had to do it because of cut-backs." He realised how lame his answer sounded, but he did not know what else to say. "Look, just ask her, stop giving me the third degree, I'm fuckin' innocent, alright."

Just then, the male officer returned.

Ignoring Gerry, he made his way over to his colleague, and whispered in her ear.

DS Carlisle nodded, and a slight smile crossed her face.

"What's he sayin'?" Gerry demanded. "What's goin' on?"

The male officer re-took his seat, without speaking.

DS Carlisle managed a half-smile. "My colleague has just

informed me that the night nurse is on her way here. She stayed back after she shift finished at our request."

Gerry managed to relax, a little. "Good," he said.

*Nancy will sort this out for me.*

"In the meantime, Gerry, how about you think back and see if the name John Salmon, means anything to you?"

Gerry turned his head to face her. "I'm presuming you're going to tell me that he was the bloke in the third bed. Am I right?"

She nodded. "You got me. No flies on you. So now perhaps you can tell me how you knew him."

"I didn't," Gerry muttered. "At least, I don't remember the name. Perhaps you can tell me how I knew him."

The DS waited for a moment. "I'd rather you told me," she admitted.

"Well, I can't, so either you tell me, or we leave it at that."

DS Carlisle flicked over a page of her notebook, then began. "You were once engaged to a Mary Stellard, is that right?"

The sound of the name evidently struck a chord with Gerry. The moment he hears it, he stiffened, and shuffled back up to a seated position.

He still regarded Mary at the one who got away. His one and only.

Even so, he was surprised that the mere mention of her name would spark such strong emotions from someone who had spent a lifetime not caring about anyone but himself.

"Gerry?"

"Yes," he snapped. "What of it? That was ages ago."

"Do you remember why you split up?" The DS pushed.

"None of your fuckin' business," he shouted. "Leave 'er out of this."

"Her father didn't trust you, did he?" the DS continued. "He paid a private detective to follow you around until he caught you with your pants down with another woman who lived in your block, didn't he?"

"Shut the fuck up!" Gerry was now beyond caring whether or not they believed him about anything. This was his personal life they were sticking their noses in, and he was not going to allow it.

"That private detective informed on you to your future father-in-law, and you were subsequently dumped, weren't you? Your fiancée wanted nothing more to do with you. Not that I can blame her, under the circumstances."

Gerry swung himself around, instinctively trying to raise his hand to slap the DS to shut her up. The restraint on his wrist halted his progress, and jolted his shoulder once again, causing a searing pain to shoot through his arm.

Despite the agony he was now in, Gerry tried unsuccessfully to wrench his hand free of the bracelet, until the male officer stood up and ordered him to stop.

"Fuck you!" Gerry spat, glaring at the officer through menacing eyes. "She has no fuckin' right to stick her nose in my life. No fuckin' right at all."

From the other side of the bed, he heard the female detective continue. "You swore that one day you would find out who that private eye was and do for him. Remember that?"

Gerry switched his gaze back to her. "So fuckin' what..." Then the thought struck him. "He was the bloke in the third bed. Is that what you're about to tell me?"

Carlisle nodded.

Gerry slumped back.

He heard the sound of the ward door opening.

"Ah, here's your night nurse," the male officer announced.

*Nancy.*

At last.

Gerry turned his head to one side and opened his eyes.

Instead of Nancy, the middle-aged African nurse who had first seen to him when he awoke the previous evening, was standing just behind DS Carlisle's chair.

Before she had a chance to say anything, Gerry groaned.

"Not her for fuck's sake, the pretty blonde one who looked after me over night. Nancy."

The DS turned in her chair to look at the nurse.

The poor woman looked terrified but was comforted by a smile from the DS.

"Mr Spicer," she began. "I was the one who was with you overnight. I was on a double-shift, and I only finished this morning."

"Not you, you fuckin' ugly bitch." Gerry snapped. "Your colleague, the gorgeous blonde bird, Nancy. The one who came in during the night."

Clearly shocked by his outburst, the nurse looked down at Carlisle for reassurance before she continued to speak. "Mr Spicer. We don't have anyone called Nancy on this ward. I was the only one on duty here last night."

"Bollocks! You fuckin' go and get 'er now, you lyin' cunt!"

"Okay, that's enough," Carlisle demanded, rising from her chair, and standing between Gerry and the nurse.

"She's fuckin' lying," Gerry shouted, his voice starting to quiver with rage. "She's probably trying to protect her colleague. Get one of the senior doctors in here, they'll tell you who I'm on about."

"As it is, Gerry," said the male officer, also standing, now. "I've spoken to the head registrar, and he's already confirmed that this lady was the only one on duty here last night. What's more, he's confirmed that they don't even have a nurse with the Christian name of Nancy working in the hospital, let alone on this ward."

Gerry spun his head back and forth between the two officers.

He could tell that neither of them believed a word he was saying, but he knew that he was innocent, and that the nurse was lying.

They had to believe him.

Gerry felt as if he was floating on air, and everything around him, including the two officers, were suddenly being shrouded by a thick haze.

The room itself began to close in around him, as his eyes grew heavy, and he sank back against his pillow.

Although not formerly under arrest at the time, Gerry was given a police guard to ensure that he did not attempt to leave his hospital ward and make a run for it. As a known villain with several insalubrious contacts, two armed officers were placed outside the door to his room, with strict instructions to vet all visitors and parcels.

Once he was deemed fit to leave the hospital, DS Carlisle returned to arrest him under suspicion for the murder of the three men who had shared his room.

Gerry was escorted down to the local police station hand-cuffed and in a wheelchair.

Having been cautioned by the desk sergeant, and reminded of his rights, he was taken to a holding cell to await his solicitor's arrival.

Once inside the cell, his handcuffs were removed, and he was allowed to lie down on the cot provided.

About an hour later, Gerry heard his cell door open.

"I've brought you some tea," said a cheery female voice. "I made it with plenty of sugar, just like you wanted in hospital."

"Shove it up yer arse," Gerry called, without turning to see who had brought it in.

"That's not very nice, and after all the trouble I took to make it, too."

There was something oddly familiar about the voice. But Gerry presumed that it just belonged to one of the multitude of officers he had seen since his arrival.

Gerry heard the cup being placed on the shelf next to his cot.

"You can fuckin' take that away for a start," he roared. "I ain't havin' nothing until me brief gets here."

"Why?" asked the officer. "It's only tea. What difference does it make whether your solicitor is here or not?"

"That's my business, now take it away before I make you wear it."

"You wouldn't do that to your little Nancy, now, would you?"

Then he made the connection.

That voice, it was her!

The nurse from the hospital.

Before his mind could consider how she managed to suddenly be in his holding cell, Gerry spun around on the cot, almost losing his balance, and falling onto the floor.

It *was* her. Nancy, the nurse. Only now she was dressed in a police officer's uniform.

It made no sense.

"What the...what are you doing here?" Gerry demanded. "What the fuck are you doin' dressed like that?"

"I'm a community officer," Nancy smiled. "This is my part-time job when I'm off shift at the hospital. Are you glad to see me?"

Gerry staggered to his feet. The sudden movement made him feel woozy, and he sat back down to help compose himself.

Once he was feeling better, he rose slowly. "Where the hell have you been?" he demanded, grabbing Nancy by the elbow. "They've got me in 'ere because they think I messed with the machines in the hospital. Do you know those other blokes who shared my ward are all dead?"

Nancy looked shocked. "No! Dead, how?"

Gerry released his hold on her and spread out his arms. "How the fuck should I know," she barked. "It had something to do with you playing around with those medical machines on the ward. You must've made them malfunction, somehow, but the point it, you used my toolkit, so now they think it was me. Where did you get to?"

Nancy shook her head. "Oh my, I didn't realise. I was just helping out that evening. I had to cover several wards."

"The doctor said there was no Nancy working there. They made out I had imagined you."

Nancy laughed. "Well, I am quite new there, so no one really knows me, that well."

Gerry could feel his anger rising. "Forget all that, what about me? You need to go and tell that Carlisle bitch that I am completely innocent, so they can let me go."

"Innocent?"

"Yes, innocent. What are you waiting for?" Gerry brushed past her and made his way to his cell door.

Hammering on it with both fists, he shouted for the custody sergeant.

Within seconds, the sergeant arrived. "Alright, alright, calm yourself. Now, what's the trouble?"

"The trouble," Gerry spat. "The trouble is I'm innocent, and this little bitch can prove it."

The officer looked puzzled. "What 'little bitch' as you so charmingly put it?"

"Her! What are you fuckin' blind?" Gerry indicated over his shoulder with his thumb.

The sergeant leaned over to see around him. "Who, exactly, are you referring to?"

Gerry spun round.

He was alone in his cell.

Nancy had disappeared. But how? There was no way she could have got past him and made it to the door. Plus there was no other way out.

He turned back to face the officer through the tiny window. "She was here just now, I swear it," he said, beseechingly. "You have to believe me, fer fuck's sake."

The officer shook his head. "Millions wouldn't," he replied. "Now keep the noise down, your brief will be here soon, you can shout and scream at him or her."

With that, he slammed the shutter, and slid the lock in place.

Gerry waited for a moment. His mind reeling with objective thoughts.

He stared at the closed shutter before him.

"Aren't you going to drink this tea then? It's getting cold." Nancy's voice trilled behind him.

Gerry felt a cold shiver run through his entire body.

He had to fight to stay upright.

After a few moments, he turned and saw Nancy sitting on his cot.

Gerry fought to hold in a scream by shoving his fist in his mouth.

Nancy patted the cot beside her. "Come and sit down," she suggested, calmly. "I can explain everything."

"Can you explain how I'm losing my mind?" Gerry asked, all the fight in him gone.

Slowly, he shuffled over to his cot, and slumped down beside Nancy.

He could feel her beside him, the same as he had when he was in his hospital bed. Her perfume, her freshly washed hair, the hit from a fresh breath mint she must have eaten recently, all the odours mingled together in his nostrils.

She had to be real!

"You're probably wondering how I managed that?" Nancy asked, as if reading his mind.

Gerry resisted the urge to reach out and touch her, even though a part of him wanted nothing more than to grab hold of her and keep her there, while he shouted for the officer to return.

Instead, he simply nodded his reply.

"You don't remember me, do you?" Nancy asked.

Gerry squinted, as if trying to recognise the beautiful face before him.

But it was no good. He shook his head, slowly.

"Think back," she continued, "about five years ago. You'd just left a pub off the motorway near Braintree. You were pissed off your head, but you didn't care. Driving without lights, whizzing through the country lanes. Ring any bells?"

Now a faint bell began to ring in his memory.

Gerry had been sitting in that pub all day, waiting for a drop-off which never materialised. By closing time, he was not just pissed, he was pissed-off, and raring for a fight with anyone who crossed his path.

The girl in the lane. He did not see her until it was too late.

She went up in the air and bounced off his hood.

"You stopped at least," Nancy continued for him, "that was something. But then, when you realised that I was still alive, instead of calling an ambulance, or taking me to a hospital, you threw me in the boot of your car, and carried on driving back to that remote farmhouse where you had been holing out, since your last job."

"It wasn't my fault," Gerry jabbered, his bottom lip trembling. "I didn't see you..."

"Of course, you didn't, you couldn't be bothered to turn your headlights on."

Gerry stood up, again too fast. His head swam for a moment as he tried desperately to remember the events of that night.

He turned back to face Nancy. "You've got to understand, I was out of my skull, I'd had way too much to drink, please."

"Do you remember what you did to me when you got back?"

Gerry did, but he refused to show it. Instead, he wrapped his arms around his shoulders and pretended ignorance.

"Allow me to enlighten you," Nancy offered. "When you got home and took me out of the boot, I was still alive, though only barely. So, what did you do next? Did you call 999? Did you try to revive me? No! You raped me, you evil bastard, right there on the grass in front of the house. And once you were finished, you threw me back into the boot, and left me there until the morning, by which time, I was dead. Then you dug me a nice big hole and buried me in it, where no one would ever find me."

Gerry covered his face with his hands. "I know, I know," he

cried out. "Look, I'm sorry, alright. I'd had a bad couple of days, and then the bloke who was supposed to come and get me never turned up…"

"So that gave you an excuse to rape and kill me, did it?"

Gerry turned to face Nancy, his eyes burning with hatred and malevolence. "Alright, alright, I fucked yer, and I killed yer. So fuckin' what? That was years ago, what d'yer want from me now?"

Nancy stayed calm and did not react to Gerry's venomous retort. "My parents are still looking for me, do you know that? They have never given up hope that I might be alive somewhere, and that one day I will come home." Nancy stood up and walked around Gerry, stopping by the door. "So, I'll tell you what I want from you, when your brief arrives, I want you to confess about what you did to me and tell them where they can find my body."

"What? You're insane if yer think I'm gonna fuckin' tell 'em anything!"

Nancy calmly walked back around him towards his cot. "Well, if you don't, then I'm going to haunt you for the rest of your miserable life. And not just me."

She pointed back towards the cell door.

Gerry turned.

There stood the three men who had recently shared his hospital ward.

Under normal circumstances, he would not have recognised them. But having been told their names by DS Carlisle, he realised at once who they must be.

Gerry spun his head around to confront Nancy. "But I didn't kill them, you did, you psycho bitch."

Nancy laughed. "Oh, they know that. But they also know my reason why, and they fully understand. You see, for one reason or another, none of them had very long left to live, and as it turns out, their ends were not going to be particularly pleasant. So, when you died on the operating table, I grabbed my chance to hitch a lift back with you, so to speak. And these three, very gallant men, agreed to let me take them over in a very peaceful manner, and in return, they have vowed to assist me in making your life hell. That is, unless you confess."

Gerry turned back to face the men.

Unlike Nancy, they all seemed to have an almost translucent appearance. It was as if they were merely visiting the here and now, awaiting Nancy's instructions.

Gerry raised his arms as if in an appeal to his fellow men. But they all just stared back at him with vacant, unseeing eyes.

"So, what's it to be?" Nancy asked, from behind.

Gerry knew that he was stuck between a rock, and a hard place.

Even if he was somehow able to wriggle out of being responsible for the deaths of the three men, once he revealed what had happened to Nancy, he would be sunk.

The alternative, however, did not bear thinking about.

Finally, he gave in. "Alright," he agreed. "I'll tell 'em everything. But you've got to promise to keep your word, too."

He turned to face Nancy.

But she was gone.

Gerry swung around to see the three men, but they had vanished, as well.

"I will, so long as you do!" The voice came out of thin air.

Gerry sank back on his cot with his head in his hands, as he heard the sound of footsteps echoing along the corridor, towards his cell.

# CAT-GIRL

Lucy swung open the back door and bounded out into the garden, her little heart full of excitement and anticipation. The arrival of a new neighbour meant the beginning of a great adventure, so far as the ten year old was concerned.

Her previous neighbour, Mr Jenkins, had been a lovely old man who made a point of always remembering her birthday, and presenting her with a huge tin of her favourite sweets at Christmas. But now, sadly, he was gone, banished to an old people's home on the other side of town. Therefore, Lucy consoled herself with the prospect of meeting brand new, exciting people, whom she could talk to over the fence.

She had spent the previous day with her nose pressed against the glass of her bedroom window, watching the removal team unload her new neighbour's possessions from their van.

Lucy had hoped that she might catch a glance of some children, especially a girl of her age whom she could bond with and become firm best buddies. But alas, there was no such sign, only men, of which Lucy could not fathom out which one was to be her neighbour.

Until today. Her mother had warned her not to bother their new neighbour the previous day, as they would doubtless be stressed and fatigued as a result of their move. But today was another story. Today she finally had the chance to introduce herself.

As she left the door, Lucy's two black cats ran through her legs, almost as eager as she was to meet their new neighbours. They both jumped the fence in unison and perched themselves on top on a couple of posts.

Lucy noticed their backs arching and their tails *fuzzing* to twice their normal thickness. She instinctively knew that something was wrong, and by the time she had reached the panel between them, both cats were *hissing* loudly.

Lucy popped her head over the fence, and immediately saw the reason for her pets' anxiety as two Dobermans rushed the fence, barking.

Lucy instinctively pulled back as the dogs jumped up and rested their front paws on the top of the low-lying fence. Fortunately, the posts were high enough so that the dogs could not reach Lucy's cats without leaping higher, which she was in no doubt that they could.

"Hecate, Lilith," Lucy called to her pets. "Get down, now!"

The two cats continued to *hiss* and *spit* at the new arrivals, almost as if defying them to try and come any closer.

They both glanced over at their owner, before acquiescing to her command.

Both cats jumped down from their perches and strolled off in the other direction. The Dobermans continued to bark, and now that they could no longer see their prey, they began running back and forth along their side of the fence.

"Ace, Bullet, get back 'ere, now!"

The shout came from one of the men Lucy had seen yesterday, unloading the removal van. He was a very large man in both height and girth, with tattoos covering most of the exposed flesh on his arms. From this distance, Lucy could see that he also had several tattoos on his face, as well. Along with a dozen or so pieces of silver attached to his ears, nose, and chin.

---

His was a frightening visage, and under normal circumstances, Lucy would have instinctively avoided such a man if she came across him on the street. But, as he was her new neighbour, she was determined not to let his appearance make her forget her manners.

"Hello," she called, trying to be heard over the sound of the dogs' barking.

The man ignored her, too involved in chastising his pets who by now were cowering in front of him while he berated them.

Lucy waited for the noise to die down. Once it had, she waved at the man and called out to him. The man looked up and frowned. He waited by his back door as if unsure whether to go back in or not.

Realising that he might be shy, although, he certainly did not look the shy type to her, Lucy stepped up to the fence and extended her hand. "Hello, my name is Lucy. We're neighbours. What's your name?"

The man stayed where he was, his frown deepening.

Finally, he called back. "Jack."

Lucy left her arm hovering, presuming he would make his way over to shake her hand in a moment. "Nice to meet you, Jack," she replied. "I presume those are your babies?" She indicated with a nod of her head towards the Dobermans.

"Eh?" Jack shouted back, evidently confused.

Lucy lowed her arm, realising that a shake was not on the cards. "I said, I presume that those are your babies. Your two dogs," she explained, just to be clear. "Ace and Bullet, was it? They're nice names."

"They're not babies," Jack informed her, sullenly. "So don't you go gettin' too close to them, or they'll 'ave yer arm off, little girl, understand?"

Lucy frowned. They certainly were big dogs, and quite capable of having someone as small as her for lunch. But she had always had a way with animals and could not imagine them ever wanting to attack her once they became properly acquainted.

When her parents had taken her to the animal sanctuary to choose a pet cat, the lady had warned them against the two black females pressed against the back of the cage, on their own. She explained that they had been left outside the home in a cardboard box and refused to let any of the staff anywhere near them.

But the minute Lucy placed her finger through the bars, both cats sat up and sauntered over to her. The lady warned Lucy's parents that they would not take responsibility if their daughter did not remove her hand in time. Then she watched with her mouth open as both cats began to rub themselves against the little girl, purring loudly.

When it came time for the staff to put the two cats in their baskets for Lucy to take home, they arrived with thick, rubber gloves on, which covered them right up to their elbows.

Upon seeing the staff, the two cats reared back, shackles rising.

"You're scaring them," Lucy informed the two helpers. "They think you're going to hurt them. Here, let me." Without giving the staff time to react, Lucy slid the bolt across on the cage and leaned in, emerging seconds later with one of the black cats. "I think I'll call you Lilith," she informed it. The cat rubbed its head against her cheek and hung limply as Lucy lifted it into its travel cage.

The staff looked on in awe, as Lucy did the same with the second moggie, naming it 'Hecate', after gazing into its eyes for moment.

Although they still felt a tinge of trepidation, Lucy's parents had to admit that their daughter did have a marvellous way with animals. To this day they still sucked in their breath whenever she bent down in the street to stroke some random stranger's dog. But the animals' behaviour was always the same.

They would allow the little girl to play with them for as long as she pleased, obliging with a sloppy kiss upon request.

They had naturally warned Lucy that she could not always expect every animal to behave in the same manner, and she always nodded her understanding and promised to be careful. But thus far, she had never come face to face with anything which did not respond playfully to her touch.

Lucy gazed over at the Dobermans as they sat obediently at their master's side.

"I don't think they will," Lucy announced, unconcerned.

Just then, Lilith and Hecate jumped up on the far fence which ringed the edge of the garden. Upon seeing them, both Dobermans raced over and began jumping up at the fence.

Fortunately for the two cats, this fence was a good deal higher than the one which separated the two gardens, so there was no way the dogs could reach them. A fact which seemed not to be wasted on the two felines.

Ignoring their barking neighbours, the two cats began preening themselves as if on display, rather than being the target of potential assailants.

Jack started screaming, again. "Stop it, now!"

The dogs ignored his command and continued jumping up and barking.

This time, Jack strode across the lawn and grabbed his dogs by their collars, yanking them brutishly back towards the back door.

Lucy gasped. "That's no way to treat your babies," she cried. "They'll come if you just call then, nicely."

Jack ignored her and threw his dogs back inside the house, slamming the door shut behind him.

From outside, Lucy could still hear Jack screaming his lungs out at his dogs. She sighed and turned to her two cats who were still in the middle of their beauty routine. "You two did that on purpose, didn't you?" she chided them. The two cats stopped their preening and looked over at her.

Shaking her head, Lucy turned and walked back towards her door.

As she reached for the handle, she suddenly heard the Dobermans whining and squealing, as if they were being battered. She could still hear Jack's muffled voice, screaming at them, and although her instinct told her she needed to intervene, Lucy knew that there was nothing she could physically do about the situation.

Later that day, Jack a couple of friends over for a barbecue.

From her open bedroom window, Lucy could hear their raucous laughter, as well as their conversation. The language they used she had only ever heard in passing before, usually from someone in the street who was shouting down a mobile or at whoever was with them.

She knew from what her parents had told her that such language was not polite, and she had never heard anyone in her parents' circle using it.

Lucy lay on her bed, reading. Both her cats were curled up next to her, fast asleep.

Every so often, she would hear Ace and Bullet barking, or growling, which was generally followed by Jack, or one of his guests, screaming at them to be quiet, and making more noise in the process than both dogs put together.

Lucy tried to concentrate on her book, but the shouting and loud talking from below continued to intrude. At one point, she heard someone ask Jack what his new neighbours were like.

Lucy put down her book, curiosity taking over, and moved closer to the open window to enable her to listen more intently.

"Next door 'ave got this annoying little brat," she heard Jack announce. "She's got these two fuckin' cats which wind me dogs up, somethin' chronic. But not to worry, I'll lure them in the house one day with the smell of fish cooking, then me two will tear 'em to shreds, and that'll be the end of that."

Lucy pulled back, shocked and appalled by what she had just heard.

No one could ever be that cruel, surely?

She looked over at her two-sleeping fur-babies, and made up her mind then and there, that drastic action was necessary.

During the early hours, long after Jack had said goodbye to his guests, and gone to bed. Lucy crept in through an open window at the back of his house.

As she landed silently on the floor, she could sense that Ace and Bullet were alert to the fact of her presence. As expected, the two Dobermans came rushing into the room, growling.

Just as they were about to start barking, Lucy shot them a stern look.

Both dogs obediently crouched down on all fours, and whimpered, quietly.

Lucy walked over to them and patted them both on their heads. The dogs licked her hand, then dropped their heads onto their folded paws.

She crept up the stairs towards the sound of Jack's snoring.

Once inside his bedroom, Lucy jumped up on his bed, and crouched on the end rail. The movement caused Jack to stir, but he did not wake. Instead, he merely turned over and continued to snore.

Spying an old cricket bat leaning up against the wardrobe, Lucy jumped down and fetched it, bringing it over to the side of Jack's bed.

With one swing, she brought the bat down on the side of Jack's head. Not hard enough to cause any real damage, but more than enough to stir him from his slumber.

"What...what the fuck?" Jack sat up and rubbed the sleep from his eyes.

Lucy replaced the bat where she had found it and turned to face him.

In the darkness, Jack could only make out her silhouette so initially had no idea who his assailant was, only that they were very small.

"Who the fuck are you?" he demanded. "What you doin' in

me bedroom?" There was no trace of fear or concern in his tone, confident that he could overpower this tiny intruder if he needed to. "Ace, Bullet, get up 'ere."

Lucy turned her ears back 180 degrees. She could hear the sound of the Dobermans making their way tentatively up the stairs, neither one, apparently, in any rush to reach their destination.

As the two dogs gingerly made their way into the bedroom, Lucy turned to stare at them. They immediately sank down on all fours and buried their eyes behind their paws.

Turning back to face Jack, Lucy arched her back. "People like you do not deserve to have pets," she announced.

Jack sat back, suddenly aware of who was in his room. "What the fuck are you doin' in my house?" he demanded. "You fuckin' little weirdo, get out!"

Unfazed, Lucy continued, "Your dogs have so much love for you, and all you do is shout at them, and beat them."

"What I do with me own dogs is me own business," Jack spat. "Now get out of 'ere before I give you a taste of what I give them."

In a single movement, Lucy pounced forward, dragging her right paw across Jack's neck. Her protruding claws ripped a huge gash in his throat, which proceeded to spew blood over his bedding.

Lucy sprang out of the way before any of it could splash her.

She stood there for a moment, watching while Jack attempted, futilely, to staunch the flow of blood. He slapped both hands across his throat, but the blood spilled out from between his fingers, until finally, he fell back against his head-board, dead.

Lucy checked her paws for any remnants of his blood. Once she was sure they were blood-free, she licked them and rubbed the back of her ears.

Turning towards the Dobermans, Lucy conveyed a message only animals could understand, and the two dogs immediately jumped up on the bed and began to tear into their former master.

Lucy left them to their task and climbed back out of the window through which she had originally entered the property.

She crossed over the roof, and silently slipped back into her bedroom.

Dear reader,

We hope you enjoyed reading *Spine Chillers*. Please take a moment to leave a review, even if it's a short one. Your opinion is important to us.

Discover more books by Mark L'Estrange at https://www. nextchapter.pub/authors/mark-lestrange

Want to know when one of our books is free or discounted? Join the newsletter at http://eepurl.com/bqqB3H

Best regards,
Mark L'Estrange and the Next Chapter Team

Printed in Great Britain
by Amazon